Shadow of Joy

A Woman's Journey
from Coercive Control and Abuse
to Courage, Freedom, and Rebuilding Identity

Jennifer Dean

Shadow of Joy
A Woman's Journey from Coercive Control and Abuse to Courage, Freedom, and Rebuilding Identity

Published by Reflek Publishing

Disclaimer: The author makes no guarantees concerning the level of success you may experience by following the advice and strategies contained in this book, and you accept the risk that results will differ for each individual. The purpose of this book is to educate, entertain, and inspire.

For more information: JenniferDean@BeyondTheShadow.me

ISBN: 978-1-968164-28-7 (paperback)

ISBN: 978-1-968164-29-4 (ebook)

Trigger / Content Warning Page

This novel includes depictions and themes of emotional abuse, mental abuse, physical abuse, sexual abuse, coercive sexual manipulation, and related trauma. These topics can be distressing especially to those who have experienced trauma or abuse.

This story may contain:

- emotional manipulation, degradation, and control
- descriptions of sexual trauma and psychological effects
- themes of power and control
- intimate partner violence

Some scenes may be graphic, and some emotional passages may evoke memories or strong feelings.

If at any point you feel triggered or overwhelmed, please pause, take care of yourself, and return to the text only when you feel safe. Your mental and emotional well-being come first.

You are not defined by what has happened to you. Survivors of trauma are strong; you deserve respect, dignity, and healing.

You are not **alone**. Healing, help, and support do exist.

If you or someone you know has experienced abuse, trauma, or sexual violence, you may find help from the following resources.

National Domestic Violence Hotline:
1-800-799-SAFE (7233)

The Exodus Project:
800-988-7499; Support@TheExodusProject.com

House of Ruth:
800-799-7233

Legal clinic:
1-888-880-7884

Woman's Law Center of Maryland:
410-321-8761

National Sexual Assault Hotline:
1-800-656-HOPE (4673)

Called to Peace Ministries Inc.:
919-374-0778; info@CalledToPeace.org; http://calledtoPeace.org

FOCUS Ministries, Inc:
630-617-0088

To my five amazing, strong, beautiful daughters
—my greatest treasures.
To my husband,
whose love reminds me that amazing men do exist.
To every woman who has walked this hard road
—this book is for you.

"I am not afraid . . . I was born to do this."
Joan of Arc

*"I can be changed by what happens to me.
But I refuse to be reduced by it."*
Maya Angelou

"You do not just survive – you rise."
Rupi Kaur

A Personal Note from the Author

Dear Reader,

This book was written with you in mind. While it is a work of fiction, it is also deeply personal. I have walked this path—a path far too many women have had to walk—and it has been the hardest journey of my life. Finding the courage to endure, stand for truth, and pursue freedom was not easy, and it never is. Through telling Joy's story, my hope is to shed light on these realities so fewer women will have to endure the same struggles. Understanding the red flags of control and abuse is essential.

My first goal is to raise awareness and help prevent unsafe relationships. My next goal is to reach those who are caught in these heartbreaking dynamics, to help them understand why they feel the way they do, and to give them the courage to take the steps needed to reclaim their lives. My last goal is for those who recognize that someone they know and love is caught in an unhealthy relationship: I ask you to give her compassion and understanding. Don't be quick to judge or blame the victim. No one truly knows what it is like to walk in another's shoes. Believe her! Offer hope, extend help, and recognize that her journey is not easy. Your support may make all the difference.

While the characters and storyline are fictional, much of Joy's pain echoes my own lived experiences.

My heart's deepest desire is that every woman who turns these pages will feel seen, understood, and reminded that her voice matters, her story matters, and **she matters.**

You are not alone. Too many women live in silence, weighed down by fear, shame, uncertainty, self-doubt, or helplessness—but you do not have to stay there. You were created with worth and dignity, and you have the right to live free from fear.

My hope is that within these words, you will find encouragement to seek truth and freedom. That you will recognize your immense value, learn to see the red flags of control and abuse, and understand that no one has the right to diminish your light.

We can choose courage. We can stand strong. We can stand for truth. And in doing so, we not only reclaim our own voices, we open the door for others to find theirs too.

We also are the example for our children; they watch our life. If we choose to protect ourselves and not stay in harm's way, we are protecting our children from abuse—emotional, verbal, mental, psychological, and sometimes physical abuse.

As you read, may you feel supported, strengthened, and reminded that freedom and healing are possible. You are worthy of love, respect, and safety, and no one can take your purpose from you. You deserve a life free from fear where you can thrive and fully be yourself. You have the right to set boundaries. You have the right to walk away from harm and choose freedom.

Remember, you are seen. You are valued. You are believed. You are not alone. Your story matters.

You matter.

Have the courage to live free from fear.

With love and joy,
Jennifer Dean

If, after reading, you feel moved to connect, I welcome you. Whether you'd like to share part of your story, offer feedback, or simply know you're not alone—I am available. You can reach me on my social media channels:

Facebook: **Jennifer Dean Novelist**
Instagram: **@JenniferDeanNovelist**
Email: **JenniferDean@BeyondtheShadow.me**

Please remember, I am not a professional counselor or crisis advocate. If you are in danger or need immediate help, I encourage you to reach out to one of the hotlines or organizations listed a few pages back.

Here's A Gift Before You Begin!

As a thank you for reading my book I wanted to give you this gift.

I hope you find your joy.

Get your free gift here:

https://www.beyondtheshadow.me/book-resources

Introduction

Desperation

"I wish he would *die*."

I hissed these words through clenched teeth. The cause of death didn't matter to me: heart attack, cancer, being hit by a car, struck by lightning, anything fatal, *anything* that would permanently and *finally* remove him from my life.

So many times I wished for his death, yet I could not act upon my desire. I hoped without apology and laughed at the irony. For *he* was pushing *me* to an early grave.

If something didn't happen, I would die.

I couldn't keep living like this.

If only people could understand what I've been through; surely they wouldn't judge me for having such thoughts. In fact, maybe they would assist. Maybe if I cast this out into the universe, like a message in a bottle, some fortunate soul would hear my silent plea and complete the wish of my heart and do what I couldn't bring myself to do. Maybe karma would step in.

Beaten down, destroyed, belittled, and broken, I was shattered into less-than pieces of a human.

I needed a way out.

His rage and destruction had eating away at the very fiber of my being . . . leaving me a shell of a human.

I didn't need the bruises on my skin to feel battered. His rage left marks no one else could see. I survived in a space between his explosions.

Then, a fragile unsteady moment opened, a small crack of light appeared. His footsteps retreated down the driveway. An engine roared to life and faded.

The house went still. Silence . . . real silence. Not the tight, waiting silence that held breath for anger. But stillness. A gap. A window. That's when instinct snapped into movement.

Go. Now. Run.

Before I could think, I was already moving.

My hands shook violently as I grabbed bags, flung open drawers. Clothes, underwear, mismatched socks—nothing made sense. I couldn't think—I packed whatever I touched.

I kept packing like I was drowning and every bag was a lifeline.

Get the bags in the car. Come back. Gather the girls. Ten minutes. Ten minutes and we'll be free.

Heaving the bags into my arms, I dragged them out to the car. As I shoved the bags into the trunk, desperation fueling me.

The sharp crunch of tires on the gravel. My stomach dropped like a stone. Nausea roared through me.

The slam of his door made my heart leap violently in my throat. Footsteps—rapid, deliberate—pounded from behind. I didn't even need to hear his voice; my body already knew. There was no escape.

A wave of panic hit like icy water. I felt on the verge of vomiting, helpless and small, wishing I'd been just five minutes faster. My pulse pounded in time to his footsteps, closing in, relentless.

"What the hell are you doing?"

This time, he stood so close I could see the bloodshot veins in his eyes and the pulse hammering in his throat. "If you think you can take my kids, you are dead wrong. You can leave, but my kids will never leave with you. I will strip you of everything, until you have no one and nothing. I will make sure no one believes you. I will see you homeless and on the street. You want to test me? Go ahead. Try me. Try me!"

Hot spittle struck my face. His nostrils flared, eyes wild with unhinged rage. He looked like a man possessed, and I knew it would take almost nothing for him to cross the line into something unspeakable.

Terror rooted me in place, and my grip on the car door handle slackened. The blinding sun seared my eyes while his stare held me captive, fear tightening its grip around me.

"You will never take my kids, do you understand?" his voice rose, harsh yet controlled as he shoved me hard against the car, the handle cutting into my back. He leaned in close. "I will destroy you."

He held me there for what felt like an eternity, his grip unyielding, like iron. His steely gaze bored into mine, cold and merciless, locking me in place. With one final shove for emphasis, he released me and turned away, certain of his power and certain he had the upper hand.

Broken, I crumbled to the ground as the gravel dug into my bare skin. There was no way out. A sharp, desperate cry tore from me, primal, steeped in agony. It carried the weight of my helplessness, the depth of pain. My nails dug painfully into my tender palms, sharp enough to draw blood. Dread hollowed my chest as my only option loomed before me: walking back into our house. Back in his grip.

Back in my prison.

With each step, I felt my dignity slip away. In one silent motion, I turned the knob. The door creaked open, and I stepped across the threshold as every piece inside me splintered.

I was a prisoner, object, body to be used, voice to be silenced, heart condemned to a life without tenderness or love. Perhaps I was born to wear this tortured mask, carved deep into my skin.

I always thought what was destined would just . . . be.

But if destiny had placed me here, I couldn't help but wonder, *must destiny always rule? How could this situation be changed? Could it be broken, could it be reshaped? How does one shatter this endless cycle? How does one escape the cage? How do you stop the endless ache?*

How do you fight back against the slow crushing of your spirit—the abuse of power, the relentless urge to dominate, to humiliate, to mock, and to belittle? How do you endure the stripping away of basic human needs, the erasure of your voice, your worth, your very self?

How do you survive when every part of you is being broken down piece by piece?

Who knew the irony of being named Joy?

As a child, my name reflected my very being. I was vivacious, cheerful as my name, and as radiant as the joy I was called. Wonder bloomed within me, spilling outward like sunlight breaking through the clouds. There was always a sparkle in my eyes, a bounce in my step, and a song in my heart—my spirit was alive and free.

I was inquisitive, the asker of a thousand questions. The aunts and uncles would look with censure, shushing me when I inundated them with countless questions, yet I was never silent or still.

My favorite pastime was running barefoot through wide fields of grass, the soft earth cushioning my steps as the swaying blades brushed their coolness against my shins. I would fly to my secret tree, where endless hours would slip away in daydreams. I was always smiling, always running, twirling, chatting—soaking up every second of my small, spectacular life.

Once upon a time, I had big dreams. I was so ready to take on the world and pave an incredible path. Adventurous and free, I saw life through happy, rose-colored glasses. To me, everything had value and deserved a second chance—or at least a new set of circumstances to improve, change, or grow.

I was determined to be a saver.

Maybe that was the problem. If that ten-year-old vivacious child could glimpse into her future, how would it have prepared her? Or cautioned her? Or would the glimpse itself have destroyed her love, vibrancy, vivid imagination, and the joyful love of life?

Snapping back to the present, with agonized truth, I realized I was simply a sweet, naive girl who had attracted a bad boy. Not just bad, but well-concealed evil beneath a façade of charisma and fun.

How does anyone learn the ability to see beneath that?

What level of perception can properly prepare one to discern the thoughts and intentions of another's heart?

Now, terrified of my own shadow and unable to rescue myself from this prison made without walls, I had lived on this earth a bit over thirty years, but it felt much, much longer. It felt like an eternity of suffering. How could I have experienced such tragedy, heartache, and anguish in just ten years of adulthood? My head hurt to a piercing ache as I thought through the full scope of my life.

As I reflected on the young girl I used to be and the woman I had been forced to become, I knew my next move could be perilous.

Possibly deadly.

Taking this chance could backfire, and cruel punishment would be the consolation. The rope of hope dangled just out of my reach . . . yet while there was breath in me, I determined I would claw myself out.

The angst to move toward freedom was terrorizing.

It was tangible. I resolved I would try, with every fiber in me.

I am but a shell, I thought. *I am desperate. I need out . . .*
Or I will die.

Chapter One

Summer 2004, *Awakening*

My childhood was idyllic—beautiful, adventurous, and free. Upon reaching adolescence, I was discovering, growing, and blossoming into a beautiful, caring, imaginative woman. As a young adult, I was full of hopes and dreams for a future full of possibilities.

Yet, I recall the very moment that marked the beginning of the shift in my personal odyssey. It was a journey that would morph me from beauty to ashes. From full of joy to a shadow and shell of the woman I was meant to be.

The moment I laid eyes on Lucas, everything shifted . . . when it really shouldn't have. There were indications, warning signs, but they are not easily detected when you are young and idealistic.

That summer—the summer I turned twenty, during my college years—felt like the beginning of everything. The season stretched wide with freedom, sundrenched adventures, and a heady rush of early adulthood.

When my best friend Charlotte called, wanting to head to the beach for the day, I didn't hesitate. Bonded together since the third grade, we were nearly one soul in two bodies, spending our days chasing the kind of moments we knew we would remember forever.

Moments later, we were tossing our new beach towels, sunglasses, and a bottle of SPF 15 sunscreen into the back seat of her weathered, white convertible Miata—the kind of car that smelled like freedom and old music. Windows rolled down, sun blazing, arms out, and wind in our long hair, we drove straight to the shore, singing wildly at the top of our lungs to Carrie Underwood's latest song, not caring how silly we sounded.

We spent the day jumping in and out of the waves and swimming out beyond them where we could float with our arms outstretched, drifting along with the rocking waves. This was my happy place. The silence was beautiful and the feeling magical; I could float peacefully for hours and hours. Floating with our faces pointing toward the shining sun, we outstretched our arms and slowly tread the rocking waves. The feel of the water as it lapped against our faces, the bright whiteness of the scattered, fluffy cumulus clouds, like fat cotton balls and the cotton-candy blue of the sky extending till it touched the water at the horizon was an unforgettable experience. It was the picture of peace.

A large wave rose and crashed over us, sending us spiraling in the frothing breakers. Gasping, we struggled to the surface.

"That was crazy!" I shrieked, coughing from the salty water in my lungs.

"I know! Let's go out and tan for a while, plus I am starving!" Charlotte replied as she stumbled toward the shore, struggling against the push of the tide. We sunbathed and devoured our slices of pizza and Boardwalk fries, drowning in malt vinegar and Old Bay, back on the shore. Life was beautiful.

"Promise me," Charlotte began. "Promise me we'll always do this, every summer. No matter how old we get, or how crazy life becomes. Promise we'll always have crazy, fun days like this."

"I promise!" I vowed, reaching over to pinky swear.

We drove home in the darkened night, while the salty warm air surrounded us and the yellow orbs shone above. Charlotte decided to spend the night, so we slipped into my house, giggling and whispering, our voices a tangled hush as we tried not to awaken my parents.

"Shhh! We have to be quiet!"

"I am!" Charlotte responded in a stage whisper. Charlotte was never quiet.

Smothering our giggles, we tiptoed our way up the old, creaking stairs into my childhood bedroom. We were fast asleep barely before our heads touched the soft linen pillows.

"Hey, there's going to be an awesome bonfire tonight. Should we go?" Charlotte mentioned over breakfast the next day. She always knew what was going on, what was worth attending, and we also heard there were going to be cute guys at the bonfire.

"Yes, absolutely!" I answered back. "It'll be a perfect night for a bonfire."

After spending a relaxing day with my parents, we retreated to my room to carefully select our ensembles for the evening, because that's the sort of priorities you have when you're twenty and carefree . . .

We drove unhurriedly, the windows partly rolled down, feeling the cool breeze waft around us and enjoying the pleasant smells of the country. The bonfire was held at a nearby farm, and the trees swirled past quickly as we drove. The farmland and fields spread out like a colorful patterned quilt. The variety of the colors ranged from pale yellowish green to golden with fields of grain, corn, alfalfa, and hay surrounding us in a storybook beauty outside the quaint, picturesque town of Chestertown, Maryland.

We spilled from Charlotte's car, our arms full of s'mores ingredients, two cozy plaid blankets, and our college sweatshirts. As we drew closer, I watched the wood catch fire, and within minutes, the entire bonfire was engulfed in a reddish-orange glow. The orange-and-red-tinted flickers grabbed upward, reaching toward the heavens, and crackled loudly with sharp popping sounds. I loved the smell of a bonfire, not caring as it seeped into my clothes and hair.

Charlotte noticed Jake on the other side of the bonfire and discreetly elbowed me, drawing my attention to him. Jake and Charlotte knew each other from college; though they had different majors, they shared similar core classes and often hung out in the same study groups. Charlotte always knew that Jake liked her but was too shy to act on his interest. And Charlotte was too busy enjoying life and pursuing her studies to focus on just one boy.

"Hey, Joy!" Jake called out. He and his friend Sebastian made their way over to us, Jake keeping his eyes on Charlotte the whole time. Addressing me was as close as he could get to speaking to Charlotte, until he could work up his nerve to speak to her directly.

"How's your summer going?" Jake nervously asked me as he kept playing with his old, torn baseball cap and running his fingers over the frayed edges. As I told him about our previous day at the beach, Charlotte finally grabbed the bull by the horns.

"It was absolutely amazing," she added, turning to him. "I think I got my entire summer tan in one day."

Jake's eyes lit when she glanced his way. A soft flush rose to her cheeks as she glowed with a bright, bubbling energy. As they began to chat, I eased back into the shadows to give them space and joined Sebastian, along with the others gathered around the bonfire.

Since Sebastian and I had been mutual friends through Jake for a couple years, it was exciting to hear him talk about his plans to join the Marines next month. Having several family members who served, I was aware of the sacrifice and honor involved. Sebastian always seemed kind and gentle, so at first it was surprising that he was willing to volunteer for such a grueling experience. But with his servant's heart, perhaps it wasn't farfetched after all.

Our conversation petered out, and I stepped closer, seeking the warmth of the bonfire. The fire crackled loudly, and I watched the flickering flames lick at the wood as it enveloped us in an iridescent orange glow. Heat penetrated far around the bonfire, reaching its arms to wrap us in a warm, suffocating hug. And that's when I saw him.

I'd been looking over the crowd of young adults, scanning their faces for familiar ones. I saw many I knew and a few I didn't. There was one guy in particular who caught my eye. His dark hair flowed loosely over his forehead and ended with relaxing waves barely brushing his collar. You could tell he often ran his fingers through his hair by the way it fell in rivulets and swooped into a gentle cascade.

I noticed he kept glancing over at me, and each time his gaze lingered a bit longer, sending chills up and down my spine. I lifted my eyes to meet his inquiring stare. My cheeks flushed hot, and I let my gaze fall back to the fire.

Rubbing my arms gently to soothe the goosebumps, I glanced over at Charlotte and Jake. Still deep in conversation, Charlotte twisted her hair nervously around her fingers. I was happy for her. She deserved to be in a relationship with a nice guy, and I knew Jake was kind. I didn't want to intrude on their conversation, so I bided my time, absorbing the radiating warmth of the bonfire. A softly strummed guitar floated through the air, and it felt natural to sway to the soothing rhythm. It was another beautiful summer night, yet I couldn't shake the disappointment that the hot guy hadn't come over or made a move. I just hoped I'd get another chance to see him.

The weeks flew by with a constant flow of events, beach trips, bonfires, and outdoor movie nights. The cute guy from the bonfire showed up at quite a few of the events, where we continued to exchange glances. I heard that his name was Lucas and he was from down south, near Texas. I was too shy to approach him, so I waited, hoping he would come up and talk to me.

And so far, by mid-August, nothing. Just the cat-and-mouse glances of hopeful possibilities.

A big, end-of-summer bash was in the works, and I was looking forward to it—one last hurrah before resuming studies, jobs, and the normal things for a serious college student. Charlotte and Jake had been dating for just over a month, and they were utterly smitten with each other. With

Jake's parents hosting the party in their open field by the river, Charlotte's excitement for the event was impossible to hide.

"Hurry, we need to go! I don't want to be late," Charlotte called up the stairs as I finished fastening the last strap on my shoe. Swinging my purse over my shoulder, I left my bedroom in messy shambles from our wild search for perfect outfits.

"I'm coming! I'm coming! Just grabbing my bag," I spoke in mock irritation as I ran down the stairs, skipping steps to hurry.

We drove with the top down and the bright sunlight streaming on our faces. Parking behind a long line of cars, we walked up the lane and crossed the field where the sounds of the party were already underway.

The harsh stubble of the cut corn scratched our ankles as we stepped carefully toward the crowd. It was late afternoon, and judging from the laughter and murmuring conversations, it seemed everyone was having a great time. Fragrant smoke rose from the cook fires, and loud squeals of delight came from those catapulting themselves into the river from the rope anchored far above in the massive oak tree.

Charlotte and I grinned widely at each other. She spotted Jake talking with Sebastian.

"You look so beautiful," Jake whispered quietly to her as she came straight to his side. "I'm so glad you are here; I've been waiting for you." Jake reached out and touched Charlotte's hand, delicately stroking her fingers while looking deeply into her eyes.

"Thank you," Charlotte responded, dipping her eyes slightly then raising them to meet his.

"I'm going to get in the water," I said, giving them some space and walked down the embankment to the water. The grass became soil, soft and silky under my feet. The silt squished between my toes, cool and earthy. Wading into the shallow, flowing water, I found a spot on the river where it slowed and pooled. Tiny minnows and crawfish were barely visible beneath the surface.

Looking up toward the group, and spotted Lucas, as handsome as ever. He was effortlessly swinging on the rope swing, like a pendulum. He plunged into the water, releasing the rope swing, yelling loud and boisterous like Tarzan. My eyes were glued to where he disappeared.

Emerging from the cool, flowing water, Lucas looked like a Calvin Klein model. Each step sent droplets flying, water dancing around him. Rivulets ran down his tan, muscled chest and defined, sculpted abdomen as he ran a hand through his loosely waved, sun-streaked hair—and our eyes met.

My cheeks burned, and I forced myself to look casual, fighting the urge to stare.

As Lucas walked toward me, my pulse began to race. *Keep it cool,* I told myself. I stood in knee-deep water and pretended to watch the minnows. But once our eyes locked, his gaze traveled slowly down my body, taking in the details of my tiny red bikini before returning to meet mine.

"Hey," he said with a drawl in his rich baritone voice.

"Hey," I responded, nervously fidgeting. My arms felt awkward, and I was unsure where to place them. Holding eye contact for a few more moments, he slowly continued past me as the water swished around his brawny calves.

Oh my God, I thought, *I should have answered with something a little bit more interesting.* With a loud sigh, I shrugged. *Oh well . . . What's done is done.*

Charlotte waded in while Jake went to hang with the guys. She grabbed a pair of floats stacked on the bank, and we waded into deeper waters while I blurted out the details. "So, the cute guy, Lucas," I whispered, "said *hi* to me when he walked by. *And* . . . he has a Southern accent, almost positive. You know how I feel about that!" I added with excitement, before telling her how awkward I felt, unable to sustain anything more than a *hi* back.

"You are gorgeous, fun, and kind," Charlotte consoled. "Don't worry, you'll get another opportunity. He'd be stupid to not talk to you again. Hey! Wanna do the rope swing? I've been dying to try."

"Let's do it!" I replied.

Charlotte went first, and in her big-personality way, got everyone's attention with her huge cannonball, her voice booming as she released the rope. I was next. Looking up at the massive oak tree, I saw its tall branches had formed a canopy. Sunlight filtered in, reflecting its light through the rich green foliage to scatter sparkles on the slow-moving water and grassy embankment. Turning my attention back to the rope swing, I jumped out and grasped onto the thick hemp rope, latching on with both hands. I felt the swish of momentum as my body propelled over the water and euphoria as I released the rope.

A yell escaped me as I plunged into the deep, cool water. I opened my eyes and saw millions of tiny bits of sediment floating and swirling around me effortlessly. I could feel the pull of the water on my body, the upward pushing of the water, the buoyancy, and the pricking of a million needles. I loved the feeling of weightlessness, effortlessly flying, and then the force of the plunge into the current.

I quickly rejoined the line of jumpers, ready for another go.

Glancing over, I saw Charlotte chatting away happily with Jake while they floated lazily on their inner tubes, holding hands to stay connected.

"Hey . . ." I heard.

Startled, I turned to see Lucas standing a couple inches behind me. His golden tan glistened over his muscles. He stood with his hands low on his hips and a half smile upon his generous lips.

My knees felt weak.

How am I supposed to respond to such a hot guy? I wasn't the kind of girl who was often approached by hot guys. Yes, I knew I was pretty—many had commented—but I was also a little shy and felt awkward when it came to talking to handsome guys. I had no trouble chatting with my girlfriends or with guys in the friend zone. But guys I found attractive—I just froze.

"Nice jump there," he said.

"Thanks," I replied, fidgeting with my fingers as all logical thought flew out of my head.

He paused. "So, what's your name? I've seen you around at quite a few of these get-togethers."

"I'm . . . Joy," I answered, with a tentative pause, like I couldn't remember my own name.

"Joy," he responded. He said my name slowly, enunciating it with his sexy Southern drawl. "That's a beautiful name, just like you."

"Thank you," I replied, wondering if he could sense how nervous I was.

"So, are you from around here?" His eyes twinkled.

"Yes, I live here and go to college here. How about you?"

"I'm from Texas, but I spent the summer here. It's pretty cool, I like it." He looked out at one of the guys plunging into the water. "Too bad summer is ending though," he said as his eyes reconnected with mine. "You . . . wanna hang out sometime?"

"Sure, that would be fun," I replied, forcing a casual tone, even as my stomach flipped and my heart threatened to burst.

He was *really* talking to me! I was ecstatic. Unbelievable. The guy I'd been crushing *on all summer long* was finally flirting with me—telling me I was beautiful, that he liked my name, *and* wanted to hang out. It felt surreal—like I was watching my own dream unfold right in front of me.

After my turn on the rope swing and emerged from the water, I noticed Lucas had wandered off. I quickly searched for Charlotte and ran to tell her what had happened, and we both squealed with delight.

About an hour later, my mouth watered at the inviting aroma of barbecued ribs and other meats being prepared. The spices and smoky fragrances pleasantly hung heavy in the air. While balancing our loaded plates, Charlotte and I carried large cups of iced tea and a stack of napkins back to our picnic table. Devouring the delicious meal, we licked the sauce from our fingers like children and giggled at each other, not caring our faces were a saucy mess.

"Hey, Joy, he's looking at you again," Charlotte whispered excitedly, gently nudging me with her foot. Stealing a covert glance, I looked toward the food tables and accidentally met his eyes. They were dark, intense, and focused entirely upon me.

He wove his way through the packed picnic tables and continued toward me with a confident saunter. My eyes grew bigger, my dread and excitement grew larger, and my stomach became a tangled mess.

"Hi, Joy. Mind if I sit?" he asked, even though by then, he was already seated. "I've seen you quite a bit today. You want to . . . go for a walk?"

My eyes glanced at Charlotte for reassurance and a little of her confidence.

"Go! I'm fine. I've got our stuff." She smiled confidently and patted our bags on the seat.

"Sure, let's go," I agreed.

As I grasped for something to say, I noticed the sun beginning to set while we wandered slowly through the adjoining cornfield, the shadows stretching longer with each step. We talked about simple things, college, small observations, nothing of great importance—but the conversation felt easy. I was still flustered by his attention, yet with each passing moment, my nerves began to settle. Lucas was fun to talk to, and I couldn't quite believe he was so interested in me. Eventually we made our way over to the warmth of the growing fire.

"I'm going to miss these summer nights," I murmured.

"I agree," Lucas said. "It's been a really cool summer. I've noticed you, but I've been a little nervous to come up and talk to you honestly. You're so pretty and I figured you had a boyfriend. I just didn't want to miss my last chance before we all head back to college." Then, catching his breath, he blurted out, "I don't know if you're seeing anyone, but I'd really like to get to know you. You are fun, and very beautiful."

I blushed a deep shade of scarlet and felt warmth flood through me. "Thank you," I said softly. "And no, I am not seeing anyone."

Nervously, I played with my fingers, picking at the pale-pink nail polish that had flecked off my nails earlier today.

Lucas reached out for my hand and slowly wove his strong fingers through mine, his gaze never leaving mine.

"Are you cold?" Lucas asked, hopefully.

"Yes . . . a little," I answered honestly, uncertain whether it was from the cooler temperature or nerves. Lucas pulled off his sweatshirt and draped it around my shoulders, gently brushing my arms with his hands as an excuse to keep me warm. The warmth of the fire was nothing compared to the warmth I felt emanating from Lucas's touch. I couldn't concentrate on anything except his presence.

"Better?" he asked, his dark-blue eyes looking deeply into mine.

Never feeling chemistry like this before, it shook me. Stepping back a few inches to make some space between us, I took a few measured breaths, letting the slow inhalations calm my fast-beating heart. He loosened his hands and slipped his thumbs into the opening of his short's pockets.

I felt nervous and anxious, not knowing where my footing was in this very new, highly charged connection. Quite literally, I was swept off my feet because I could not feel them, nor the ground beneath them. And I wasn't even sure how to keep the conversation flowing.

Thankfully, Lucas filled the void, chatting casually about his summer and his thoughts about entering his senior year at college. He was transferring to the college nearby to be closer to extended family—the same college as mine.

It's fate, I thought briefly, my head swimming. He was determined to finish his degree in engineering and jump straight into the field, and the more he spoke, the more his excitement seemed to build.

Charged by his energy, I talked about my desire to get my teaching degree. I loved children and couldn't think of anything more fitting than being a teacher. I didn't just want to teach, I wanted to inspire students to be more than they could imagine, to know the sky was the limit for their dreams.

Realizing how much I was disclosing, I paused and gazed out into the sky. The sun had now fully set in a riot of lavender, fuchsia, and magenta colors as the sun's golden orb fully sunk below the horizon, and the vibrant colors melted into night like liquid lava. Lucas continued to talk as he stood close to me, our skin barely glancing against each other's arms.

As the colors disappeared from the horizon into the darkness of night, Lucas put his arm around my hips. Ever so slightly, he stroked his fingers cautiously and slowly along the bottom trim of the sweatshirt. He paused, and feeling no resistance from me, his fingers slowly burned a trail on my bare skin, shooting flames up my back and over my skin.

My breathing paused, ceasing for a few moments as my body processed the intensity his fingers created. *Breathe!* I told myself. As the fire's glow deepened, his fingers traced the curve of my spine, each slow stroke set my flushed skin ablaze.

Oh God . . . how is he doing this to me? The thought fluttered through me as excitement flooded my chest. Lucas kept talking in that low, enticing Southern drawl as his words wrapped around me as gently as his fingertips. The shadows hid his touch, but I felt every breath of it.

Glancing away from the fire, I saw Charlotte and Jake loosely holding hands as they came to stand beside us. Even in the darkness, Charlotte's eyes took in much as the firelight illuminated our faces, casting a glowing aura of light around us. With a slight raise of her brow, she assessed the situation. My face flamed crimson. Embarrassed, I tried to act natural as Lucas's hand moved to hook into the back loop of my jean shorts.

"Loving the bonfire?" Charlotte asked, with a touch of sarcasm and a raised brow.

"Absolutely," Lucas answered, either ignoring or oblivious to her pointed tone.

Trying to calm my racing heart, I shifted my gaze back to the fire as Jake and Lucas started talking about sports. Charlotte grabbed my arm, pulling me a few feet away.

"That's . . . moving a bit fast!" she whispered sharply. "I know you've had a crush on him all summer, but be careful, okay?"

"I *am* careful. Nothing happened," I defended, heat rising in my cheeks—more from irritation than embarrassment.

Charlotte shot me a look. "Nothing horrible . . . but he definitely had his hand up the back of your sweatshirt. Joy, you never do that."

"I'm fine. Really," I said, meeting Charlotte's concerned eyes.

"That's just not like you—to move so fast." Worry clouded her expression, her brows knitting together. "Just be careful, okay?"

"I will. I just feel this instant chemistry with him, like nothing I've ever felt before. But I'm good, I promise. Don't worry!" I squeezed her arm in assurance. "I'll be careful."

Charlotte's expression softened, and she pulled me into a quick, grounding hug. The knot in my chest loosened, and for a moment the night felt calm again. Laughter drifted from the others, and the mood picked up as everyone migrated toward the table being set up for s'mores. Charlotte and I grabbed our skewers, loading them with marshmallows, while everyone debated the usual—how many marshmallows to use, do you lightly toast them or scorch them, and so on.

I continued to pile copious amounts of marshmallows onto the end of my skewer.

"Seriously, Joy, six marshmallows?" Jake exclaimed. "Is that necessary?"

"Of course!" I explained, "Haven't you heard about roasting all your marshmallows at once, so you have all you need to make the best s'mores and you don't have to keep roasting them?"

"No, I haven't," he laughed. "I just think you want a ton of marshmallows!"

"Maybe." I shrugged. "You'll never know!" I plunged my marshmallow-loaded skewer near the hot, glowing fire.

The heat from the fire slowly toasted the marshmallows as I rotated them for perfection.

"Hey, Joy," Lucas called. "Make me one?"

"Sure!" I answered, more than happy to accommodate his request before making my own.

After enjoying way too many s'mores, Charlotte and I stretched out on our quilt beneath the stars, sugar-drunk and happy, talking about how this felt like a perfect ending to a spectacular summer. Propping my head up on my arms, we continued talking about tomorrow's "back to reality" when I noticed a pair of feet next to us. I looked up to see Lucas slowly bending his tall frame down to squat next to us.

"Room for one more?" he asked with a slow smile.

We all resumed our conversation about returning to college and "adulting."

"Gonna miss these nights though," he replied, looking at me. Then he reached out and gingerly grasped a curly lock of my hair that fell onto the checkered quilt, playing with it between his thumb and fingers. The goosebumps returned to my arms. It was enticing, and I didn't want to move away.

As the fire began to dwindle, the group began to dissipate one by one. Reluctantly, I began folding the quilt, gathering our items and s'more leftovers. Lucas stood next to me with his hands shoved into the pockets of his shorts.

"Want me to walk you to the car?" he asked.

I glanced over and saw Charlotte deep in conversation with Jake.

"Yeah, I'd like that," I responded, looking up for a long moment into his clear, liquid-blue eyes.

Lucas reached out, touching my hand, and wove his long fingers through mine. I looked up at him, seeing unhidden attraction in his eyes. A ripple of warmth rose up my arm, and I liked what I saw. This was new territory for me: I had a heightened awareness—every sense tuned to his presence.

Walking through the cool grass, my mind raced with introspective thoughts. I knew I could be a bit of a wallflower sometimes, not usually central to the excitement. Being at the center of his attention was making my head swirl, and I wasn't sure how to maintain it.

This must be what it's supposed to feel like, I thought. *To finally be noticed and included.* My hand felt warm and small in his.

Reaching the car, he opened the passenger back door, and I placed the tote on the seat.

I turned after shutting the door and looked up, straight into his magnetic eyes.

He moved closer, just inches away from my body.

Pausing. Hovering.

I felt the smooth metal of the car pressing against the bare skin on the back of my legs as I fumbled nervously with my hands at my side. He took one step closer, until his leg was wedged between mine. I felt the brush of his shorts against my thigh, the curly hair on his thigh tickling my leg.

The anticipation and the closeness of his body heightened my senses, and I could barely breathe. Placing one hand on the car, next to my shoulder, he took his right hand and slowly touched my cheek. Then, running his finger down my neck, he cupped the back of my head and pulled my head gently toward him. His lips came close and hovered over mine. A soft breath touched my face. I could smell the marshmallow and chocolate.

One, two, three breaths. Shivers raced down my spine.

"Can I kiss you?" he whispered softly.

"Yes," I breathed, allowing my eyelids to flutter closed.

When his lips caressed mine, I lifted my arms in response, cupping his head and moving to the magic of the moment. He kissed me deeply, then demandingly.

And I couldn't get enough.

His muscular arms wrapped tightly around me in the darkness, effortlessly lifting me and holding me suspended while his mouth worked itself down my neck. When my feet touched the ground again, his fingers gripped my sweatshirt, tugging at the neckline to leave a trail of hungry kisses. Gasping for breath, we paused.

"Joy, I am so into you," he whispered in his sexy Southern drawl. "When can I see you again?"

I could barely stand. He didn't release me but held my body close.

"Soon," I managed to say.

"Okay, soon it is," he responded.

Slowly, Lucas released me, touching my cheek one more time, then turned and walked into the darkness. "See you soon, beautiful Joy." He cast a look over his shoulder, holding my eyes in an entrancing gaze.

Breathless, I fell against the car.

Who knew this was an omen? A strikingly similar setting with drastically different emotions and lasting, impactful results.

I was hot and sweaty from the passionate moment but quickly chilled as a cool breeze blew over my damp skin and I became lost in this world of swirling, intoxicating emotion.

Chapter Two

Summer 2015, *Present Day*

"I did it," I whispered, almost unbelieving.

One week into freedom, and the sun was shining differently. It seemed brighter, more glorious. The birds chirped louder with their happy symphony and their song was somehow sweeter, more vibrant. Nature seemed surreal, like I was seeing it for the first time; yet how was that even possible?

I felt this kind of lightness. It was foreign, almost unrecognizable. I noticed what was missing . . . it was the palatable fear that constantly gripped me—suffocating. This feeling of freedom was so new, it reminded me of one who was deprived of oxygen and finally allowed to gasp pure, clean air. Imagine filling your lungs for the first time and exhaling in relief. Then the next breaths come easy.

That was me.

I could finally breathe, live, laugh . . . This is wondrous. Strangely beautiful.

How can one person's influence so penetrate your life, that everything drastically shifts with their absence? What power did he have over the sun? Over the birds?

My only thought was, his negative energy must summon such grey clouds that choke the light—morphing what should be unspoiled, guileless and free into something heavy, oppressive, suffocated. What was innocent became twisted and burdened under a weight that shouldn't have even existed, bending anything that was simple and pure into a subdued, muted shadow of itself.

The weight of his control had stripped me of my ability to live in my authenticity and smothered the vibrancy of my life. Now, the sun was allowed to filter in, and my senses were awakened to things I had long forgotten.

Remembering back to that fateful summer, the one that changed my life's entire trajectory, there were clues I'd missed. When you're twenty, love is like the love you dream of, a storybook love. Prince Charming rides in on a white horse and sweeps you off your feet. It is a heady, sweeping, intoxicating feeling you feel powerless to control. And because it's what you wish, your carelessness, lack of insight, letting down your guard, is just a way you grow into more "love." That's what love is when you're twenty, all dreams and little wisdom.

It's a love you fall into when discernment is still learning to walk.

Charlotte warned me when she saw how quickly Lucas crossed a boundary just a couple of hours after the first words were spoken between us. She wasn't being judgmental; she picked up on something I'd missed. Perhaps if the shoe had been on the other foot, I would've been the one warning her; but Jake treated her with such care. I never saw him demand anything contrary to her values.

The conflicting emotions I felt about his love-bombing were quickly brushed aside. *Maybe I just wanted love too badly.* I was in love with love. I was leaning into the feeling of being noticed and included. Within minutes, he was telling me how beautiful I was, how he'd had a thing for me all summer, and within hours after our first exchange, we were making out like crazy. Love is supposed to make you do crazy things; you're supposed to be overwhelmed, out of control, giddy . . . because that's what we think love is—when you're twenty.

Ten years later and finally free, I realized after all I had endured, my senses had been dulled. Now, I noticed the sound of the chattering squirrels, the damp smell of moss, leaves, and peat, and the rich perfumed fragrance of honeysuckle that curled around me like a whispered memory as I wandered down the sun-dappled street.

I felt light.

Carefree.

Something I hadn't felt since that summer of my twentieth year. I could taste this freedom, and it was sweet.

Refreshing. Breathable. Effortless.

Beautiful.

Chapter Three

What Glitters Isn't Always Gold

"Want to get a pizza?" said the text. "I'm outside."

What? Who??

Launching off the couch, I pulled the curtain aside and peered past the flowering dogwood branches. There he was—Lucas, lounging in his convertible with the top down, a wide, mischievous grin aimed straight at my window. His aviators perched on top of his head, tangled in the sun-kissed waves of tousled brown hair.

Snatching my phone, I fired off a quick text: "Five minutes!"

With urgency, I stripped off my cozy sweatpants and pulled my tank top over my head, slipping into a pale-pink strapless sundress that brushed just above my knees. Nude flats slid onto my feet, a sweep of gloss kissed my lips, and mascara accentuated my lashes. Casting myself a quick glance in the mirror, the girl staring back at me was almost unrecognizable. Eyes sparkled with anticipation and cheeks glowed with a flush of hope. She looked light and carefree, luminous, as though joy itself radiated from her skin. I couldn't help but smile; for the first time in so long, I saw not just myself but the possibility of something new—something amazing.

Full of anticipation, I ran down the stairs and out the front door. I told myself not to appear too eager, forcing myself to walk at a normal pace down the flower-lined sidewalk to the edge of the lawn where Lucas sat waiting. With his tanned arm hanging out the window and the other resting on top of the wheel, he looked unbelievably hot.

"How'd you get my number?" I grasped the door handle, swinging open the car door and flashing a quick smile in his direction.

"Jake," he answered.

I laughed lightly. "Makes sense."

"Well, it's soon," Lucas stated. ". . . Soon enough?"

I laughed, "Yes, it's perfect."

"Got a favorite pizza place?"

"Yes actually! There is this cute little pizza place that overlooks the water. They make the best woodfire pizza and root beer floats. Let's go there!"

The wind whipped through my hair, tousling it recklessly. I laughed and moved the hair that kept flying into my mouth, pushing my sunglasses on my head to secure my hair.

"You look so beautiful." Lucas kept glancing at me while he drove with a grin on his perfectly chiseled face.

Beaming, I held onto his hand a little tighter and let the wind whip my hair.

The large wooden door was framed by climbing English ivy, giving it a charm all its own. As Lucas pushed open the door, my eyes wandered instinctively about the room. The decor greeted me like an old friend. Dripping white candles illuminated tables, plates imported from Sicily adorned with bold yellow and blue flowers added a vibrant touch alongside matching red metal chairs. The warm, intoxicating aroma welcomed us in, wrapping around the soft hum of voices and bursts of laughter from couples tucked into cozy tables.

When our order was ready, Lucas stood to collect our pizza, and I carried the foamy drinks made in large clear mason jars. We stepped out through the large wooden back door, propped open by a rusted metal chair, and found a spot overlooking the wide, slow-moving river, its surface glinting soft blue in the light. Setting the pizza box between us, we each reached in, pulling out heavy, cheese-laden slices, with steam curling up as we took our first, eager bites. Biting into the delicious flavors of ricotta and mozzarella cheese, basil, and richly seasoned sauce, I could taste the complimentary flavors of rosemary and oregano.

Lucas paused, his gaze locking with mine, and searched my wide hazel eyes as if they held a hidden secret. When he spoke, his voice dropped to a low husky whisper, "Joy . . . you're so beautiful. I know you probably hear this all the time, but honestly, you're the most beautiful woman I've ever seen."

I dipped my head, feeling a blush rise to my cheeks. "Thank you," I whispered, the words scarcely louder than a breath. Setting my slice of pizza on the box cover, I slowly—almost shyly—lifted my gaze until it met his steady, knowing one.

He leaned in, fingers brushing softly against my cheek—a touch so tender it made my breath catch. Then slowly, deliberately, he lowered his head and kissed me. His lips found mine, gentle and insistent. The kiss lingered, unhurried, electric, sending sparks through every nerve. When he finally pulled away, my senses were spinning. A flash of heat swept across my skin, tingling and demanding. All at once, I wanted to forget everything else, including the pizza—and just toss it into the grass and lose myself in his kiss, again and again. My fingers rose unconsciously to my lips, tracing the memory of the kiss, craving every bit of it.

"I love kissing you," he admitted as he held my gaze with power.

I tore my eyes away for a moment, trying to steady the wild rhythm of my heart.

Reaching for my root beer, I took a slow, long sip, letting the cool, fizzy sweetness linger, anything to anchor me, if only for a moment. Lucas rose, extending his hand to me. I slipped mine into his, and with a gentle pull, he drew me into the warmth of his chest.

Wrapping his arms around my slender waist, he suggested, "Let's walk."

We walked and talked, learning more about each other and I savored the feeling of my hand in his, it felt safe and warm. I felt special, admired, and adored.

The sky was soft and dusky when we returned from the river. My hand still tingled from his. We stopped in front of the car, and Lucas brushed a strand of hair from my face. "I can't remember the last time I felt this, complete and at peace. There's something special about you."

My whole body lit up. For the first time in years, I didn't want a date to end. As we drove home, my mind kept replaying it all—the laughter, the way he listened, was tuned in to me, how he seemed to really *see* me.

Later that night, Lucas texted, "Can I see you tomorrow?"

Sitting curled up among the soft throw pillows, I couldn't hold back the smile spreading across my face as I texted back, "Yes."

The next night, as the sun was kissing the horizon, Lucas knocked on the front door with an array of flowers so huge, they could not be hidden behind his back. They weren't just any flowers; they were my favorites. *How did he know?* The bouquet overflowed with hyacinths, lilies, and tulips, their intoxicating fragrance spilling into the air.

"These are for you, beautiful Joy." Lucas placed them in my waiting arms.

I buried my face in the delicate blossoms, inhaling the sweet, mingling fragrance until my eyes fluttered closed. I couldn't help but smile. "I love them. Thank you!"

"I couldn't stop thinking about you," he admitted, his voice low and sultry. "You've been haunting my thoughts."

As I slid into the passenger seat, I noticed the spotless car, shiny chrome, leather seat buffed to perfection, and the music low and mellow. The cool, warm evening air swirled around us, engulfing us in its comforting presence.

"You look incredible," he commented with admiration in his eyes. "I've thought about you all day, and I couldn't wait to see you tonight."

I laughed softly as I straightened the hem of my ivory wrap dress that flowed in soft folds, ending above my knees in a gentle waved trim. My simple gold necklace and diamond studs were my only jewelry. I had chosen a dress that still felt like summer, soft and light, the fabric light enough to catch the breeze, but warm enough for the fading late summer's sun. I let my hair fall freely, the natural waves sweeping over one shoulder, almost brushing my waist as the sun caught glints of caramel among the soft, chocolate waves.

I saw the way his eyes swept over me, capturing the details, and I felt exactly how I'd hoped to—effortless, beautiful, and seen.

We drove to a small bistro tucked behind the old theater, the kind of place that strung dozens of threads of fairy light across the ancient ceiling. The air smelled like herbs and rain; the windows thrown open to catch the breeze. The hostess directed us to a table set in the dimly lit corner half-hidden by vines decorating the old, timeworn walls. We enjoyed the romantic ambience, soft music, and twinkling lights.

Lucas reached for my hand before the menus even arrived. "I don't know what this is," Lucas admitted softly, "but I've never felt connected to anyone like this before."

His words sank deeply, resonating in my heart, warming me in a new and exciting way. We chatted through the evening about the things we loved, my favorite books, the way I loved coffee, the sports he loved, how he craved adventure, and all the places I dreamed of visiting one day.

After dinner we walked along the river again. The full moon cast its light down upon us, and starlight danced on the dark water. Lucas slipped his jacket off, resting it upon my chilled shoulders. He leaned in, brushing a gentle kiss on my temple.

It was a perfect ending to a date I'd only dreamed of. As I lay snuggled in my down comforter at home, I felt enraptured as if in a dream, wistfully wrapped in the joyful bliss of young love.

A few weeks flew by in the soft, golden rush of romantic dates, long walks, late-night talks and kisses that left me breathless. Lucas had a way of making everything seem larger than life. The way he looked deeply into my eyes, as if seeing into my soul, the way he seemed to know exactly what I desired and loved. Before I'd realized, he had woven himself into my everyday thoughts, my every moment. Every morning began with his text, brightening my day like the sunrise, and every night ended with his voice, deep and sultry, comforting and safe. It felt like love—dizzying, consuming, and irresistible.

I was convinced.

The evenings spent on the porch swing with stolen kisses captured our perfect evening. I noticed that Lucas saw everything about me—when I changed my nail color, a new outfit I'd chosen, when I seemed tired, he seemed to know when I wanted to do something fun and exciting or slow and relaxed. Sometimes I caught myself wondering how this happened all so fast.

Maybe too fast? Yet it seemed to be a perfect fit. *Maybe that's fate.*

All worries diminished the minute his smile rested upon me. It lit the very center of my being. I felt alive.

Late September was a flurry of early fall activities. I had been counting down the days until the fair opened—the smell of caramel apples, the glow of the lights, the rush of the rides, and the sounds of laughter rising on the cool air, reaching even the farthest parts of our small town.

Our friend group had planned to meet on Friday night for the opening of the fair, and I could hardly wait. Charlotte and I spent the afternoon in my room, music blasting as we tore through half our wardrobes to find the perfect mix of cute and casual. In the end we settled on denim jackets, stone-washed cutoff shorts that barely skimmed our thighs, and flowy crop tops paired with cowboy boots—the kind of outfit that felt like summer refusing to let go. Charlotte was a flurry of excitement, twirling in front of the mirror, already daydreaming about Jake. Her laughter filled the room, bright and unstoppable.

The Chestertown Fair was the highlight of every fall—the one weekend in fall the whole town seemed to come alive. From the youngest kids clutching cotton candy in their sticky little hands to couples who'd been coming since high school, everyone gathered to celebrate. From the charming old couples to young, starry-eyed lovers, romance bloomed beneath the midway lights, sparked on the rides, while chivalrous young men vied to win prizes for their sweet, innocent ladies.

The air was thick with the scent of grilled meats and wood smoke; every corner offered something tempting—meats grilled and smoked to perfection, roasted corn brushed with butter, caramel apples glistening on skewers, large wedges of watermelon, fresh and ripe, and brewery tables loaded with local brewed beer and ciders.

As dusk settled, the fairgrounds began to glow, strings of bulbs flickered on above the crowd, music from the local country band filled the air, and laughter echoed through the cool September air. The sounds of the fair traveled far. Even miles away, you could hear the faint laughter, the hum of the Ferris wheel, and the echo of the tinny country band. It traveled across the small country town, brushing over the wide-open farmlands, and was carried across the country air, slipping over fences and reaching the farthest corners where only the crickets and the wind kept company, down to the softly flowing river, catching the unsuspecting traveler by surprise.

By the time the sun had slipped behind the trees, Charlotte and I had arrived at the ticket booth looking impatiently for Lucas and Jake. Lucas was already there, leaning against the fence, his smile lighting up when he saw me.

"There you are! You look so beautiful." He took my hand. "I thought you'd never get here."

The noise and chaos faded as he linked his fingers through mine. Charlotte found Jake, and together we moved through the fair, laughter trailing behind as we wove our way through the crowd. The guys tried their luck at ring toss and balloon darts. Jake won a fluffy, oversized teddy bear for Charlotte that she hugged tightly to her chest. My cheeks ached from smiling. I felt light and carefree, carried by the rhythm of the night and Lucas's presence.

We shared caramel apples as our fingers brushed, piping-hot ears of corn laden with dripping butter, and piles of smoked meats. My hair whipped across my face as we rode the dizzying rides. Then came the Ferris wheel; Lucas insisted we save it for last. We climbed into the small car as the cool air brushed my legs, and goosebumps rose on my skin. Below us, the fair became a swirl of lights and motion, and the music faded to a distant hum. As we reached the top, the wheel came to a screeching halt. I screamed and clutched onto Lucas's arm as the cart went from a swinging motion to a violent halt. Finally, after several moments, the gentle swinging began, and the car rocked gently in the wind. It felt like time stopped. The whole town was spread out beneath us, the smell of popcorn drifted upward, hay flew gently on the breeze, the night sky stretched endless and clear.

"It's so beautiful," I whispered, taking in the beautiful sights.

"You are," Lucas whispered in return, gazing deeply into my hazel eyes.

We were caught in this moment of excitement and bliss, and before I could respond, Lucas leaned in, his lips capturing mine. The kiss was soft at first then deeper, pulling me in as everything fell away except Lucas and me.

When the Ferris wheel finally lurched forward, I laughed, dizzy and breathless, my fingers still intertwined through his. The fair lights shimmered below like a thousand tiny stars, and in that moment, I was sure nothing had ever felt more perfect.

One warm, early October evening, he gently grasped my hand and led me down toward the gentle flowing water as the grass brushed against the skin on our feet. We walked down the path and chose a secluded spot under a large, cascading willow tree. The branches cast a private curtain, and Lucas pulled me comfortably next to him on the ancient stone bench. Sitting with my head rested against his strong shoulder, he draped his arm protectively around me. The curtain of willow branches lent a romantic aura, and I rested my head against his shoulder, relaxing peacefully in this fairytale moment.

Lucas looked deeply into my eyes. "I don't want to see anyone else. I don't want to think about anyone else. I just want you. I want this. Be my girlfriend," he murmured. "Will you go out with me?" He raised his hand to my face, gently securing a fallen lock behind my ear.

The words sent a shiver through me. Part thrill, part disbelief. No one had ever seen me the way Lucas did. He saw me so completely.

"Yes, I want you to be my boyfriend." My heart soared as I said the words, and a smile spread across my glowing face.

Lucas pulled me onto his lap, his lips claiming mine. Each kiss drew me closer and closer into him, until I was completely lost. His lips traced my neck, brushing my ear, and kissed a path down my throat. I was suspended in the moment, and every nerve screamed for more, yearning for another touch, another kiss.

His arms wrapped around me with a hunger that clung and kindled, awakening something deep inside of me. My fingers slid into his hair, then clutched tightly, as if letting go wasn't an option. I lifted my gaze and looked into his eyes, seeing a world reflected back that left me breathless—everything I had ever dreamed of, all at once, too fast, too much, and I was swept off my feet before I could even find solid ground.

Chapter Four

Fall 2020,
Present Day

I found myself thinking how life was different with just the four of us. It was good. Peaceful. New. I wanted to make new memories, ones that held the warmth of happiness. Little by little, the girls and I began stitching new pieces to the quilt that shaped our lives—laughter echoing in the kitchen, Saturday morning filled with pancakes and sticky fingers, late-night movies with fresh-popped popcorn and homemade cookies, and long neighborhood walks picking flowers and stopping for tasty snow cones in the mid-summer's heat.

It was a beautiful remaking of our lives. Every new, happy memory was painted over ones that brought pain. I purposed to build an environment that flowed with peace, joy, and love—one where we could be free to be ourselves. In this time, it required much grace. Grace to forgive, grace to let go, and grace to embrace our true selves and look toward a wholesome and fulfilling future.

As the months turned into years, I saw healing and growth. I learned when a person is away from the source of trauma, their brain and body innately begin to repair. The body brings itself back to a place where growth can occur. How amazing it is, how the body and mind work. If you can be in a place free from fear and restriction, you grow. You heal. That's how it was meant to be–how we were created.

Stepping into the Pizza Shoppe with my girls was like stepping back in time. I could see Lucas and I secluded at a tiny table for two, romantic and entranced with each other. I could see us whisking away to the riverside for a romantic picnic, nestled together by the flowing riverbank, and I remember sneaking in a few minutes before closing to share a foamy root beer float while staring deeply into each other's eyes.

The memories were strong and haunting.

We were surrounded by the warm Italian decor, the faint hum of music drifting like salt on the air, the heavy fragrance of herbs that clung to every memory I carried with me, and the slow, sultry music. For a moment, the past closed in, but I held tight to my resolve. I was determined to start fresh—to create meaningful moments and reestablish and build new memories that brought smiles and joy. I believed deeply in the power of healing, in giving the body and spirit room to reset. I learned that children who grow in the shadows of domestic abuse often carry invisible wounds; they struggle with identity, with self-worth, and with the very sense of their value and purpose.

I wanted my daughters to know a different story.

"A table for four, please."

"One moment, please," the hostess responded, smiling kindly, looking sharp in her black form-fitting dress and patent leather heels.

"Right this way." The cheerful hostess beckoned, guiding us to a small table set for four. It was tucked in the shadows, softened by the glow of numerous dripping candles of varying height, their flames flickering like whispers. The table overlooked the slow-moving river with a surface that caught glimmers of light.

"Here, girls, choose a seat please." I pulled out a chair.

They scrambled for position, tugging at the chairs in competition, as if the best seat were a trophy to be won.

"I get the river view," Ivy declared triumphantly, sliding into her selected chair before anyone could protest.

"You always get the best seat," Mia groaned, though her grin gave her away.

"Ya, no fair!" chimed in Rose, her dimples betraying her mock irritation.

Soon the whole table was alive with teasing and laughter, bubbling over like champagne.

I sank into my own chair, letting their joy wash over me. The weight in my chest felt lighter, as though the flickering candles had burned holes through the darkness, letting in something brighter.

This was what I wanted—not perfection, but moments like this, where my girls could simply be young and happy, carefree enough to argue over who got the best chair.

Life didn't have to be perfect to be good—just free of damaging trauma. I knew raising three girls, especially as I looked forward to the rest of the teen years, wasn't for the faint of heart—but it was more than possible with stability, safety, and love. I smiled through dinner, listening to their chatter about favorite singers, secret elementary and middle school crushes, favorite movies, and how they'd suddenly developed a strong dislike of country music. Their tastes shifted like the rising tide, and I let my smile linger, soaking in these small, ordinary moments that felt like everything.

As we walked out of the quaint restaurant, I cast a glance back, trying to imagine it through my daughters' eyes. To them, it was probably just an old-fashioned restaurant, not particularly exciting, with old metal chairs and an overabundance of candles, not like the cool fast-food restaurants that had popped up everywhere. Yet to me, every detail carried a sense of nostalgia and memory. Hurrying to catch up to the girls, I left my lingering thoughts behind. Our present was full, our future promising.

I pictured a future bathed in light and calm—a life where past trauma was replaced with joy, laughter, and a deep sense of peace. A world where my daughters could carve their own paths and understand their worth. They would learn the power of healthy boundaries, the courage to speak the truth, and the bravery to follow their hearts. It was to be a life where mistakes were lessons, not scars; where growth was celebrated, and love was abundant. New memories were waiting to be made—adventures to share, quiet moments to savor, and holidays to rejoice in. Most of all, it would be a life with space to simply be ourselves.

In this new beginning, where we chose to stand for truth and authenticity, joy was no longer fleeting; it was steady, resilient, and ours to grow into and claim.

Chapter Five

Under the Spell

Lucas's zest for life was contagious. His energy trailed behind him like a glowing aura, pulling me in with an irresistible force. The way he desired me so completely was intoxicating, and in that moment, I was utterly, unreservedly happy.

Rational thought slipped away as I became entranced with blissful love, a storybook romance, and a perfect future—every girl's fairytale dream.

Since attending the same college, Lucas and I had become inseparable. In the months that followed, we stole moonlit walks and long drives down quiet country roads, often parking on dimly lit streets where kisses ignited the night. Back home, my old, checkered quilt became our sanctuary as we lost ourselves in whispered laughter and freely given kisses. It was intoxicating, addicting and began escalating quickly. I felt I could not withhold myself; he was an addiction I didn't want to quit.

October came in full swing with bright oranges, fire reds, and translucent yellows that painted the trees.

It was one of those perfect afternoons when the air felt golden. I was heading to my car after class when Lucas's text buzzed, "Let's go for a picnic."

"I'd love that!" I texted back.

By the time I returned home, his car had already pulled into the driveway. The sight of him waiting sent a rush of excitement through me. I yanked a cozy sweater from the coat rack, in case the evening air turned crisp and sprinted to join him in the passenger seat.

He greeted me with a lingering kiss. "Look what we have!"

In the back seat, an overflowing picnic basket stuffed with delicious-looking goodies—cheeses, prosciutto, olives, strawberries, blackberries, fresh bread, little jars of jam, and a cheap bottle of Riesling.

"This looks amazing," I exclaimed. "It's been such a stressful week with studying and tests, I could use an afternoon of fun." A huge smile spread across my face, impossible to hold back.

"My thoughts exactly," he responded, reaching over to intertwine his fingers through mine as we sped toward the countryside as the vibrant scenery rushed by in a blur of color.

"This is perfect," Lucas decided, pulling off the road beside a wooded area where a gentle, meandering stream wound through the trees and bright fall wildflowers painted the ground. He lifted the picnic basket effortlessly while I carried our sweaters and quilt. Walking close to the water, I chose a spot beneath towering maple trees ablaze with autumn colors, the canopy stretching overhead and opening onto a grassy expanse.

Spreading out the quilt in the shadow of the massive trees, sunlight broke through the leaves to filter its dappled light on the ground below as the sun warmed us deliciously on this mild day and we settled comfortably on the quilt.

Ceremoniously, Lucas poured wine, handing the first glass to me. We toasted our little date and drank the light, refreshing wine, the citrus and apple flavors melding together. Nibbling on wedges of cheese, berries, and soft-baked bread, I felt the heady feeling of slight intoxication. I was calm and relaxed, and I laughed freely as Lucas shared bites of strawberries with me.

He leaned closer, his lips brushing mine softly as first, then deepening with longing. Gently, he took the wine glass from my hand and set it aside. One arm slipped beneath me, drawing me against his chest. Our bodies pressed together as his gaze locked on mine—then his head dipped, and his lips found me once more.

Our tongues moved in a fiery rhythm, his kisses unraveling every guarded part of me until I was swept into a passion I never wanted to end.

"Oh, Joy," he groaned, pulling me close. The gentleness was gone now. His heartbeat thundered beneath his sweater, and his eyes burned with deep longing.

The world around us seemed to blur and fade until there was only the warmth of his touch and the quiet rush of our mingling breath. The quilt draped around us, cocooning our warmth as the air grew cool. The sun melted in a riot of radiant hues, and the hush that followed was sacred. As darkness began to draw close, I wished this moment would never end.

Driving home, the dusk breeze whipped through our windswept hair. Sunglasses perched atop my head, one leg folded on the seat, my arm wrapped loosely around it as I tapped my toe to *Amarillo Sky*.

Life was perfect.

We stole every spare moment—kissing, laughing, and falling deeper into each other, seizing every chance we had to be together. In the meantime, Charlotte and I had barely connected since college began. When she reached out to grab coffee, I claimed I was busy or already with Lucas. A twinge of guilt always followed, but it never outweighed my eagerness for one more moment with him.

"Girl! Are you ever gonna make any time for me?" she insisted over the phone.

"I know . . . okay, how about tomorrow afternoon we grab coffee?" I replied, my guilt pressing heavily. I had brushed off my best friend one too many times, and we both knew it.

"Perfect!" she answered, relief filling her voice.

I shot a quick text to Lucas. We agreed to push our date back a couple hours so I could make time to hang out with Charlotte. I missed my best friend too much to skip another opportunity to be with her.

Planning my outfit for our coffee date, I sifted through the closet, my fingers landing on the perfect pair of pale-blue skinny jeans that I paired with a tight lavender ruched top, the color reminding me of a bloom just beginning to open.

Shortly after noon the following day, I peddled my bike toward the local coffee shop, tucked between my favorite used bookstore and the little antique shop. Fall had arrived with warm days and chilly nights. I couldn't help but admire the way the leaves fell, collecting in no particular order across the earth's soft floor. I felt the crisp, colorful leaves crunch beneath the tires of my bike with every turn of the wheel. Braking to a stop, I hopped off my bike and leaned it against the solitary scarlet maple tree in front of the little cafe.

Pushing the door open, the bell jingled a happy *hello* to announce my entrance, and Charlotte turned. "Hey, girl, missed you!" she said, enfolding me in a welcoming hug.

I returned her warm hug, then we placed our order with the chatty waitress and caught up on gossip and life. My caramel macchiato arrived with Charlotte's lavender latte. Sipping our frothy brews with enjoyment, we relaxed with a few contented sighs.

"So, how's it going with Lucas?" she inquired. "Tell me!"

"Amazing!" I replied, as I tucked a stray lock of hair back into my bun. "We've been dating about two months now. It's been wonderful. How about you and Jake?"

"It's going really well. Jake's so kind and thoughtful. He's always sweet to me, and the family loves him. I want to see how things go for about a year or so, but I have a very good feeling about this." Charlotte's eyes sparkled with future dreams. "I love being with him."

"I'm so happy for you." I clasped Charlotte's hand, and she returned the knowing reassurance.

"Make sure though," she offered, "to make time for friends! I know it's fun and exciting in a relationship, but it's healthy to have your own space and time with your own friends. I have to make myself do that, otherwise I'd spend every free second with Jake too."

"I know, you're right," I admitted, my voice soft. "I just . . . I love being with him. Every spare second, I want to be with him. He's fun, exciting, and there is this *spark*—you know! The way he looks at me . . . like I'm the only person in the world. It's kind of amazing." My words drifted out like a sigh, dreamy . . . full of that wild, weightless feeling of falling in love.

"Girl, I get it. Just find your balance."

We chatted a bit more about our college semester, the struggles and challenges, what we were loving, then hugged a tight, happy goodbye. After returning home, I kept glancing down at my phone with curiosity. I'd expected to hear from Lucas about our evening plans.

That was weird, I thought, brow scrunched.

After talking to Lucas earlier in the morning, I hadn't heard from him in several hours. *Usually, he texts all the time.* Another hour passed and still nothing. Feeling confused, I texted him to confirm our plans and waited to hear his reply.

Nothing.

Sitting on the overstuffed couch, I chose to get lost in a long-forgotten book as the afternoon drifted. Periodically I checked my phone, curious. And another hour went by.

No reply.

I called. It went to voicemail. Feeling uncertain, by eight p.m. I decided to get a small bite to eat, then turned my attention back to finishing my book.

"I thought you had plans?" Mom said as she popped her head around the corner, "Are you staying in tonight?"

"Apparently so," I answered, my brow scrunched in concern. "Lucas hasn't responded."

"That is odd." Mom's expression tightened in worry.

By eleven p.m., sleep was already tugging at my eyelids. Drowsy, I staggered upstairs and sank beneath layers of thick, warm blankets.

The next thing I knew, morning sunlight splayed soft rays across my eyes. I blinked against the warming light, stretching out my long limbs. Outside the open window, autumn leaves blazed in a riot of color on the tree branches.

Reluctantly, I slipped from my bed, wrapped myself in a white, fluffy robe, and cinched the belt snuggly at my waist. My feet found their way into fuzzy slippers, and I padded down the wooden stairs toward the comforting sounds of life stirring below—and the welcoming promise of coffee.

"Good morning!" Mom cheered from across the kitchen as she mixed up muffins of some sort. "Sleep well?"

"Yes, I did," I answered sleepily as I grabbed a mug and poured the hot brew into my cup.

"It's definitely a gorgeous day." Mom smiled. "Any plans?"

"None that I know of right now. Lucas and I were supposed to go on a date last night, but maybe he fell off the face of the earth, I don't know. So . . . we'll see." I yawned, letting out a tired sigh of annoyance. "What are you doing today?"

"I'm going to run to the farmer's market and get more mums and flowers to plant. I'd like to get a head start before it begins to rain. Want to come?" Mom inquired.

"Maybe, let me think about it." Glancing down to my phone, I saw no alerts. Turning the phone facedown, I decided to put it out of my mind.

I finished my coffee while Mom and I chatted. The timer chimed, and as soon as Mom pulled the muffins from the oven, I selected a piping-hot raspberry muffin. I split into its fluffy softness, and a burst of steam billowed out from the middle. I took a bite and immediately felt it melt on my tongue in hot raspberry deliciousness.

By mid-morning I still had not received a response from Lucas. I decided to give him a call. It rang several times, and on the fifth ring, he answered.

"Hey," Lucas said, his voice heavy with sleep.

"Hello?"

"Ya, hi, what's up?"

"I called you last night . . . We had a date, and you didn't answer or call me this morning." I explained, "Is everything okay? I was worried." I flicked at a chip in my nail polish, trying to sound casual.

"Ya, I got busy with the guys."

"We had a date . . ."

"Ya, well, you pushed it back to hang with your friend, so Jimmy called with plans, and I got busy." He sighed, the sound sharp with irritation.

"Umm, I asked if you minded me pushing back the time. You said that you didn't, especially since I explained I haven't seen Charlotte in, like, forever," I reminded him, brow scrunching in confusion. "You said you were okay with it."

"Ya, it's fine," he said. "I ended up with plans with the guys, and we hung out late with a bunch of friends at the bar."

I stood dumbfounded. "And you forgot to tell me? Then you went out and hung with a bunch of people at a bar when we were supposed to be on a date?" I started pacing, anger rising at his less-than-honest behavior. "Who did you hang out with?"

"Jimmy, a couple guys, and a few of their girlfriends," his voice easy and unbothered.

I froze. "You hung out with girls too? That's not cool." The heat of anger crept up my neck.

This feels wrong. I had never seen this careless side of Lucas, and I didn't like it. Again, I replied, "We had a date!"

"Hey, you were busy." His voice sharpened, cutting through the pause between us.

"Not in the evening," I said, my voice rising an octave.

"Well . . . next time," Lucas said ever so smoothly.

I was pissed. *The audacity.* I ended the call, slamming my phone on the couch before pacing the room to work out my frustration.

I didn't understand. Grabbing my phone, I ran up the stairs to call Charlotte and vent.

"What?" she exclaimed. "That's not okay. If Jake did that, I'd be furious."

"Ya, well, I'm mad! I mean, yeah, he can hang out with his friends, but we had a date we agreed on, and he should've communicated to me if he couldn't go. Not just ditch me to hang out with the guys and some other girls . . . like, what the hell?" I picked the pink nail polish off my manicured fingers and flung it to the floor.

"*Exactly.* Well, don't you have plans to go to the movies tomorrow? I wouldn't go." She stated firmly. "Teach him a lesson."

"Ya, we do," I hesitantly answered. "I'll think about it."

"You'd better. That's not cool," she sternly lectured.

Trudging down the stairs, I saw Mom heading out the door with her purse slung over her shoulder. She turned back, with her hand pausing on the knob. "Wanna come?"

"Sure," I said in a depressing low voice.

"You okay?" Mom asked, her brows furrowed deeply in concern.

"Ya, I'm fine," I answered, "just stuff."

"Okay," she said in a consoling voice, "will Starbucks help?"

"Most definitely," I answered with a genuine smile.

Feeling a bit better, we headed out to the farmers market with a very important stop, first at Starbucks, to get my favorite pumpkin spice latte . . . extra hot.

The next day was unseasonably chilly. October winds blew cold, and brilliant fall leaves swirled about in little cyclones. It was not a day to be hanging outside. I cozied up in the house with a large mug of Earl Grey tea and a big book, cocooning myself in a cozy throw as tree limbs bowed deeply in the chilled wind, creaking like old bones about to snap.

I had worked my way through half the book when my phone vibrated.

Hesitantly picking up my phone, I looked at the screen.

The text read: "Pick you up at 7:00, see you for the movie."

After a few long moments, I replied with only "?"

"Sorry about yesterday," Lucas responded.

That did not feel like a genuine apology, but did I need to make a big deal about it? *Maybe not.* He did—*sort of*—apologize.

"Okay," I texted, with a quandary of mixed feelings.

Brushing aside my nagging doubts, I climbed the stairs, determined to rinse off my nerves in a hot shower and get ready for the movie. Maybe if I got ready, smiled, showed up, it would work itself out.

Lucas pulled up to the end of my walkway a few minutes after seven p.m. Cautiously, I walked down to join him, hoping he would initiate a meaningful apology or something. Instead, Lucas acted nonchalant. He looked handsome with his hair waved across his forehead, sun streaks still visible throughout. Leaning over, he gave me a quick peck. Noticing my less-than-usually-responsive kiss, he paused and looked at me confused, a bit irritated.

"What's wrong?" Lucas asked. "Are you still upset about last night?" Not waiting for a reply, he rushed on with cool instruction, "Relax . . . it's not a big deal. I said I was sorry."

I gripped the edge of the seat, jaw tight, hands clenched at my sides. Frustration and disbelief rose in my chest at his flippant response.

"Seriously, don't ruin tonight. I want to have fun." He looked at me with slight disapproval.

His behavior made me feel bad for having genuine feelings, I felt sort of guilty.

I didn't want to be the cause of arguing or ruining our night, so I forced a smile on my face and focused my attention on the road ahead.

"There we go," he said, patting my knee consolingly, and drove on toward the theater as the sun began to set in the western sky. Even with the inspiring beauty, I tried without success to liven my mood. Unprompted tears began to blur my vision as we drove. I felt an inner sadness growing at his inability to recognize his responsibility in hurting my feelings and his lack of truly trying to make up for it.

I tried to enjoy the date, but I couldn't. I didn't complain, but my heart wasn't in it. I felt jumbled feelings—confusion at his random change of demeanor, anger at being ghosted, betrayed at his hanging out with others without a thought of including me, and injustice at how he was expecting me to just dismiss it, without a care.

This wasn't him! Not the Lucas I knew.

It felt wrong to have genuine feelings and be told to shove them inside to not cause disruption to our date night. Yet Lucas acted as charming as ever . . . smiling, charismatic, and chatting with anyone who crossed our path. When the date was over, he pulled up to my house, the car ride as quiet as the night. I pushed open the car door into the bright moonlight casting its light on the front of the house, and I stepped out of the car.

"No kiss goodbye?" he admonished.

I paused and slowly leaned back in to give him a small peck on the lips.

"When you stop sulking, call me. You were rather cold tonight."

I froze, in shock at his callousness. Slowly I closed the car door, hurt and confused.

Without a backward glance, I walked up the sidewalk alone, with scattered leaves underfoot and a cold breeze chilling deeper than my bones. Pushing open the front door, I shut myself in the house and leaned back against the inside of the door, pausing to digest what had just happened. My thoughts were a mess. After a long moment, I turned toward the warm foyer with the fireplace ablaze where I could see Mom and Dad sitting comfortably on the living room couch reading their own novels, Mom with her slippered feet propped on the mahogany coffee table.

"How was it?" Dad asked.

Mom looked up toward me.

"It was good." I really didn't want to talk about it.

"Okay," Dad responded, "want to join us?"

Plopping down next to Dad, I sank into the softness of the couch and leaned into his strong shoulder, soaked up his companionable love.

"Want to grab a book and read?" Dad suggested, his voice gravelly and low.

"No, I just want to relax for a bit," I explained.

"Okay," he said as he patted my knee and turned back to concentrate on his book.

After some moments of soaking up the comfortable atmosphere, I felt myself drifting drowsily.

Although my parents could read until late into the night, I pushed myself up, muttering tiredly, "I'm gonna go to bed now, love you guys."

"Okay, honey, good night," Mom replied, glancing up for a quick second and then down to the book drawing her attention.

Dad blew me a kiss then tugged his blanket more cozily around himself. Dragging my feet upstairs, I collapsed onto my bed. I sank into the assortment of decorative pastel pillows, pushing a few aside before snuggled into my covers. The blankets swallowed me up, and I was sound asleep before my arm even fell back on the mattress.

Morning dawned grey with heavy clouds. Rubbing sleep from my eyes, I rolled over to reach for my phone.

Four missed texts. All Charlotte.

Okay, fine, I thought, *I'll just call her. That will be easier.* I dialed Charlotte and she answered immediately.

"Hey! I've been trying to get a hold of you!" Charlotte said. "So . . . what did you do last night? What happened?"

I told her the whole story and how utterly confused and miserable I felt.

"Oh my god, Joy, that's not okay!"

"I know, I know . . . but do you think making waves is right?" I wondered aloud.

"Having boundaries is!"

"I get that, but I was upset with him, and he said he was sorry, then he expressed he just wanted to have a good night and didn't want to keep going over it . . . But I feel like his 'I'm sorry' wasn't really genuine . . . it felt sort of, just . . . brushed under the rug.

And he thinks I'm supposed to quickly forget about it and just move on? I don't feel right about that. And I don't know why suddenly he is acting like this." I sighed. "But also, I don't want to be bitchy or overly sensitive."

There was a long pause. Charlotte sighed heavily. "You would have sounded bitchy if he apologized profusely and sincerely and then you still held a grudge against him. But that's not you . . . I don't think that's how you acted. And that's not being overly sensitive when you respond with honest feelings to his rude actions."

"You're right! That wasn't how it was. It was valid to be bothered by that!" A rush of understanding came over me as her words illuminated the truth, and tears leaked from my eyes. I was glad my friend was in my corner. And a soft comfort took root—steady and grounding.

"Why don't you take some time away from him, just do other things, and give him a little space?" she suggested. "I think it would be good for him to think about his actions, especially since he treated you without thoughtfulness."

"Yeah, I think you're right." I hated to admit she was right. "It's just hard because . . . I really like him, and I like spending time with him. When I'm not with Lucas, I'm wondering what he's doing, and I have a million thoughts going through my head, then I miss him terribly . . . but you're right." I leaned back, letting my shoulders relax. "Okay, I'm gonna go, thanks for chatting with me." I breathed deeply. "You always help me feel better and think smarter." I smiled.

"I feel the same. I love you and just want you to have a healthy relationship. Have fun today, okay?" Charlotte suggested in her perky tone. "Especially on this dreary day, we need it!"

Walking down the wide wooden steps, I slid my hands down the banister, feeling every worn groove, nick, and childhood memory as I descended. The aroma of homemade waffles surrounded me, and I could feel my empty stomach growling loudly in response.

"Good morning!" I cheered.

"Morning!" Mom answered with a smile. "Dad just left for work, I made waffles, there are plenty left."

"Oh amazing! What a perfect breakfast on a dreary day."

Sitting at the little kitchen table, I dug in to enjoy my decadent breakfast. Mom walked over with two steaming mugs of Columbian coffee, setting one down in front of me. She eased herself into the other chair facing me.

"Do you like it?" she inquired with a knowing smile.

"This is fabulous, Mom!" I said. "I haven't had waffles like this in . . . almost forever. Thank you."

"Well, you looked kind of low last night, so I thought I'd make a pick-me-up breakfast to cheer you up." Mom smiled.

"You certainly did," I gushed. Sipping the frothy whipped cream on my coffee, I let out a contented sigh. My favorite.

"So, what's the plan for today?" she asked.

"I don't have class until two p.m., and it goes until nine, so I might relax here until then." I drummed my fingers on the table, pausing as the rhythm bounced through my thoughts. "Although . . . I might leave a bit early to hit the library."

"Sounds like a plan. I have a few errands and appointments today, so I'll be heading out soon," Mom explained as she tidied the counters.

I gazed outside at the dreary sky for a long moment over my cooling cup of coffee. The sun was valiantly trying to appear, but it would be in vain. The clouds were thick, grey and heavy, hanging low, almost touching the ground, and the wind whipped the drying brown and red leaves into stray piles across the lawn.

With this kind of weather, a cozy sweater and thick scarf was certainly necessary.

I dashed upstairs to get ready. After a quick shower, with my hair still damp, I swept the thick strands into an elegant chignon at the nape of my neck, tugging out a few whisps to softly frame my face. Adding a touch of burnt-orange lip gloss to my generous lips and a few swipes of mascara, that was all I needed. I stuffed my college books into my bag, flew down the stairs, and left the warmth of the house to the windy chill of the outdoors.

Locking my bike on the rack, I entered the vast, dimly lit library searching for a secluded spot to study. I had barely settled in when I glanced up and saw Lucas walk in with another college coed. They looked cozy, chatting as if they were close friends. My chest tightened; a knot of confusion, shock, and discomfort twisted inside me. *What is he doing? Is he . . . cheating on me?* I tried to force my eyes back to my books to focus on studying, but it was impossible.

My thoughts raced, tangled in disbelief with a rising storm of anger. He guided her over to a selection of books, his hand resting on her lower back. She looked up at him adoringly and giggled as he whispered something into her ear. My stomach flipped.

I'd seen enough.

I popped out of my chair, flying across the library to make my presence known. As I neared them, Lucas happened to raise his eyes and meet my furious ones.

He subtly moved his hand from her back to the books piled beside them. "Hi, Joy, have you met Ashley? She's a new transfer and needed someone to show her around the campus. I was volunteered." He shrugged nonchalantly then smiled.

With calculated control, I moved my gaze over to hers and replied, "No I haven't. Hello, Ashley, it's a pleasure. I'm Lucas's girlfriend." My eyes returned to glare at Lucas.

Lucas turned to Ashley. "I hope that was helpful. If you need any more help, you know where to find me."

She smiled demurely and nodded, then gathered her books and headed farther into the library.

"What was *that*?" I hissed, leaning closer, my fists clenched at my side.

"What?" he whispered back, tilting his head with a mock look of confusion.

"*That!*" I shot back, gesturing wildly toward Ashley, my voice trembling in anger.

"Um . . . . helping a student. It was nothing—don't get all jealous." He said it casually, as if flirting with another pretty girl was the most normal thing in the world. He leaned back slightly, one hand resting lazily on the table, brushing off my tension as easily as dust.

I didn't want to be accusatory, but I also was not blind or stupid. Even if he was only trying to assist a new student, his body language was completely unnecessary and flirtatious.

"That was *not* nothing."

I spun around and stormed across the library. Collecting my items in a hurry, I strode angrily out of the library, my footsteps quick and sharp against the floor. My breath came hard and uneven. Once outside, I paused, pressing my back against the cold brick wall. The chill grounded me just enough to catch my breath, yet my chest burned with fury. Beneath that, disbelief churned.

How could he possibly think that was okay, that any of it was acceptable? I knew in my gut what was right and wrong. And I was furious. What had gotten into Lucas?

The rest of the day slipped by in a forgotten haze. I couldn't remember a single thing from any of my lectures—the words, the discussions, even the assignments were all gone from my mind. By the time my classes ended, the hours felt like a blur. I pedaled home on auto pilot, stashing my bike in the garage, and hurried inside to the warmth of the house.

I tried calling Charlotte repeatedly—it went straight to voicemail. Deciding to call it a night, I crawled into bed, feeling hollow. I cradled the soft pillows, hoping their warmth could fill the quiet ache. Nestling as deeply as possible into my blankets, I couldn't quite name the emptiness I felt. Finally, sleep came.

Moving robotically for several days, I did only what was necessary, my mind trapped on an endless loop of that scene replaying over and over. I didn't imagine it—his behavior was overly friendly, unmistakably flirtatious. Too obvious. We'd been dating exclusively for a while now. There was no excuse. My chest tightened, a sharp ache of betrayal slicing through me, unable to shake the sting.

How dare he flirt and act cozy with another girl. How dare he guide her around with his hand on her low back! Seriously? Thinking about it made me even more furious. I could not shake the image—the way his hand rested on her lower back, the way she looked up at him with that coy, flirty gaze. The way he looked at her . . . was the way he should be looking at me. It twisted in my gut. And I felt a seething rage.

Confrontation had never been my strong suit, so I kept my distance. I didn't reach out to Lucas. *I'd rather not talk to him anyways,* I decided. *I'll focus on my schoolwork and push him to the back of my mind. I'd rather be alone and quiet. And angry.* He wasn't turning out to be the guy I thought he was. He obviously didn't seem committed to me, and I didn't want to play second fiddle. If he was as in love with me as I was with him, then I expected to be the only one who captured his attention. I didn't want him flirting or hanging out with other girls.

I would never do that to him, and I expected the same obvious loyalty.

I didn't want a man not fully dedicated to me.

A few weeks passed and I buried myself in finishing several papers. With deadlines looming, I declined all of Lucas's calls and threw myself wholeheartedly into my studies, using the work to keep my mind off everything else.

One afternoon, while studying at home, my phone chimed sharply, breaking my concentration. I flipped it over and saw . . . the text.

"Come outside." It was from Lucas. Then, a second text immediately followed: "Please."

I did not want to talk to him right now. Maybe never.

I flipped the phone back over.

"I'm not leaving. I can stay all day," he texted.

"Oh god," I groaned out loud.

"Just two minutes, pls," he asked. "If you give me two minutes, I promise I'll leave."

"Fine," I finally replied through text.

What, no! I thought, frustrated with myself for giving in.

Resting my hand for a long minute on my forehead, I contemplated the dilemma.

Finally, I pushed myself up from the desk chair and walked hesitantly down the stairs and toward the front door. Pausing with my hand on the doorknob, I gripped the knob so hard, my knuckles turned white. I released the knob as doubt surged through me, sharp and sudden. Then I reached for the knob again.

Should I even open it? I let go again.

After a long moment, I cracked open the large, wooden front door and stood framed in the doorway, the cool air from the courtyard brushing against my face.

"What?" My voice came out flat, stripped of any emotion.

Across the courtyard, he stood still, one arm tucked behind his back. "I have something for you," he said. The echo of his voice drifted between us, swallowed by the quiet.

As he crossed the courtyard, the hidden arm came forward —an enormous bouquet of scarlet-red roses, each one in lush, velvety bloom, their heady fragrance spilling into the air, intoxicating and impossible to ignore. When he reached the edge of the front steps, he extended the bouquet toward me, his eyes searching mine.

"I'm sorry," he began softly. "It was a misunderstanding; I really am sorry. It was stupid. I don't want to hurt you. It's you I love. There is no one else who could ever possibly fill my heart. I'm really sorry." The words tumbled out, his eyes heavy with regret.

I stayed where I was, the doorway a quiet barrier between us. The perfume of the roses drifted, rich and impossible to ignore, but I kept my face composed, feigning detachment.

After a full minute I relented with a simple "Thanks."

The roses were beautiful. My eyes kept stealing glances at the delicate petals releasing the most glorious aroma.

"Please, let me take you out. Just dinner. Let me make things right," he suggested as hope flickered in his eyes, that glint he used when he wanted forgiveness. "Let's put the roses inside and let me take you out on a date. Please."

His hand found my elbow, fingers gently tracing a path down my arm until they curled around mine. He stepped closer, the doorway shrinking between us, his nearness warm, practiced, disarming.

His touch drew me in, though I tried to resist. My fingers slackened around the door, and it drifted open as I cradled the roses in one arm. The air around us thickened, heavy with the scent of flowers and something unspoken. Stepping into the foyer, his eyes flicked toward the kitchen. "Let me help you find a vase," he offered.

Without a word, I followed, my movements mechanical. I was suspended between anger and the fragile illusion of his sincerity—caught in the pull I knew too well.

"Let's go to your favorite restaurant," he said from behind me and placed an empty vase on the counter. "I need to make it up to you."

Trying vainly to ignore his advances, I leaned over the sink to trim the roses, pretending his presence didn't unsettle me. The nearness of him pressed in anyway. He wrapped his strong arms around my midsection, gently pulled me close to his chest. My body remembered what my mind was trying to forget. Slowly, his head dipped, brushing the back of my neck, lips tracing the sensitive curve of my ear, leaving a trail of fire and tension down toward my shoulders, each kiss more intentional than the last. His warmth pressing close, breath hot against my skin. He lingered near my shoulder, leaving a magnetic intensity that left me unsteady, a quiet tremor in its wake.

"I'm sorry, babe. It didn't mean anything. I care about you. Let's make up. Please let me make it up to you. It will never happen again, I promise."

My emotions tangled in a knot—anger and hurt clashing with a flicker of something softer. His words carried a sincerity I couldn't quite dismiss—and the magnetic pull of his presence chipped away at the walls I had so carefully built. I stilled—caught between the resistance and the pull I couldn't deny. Methodically, I placed the roses in the vase and filled it with water, each movement deliberate, grounding myself. Then I turned to face him. My gaze lingered on his eyes. I looked for any trace of insincerity, but instead I was met with a raw, overwhelming blend of sadness, regret, hope, and concern.

After a long moment, I relented. "Fine, but don't ever do something stupid like that again. I'm serious, or don't bother ever coming back," I said, my voice growing louder and stronger with each word.

A relieved smile spread across his face, his shoulders heaved with a deep sigh. He tugged me gently toward the door, guiding me down the steps, with hurried energy. His grin was radiant as he opened the passenger door, sweeping his arm out with a flourish, and pressed a quick, warm kiss to my lips. Carefully shutting the door beside me, he rounded to the driver's side, sliding in with effortless agility. The door clicked shut with a firm thud, and then we were off. His hand found mine, gripping it with a quiet insistence, as we sped toward town. A blend of anticipation, relief, and something unspoken lingered between us as he steered us toward my favorite restaurant, the Pizza Shoppe. The same place we had our first date.

Unconsciously I smiled, tapping my foot to the music, as relief flooded me.

“I like to see you happy,” Lucas commented with a grin and a gentle squeeze to my hand.

I decided to let the situation pass. He seemed regretful, sincere, and apologetic.

I really love him, and I know he loves me . . . I just hope something like this never happens again.

Walking into the Pizza Shoppe, we were seated in a small nook decorated with a smattering of dimly lit candles, all varying in height. Faint instrumental music played in the background, adding to its eclectic charm. And I felt happy again.

A couple hours later, we pulled up in front of my house. Lucas stopped just short of the driveway, his hands resting on the wheel before he turned toward me. His gaze held a quiet sincerity as he leaned closer, guiding my face toward his. His lips met mine in a gentle kiss that quickly deepened, sending flutters through my stomach.

“You are the only one for me,” he whispered, his breath soft on my ear. Pulling back, he paused, gazing deeply into my eyes, as if looking into the depths of my soul. “Goodnight, sweet Joy. I’ll see you tomorrow.”

A heady feeling of lightness enveloped me as I stepped out of the car and walked inside the dimly lit house. I felt I was in a dream as a gentle smile lingering on my face.

Chapter Six

Fall 2015, *Present Day*

I sat in silence—the kind that settles around you when reflection becomes inevitable. Crickets sang in the distance, their rhythm syncing with the creak of the porch swing beneath me.

A gentle breeze stirred the autumn air as the sky deepened from lavender to indigo. From the safety of my porch, my thoughts drifted backward, threading through memories and versions of myself I had long outgrown. It struck me then—being gentle, agreeable, soft-hearted, and forgiving wasn't just my nature, it was my trademark.

It was a quiet beacon to those who saw empathy not as beauty but as something to bend. Perhaps, without knowing, I had been a magnet for the kind of man who thrives on the light of others—until he dims it.

Why is that? I wondered.

This wounded and damaged soul concealed himself behind a well-crafted façade of feigned humility, false concern, and a whirlwind of swiftly moving romance.

How can it be that the more compassionate you are, the more they take advantage of your heart, and the more they fixate on destroying your authenticity?

What do they truly gain by standing taller only after crushing one beneath them?

Lightbulbs were going off in my brain, and the dots were beginning to connect.

My mind traced the full scope of my life as sobering clarity settled in. My natural warmth—eager to please, slow to confront—had been like a flame to someone drawn not by affection, but by the promise of control.

What twisted sense of power does this kind of person gain by finding triumph in breaking down another? By unraveling confidence, dimming self-image, and turning emotions into scattered ash?

Without firm, healthy boundaries to guard my spirit, I had unknowingly made myself vulnerable to a point where dominance could masquerade as love. It was a lesson carved in hindsight.

Kindness without limits can become a silent invitation to be used.

If only I had known.

How could I have missed the signs of his darkness? If only I had recognized them and listened to the quiet warnings my heart tried to give me.

I can see now: abusers are the best manipulators, the best pretenders.

It certainly takes a deeply aware, well-informed mind to spot the subtle traits of coercive control or narcissism at the start. You must be sharp enough to catch the red flags others miss—when the charm feels a little too rehearsed, when the concern never quite reaches the eyes, when you feel pressured to adapt to their wants, and when their change is not sincere.

Now I see it. But it took years.

Way too late.

I thought how depleted I was, how I had lost myself, how I had lost my personality, my excitement for life, my peace, and my voice. Nearly every day brought a new eruption—some unpredictable storm of anger, manipulation, or emotional chaos—all rooted in his unrelenting need for control.

Living in that kind of madness, where peace was a stranger and drama reigned, wore on my soul, like a slow erosion. And I didn't even realize what was happening.

As the porch swing traced its slow, familiar arc, its rhythm reminded me of the well-worn paths we sometimes walk—paths that feel familiar, even comforting, despite being anything but safe. When something is unhealthy but routine, we stop noticing the signs. We miss the warnings waving all around us.

I had been blind. Oblivious to control.

I didn't know what *love-bombing* was or *gaslighting*. I didn't recognize the way his charm masked manipulation, or how the storm around him had already begun closing in. I didn't see possessiveness as danger. Or the way my autonomy was slowly eroding—through dismissiveness, through secrecy, through pressure and a lack of mutual respect.

I didn't understand why my feelings were met with criticism, why sensitivity was treated as weakness or how every disagreement seemed to end with my words twisted, my worth diminished, and myself blamed.

It hadn't always been loud. It had been somewhat quiet, gradual. That's what made it so dangerous.

Why did he seem so wonderful in the beginning? Why did it shift to behavior that caused the soul to ache?

I see now.

I kept trying harder to make up for his lack—filling gaps his poor behavior made. The harder I tried to have a happy, smooth relationship, the more it was on me and the less he invested in working toward a healthy, reciprocal relationship. Increasingly, I had to shove down my genuine feelings, my disappointments, hurts, aches—until I had to shut off my authenticity just to exist.

Instead, I presented what *he* wanted to see—just to appease. Only then did things go smoothly. I had to please him, not disagree, not make waves, and never express honest feelings or thoughts. I could never put any restrictions or requests on him.

As I gently pushed the swing, my looping thoughts continued to reflect on the decade that had unraveled me. Over time, the weight of the relationship had shifted, subtly at first, until it rested entirely on my shoulders. His moods, his needs, his chaos . . . I carried it all. I took on more and more until there was nothing left for him to hold but the echo of his own inaction. Whenever I asked for help or dared suggest balance, I was met with silence so sharp it cut, or rage that left me hollow. The message was always clear: there was a price for wanting more. So, I kept the peace. I kept serving. Even as it slowly cost me pieces of myself.

I lived in a constant state of fear and uncertainty, never knowing when the next silent treatment would begin. Or when blame would be flung in my direction. Criticism was constant as the changing wind; sudden explosions came without warning. When he wasn't turning away from me, he was turning others against me, quietly pulling strings to sabotage.

Who can bear this and survive unscathed?

No human.

It was the un-freedoming of me.

It was the slow dismantling of who I was. It was the tearing apart of Joy itself—my name, my spirit, my very essence—shattered piece by piece until I was almost unrecognizable, even to myself.

Charlotte once shared with me the phrase "coercive control." She described that it began slowly, with promises cloaked in concern, assurances, and invasions that looked like protection, but eventually felt like slow suffocation. Control.

The day Lucas brought me roses to apologize for humiliating me, was that a fair trade for disloyalty? The important things seemed easily replaceable to him—honor, truth, and character. You can't buy your way out of these with flowers and expensive gifts.

Truth, honor, and integrity became a mirage, and behind the carefully constructed façade, something darker pulsed—manipulation masked as love, control masquerading as care.

Over time, the erosion began—rights weren't taken all at once—they were quietly dissolved, piece by piece. My choices stopped being mine. My voice no longer echoed with certainty. Until one day, whether through escape or release, I woke to find myself . . . unfamiliar. A stranger in my own skin. A shell. A shadow of Joy.

I had to learn again the simplest of things—how to choose what I preferred to eat, what I liked to wear, and how I wanted to feel. Everything had been under scrutiny and criticism. Decisions that once came as naturally as breathing now felt paralyzing. I had to unearth my thoughts from the wreckage of someone else's will. His voice in my head was so much louder than my own.

How long does it take until his voice dims? Or is silenced? I wondered. And how long would it take to rediscover what joy meant? What I wanted? Who I even was?

What remained, in those first steps toward freedom, was not the vibrant woman others knew—but a shadow, trembling and raw, broken into pieces—just dust, less than dust—trying desperately to remember how to be whole again.

As I reflected on the irony, I remembered reading a magazine article about an unusual fish in the bottom of the ocean that would hunt its prey by dangling an iridescent light that grew on top of a tentacle at the top of its head and hung down in front of its face. It would glow, looking beautiful, and attract smaller fish, then when the unsuspecting fish came close, it was too late. This monstrous-looking fish, now in plain view, would devour the smaller fish. Then the hunter would go back to woo another unsuspecting prey to feed its insatiable appetite.

That, plainly said, was what it felt like being selected and stalked by a narcissistic man, consumed and controlled until they completely devoured you, until there was nothing left of you at all.

I became a bullet-ridden shell of a human. Those bullets were his words, cruel actions, neglect, force, anger, rage, control, his hands, manipulation, rejection, threats, contempt, and betrayal.

My mind drifted back to the moment the fairytale illusion began to crack—when the mask he wore so effortlessly began to slip, when all this became the beginning of my reality.

The charm began to fade and was replaced by cool indifference. Lucas grew deliberately distant; his presence became a haunting shadow instead of a comfort. Control crept in where kindness used to be; neglect took the place of care. It was then I began to understand I had never known the real him, only the version he wanted me to see.

Chapter Seven

Built on Hollow Vows

Life was wonderful. I was getting married! I had dreamed of this my whole life and had planned my wedding down to the smallest detail in my mind. I always wanted to get married and have a family, though my plan was to graduate first. But when love sweeps you off your feet, why wait? —that's what Lucas said. Why pass up the unexpected joys of life?

I didn't want to lose what we had. We both were smart, capable, and ambitious. I believed we could juggle marriage and college—that love and determination would be enough. Plus, Lucas insisted he was almost finished and would soon have his career to support us while I completed my final year. It made sense. Even though it was a whirlwind of a romance—less than a year together—it felt like everything I had ever dreamed of, and I became swept up in the tide of Lucas's passionate love.

With only two short months until the wedding, the day was approaching quickly, yet most of the details still fell squarely on my shoulders. I wanted it to be perfect. Lucas always seemed so busy and didn't have time to be helpful. But I was okay with that, I reasoned, his major was more demanding.

I pushed myself, knowing the deadline was rapidly approaching. *Work harder, work faster,* I thought. *Push, push, push!* I studied and planned the wedding in full force.

Amid the busy pace, I noticed there were times Lucas and I were at odds.

That is normal, right? Relationships aren't perfect.

Several times I needed Lucas to accomplish a task for the wedding or help with important details, and again, he was "too busy" or had a valid reason why he could not.

I realized many guys aren't into planning the wedding, but we were in college, and I was studying full-time as well. *I needed him.*

Feelings of frustration grew within me. We should have been planning this together, yet instead of insisting on what I needed, I kept the peace—shrugging it off and doing it all myself.

It was the day to sample the menu options for the reception. We picked a superb wedding caterer, and I was excited to sample the cuisine.

"Honey, the menu sampling is in an hour," I texted. "Let's meet at my house, we can drive together."

"Babe, sorry I forgot to tell you, I have a study group that I can't get out of. I was picked to lead it. Just go and decide. I trust you," Lucas texted back, excusing his responsibility.

Calling him immediately, I asked, "Are you serious? This is important; we both need to decide. I don't want to do this alone. Can't you skip the study session and make it up later? This is our wedding."

"No, I can't. I'm sorry. You can do it—whatever you pick will be fine," he said, his voice thinning at the edges, like a thread pulled a bit too tight.

"Fine," I responded despondently after a lengthy pause.

"Thanks, doll, you're amazing," he replied, now more upbeat.

I hung up. It was a letdown to have to do another important wedding task by myself. *I might as well marry myself,* I murmured as I drove downtown to meet the caterers.

Pulling up to the caterers, my phone chimed.

"How's the sampling going? You guys pick anything out yet?" Charlotte texted.

"Just pulling up," I responded, "here by myself."

"What? . . . Why?" Charlotte texted.

"Lucas said he couldn't make it. Study group. Bummed," I texted.

"That sucks. He should be there with you," she insisted.

"I know. But what can I do? I can't make him come. I don't want to make a big deal about everything," I explained, "but I wish he was here."

"I'd totally come with you, but I have a class in thirty minutes," Charlotte responded.

"Thanks, I'd love that. I get it though, no worries," I responded before sliding my phone into my purse and heading inside the shop.

After browsing and sampling the food selection for the reception, I chose several savory appetizers and a main course that tempted the palate—crisp spring rolls beside delicate seafood bites and golden focaccia with rosemary and thyme, nestled near lamb chops crusted with herbs. Vegetables curried with rich cardamom drew me with its addicting fragrance. The crème brûlée shimmered with a caramelized sheen. The aromas were intoxicating, and every morsel tasty and addicting. I finalized the order after the difficult but delicious decisions were made.

Stepping outside, I spotted a small coffee shop next door boasting the best homemade scones in the state. Deciding I deserved a treat, I ordered a hot lavender latte and blueberry scone. Choosing a seat by the large open window, sunlight spilled across the table as I lifted the frothy lavender latte to my lips, savoring its calming floral warmth. The scone was perfect. Crystallized sugar glistened on its slightly crisp exterior, while the inside offered a melt-in your-mouth softness, sweet and tender enough to make the moment feel indulgent. For a brief while, I let myself sink into the calm comfort of the café, the world outside fading as the simple pleasures grounded me.

Looking over the garden beds, I was met with a riot of spring colors putting on a beautiful display while the tree-lined streets were laden with bursting white and pale-pink blossoms. Unconsciously, I tapped my toes to the comforting, coffee shop music. The peaceful sounds happily serenaded, I allowed myself to get lost in the music and vibe.

Reality broke into my enjoyment when my phone alarm notified me of my next obligation.

3:30 Class. The alarm chimed again. Collecting my purse, I exited the shop and headed toward college.

"How was it?" Lucas texted as I focused on driving.

"Fine," I replied after a few minutes. "I ordered everything."

"Awesome! You're the best." He gushed, then immediately shifted gears: "By the way, the shoes you got me keep giving me blisters. Would you return them?"

The wedding details I had just shared vanished in thin air, replaced by his trivial complaint.

A quiet, heavy ache settled in my chest as I crossed another major milestone alone. Beneath it all, I felt that deep, intrinsic loneliness that comes when you realize you're the only one carrying a special memory. Heading to class, I was in a sober state.

Later that night, the doorbell chimed a welcome. Running down the stairs to the front door, I peered through the peephole and saw Charlotte. Swinging open the door, I immediately embraced her, pulling her quickly inside.

Charlotte pulled back to look into my hazel eyes discerningly. "How are you, girl?"

"I'm fine." I tightly squeezed her. "It's so good to see you."

"I had to come over and check on you," she earnestly replied, searching my eyes with her wide green ones. "Are you sure you're okay?"

Pulling her into the living room, we sat on the couch facing each other. Hugging a pillow, I began to relax.

"How are you honestly doing?" she questioned, brow furrowed and eyes searching mine.

"Okay, really. It's a bummer when I have to handle things alone." I nervously picked at the loose embroidery threads on the pillow. "But I get that life isn't always how we'd prefer it to be."

Charlotte leaned forward and took my hands in hers. Looking deeply into my eyes, she shared, "Yes, that's true, but you also deserve to be in an equally shared relationship. It needs to be mutual and reciprocated. Otherwise, it's all on you and that's not balanced."

"I know. But I struggle with knowing when to be assertive–saying what matters to me and striving to be flexible." I fidgeted with the tassels on the pillow.

"You need to be true to yourself. What is it that you honestly desire? Share that! It's important to communicate and expect to be respected. Your life and future should flow from that. You also need to communicate your desires and needs," Charlotte explained. "Jake supports me. He supports my desires and puts me first, and I support his desires as well. That's important to us and to our future. If he didn't, as much as I love him, it wouldn't be healthy. And I wouldn't be able to stay in a long-term relationship with someone who practices selfishness and insensitivity, and he feels the same way."

Truth resonated within me. Charlotte was right. It was hard to verbalize, but my gut feeling, the one I kept pushing down, was this relationship was already headed in an unhealthy direction.

Yet my desire of wanting a romantic relationship overrode sensible advice. I was seeing red flags, but chose to brush them away, thinking if I ignored them, maybe they'd go away.

If I loved more, served more, and was more pleasing . . . it would all work itself out.

Unfortunately, that's not how it works.

The moment had arrived. The wedding was filled with timeless beauty, radiant joy and an unforgettable anticipation, becoming a cherished tapestry of memories. It unfolded like a dream and my soul hovered and floated above each beautiful moment. The swell of the music, the tears, and for one perfect moment, the world hushed and watched in awe. All I felt was love and awe wrapping around me in the most glorious splendor.

We were whisked from one table to another as each one gushed over the beauty of the bride and groom and the magical ceremony.

"I don't know how you did it, but it is beyond spectacular. I can't believe you guys planned this yourselves without a wedding planner. How did you do it? I need to know, especially with our wedding happening next summer," one guest asked.

Before I could answer, Lucas took the lead. "It's amazing, isn't it? It was a lot of work, but you know, it was important to us, so it was easy to dedicate the time we needed to make this day happen. We all have hidden talents up our sleeve." He smiled.

I felt odd. *Why is he taking the credit when he basically did nothing but show up today?* I smiled through my conflicting feelings and decided to brush it aside.

Maybe he was just trying to be polite.

I continued to immerse myself in my magical day, and this occurrence became one of many memories to be buried under the rug of conflicting and uncomfortable feelings.

The year swept by, and soon, six months pregnant and blooming with maternal beauty, I stood frozen, with eyes wide. A stark look of terror was etched across my face as I watched fury unfold before me. Lucas raged with a force I could neither stop nor escape.

"Who told you that you could waste money on stupid things!?" he exploded, nostrils flaring.

I sputtered in defense, "I . . . I was trying to collect a few things for the baby. I happened upon the clearance, and it was too good to pass up. We barely have anything for the baby yet. I just wanted to . . . prepare." I fidgeted with my hands.

Lucas glared at me, leaning closer to my face. "You do not spend money without my permission. Is that clear?" Nostrils flaring, he breathed heavily in my face. I blinked, trembling, wishing I was anywhere else. My lips quivered out of my control and my hands began to shake. Tears formed, unwanted, while he glared with harsh, narrowed eyes.

Stay strong, I said in my mind. *I didn't do anything wrong. Why is he lashing out?*

I searched my brain for the answer. *I don't understand. This doesn't make any sense.*

"Do. You. Hear. Me?" he said, as he jabbed me in the chest with each word.

"Ow!" I cried out. "Don't do that!" I snapped back, pushing his hand away.

He shoved his finger inches from my face. "Do not forget what I said, is that clear?"

I trembled. Covering my sore chest with my hand, I turned and fled upstairs. Lucas stalked into the living room and grabbed the TV remote, then all I heard were the muffled voices drifting upstairs.

I lay in bed alone, my soul aching as a single tear made its way slowly down my cheek and was lost in the sheets. Hugging my belly, I rocked slowly while my thoughts tortured me.

I am his wife! I am carrying his child! Why would he hurt me? He doesn't usually react so angrily, I thought. I searched my brain to figure out what caused his explosion, to remember back when he began to change.

For the first several months of our marriage, it had been almost perfect, romantic, effortless, with hardly any bumps in the road. Lucas brought flowers, surprise gifts, and took me to restaurants regularly. He told me he loved me more than anyone he had ever loved, that I was the only one for him. When he acted insensitively, he would apologize, and I would forgive quickly, moving on as if nothing had happened. And yet, somehow, he always got his way.

I began to notice subtle irritations that flared when things didn't go according to his preferences. He insisted on doing only what he wanted, always offering excuses when he didn't. Since he loved being the center of attention, his mask was perfectly in place. In public, he was always charming and fun. Things seemed to go the way he wanted, and he was happy when everyone agreed with his ideas.

Mastering the art of grand gestures, he showed lavish displays of affection to wrap his apologies. Each bouquet, each surprise weekend, each perfectly timed kiss was a bandage over a wound he refused to treat. Thinking back, I realized I was swept away by the shimmer of the moment and promises laced in gold. But beneath the velvet of romance, his patterns remained—unchanged, untouched, unrepentant.

It was all about him.

Staring at the two pink lines, I held the pregnancy test with quivering hands.

I had been feeling poorly—exhausted and nauseous, the general under-the-weather feelings. I blamed it on my intense semester, finishing senior year and working part-time. I was dedicated to my studies and wanted to finish with excellence. Looking at the pink lines, I realized how everything was plummeting into a fast forward direction. We had planned to wait a couple years after I was established in my teaching job, but apparently life had other plans. Anxiety rushed over me as I thought about my graduation, my commitment to my upcoming job, and now a baby. It felt overwhelming.

"It's okay, babe," Lucas comforted. "This is amazing news, we are going to be parents!"

"I know, I'm so excited, I can't believe I'm going to be a mom," I said, running a hand through my hair while I paced the room. "But I didn't think it would be so soon. I mean, I wanted to teach for a few years first, then we would try . . ." My shoulders slumped as I sank onto the couch. "I'm just so overwhelmed, and I feel like crap!"

"There's no rush to get into teaching," Lucas said, his hand sliding down my back in slow, comforting strokes. "You'll always be a teacher. You could stay home with the baby for a couple years, then go into teaching. Our baby is important—we don't want to stick our kid in some day care." He leaned closer, his voice gentle but insistent. "Let's think about it. We need to do what's best for our child. We need to make decisions that might be difficult but are best for our baby. We can't be selfish."

He meant I can't be selfish. But was it?

I ran my fingers through my hair, feeling tension twist in my chest. "I don't know, I do want to be home with her, but I also don't know if I want to give up my job. I've worked hard for my degree. And I'm really looking forward to working," I admitted, my voice tight. "It's a lot to think about."

"This is important. You need to trust me," Lucas urged, his lips pursed.

I didn't like how his words made me feel. Backed in a corner, guilty for wanting something for myself, I wrestled with my desire to be a mom while still pursuing my career. I had always wanted both.

"It's the right thing to do," Lucas decided, his tone final, almost commanding. "Trust me." He patted my back and pushed himself up from the couch, as if signaling the conversation was over, the decision already made.

I hated the way my choice felt dismissed, overlooked. The ache of having my voice ignored settled deep in my chest.

After marriage, I noticed I had to work harder for Lucas's approval and attention. To please him, I needed to cook the meals he preferred, agree with all his ideas, and keep the house perfectly clean—anything less invited criticism. I was trying my best to be a good wife. I wanted him to be happy and loving toward me. My heart yearned for tender looks, cuddling, kind moments, and passionate lovemaking. Yet it seemed almost nothing was good enough to make him truly happy with me.

With my focus and attention on the upcoming little one, Lucas seemed more irritated, almost resentful, and demanded perfection. With a shuddered sigh, I cradled my abdomen and drifted off to sleep. I slept soundly, my hair fanned across the pillow, and my face finally relaxed.

Morning light spilled through the curtains, flooding the room with gold. I blinked against the brightness, stretching until the ache in my back eased and warmth settled over me. Lucas had left early for work, and for once, the house was entirely mine.

A brand-new day, and it's all mine, I thought smiling to myself. It was one of those perfect, sunny Saturdays that made the world feel fresh and full of promise. Tonight, we'd celebrate Dad's birthday. The thought filled me with a happy excitement—I'd always loved special occasions.

Brushing aside the curtain, I pushed open the window and breathed in the sweet, heady fragrance drifting inside. Letting the fabric fall back into place, I smoothed the bed and slipped into a simple summer dress. A splash of cool water on my face, my hair twisted into a loose, messy bun, I took a deep breath and braced myself for the day ahead. Being six months pregnant didn't slow me down too much, although finding energy to last the full day was a constant issue. I began brewing an inviting cup of coffee, thankful at least I could tolerate my favorite morning brew.

Today is going to be a beautiful day, I decided.

By afternoon, the sun hung lazily over the front yard, its warmth wrapping around me like a soft banket. I settled into the lounger, eyes drifting closed as the hum of nature lulled me toward sleep.

I startled awake at the sound of footsteps crunching up the drive.

The mailman 's cheerful voice called out, "Nice day for a nap, ma'am!" His old eyes crinkled with a grin.

"Yes, it is beautiful today," I replied, stretching on the lounger as I eased the slight tension from my cramped muscles. Rising from the chair took a bit more effort these days—six months pregnant and moving slower than I liked. I glanced up at the sky, realizing the sun had dipped lower in the horizon than I'd anticipated.

I can't believe I slept so long! I hurried inside.

The clock read nearly four. Lucas would be home soon. Quickly, I tidied the house, washed dishes left in the sink from last night, and threw in another quick load of laundry. I heard the front door open just as I folded the last of the laundry, stacking the warm clothes in neatly folded piles on the laundry room table. A moment later came the familiar clink of the keys hitting the counter, followed by the soft release of the refrigerator door opening.

"Hey, I'm home," Lucas called out. "So, what's for dinner?" He dug through the pantry, looking for a tempting snack.

"Not sure right now," I answered. "I'm finishing up the laundry before we leave for Dad's party. I was thinking I can throw together a quick salad for us before we go."

"Salad?" He paused. "Why do you think I want salad for dinner?" His ire rose. "I'm a working man, I want dinner, not a stupid salad. What have you been doing all day anyway? Sitting your lazy butt down? Being useless?" His mouth twisted, eyes filled with disdain as he stared me down—as if I were nothing more than a disappointment.

"I'm sorry!" I sputtered, startled by his unexpected, angry response. "I fell asleep for a bit, but the baby makes me so tired. Then I got caught up with housework and lost track of time." I shifted the laundry basket to my hip. "Anyway, we are going to my parents'. I am sure we will have food there."

Lucas walked over to look me directly in the eyes. "I work hard to support this family. That is something you know nothing about." His voice escalated with every word. "I expect you to take care of your responsibilities and actually do something around here." He glared and in a measured breath spewed, "You . . . are useless." He looked at me with harsh disapproval, then turned and walked away.

I took two steps back, trembling and hurt. Tears blurred my eyes even though I tried to force them away. Setting down the overflowing laundry basket, streams of tears escaped and spilled over, running down my pale cheeks, and dripped into the folded towels, making dark blotches where they landed. Brushing away the escaping tears with the back of my hand, I turned and walked upstairs to the bedroom. I didn't understand why Lucas would get angry and explode over something so small.

I'm not useless! I'm not a bad wife, I said to myself.

"Look," I said, glancing over my shoulder as I reached the top of the stairs. "Can we not fight right now? We have to leave in half an hour anyway."

"You can go by yourself, I'm not going," he said dismissively, with just a hint of a vengeful glance.

"But this is important! It's Dad's birthday," I cried, my voice raised with urgency.

"I don't give a damn whose birthday it is!" he spewed. "Go by yourself."

The darkness reached for me, curling around my thoughts like tentacles, strangling any light that dared to surface.

Panic welled up inside. *Why does this happen every time there is something important to me?* I cried, wiping furiously at the tears that continued to spill.

Stop crying. Stop crying! I told myself as I ran into the bedroom, shutting the door and collapsing against it. Closing my eyes, I tried to breathe slowly to calm my racing heart. After a few moments, I headed into my closet. I flipped through the dresses mindlessly, seeing nothing. Feeling robotic, I picked whatever my hand landed on and dressed methodically while mascara kept running messy trails down my cheeks.

Stop crying! I commanded. In vain, I continued patting my cheeks dry with a towel grabbed off the towel rack. I stared at myself in the mirror, looking deeply into my own eyes. I clutched the towel in my fist until my fingers turned red then pale from the pressure, and my chest began to heave with suppressed sobs. My heart felt like it had been pierced with a knife—once again.

Hopeless. Broken.

Confused.

Why is this happening? Why does something always go wrong? Why is this so hard? Shouldn't marriage be easier?

I felt I was doing all the work, making all the adjustments, walking on eggshells . . . I was trying to be perfect. I really was trying.

Sometimes things would seem fine, no major bumps in the road, as long as I was agreeable and unconsciously crossing all my T's. Yet it seemed we would circle back to another unexpected explosion.

Staring long into my own image, I solemnly told myself, *I want to be happy and enjoy today.* I exhaled slowly. *Okay, let's do this. I can do this alone.*

As the sun set behind the trees, I drove my old Chevy Malibu toward Mom and Dad's house, perched on a little grassy knoll surrounded by blossoming dogwood, crab apple, and magnolia trees. It was unseasonably cool for a summer evening, and the soft air drifting through the open window steadied me. Taking a deep, calming breath, I walked up the picturesque courtyard to the oversized wooden front doors. My hand rested on the knob. *Breathe.*

I arranged my face to look unstrained.

Pushing open the door into the joyful foyer, I called out, "Happy birthday, Dad!" Smiling, I reached out for a hug. "I love you," I whispered.

He was a tall man with more salt than pepper hair, warm eyes, and a big smile. He was a strong, big bear of a dad, yet still a teddy bear. Mom walked over and held me in her warm, motherly embrace.

"How are my girls?" she asked, smiling with her bright eyes and cheery disposition.

"Where is Lucas?" Dad questioned, looking toward the door concerned. "Is he on his way in?"

"No. It's just me tonight," I explained as a somber feeling enveloped me.

"Okay . . ." Dad looked into my eyes for a long moment. "You okay?"

"Yes, he just had a long day," I offered as a quick excuse. I did not want to shower sadness on Dad's birthday. He was much too special to douse his day with my problems. "Let's celebrate!" I cheered, redirecting and guiding them into the brightly lit living room amid family and friends.

The room emanated a warm glow with softly muted colors as the stone fireplace blazed with a crackling fire. Choosing to push the sadness back into a corner of my heart, I made the effort to rejoice with my family on this special night.

Sitting on the cozy couch, I looked from Mom to Dad. *Is marriage always this hard?* I knew they had their struggles, but I never remembered Dad being mean or angry toward Mom or me. Frustrated, yes, sometimes. Impatient, at times, but not intentionally cruel with the intent to wound.

Focusing back to the happy chaos surrounding me, a small smile played upon my lips. I watched Dad open his gifts amid the admiring ooohs, aahs, and laughter. Snuggling into the coziness of the couch, I pulled my legs up into a more comfortable position, trying to exhale my sadness and inhale their joy.

Mom was handing out steaming-hot mugs. Taking one gratefully, I sipped the hot chocolate topped with mounds of rich whipped cream and shavings of dark chocolate, Dad's favorite drink and necessary birthday tradition.

Mom came over, scooching on the couch next to me. "How's my baby doing?" She tenderly patted my belly.

"Good," I genuinely admitted. "She makes me tired a lot."

"Don't I know." Mom smiled. "You had me so exhausted, all the time! I could have slept for days," she laughed, "weeks, even!"

I smiled warmly. The evening wore pleasantly on and was a soothing balm for my soul. After sharing hugs and happy wishes, I stepped outside. Darkness overshadowed the sky, and the sound of crickets and night creatures serenaded us, as the cool of the evening wrapped its arms around me.

Driving home, my thoughts consumed me. I didn't want to burden my family with relationship sorrows. *I mean, it's not that bad,* I argued with myself. *I don't want to make a big to-do about nothing. What would I even say? That sometimes . . . he is . . . not very nice? Many others have it far worse. It's not like he hits me. So why should I be complaining? Maybe he's going through something. Maybe it's just stress.*

I missed the romantic, playful Lucas who loved to hug, kiss, and spend countless hours with me. Turning on the music for the short drive home, I let the peaceful melody waft over me.

Chapter Eight

Spring 2015, *Present Day*

My mind drifted back to the present. I couldn't help but think how strikingly different Lucas seemed initially from who he ended up being. I thought of his intense eyes and ready laugh. He was always full of charisma and presented a fun, easygoing persona.

How interesting that none of this accurately portrayed him at all, I mused. You definitely can't judge a book by its cover.

Sadness tugged at my heart for what could have been.

If only he had chosen to be kind. If only his arrogance, need to control, and belief that he had the right to punish anyone who didn't strictly adhere to his impossible demands—hadn't destroyed everything.

I pushed these thoughts away. The scars would always remain on my heart, like ugly, purple raised lines etched into my fair skin. It would be a constant reminder, sensitive to the touch. I decided instead to grow and heal beyond the pain. I was determined to not allow him to steal my future even though he had destroyed my past.

I let my gaze drift toward the girls and watched as they played, running happily and carefree while I lay on my checkered quilt. I watched Rose, my five-year-old, bright bit of sunshine, dart across the grass with a floppy handful of dandelions clutched lightly in her hand. I was unable to hold back the laughter as they bobbled crazily in her exuberant race.

Then there was Mia, my eight-year-old bundle of energy and humor. She breathed life and passion into each day. Her effervescence spilled into every corner, lighting the world around her. She reminded me of myself.

"Look, Mommy!" she shouted happily. "Look at me!"

Mia tried her best to perform several cartwheels in a row, ending up in the evergreen bushes.

"Look, Mommy! The bushes got in my way!" she exclaimed, brushing bits of twigs and bramble out of her hair.

"Yes, they did!" I responded, unable to contain my laughter. "And you still did such great cartwheels, even with those bushes!"

I saw my beautiful Ivy, my contemplative one—wise and thoughtful beyond her ten years. There she sat in a patch of violets serenely picking wildflowers, an old soul whose eyes seemed to hold experiences far beyond her tender age. Her mannerisms were thoughtful and deliberate. Even in situations of chaos, she had learned to remain composed and calm. She carried an air of responsibility, and I wished to remove any burdens that had been placed upon her too-young shoulders. I wanted her to feel the joys of childhood without the burden of adult responsibilities, to be carefree without a worry pressing on her little mind. I blew her a playful kiss and saw her eyes brighten with a joyous sparkle. I loved her beautiful heart fiercely.

Breathing in the fragrance of blooming wildflowers, I watched my girls play with unbridled joy. Their smiles, their giggles, and their laughter rang out like music, a melody that wrapped itself around me. Yet, beneath that sweetness I longed for the quiet, long-forgotten peaceful moments that once restored my soul. With a resigned sigh, I reminded myself, it is the timeless dilemma of mothers everywhere.

Through the overgrown grass, Charlotte made her way over with her two spirited boys in tow. "Sorry we are late!"

Charlotte called. "You know how it is with these boys. Not a moment of peace at all!"

"Oh, it's fine!" I replied. "It's so beautiful out; I could sit here all day and enjoy this weather."

"Me too," Charlotte sighed. "But more than likely, the boys will break something or climb something or make me chase them. I have given up on expecting any peaceful or relaxing moments with these two!" she said with a twinkle in her cheery green eyes.

"Only you could handle them! It's a good thing you have enough energy for both of them!" I laughed easily. "I would never make it."

We chatted happily as the children played and teased each other and the boys chased . . . everything. I noticed how happy I felt. It was a peaceful kind of happiness—one that settles in your bones. It had been a long time since I felt this serene. It was a wonderful feeling, and I wanted to stay in this moment and hug myself.

"You look good," Charlotte commented, as she took a moment to really look at me.

"I feel good," I answered with a lilt in my voice. "I feel mostly normal. More like myself."

"And you will," Charlotte replied. "One day at a time."

"Thank you for being my friend through everything." I gently touched her arm.

"Of course I am here for you. You have been here for me too. You've been my best friend forever. Since third grade!" Charlotte replied warmly, enfolding me in a tight hug.

We chatted and entertained each other with silly stories of our children as the afternoon passed.

"Let's collect these silly monkeys," Charlotte suggested.

"Yes," I readily answered. "They are about to crash."

In a joyful flutter, we collected toys, gathered the quilt, corralled the children, and said a happy goodbye.

Once we arrived home, I settled the girls for a short, quiet time, soaking up their generous, warm hugs. My girls, my angels—I truly loved my beautiful gifts from heaven. *How would the years treat them with the memories? No one escapes unscathed, especially not the innocent children.* I breathed a hopeful prayer heavenward and landed a soft kiss on each brow before shutting the door behind me.

As I sank into my rocking chair on the old front porch, its gentle creak matched the rhythm of my thoughts, back and forth. I moved slowly, deliberately, as my mind slipped once more into the past, to the night Ivy was born on that snowy winter's eve . . .

Chapter Nine

All Her Effort, All His Anger

It had been a difficult pregnancy at the end.

Soon this little baby will be here, and she will be mine to hold and love, I thought longingly as I stroked my rounded belly. The contractions had been growing stronger and more frequent.

"We need to go!" I urged. "It's really hurting!" Pain radiated from my back, gripping my stomach like an iron vise. I could barely speak as sharp, piercing pain intensified.

Lucas gathered the bags in one armload and supported me as I staggered to the car.

"It's okay," he reassured, as he held me up with one arm tightly secured around me.

It had been a hard year. Sometimes Lucas flipped out, causing me to cry in frustration and hurt, then he would swing to the opposite and be the fun-loving guy with whom I fell in love. Although, I noticed Lucas had been more kind as my due date approached.

Maybe he had been going through a rough patch. I glanced over, searching his face. His eyes were focused on the road, and he looked with calm intent as he wove through the traffic on the way to the hospital. I tried to shift my coat more comfortably to drape over my chilled body between sharp, deepening contraction.

"Honey, we're five minutes away." Lucas quickly squeezed my leg, then gripped the wheel with two steady hands.

I loved this side of Lucas. The side that seemed to care. I desperately hoped this would last. My heart craved to be loved, and I loved easily in return.

After an hour of pushing, beautiful, squalling Ivy came into the world. All six pounds and twelve ounces of a perfect miracle. I could not hold back the tears as a welling of love so deep filled my heart toward this tiny, perfect little human nestled closely to my chest. Her tiny fingers curled instinctively around mine. Fingers so small, all five could barely grasp around my pinkie finger. The simple touch sent waves of warmth through my entire body, and I was caught in the awe and wonder of this tiny, wondrous miracle.

Lucas looked down proudly at baby and mama. "You did good," he said softly. "Can I get you anything?" he asked as he gently cupped baby Ivy's head.

"No, I am perfect." I kept my focus on my beautiful baby girl. My heart overflowed with more love than it had ever held. Closing my eyes amid the lights, I tuned out the beeping noises swirling around me and the antiseptic smell, and I let peace wash over me. *God, let this be a new beginning.* The beauty of birth, the joy of being a new mother, the wonder of it all enveloped me in its warm comfort.

One month into recovery, and I was truly exhausted. *How does a mother ever catch up on sleep?* I wondered, after spending endless hours rocking baby Ivy throughout the long night. The cries of the upset baby wore on my sanity, each wail echoing through the walls of my chest. My body ached with fatigue, eyes heavy with countless sleepless nights, yet with every tear, I felt my heart swell even more. Love wrapped around me like a weight and a gift all at once. It was hard being a parent—harder than I imagined—but in the same heartbeat, it was the most consuming, breathtaking love I had ever known.

I am doing so much of this by myself. This thought would interrupt me often. Other than an occasional diaper change, I *was* doing it all. I ached to have an active partner. *What does that even feel like?* I wondered. I had no idea what it felt like to have a partner who shared in the sleepless nights or busy days. Lucas's job took precedent to everything. Since he had a "real job," he insisted he couldn't pitch in the way a parent should. That left me feeling like a single mom.

It was two a.m. when baby Ivy's piercing cries shattered the silence, yanking me out of the fragile sleep I had finally found. The cries cut straight through the darkness, sharp and relentless. My body felt heavy and weighted, like lead holding me to the mattress, but I rolled over and nudged Lucas weakly on his shoulder.

"Can you please get her? I am so exhausted," I whispered, my voice thin and worn. "I've hardly slept at all."

Lucas barely moved. He grunted and adjusted himself more comfortably.

"Lucas, please!"

He shifted slightly and muttered, "I've got to work in the morning . . . that's your job."

"Lucas, I can't . . .," I begged with mounting frustration. "I need help!"

"I have to work. Take care of it," he demanded, tugging the covers tighter around himself, cocooning himself in the comfort of the soft quilt. Within moments, his breathing deepened into a steady rhythm and his snoring waved with the cries of baby Ivy.

Unwanted tears blurred my vision before spilling over, hot and relentless, born from utter frustration and sheer exhaustion.

"God, I can't do this alone!" I cried aloud under the weight of my desperation. Words spilled out into the darkness as a release, asking for help in the midst of my helplessness. But the only answer was relentless wails.

Stumbling down the dim hall into Ivy's room, my body sagged with exhaustion as I collapsed into the rocking chair and gently gathered Ivy close to my chest. Her little arms flailed in frustration, tiny fists striking the air until she was comforted. I pressed my cheek against her soft skin, breathing in her comforting baby scent and positioned her for nursing.

Her tiny baby fingers clutched the neckline of my nightgown, clinging with desperate strength, fragile yet strong. Finally, her little rosebud mouth rooted and found me, latching with instinct, and a steady rhythm settled between us.

My lungs released a trembling long exhale, and I let this precious bundle bring comfort as only a baby can. Gently rocking us, I marveled at my little amazing treasure.

How precious and delicate, I thought. To love this baby is worth it. I loved her so much it made my heart ache. *I have never loved anyone as much as this little one.*

The unparalleled love I found for this little one soothed the raw ache left by the gaping absence of a tender love from my spouse. Nothing could ever replace the tenderness and partnership I longed for—there would always be that hungering void, an unfulfilled ache, but Ivy's presence filled my heart in ways I never thought possible.

I discovered in her a love so consuming it both healed and hurt at the same time.

One sleepless night bled into the next, and one weary day blurred into another. I lived for those rare moments of connection with friends, yet those moments stretched fewer and farther between. Exhaustion swallowed nearly everything, tethering me to the sole care of baby Ivy. Days blurred into weeks, yet spring blossomed again in glorious color.

My phone buzzed. "Let's meet in the park at noon," Charlotte said. "Can you make it?"

"Yes, let's!" I replied, a spark of gratitude in my voice for the chance to see my best friend. "We can chat while the babies nap."

Rushing through my morning, I threw open the windows, letting the fresh perfumed spring air flood the house. The breeze carried the delicate scent of lilacs as it drifted softly throughout the house. With the diaper bag packed full of baby essentials, snacks, and a bottle of water for myself, I nestled Ivy securely in her stroller. Pushing her gently, I set off toward the neighborhood park, feeling the morning breeze and warm sunshine on my face. I spotted Charlotte in the distance, her flaming chestnut locks catching the sunlight, as gorgeous as always. Embracing with a tight hug, we began our stroll around the park, drinking in the beauty of spring and companionship of each other.

"I've missed you so much!" I said, my voice catching with warmth. Seeing her after too long of an absence made my chest ache with the kind of longing only a dearest friend can stir.

"Me too!" Charlotte exclaimed, her voice full of excitement. "How are you surviving babyhood? Are you getting any sleep?"

"I love her to pieces, but she definitely is not a good sleeper. I don't think I have gotten more than two hours in a row," I answered. "How about you? Are you getting any sleep?"

"Gosh, about the same. Jake is so great though. He takes a lot of night duty so I can try to get some sleep, since I have the baby all day while he is at work. He's such a doll, I don't know how I could do this without him." Charlotte affirmingly said, "I'm sure Lucas is just as helpful."

"Yeah, he changes diapers sometimes, but . . . you know, his job is pretty demanding." I caught myself unconsciously making excuses for him. "He needs to sleep."

"Wait." Charlotte paused. "Lucas isn't helping you at night?" She held my gaze, her eyes full of concerned sincerity, as if searching for the truth I was trying to hide.

"Well, you know, he's working during the day, and I'm staying home with the baby, so I guess that that sort of . . . falls on me," I stammered, my answer coming out sheepishly, embarrassed by the truth.

"No, that does not *just fall* on you. Lucas is Ivy's father. He's your husband!" Charlotte stated emphatically, her voice firm and unwavering. "It is his responsibility to help with Ivy."

I twisted a blade of grass around my finger, my movement small and restless, betraying my unease.

"How many nights have you been taking care of Ivy by yourself?" Her tone was gentle but insistent. "Be honest." Her eyes refused to break contact with mine.

"Every night," I replied, my eyes dropping to the ground. A sick feeling grew in my stomach. *Was I betraying Lucas for opening up?* The weight of exhaustion and guilt pressed down on me.

Charlotte broke into my thoughts. "Are you serious?" Charlotte exclaimed, aghast, her eyes wide in disbelief. "Joy, that is not okay! You cannot be doing this all yourself, you're going to go insane!"

"Charlotte, I can't make him help me. I have asked so many times for him to bring me the baby or take a feeding so I can get a couple hours of sleep. But he gets irritable and loud and . . . and he refuses. There's nothing I can do!" I blurted. "He insists because I am home with the baby and he is working, that it is my job to take care of her."

"Do you realize this is wrong? You both are parents. You both are supposed to share the responsibility." Charlotte stressed the importance, "Yes, he's working at his job. But you're taking care of Ivy twenty-four hours a day. He works eight hours." Charlotte's eyes filled with concern. "He should be sharing the responsibility when he is home."

"I don't know what to do!" I helplessly admitted. "I've asked so many times, and each time, he gets louder and more insistent. I don't like it when he escalates, but also, I feel it is my responsibility because he is working and I'm at home."

"That's not true. You can't feel guilty just because he put the whole responsibility on you." Charlotte reached out, grasping both my arms as her eyes filled with worry.

"It's just hard, because if I push, he gets rude," I explained. "He'll get assertive. You know it always has to be his way. He's changed a lot from when we were dating or . . . maybe, I just never noticed these things about him before."

"I can't believe Lucas is like this," Charlotte admitted in disbelief, sighing sorrowfully. "He always seemed pretty easygoing around all of us."

"Yeah, well . . . not at home," I admitted.

"Joy, this doesn't sound good at all," Charlotte pressed, highly concerned.

"It's fine, it's just . . . not easy. I'm exhausted from taking care of Ivy. I don't have the energy to fight him on these issues, and I don't want Ivy in an environment that is escalating. It's not healthy for her to hear her parents yelling. So, I just do what I have to do."

"I'm sorry," Charlotte uttered in brokenness. "Maybe Jake can talk with him."

"No, no please! Don't ruffle the feathers. I can't handle more right now," I pleaded, trying to express the urgency. "He'd get so angry."

"If he gets worse, you tell me," Charlotte pressed.

"I will. I'm trying my best right now. As long as I don't make a big deal about things and don't ask him to do much of anything, it's okay." My shoulders trembled as I succumbed to sobs. "It's just . . . I kind of feel . . . all alone."

Charlotte gathered me into her arms, holding me together while I fell apart.

After a long moment, I breathed deeply, stilling my sobs, exhaling in slow, meditative breaths.

"I'm hoping he gets better as Ivy gets out of the infant stage," I shared wistfully.

"Ya, well, let's hope," Charlotte said unconvinced, her trademark objectivity shining through.

I pushed the stroller around the rest of the track surrounding the park, more somber than before, as an uncomfortable feeling settled in the pit of my stomach—a feeling of impending dread. Somehow, I knew it wasn't going to get better or easier. I realized the man I thought I'd married was not the man who lived with me now.

And I felt betrayed, tricked, and deceived.

I had made the biggest mistake.

I felt like I had one leg knee-deep in quicksand. *Is it too late to get out? Or will I drown if I stay? Is it wrong to leave? Would I be quitting, or giving up?*

Swirling thoughts and doubts assaulted me.

I looked around and saw the blossomed trees, heard the joyful birds chirping a cacophony of lilting music, and felt the warm sunshine on my face, but it could not touch the deep sadness that had entered my soul. Somberly, I finished the stroll with my dearest friend. And we parted with a long, tight hug, full of comfort and meaning.

Walking home, Ivy slept soundly, so I allowed my thoughts to drift deeply. I felt time stand still, and I saw my life play out in my mind—a life of sadness, aloneness, and no partnership.

How was I going to live like this?

Why was my life so difficult when I saw my friends happy, sharing life together, loving each other and working through struggles together?

Helpless. That is how I felt. *Unfair.*

I couldn't change Lucas. He obviously didn't care about changing, improving, or sacrificing for his wife or baby daughter. He became irritated any time I asked him to do something for me or the baby's benefit. He only did what was most beneficial for himself. His much-used phrase was, "You have hands, do it yourself."

Pausing in the shaded driveway, I sighed in defeat before rolling the stroller into the garage. Lifting the carrier inside, I glanced down at Ivy, still sleeping with her long eyelashes fanned out upon her soft, pink cheeks. The gentle rise and fall of her chest told of her deep slumber.

Entering my home, I set the carrier down in the foyer to give my aching arm a moment of rest. Lucas lounged on the couch, eyes fixed on the screen as explosions echoed through the living room, the surround sound rattling the walls.

Walking over quietly, I cringed at the loud volume. "Would you mind turning it down a little? Ivy's still napping, she needs to sleep longer," I said, forcing my voice to stay calm.

"She'll be fine," Lucas commented, completely absorbed in the action unfolding in front of him.

"Please," I pleaded, a bit more strongly. "I don't want to have to nurse her again so quickly."

Exhale . . . "Fine," Lucas said as he barely lowered the volume.

There is no point arguing, I thought, *he's not going to budge willingly.*

Hefting the carrier upstairs to Ivy's room, I shut the door quietly, hoping she would sleep through the echoing volume. As I tiptoed softly out of Ivy's room, her sharp, rousing cry rose above the volume floating upstairs. My shoulders tensed. Frustrated, I headed back across the room, knowing my chance of a moment's peace was now gone.

While settling Ivy to nurse once again, Lucas stuck his head into the room asking, "Hey, what are you making for dinner?"

With rising frustration, I replied, "I just got home and now I have to nurse. Can't you just make something?" My eyes bored into him with intensity and irritation.

With eye bulging, Lucas replied, "I just got home from work . . . What did you do today? Hang out? Have fun? Must be nice to not have to work and expect me to do everything!"

"I finally got to see my friend after over a month! I haven't been out at all, and you go out at least three or four times a week," I defended, my volume increasing at his audacity.

"Well, I have a job. I work hard and I deserve to have a break. You stay home and do nothing all day except—watch a baby," Lucas said, glaring at me. He slammed the bedroom door with such force, the window rattled, and his boots loudly struck the steps as he descended.

Jumping at his volatile outburst, I tried to settle a now startled, wailing baby. Crying with vigor, Ivy was clearly distressed by the loud explosion that invaded her peaceful nursing. Panic rose in my throat. Watching a fussy baby all night, trying to maintain the house, groceries, and meals . . . without a functioning partner, all without sleep was almost impossible. I felt with certainty I was going to lose my grasp on reality.

I could go crazy.

Anger, frustration, and exhaustion swirled around me. I was so angry, yet I didn't want to explode or cause more trauma in front of my baby. This stifling environment of control was overwhelming. I couldn't define it with words, but I knew within myself this was not right. It was not okay.

This was not normal.

I tried to calm myself and baby Ivy. After nursing Ivy, I settled her little sleeping form in the crib, kissing her softly on her forehead, then tiptoed quietly across the soft rug, silently closing her door.

Walking downstairs into the kitchen, I opened the refrigerator, trying to think what I could quickly prepare. Drawing a blank, I settled on something easy but filling.

I'll make a three-cheese grilled panini and soup on the side, I murmured to myself.

Once the meal was ready, I cradled the hot bowls of soup on their plates, oven mitts shielding my hands, and in careful, measured steps made my way to the table, calling Lucas to dinner along the way. From his comfortable perch on the couch, he stretched, then sauntered into the kitchen.

"What is this . . . grilled cheese?" Lucas's eyes narrowed in disgust while he lifted the plate for inspection. "This is lunch. You think I am having grilled cheese for dinner?" he demanded with nostrils flaring.

Frustration and overwhelm flooded me.

"You've been hanging out all day, and you think grilled cheese constitutes dinner?" His beady eyes glared at me, and his voice gained volume with each word. In a sudden rage, he hurled the plate across the table. The sandwich tumbled through the air as the plate shattered on the floor, sending shards flying. The bowl of soup was knocked over, sloshing hot liquid across the table and onto the floor.

Panic pinned me to the floor. My lungs waited for an order to breathe.

Every heartbeat hammered. It seemed to echo outside my body.

Beyond the roaring in my ears, Lucas rammed his chair against the table, stormed into the other room, and grabbed his keys.

"Clean up this mess. I am going out to eat. This is ridiculous. When are you going to learn?" he fumed, slamming the door on his way out. He was gone before I remembered how to breathe.

Silence met my ears. Deafening silence.

Standing by the table, I looked down and saw one of the oven mitts had slipped off my hand and had fallen to the floor, the other, dangling precariously, was about to fall.

I shook off the remaining mitt and felt a surge of something . . . fury, humiliation, terror, and rage. All these emotions welled up inside of me, colliding in a storm that seemed to lift me out of myself.

I turned away from the disastrous mess, storming over to collect a roll of paper towels. I could not see past the flood of angry tears streaming down my face into the sloppy mess I was unsuccessfully trying to clean. Soup dripped and pooled from the table onto the wet floor. Wiping the soggy mess into a pile, I scooped it into the trash, mopped the floor, and scrubbed the entire table.

Through blurry eyes, I completed the unnecessary task and sank onto my heels, staring at the situation—stared into the emptiness, the hurt, the ache—as waves of helpless anger flooded over me. After several long moments, I pushed myself up with shaking arms, gathered my now-cold sandwich, walked into the living room, and sat—hopelessly on the couch. Absently, I took mindless bites, tasting nothing, and cried, soaking the sandwich with my tears. And then I sat.

Alone.

Abandoned.

Broken.

In robotic movement, I placed my dishes in the sink, climbed the stairs, and slipped into bed, not even bothering to change.

I felt so very alone.

How was I going to live like this?

Was I wrong for going out with my friend?

I felt guilty for not completing everything expected—*but also how is that even reasonable? A husband should not be cruel or mean. There is never an excuse for being cruel!* I said all this to myself, and with shuddering, quiet sobs, I fell into an unsettled sleep.

Heartbroken.

I found myself tiptoeing through my days, trying to check all the boxes. I formed a subconscious checklist of everything I needed to accomplish. Clean the house, check. Make dinner, check. Care for Ivy and don't ask Lucas for help, check.

Bury myself in being a homemaker, check.

Mom came to help as much as she could, but I hated asking too often. It would also tip them off that Lucas wasn't much help. I didn't like the person I was becoming—quieter, smaller, stretched thin. I felt as if piece by piece, my own self was winnowing away. Yet when I did everything that was expected, Lucas seemed happier with me. Maybe my purpose as a wife was to make my husband happy.

Was that wrong?

Then why did I feel I was abandoning myself?

"I'm having the guys over tonight. We're watching the game," Lucas informed me one Monday before he left for work. "I'll pick up snacks. When Ivy is down for bed, would you make a pot of chili?"

"Umm . . ." My brain searched for the correct answer. I didn't want to have a bunch of guys over after a long day with a fussy baby. I'd rather have a quiet evening. But I couldn't say no. If I did, I knew Lucas would be upset. I felt stuck between expressing how I honestly felt and backed into the corner to do what he wanted.

"Do you have a problem with that?" he asked pointedly, his eyes widening.

"No, I just didn't really want to have a bunch of guys over. Ivy's been so fussy and they'll probably wake her. And then making more food . . ."

"They are coming over. It's my house. I'll tell them to be quiet, it will be fine. Why can't you make the chili? What do you have to do all day?" he pointed out.

His words felt insulting. I know it's also his house, but his words made me feel like he's the only one who can make decisions who comes to our home and when, as if my say didn't matter. And why should I have to cook for his friends? His friends were nice, and I usually enjoyed cooking, but I didn't have the energy to cook a big meal when I was already tired and just wanted to relax.

Feeling guilty for not being agreeable, I heard myself say, "Fine, I'll make the chili."

I really didn't want a fight.

The evening stretched long. I could hear cheers from the guys as I wiped away the crumbs they'd left on the counter from their snacks. Too tired to even enjoy a bowl of chili, I crawled into bed close to midnight as the echoes of the game drifted through the walls. I tried to block them out so I could sleep before Ivy awoke for her feeding.

Morning came with an overcast, hungover feeling. My body felt the same. Needing coffee to start the day, I was stopped to a halt when I entered the kitchen. Lucas had already left for work, the sink was stacked full of dirty dishes, and remnants of party clutter was spread throughout the kitchen and living room. Feelings of overwhelm flooded me. I couldn't keep tears from springing to my eyes. *How am I supposed to be a happy, easygoing wife when I feel so taken for granted? I feel like a maid.* I wiped the tears away and hurried to clean the rest of the mess, knowing my few minutes to relax were gone.

I longed to have a happy marriage, but the only way to make that happen was to reshape who I was to conform to Lucas's preferences. I always had to cave, give in, agree with him and forget what I wanted, what my desires were, and any goals I might want to pursue in life. I felt I was betraying myself. *But what else could I do?* I was being pressed against the very grain of my true self.

Several moms, including Charlotte, had planned an overnight trip to the beach, and excitement flooded me as the day approached. I'd been looking forward to this getaway with great anticipation. The beach was my happy place, and being with friends and relaxing was much needed.

Two days before, Mom called. "Joy, I am so sorry, but I'm sick. I won't be able to watch Ivy for your trip. I feel so bad, can Lucas watch her?"

Feeling a sinking disappointment, I pushed it down and said with understanding. "It's okay, Mom. I'm sorry you're sick. What's wrong?"

"I'm not sure, probably the flu. I've been so achy and feverish. I can barely get out of bed. Dad's been amazing of course," she answered, "but I hope he also doesn't get sick."

"Just rest, it's okay. I'm sure I can figure it out," I assured her. "Let me know how you're feeling tomorrow."

"Okay, honey, I'm going to go and take a nap," she answered softly.

Ending the call, I knew this would be hard to fix. Hoping Lucas would be understanding, I called him at work and explained the situation.

"Oh, sorry your mom's sick," he replied. "But I can't help you."

"Why can't you watch Ivy?" I started pacing the living room in frustration. "I have her every single day, and I've been looking forward to this trip all month. Mom just got sick, you could watch her Friday night and Saturday," I explained. "You aren't working."

"I'm not doing it," he said clearly. "Sorry, can't help you."

"Lucas, she is your daughter, you are her dad. It's also your responsibility to watch Ivy. Why are you being so stubborn?" I begged.

"I'm not doing it. I have plans. That's final. Stop being demanding," he said with finality.

I sank into the couch, my whole body sagging under the weight of disappointment. I needed this time with friends. Taking care of Ivy every single day was exhausting and getting away with friends meant so much to me. I needed a break. Tears burned my eyes as I ended the call. I tossed the phone onto the cushion beside me and let the bitter sting of frustration wash over me.

This isn't fair. Why do I always have to compromise and give in? Why can't I ever get a break? Feeling helpless and frustrated, I grabbed my cell phone and walked out the back door.

Sitting on the bottom step, I called Charlotte.

"I'm not going to make it," I blurted out.

"Why? What happened?" Charlotte answered in concern.

"Mom's sick, and it's just not going to work out," I shared, feeling guilty that if I disclosed the full reason why, I would be making Lucas look bad, so I only admitted the partial reason.

"Oh, no! I'm so sorry. Is there any other way you can come? We've been looking forward to this."

"No, I need to stay and help her. I'll have to go another time," I offered as disappointment filled me.

"Oh man, we were going to have such a blast . . ."

"I know."

After I hung up, I felt an ache of unfairness. I rarely got a chance to do something for myself. And again, it was squashed. How can Lucas think it's okay to refuse watching Ivy so I can get a break, and still demand his time out to have fun however he wants?

It was so wrong it made me livid. Yet again, it seemed I had to shove my feelings inside, be a good wife, shut my mouth, and live with another disappointment.

Don't rock the boat.

I felt like someone enclosed in a tight space that kept getting smaller and smaller. It was a pressing, suffocating weight. I had no voice, and no decision-making power. Lucas decided everything—what we did, where we went, how I spend my time. He could veto anything he wished, and I had no power to make what I desired come to life. Whatever Lucas wanted was what happened. My needs and desires were brushed aside, my opinions dismissed before they were even formed. Somewhere along the way, I stopped being his partner and became his servant, trapped between wanting peace and mourning the loss of myself.

Strapping Ivy into her carrier, I took a long walk down to the river. Meandering along the mossy bank, I let the sounds of nature quiet my frustration and anger. But the storm inside me only swelled with a tangle of feelings I couldn't unravel. My sense of authenticity blurred, as if who I truly was no longer mattered. Instead, I was reshaping myself into something that served the family—meeting every need but my own. My essence was pushed aside, fading little by little, until all that remained was a polished image of the perfect wife and mother, stripped of joy.

I grieved that loss, because deep down I knew it was wrong. Yet I couldn't see a way to hold onto myself and keep the peace in my marriage. Sitting on the flat rock at the river's edge, I dipped my toes into the cool water, stirring gentle ripples with my feet as tears fell, soundless and steady.

Chapter Ten

Summer 2015,
Present Day

Startled awake, it seemed I had fallen asleep on the couch and dreamed my past. The scenes played out with such vivid clarity they did not seem like memories. I could taste the tears. I could feel the sadness. I wiped my face to check for tears, but there was nothing. Dry.

I felt the constricting in my throat. Standing slowly, I went to check on the napping girls. Silence came from the girls' room. I leaned against the wall, feeling the coolness ground me, letting the reality of my present life settle over me.

I was okay. My girls were okay.

I didn't think these flashbacks would ever end. Why did they have to come and torment?

I wanted to move on and not carry the weight of paralyzing trauma. I didn't want to relive even one moment of my past.

Yet the flashbacks still clung. They were unwelcome shadows twisted into nightmares I couldn't outrun. I didn't know how to make them stop. Talking to Charlotte always seemed to help. Her advice had a way of grounding me.

"Can we talk?" I texted her.

The next morning, I sat in Charlotte's living room, holding a steaming mug of coffee as she sipped her cup of lavender-infused tea.

"How does one heal from all this trauma?" I implored Charlotte. She was the one who knew me better than anyone.

"I don't know. . . time? Lots of space?" Charlotte suggested. "A brand-new beginning? Just take one day at a time," she reassured me. "One day of freedom after another. You have me and your parents. You aren't alone. Slowly you will remember yourself. Maybe, one day at a time, you will find yourself piece by piece amid the wreckage. I know it seems impossible, probably like you've forgotten who you even are. But you will remember." She rubbed my back gently, soothing and comforting me. "I know you will. You are stronger than you know."

Sighing, I knew in my heart I was free. But the terror of being imprisoned in abuse, without being allowed the power to make decisions, without the freedom to think and act as I would instinctively, with all the broken pursuit of desires and dreams, felt like it had stunted my emotional growth.

In almost ten years of marriage, I had regressed. The joy I naturally exuded had been slowly stripped until I was a shell of myself.

How many months or years into freedom would it be until I felt all the puppet strings permanently severed? Would I ever be fully emotionally free?

I told Charlotte I honestly didn't think anyone could truly understand the level of anxiety, fear, and self-doubt one feels in every cell of their body. It takes you back to square one of panic, just hearing their voice, reading their text, or reliving an experience. I knew from experience it can take days to feel normal after an occurrence. Some people think once the threat of abuse is removed, you should easily be able to move on without the lingering trauma.

It is just not that simple.

There is nothing simple about abuse.

You can't suddenly wipe away the effects of years of trauma or the damage to your brain, your emotions, your body, or your cells. Abuse causes damage to your brain as it changes the way you were authentically made, rewiring your brain. Many victims suffer memory problems, difficulty concentrating, chronic headaches, mood changes, impaired cognitive function, depression, dissociation, emotional dysregulation, and C-PTSD. Many are long lasting, even permanent.

There is no simple fix.

After leaving Lucas, I began reading and researching how to heal from abuse. One study I read explained that a high percentage of women who live in or lived in a destructive marriage, with abuse and coercive control, become ill with a variety of cancers and auto-immune diseases. Many struggle with insomnia, paralyzing fears, C-PTSD, and major trust issues, and most die early, years before their abusers. The body cannot handle bottling up years of trauma. If it isn't released in healthy ways, it will find other, often-toxic ways to surface—ways that harm an already broken person. The fight to reclaim what was broken, stolen, and destroyed is relentless—and it leaves scars even as we move forward.

I could feel the atmosphere shifting. The heavy weight of fear, panic, and anxiety was lifting, slowly but surely. Each day brought a small sense of freedom, a little more breathing room in my own life. But I knew it was a process—a long, gradual one.

It would take time and patience. With myself.

Chapter Eleven

Shattered Beneath the Skin

One day, I found myself reflecting on how deeply thankful I was for Mom, Dad, and Charlotte. Yet in my gratitude, I wasn't fully honest with them about the daily trauma I went through. A heavy cloak of embarrassment and shame clung to me, making it impossible to utter the words. Silently, I had suffered—agonizingly and relentlessly—while trying to keep the peace by pleasing an unpleasable man. It was a constant balancing act, like walking barefoot on broken glass. My own spirit fractured again and again under the weight of fear and despair.

Don't quit. The voice in my head told me, If I quit, I'm a failure.

Wracking my brain to find the "thing" that would work to fix my marriage, I wanted to help my husband become a better man. I thought about my vows: "for better or for worse." Doesn't that mean you have to stick it out even through the worse?

One evening, I escaped with Ivy over to Mom and Dad's for a desperate break. Ivy curled up on the couch with Dad, giggling in her little toddler voice as they played a game together. As Dad kept her happily distracted, I sank into a chair, shoulders shaking, as silent sobs spilled out. I cried, "Please pray for me. This is so hard!"

Mom sat down beside me, her face etched with worry. Her voice trembled as she wrapped her arms around my trembling body. "Honey, what happened, would you tell me?"

"He yelled at me over something so insignificant! I can't even remember all the details. I just hate it when he treats me this way." I buried my face into my hands. "It's usually over things that don't make sense to me. I feel confused, and it makes me question whether or not I'm right or wrong or what I should have done differently."

I felt I couldn't go into all the details or it would be too revealing of my husband. I also didn't want to be thought of as a failure, and I didn't want Mom and Dad to think badly about Lucas. Which was the lesser of two evils: to be completely transparent and have Mom and Dad hate him, or keep things between us, hoping the problems would resolve?

I couldn't tell Dad the things Lucas said and did to me. Dad would want to hurt him. I didn't want to be the catalyst that caused a huge explosion. I was stuck between two impossibilities.

Despite this impossible quandary, I did the expected thing, and I went back to Lucas. I knew in my head, it was the proper thing to do. The more I tried to be a perfect wife, the more pieces of myself seemed to slip away, and I didn't know how to fix it. Being strong and assertive didn't work, and being more submissive and accommodating was also not working. I was trapped by two impossible choices, and no matter what I did, the situation remained tumultuous and exhausting.

At seven months pregnant with my second baby, I was carrying low—so low every step sent grinding pressure through my cervix. My body protested every movement. Chasing after a toddler while growing another human was no small feat. I needed a well-earned break. I couldn't remember the last time I left the house for fun. Every single moment of every day was consumed with caring for Ivy and issues with my pregnancy. The weight of it all pressed deeply—emotionally and physically. My thoughts scattered and my mind was in a numbing trance.

Lucas stretched out comfortably on the couch, caught up in another movie marathon, choosing to be unaware of all I was trying to handle on my own. Walking over, exhaustion evident upon my face, I tentatively sought out Lucas's help, "Would you please watch Ivy and feed her lunch so I can rest for a little while?" I set down the wiggling toddler in front of Lucas.

After a lengthy pause, his annoyance at being interrupted was obvious. "What do you need to do? he asked finally, his eyes flicking between me and Ivy, his voice sharp. "What is so urgent for you?"

"I need to go upstairs and get some laundry done and rest for a little bit." Exhaustion was written plainly upon my face. "I shouldn't be longer than an hour and a half or two."

"Fine," he said in a disinterested voice, his gaze cutting back to the television. "Where is her lunch?"

"Just make her a sandwich and cut it into small pieces. Please watch her when she eats so she doesn't choke," I explained.

"Go make her a sandwich and bring it to me." Lucas fixed his attention entirely on the television. "Then I'll feed her."

Exhausted and irritated at his laziness, I pointedly shot back, "Can't you make her lunch and feed her?"

"I am not getting up. If you want her fed, bring me her food," Lucas demanded. "Otherwise, do it yourself."

I turned to face Lucas sprawled on the couch. I wasn't blocking the screen, but I stood close enough to demand his attention. The weight of exhaustion pressed hard against me, and the sharp edge of resentment sliced through my words. "You can make her lunch." I stomped my foot, letting the sound carry my frustration around the room. "I am exhausted, and you barely lift a finger for your own daughter. Stop expecting me to do everything. I am not the only parent here. I can't do this alone."

Lucas's eyes bugged out. "What did you say to me?" His slowly pushed himself up from the couch. Storming toward me, he stopped inches from my face, his jaw clenched tight while he balled his hands into fists, clenching and unclenching.

The room shrank. I cowered in fear.

"Do you think that you can talk to me like that?" He jabbed me in the chest. "Do you? Who the hell do you think you are?" he roared.

"Stop!" I tried in vain to push his hand away. "Don't poke me!"

Lucas shoved my shoulders hard. My body slammed against the wall.

"Ow! Stop!" I screamed, as pain shot through my back and skull. "Why are you hurting me?"

"Don't ever disrespect me! Do you understand? Without me, you have nothing. Nothing! You understand?" He raged, jabbing hard into my chest again. "Now, you can do it by yourself."

For a heartbeat, time stopped. His rage, my agony, the silence. The room felt impossibly small—the couch, the TV, even the scattered toys around Ivy seemed to shrink, pressing in on us. I could feel my pulse thundering in my ears, my chest tight from both fear and the lingering pain of the jabs. He stared venomously, as if challenging me to respond—or cower in submission—or break.

Finally, Lucas stalked away into the bedroom, slamming the door. Our wedding picture—the one I cherished most—tore from the wall, its frame crashing to the floor. The glass shattered in countless shards, each one a jagged reminder of what was breaking around me. Sliding down the wall, I collapsed into broken wreckage. Trembling, I wrapped my arms protectively around my belly, terrified for me and my baby. My shoulders shook violently, my chest heaving, as sobs tore through me uncontrollably.

Tiny hands touched me.

"Why Mommy cry?" Ivy asked in her gentle, little toddler voice as she nestled herself into my lap, clinging tightly to me.

I sobbed harder into my hands, heartbroken that my precious girl had to witness my unraveling.

Tiny eyebrows wrinkled in concern as she looked up to gaze deeply into my eyes.

Stifling my sobs, I tried to compose myself and calm my trembling. Wrapping my arms around her, I hugged

Ivy tightly, holding her close to me, feeling the warmth of her little body. Resting my head against hers, I allowed her presence to infuse me with calm.

"It's okay," I reassured her and myself, focusing to calm my breath and breathe slowly, deeply, and methodically. "Mommy will be okay."

"Why Mommy sad?" Ivy asked.

"It's okay, baby," I said with forced calm. "Let's go outside. Do you want to see the flowers?"

"Yes, Mommy, flowers!" Ivy answered.

Stroking my belly protectively, I eased myself up, wincing as a sharp pain cut through my back, mirrored by an even deeper ache that pierced my heart. I grasped Ivy's tiny hand as small fingers wrapped around mine, anchoring me. We walked out to the flower garden in silence.

Even after several minutes, the trembling lingered and a strange sense of disconnect hovered. Nothing felt real.

Did this really happen? Did I just imagine this, or did I actually experience this?

My thoughts tangled in unbelief. I stood suspended between reality and a nightmare, the moment too sharp and horrible to digest. I tried to push aside my shock and focus on little Ivy and the beautiful flowers blooming in the little garden. Yet I felt a surreal detachment—like I was watching someone else's story play out—terribly.

This couldn't be mine.

"Look . . . pretty flowers." Ivy's voice snapped me to reality.

I blinked hard. Focus! I shoved the shock down like a stone to the bottom of a well. Focus on Ivy. Focus on the garden. Her little hand gripped tightly to mine, and that was enough to pull me back—for now. "See the bright colored petals . . . how pretty they are? Feel them," I said to Ivy as I reached out a trembling hand to touch the petals, rubbing my finger gently across the velvety softness.

Ivy reached out her chubby little fingers to caress the soft, delicate petals.

"Smell the pretty roses, they smell so delicious," I said, bringing my nose close to inhale the fragrant scent.

She leaned over to bring her tiny little nose close to smell the invigorating fragrance. "I like flowers," said Ivy. "Mommy like flowers?"

"Mommy loves flowers! I love flowers, I love trees, I love blossoms, it's all so beautiful." I tried to keep my voice sounding normal.

"Pick some, Mommy?" asked Ivy.

"Sure, baby! Let's pick your favorites." We wandered slowly through the garden, picking a beautiful bouquet to place in the kitchen window. Sitting on the soft grassy lawn, the freshly cut blades tickled the bare skin on our legs as I situated Ivy in my lap. As I braided a delicate daisy crown for Ivy's hair, a sense of peace slowly began to settle. Nature had a way of consoling me. It brought calm to my chaos. The beauty of the colors, the intoxicating scents, the breeze tickling my face . . . all this moved me in unparalleled ways. It restored a feeling of wholeness when everything around me was falling apart and being shattered into pieces.

Focusing back on Ivy, I said gently, "You look so beautiful, like a little flower princess."

Ivy giggled and smiled. Her dimples appeared on her flushed cheeks. She patted her crown vigorously, causing it to sit askew on her curly blonde head. "So pretty, Mommy!" Ivy said gleefully. Her little curls peeked out all around her flowered crown and her lips were set in a delightful smile. We stayed outside in the peacefulness for as long as I dared.

"Hungry, Mommy!" Ivy piped up, and I realized nearly an hour had quietly slipped by.

As we stepped into the house, a small measure of calm began to settle, though the lingering weight of trauma still pressed beneath the surface.

Lunch was quick and simple, and Ivy's chubby cheeks bore sticky smears of her meal. Wiping the traces off, she began to yawn. Lifting her little body, I carried her upstairs as her legs straddled my extended belly and placed her gently in her bed for a nap. Slipping out of the room, I stared solemnly out the large, open window overlooking the wide expansive yard and spent several somber moments contemplating.

My brain mulled over and over what had occurred. I was not sure what to do or how to handle this. It seemed things were always escalating for no valid reason.

Was I not able to ever honestly express myself when frustrated? Could I never speak about my needs or Lucas's responsibility as a dad? Why did things seem unfair? Did I really have to be a doormat without any allowance to communicate honestly?

This was wrong.

I continued to question within myself. How could he demand preferential treatment yet give zero helpfulness, mutual respect, or kindness in return? I did not know what to do. No decision seemed to have a possible good outcome.

How drastic does my decision need to be? And is it fully warranted?

So much was happening that was wrong.

I yearned to spill everything to Charlotte and Mom, but humiliation and embarrassment hovered. I shouldn't have to deal with this.

I felt wronged, assaulted, and livid. But then, a guilty thought arose.

Maybe, I shouldn't have raised my voice and accused him. Was I also to blame? Was it my responsibility for causing his reaction? If I had just done what he asked without causing a situation, would he have even blown up? If I was more tolerant and serving, he probably wouldn't react.

But it's also true that he should act like a father and help take care of his own child. I was doing almost everything at home. It couldn't be wrong for me to state the obvious and expect help.

I couldn't keep all this turmoil inside. This circular thinking was driving me insane. I needed a safe place to talk. I reached out to a couple married friends, hoping they might help me understand what I should be doing differently. Their eyes lingered on me in quiet skepticism, as though my words didn't quite add up. It took everything in me to voice even fragments of the heartache and trauma I was carrying. Each admission felt exposing and humiliating.

As I stumbled through pieces of my pain, the words felt shameful once uttered, too raw, and too personal–exposing. It felt as though I were peeling back layers I had worked so hard to keep hidden, trying to convince myself it wasn't real. I was asking for clarity, for reassurance, yet instead, I felt doubted. Their disbelief landed like a quiet rejection, their doubt of my brokenness and pain, and unwavering faith in Lucas's goodness was a piercing betrayal. It left me questioning not only my story, but my worth for even telling it. Maybe speaking up at all–was a mistake. To them, Lucas was charming, easy, the fun-loving life of the party. My truth didn't match the man they knew.

I had to be careful what I revealed about Lucas. I knew he could twist the truth in a heartbeat, portraying me as irrational or overreactive if questioned. I didn't have many safe people to confide in anyway.

It must be mostly my fault—he tells me that I'm difficult—that I need to be more patient, less sensitive, tougher. Most of our friends didn't believe me anyway. I tried endlessly to fix whatever was supposedly wrong with me, but I never seemed to get it right. No one else had a problem with Lucas, so maybe the problem was me.

Something was wrong with me.

This confusion was constant. People say it takes two to tango . . . so I must also hold the blame. I just didn't see what I was doing wrong—unless I needed to disappear inside myself completely to make him happy.

What about me made me unlovable?

Lucas grabbed his keys, slamming the door on his way out. I didn't even care where he went. The weight of the trauma and the chorus of inner voices became unbearable. I needed to leave—where, I don't know. I packed our overnight bags, deciding to spend the weekend at Mom and Dad's. I wasn't even sure what I would say to them; my emotions were a tangle of confusion and fear. I didn't want to meet Lucas's contemptuous eyes, hear his accusations or face his demands. And I didn't want him to touch me. I just wanted to be as far away from him as possible.

Quietly, I packed a little bag of toys and toddler items for Ivy while she napped.

When Ivy awoke, I had just finished. "Want to go to Grammy and Grampy's?"

Ivy bounced on her toes, her excitement barely contained. "Yes, Mommy, Gammy, Gampy!"

Taking her little hand, we quietly left the house. I carried both bags out to the car and headed straight toward Mom and Dad's. Still, I didn't know what I was going to say, or how much to disclose. Maybe I'll just tell them we had an argument or that we missed them and wanted to spend time with them. Either way, I knew they were going to see through this thin veneer.

I felt a little better the farther I drove away, as space accumulated between Lucas and me. Driving up to the house, a peaceful calm began to settle. My parents' home always had an environment of tranquility, the smells of homeyness, and the all-encompassing warmth of love.

Dad was in the front garden bed surrounded by pots of colorful petunias, zinnias, and vinca, kneeling amid the summer flowers.

"Hi, Dad!" I called. "We were missing you guys, so we thought we would come and visit."

Dad pushed himself up and took off his work gloves, clutching them in one hand. He enfolded us in a big bear hug, being careful of my belly, then gave butterfly kisses to Ivy. His tenderness caused an ache deep inside.

I averted my eyes, choosing to turn my gaze on the garden bed instead. "Love the flowers! They're so beautiful. I know Mom loves as many flowers as possible."

"I missed my princesses! How are my girls?" he asked, his voice gentle, the warmth and love in it spilling over naturally, and I felt tears rise that I hadn't even realized were there.

"Good . . . Dad," I answered. My chest tightened as I tried to swallow the lump in my throat, as a wave of ache and longing threatened to overflow. His gentle kindness opening the wall guarding my emotions. I glanced away, desperate to hide the tremor in my face, and bent to pick up our bags.

"Let's go inside and find Grammy and give her big hugs," I suggested to Ivy. "And let's play with the doggie!"

Giving Dad a quick peck on the cheek, I hurried Ivy up the flowering courtyard to the oversized dark-walnut doors.

Pushing open the heavy door, I called out, "Hi, Mom! We're here. Surprise!"

"I love surprises!" Mom said as she walked around the corner and enfolded us both with a big hug, kissing us on the cheeks with a little kiss on my belly. She paused and looked into my eyes, contemplating. "Is everything okay?" she asked when she saw my eyes bright from unshed tears.

Looking at Mom, I paused and darted my glance to Ivy. "Here, Ivy, how about you come to the living room and play with your toys and the doggie?" I gently escorted her into the cheery living room.

Once Ivy appeared content, I walked with Mom into the kitchen. Ivy's happy little chatter assured me she was fine, so I settled into a chair, trying to sort through what to say–how to explain all of this.

"No." I blurted in a jumble of words, "I don't know. We had a fight; he's always so angry. I . . . I don't know what to do. He always blames me and says it's my fault for things. He never accepts responsibility for anything he does, and I'm just so angry. I don't want Ivy to be in the middle of that either. I just thought, maybe we would come over here for the weekend and hang out with you guys, if that's fine. I just can't go home right now!"

"Of course, honey, it's fine! We're so happy to have you." Mom reached over, enfolding me in a tight, comforting hug.

"We'll hang out, and we can bake a dessert, watch a movie . . . you know we love to spoil you and Ivy whenever we get the chance! I'm sorry that happened. Marriage is not easy." Mom comforted and assured me, "There can be a lot of ups and downs."

I nodded in agreement but did not want to say any more specifics. It was too traumatic to relive, and I decided to just shove it in the farthest corner of my mind.

"Want some tea?" Mom reached for her vintage red kettle.

"Yes, I'd actually love some," I answered.

I went to check on Ivy and saw she was unsuccessfully trying to cradle the squirming toy poodle like a baby doll.

"Mommy, look! Baby!" Ivy exclaimed. Ivy's sweet cheerfulness made me feel happy.

I joined in the laughter at their silly scene, rescued the puppy, and breathed out the stress. It was good to be home; it was nice to laugh and feel peaceful.

Relaxing together, we snuggled under a thick blanket, watching a funny movie while enjoying warm, homemade brownie sundaes. I was reminded how much I loved hearing the deep, belly laugh of Dad and Mom's soft, lyrical laughter.

The peace it brought was soothing to my soul.

Sunday dawned bright and sunny. Stretching out the kinks in my back, I remembered I was in my childhood bedroom. Gazing at the photo-filled walls, I reminisced at the pictures, sports awards, and teenage decor. A flood of happy memories resurfaced.

Ivy was still in dreamland, her little body lay curled next to me as her lashes splayed across her flushed cheeks, her mouth slightly ajar, and her lavender blankie grasped tightly in her tiny fist.

So beautiful and innocent.

Brushing my fingers gently over the rounded mound of my belly, I caressed the baby inside, whispering, "I love you, little one."

A little jump of a baby's foot pushed out against my bare skin. So beautiful. I took a moment to cherish and tuck away the memory.

The aroma of coffee brewing drifted upstairs, and its intoxicating scent wrapped invitingly around me. This gave me the incentive to push myself out of bed and carefully climb over the sleeping little one. Quietly, I slipped from the room and silently shut the door, hoping to let Ivy sleep as long as possible.

"How did you sleep?" Dad asked with eyes twinkling.

"Really good, actually!" I replied earnestly, stretching one last time.

"I made you coffee," Dad said as he poured a large mug. "Hot the way you like it and in the largest mug."

"Thanks, Dad, you're the best." I leaned in for a side hug. Taking my steaming coffee outdoors, I sat in my favorite Adirondack chair that faced the blossoming trees and the colorful horizon.

Balancing my mug of coffee on my big belly, I thought, A perfect shelf, and laughed, being careful that the jostling of my belly didn't disrupt my brew. Enjoying the peaceful sounds of nature, I admired the delicate, blossoming trees and glorious rosy-pink sunrise.

If only every morning could be this peaceful, I mused blissfully. I invited the beauty of nature to wash over and console me. After the peaceful weekend, almost regretfully, I left as the morning was ending, and we headed back home.

Pulling into the driveway, the panic returned. It gripped my chest, making it difficult to breathe. I took a moment to pause, my hands tightly gripping the wheel. After several minutes, I gathered the bags and we headed into the house, hoping for a peaceful entry without any confrontation.

Gripping Ivy's tiny hand, I walked cautiously into a quiet home. Setting my items down, I was glad Lucas was nowhere to be found. After depositing the bags in the bedroom, I settled Ivy in the living room to play with her toys and put on a cheery Strawberry Shortcake video.

I noticed the dishes were piled high in the sink, and the living room and kitchen were in complete disarray. It was a disaster. Obviously, Lucas didn't think it was important to clean up after himself. Or it was my punishment for having a boundary. Overwhelm flooded over me. Tired, pregnant, and returning after an emotionally brutal few days to a house that looked like a bachelor pad was not appreciated. I wanted to leave the disaster. But if I did, no one would touch it. I knew with certainty that Lucas would never lower himself to clean. It was again left to me.

After nearly three hours of cleaning—vacuuming, scrubbing the floors and bathrooms, tidying the bed, picking up all the dirty laundry, and starting a load of wash—I finally collapsed onto the mattress in complete exhaustion. Ivy had been rubbing her eyes in tiredness. After seeing her yawn numerous times, I had laid her down for a late nap, grateful for the small window of rest it gave me. I slept hard for two hours, only waking when Ivy's restless little sounds drifted into the room.

"Okay, Boo, let's go in the kitchen and make some dinner," I suggested cheerily.

Looking in the freezer to see the options, I pulled out chicken, quickly thawed and seasoned it with cumin, garlic, salt, paprika, chives, and a pinch of cayenne, and set it in the air fryer to cook. Deciding to put sweet potatoes in the oven, I seasoned them generously with brown sugar, cinnamon, and cloves.

Just as I set everything on the table, Lucas walked in the front door. Overwhelming waves of anger and humiliation crashed through me when I saw him. At the same time, a sharp awareness rose in my chest—I had to steady myself, had to make sure the atmosphere stayed safe and calm for Ivy. These feelings conflicted inside of me, pulling me in opposite directions. Lucas glanced at me with utter indifference, as if nothing had happened, nothing had been said, nothing had been broken. Without a word, he pulled out his chair, sat down, and served himself an enormous portion.

Then, as if flipping a switch, he looked over at Ivy and broke into a warm smile. "Hi, baby girl. How are you?" He didn't look at me, didn't speak to me, didn't acknowledge my presence at all.

I may as well have been invisible.

Lucas's continual rejection and disapproval had pierced my heart in the cruelest way. I would have settled for crumbs of kindness—anything—but there was nothing. And though I felt relieved he wasn't indifferent or unkind to Ivy, his dismissal broke my heart.

I refused to look in his direction as my eyes blurred with unshed tears and focused on strapping Ivy into the highchair.

Prepping Ivy's food, I set her plate on the tray, placing the toddler fork in her hand. Dishing the remaining food on my plate, I saw the chicken was mostly gone, so I filled my plate with the remaining sweet potatoes.

Resentment welled up inside. *Well, that's one way to stay slim—having an unthoughtful and gluttonous husband. Seriously, what kind of husband is so selfish that he doesn't even consider his pregnant wife or child,* I thought in disgust.

I wanted to shoot a rude comment in his direction but refrained. It wasn't worth it. Dinner was silent except for the happy chatter of Ivy. Lucas focused on his plate except for a few sweet words said to Ivy. He continued the silent treatment, and I assumed it was a punishment. But for what, leaving for two days after he assaulted me? Was he going to act like I wronged him and not the other way around? *Unbelievable.*

I preferred the quiet to rude comments, but I also longed for a genuine apology and a broken husband who chose to change.

I just wanted love.

I was trying everything I could think to do, but it all invited his scorn.

Well, I consigned myself, *I guess I am going to have a few quiet days.*

When I felt hurt by Lucas, my emotions tended to cut him off, and I would go numb. To distract myself, I focused all my energy on Ivy. I worked hard to create extra-fun playtimes, homemade kiddy crafts, and basically anything to replace the stirring up of the agonizingly painful hurt caused by my emotionally absent and aggressive husband.

And so, I lived . . . day after day, month after month, walking on eggshells, overly tending to the home and parenting, and losing pieces of myself, settling for mere crumbs of kindness, and bit by bit, I no longer recognized myself.

Sometimes I would sit at my vanity, staring at my reflection searching for the girl I once knew. I looked for the sparkle in my eye, the ready smile upon my face, or the spark of mischievousness. Nothing appeared. An empty shell was all that remained. A canvas with its authentic charm erased. A painting with the artist's defining touch permanently scrubbed clean.

What remained?

An obedient wife. A maid. A nanny.

A woman who had been forced to behave with the limitations of a child.

No independence. No individuality.

No longer did I feel the newness each day. I began neglecting my friendships as my days were consumed with the care of Ivy, the home, and managing a very tiring pregnancy, yet my heart continued to ache for companionship and love. I forgot what it felt like to be admired, to be flirted with, and looked upon with desire.

I longed for my husband to want me, to look at me tenderly, hold me and make love to me. More than anything, my heart longed for connection, companionship, and bonding.

Everything I did, I secretly hoped my husband would finally approve or notice, and be pleased, looking upon me with tenderness and kindness.

It was not to be.

The more pleasing and sacrificing I was, the more he expected and the less he noticed me. To him, I was raising the child and maintaining the home.

Regularly after work, Lucas would relax or go out with friends.

"Where are you going?" I asked, disliking his secrecy. Lucas puffed out his chest in his threatening way, roughly replying, "It's none of your business. You're not my mother. I don't answer to you."

His harshness and dismissiveness etched a bigger hole in my heart. I'd heard conversations from our mutual friends, how he was hanging out with everyone, going out to dinner, partying, and living life . . . all without me.

Everyone probably thought I didn't want to join, or that I wasn't fun anymore. *What did he tell them about me?*

"Lucas, I really want to come and have fun. I don't like being left out," I tried to explain.

"You've got the baby to take care of. I'm not going out and having to do it for you, that's your job. I'm not running around taking care of a baby when it's my time off. That's my time to relax. I want to enjoy myself, and I don't need you hovering and asking me to do things for you," Lucas said. "If you go out and get a real job, then we'll talk."

"Lucas, I'm your wife, I should be included in things! These are my friends too. And if we do go out, yeah, I might need you to help with Ivy. You're her father, my husband, and I'm pregnant," I pleaded.

His words pierced me. "See, you're already being demanding. That's not how it's going to be. I am not going to be around you when you are demanding or needy. I draw a line, and I will not tolerate you telling me what to do or making demands of me," he coldly reprimanded.

"I am not making demands," I said, as my voice broke in sadness. "I am explaining to you that there may be something that I might need help with."

He brushed me off with disinterest and contempt. "You have hands, figure it out yourself." With cold finality, he walked away.

In doing so, Lucas walked out of my heart. I felt dead toward him.

Walking to my bathroom, tears blurred my vision. Blindly, I locked the door behind me as heaving sobs welled up inside, threatening to spill out. My knees gave way, and I sank to the floor, trembling, hands clutching over my mouth, trying to hold in the storm of grief that had been building for so long. A resignation of solitude settled upon me as massive sobs erupted into huge racking cries, and pieces of me spilled across the tile.

I screamed, "Why?! Why do I have to go through this? I hate him so much!" I pressed my stiffened body into the towel, screaming into it as my hands fisted the fabric in desperation. Crying with sheer venom, my sobs racked me from the inside out, hot tears streaming, voice hoarse and breaking, until there were no tears left to cry.

My chest shuddered, shaking breaths that slowly stilled, until all that was left was an occasional trembling as remnants of grief shook through me. I lay on the tile, hair streaming across the cold floor, completely spent, every fiber of me aching and raw, as though the last pieces of my heart had been crushed and scattered carelessly across the bathroom.

I closed my eyes and let my mind go blank.

Thinking nothing.

I don't think I can do this. I really don't. Something must change.

Chapter Twelve

Winter 2016, *Present Day*

I clearly remembered that moment. It was a moment when everything shifted in my mind. It was when I knew absolutely there was no longer a possibility of a normal, functioning marriage. It was when I realized I was imprisoned. I had been trapped.

Opening up about my traumatic memories with my counselor was an act of raw, soul-deep courage, one of the hardest things I had ever done. Each memory was heavy, yet necessary, as if I were slowly lifting pieces of the weight I had carried far too long.

These hours spent in my counselor's little office were invaluable. Her office held the comforting fragrance of sweet pine and neroli that drifted from scented candles nestled in cozy little places. The dim lights, neutral decor, and soft, fluffy pillows all enhanced the atmosphere of peace. Soft instrumental music serenaded the soul. I loved my time spent with her, as it soothed the ache the memories stirred. Each hour, I felt I gained back one more piece of the disappearing puzzle named Joy, as I was learning to piece myself back together, one missing puzzle piece at a time.

After all the hurt and trauma, I was beginning to be honest about my feelings and emotions. And it was liberating and normal. I was beginning to understand what it meant to live free from fear. It was healing to feel anger, irritation, frustration, or just communicate something important without rage attacking me in the face. It was wholesome and renewing. I had held so many of my feelings captive, afraid to speak—out of fear of the consequences. One by one, I began releasing my feelings from the invisible prison inside my body—fear of him, of his anger, of his punishments, his retributions, and his coldness.

Now, somehow, in my mind, I felt I was on a clear path toward freedom. It was a wonderful feeling relearning to be authentically myself.

Honest. Myself. Alive. Choices. Decisions. Options.

All the things I had been forced to live without. It was wonderful to feel appreciated, loved, acknowledged, respected, heard, and validated by people who cared. I realized I had spent years being trained to not express my needs. Now, I was having to relearn how to speak for myself, advocate for myself, and practice using my authentic voice while not living in fear of others' responses. I was not choosing to be around those who tried to manipulate me into feeling guilty for not being a better wife or for not suffering more. I learned it is better to have a broken home than to be broken and destroyed in your home, and that included the lives of each child.

It was healing to have the counselor explain the things that many victims of abuse struggle with, and it brought much clarity and understanding.

I began to understand there is a cycle that tries to drag us in, confuse and trap us. And the abuser's behavior can have many differing effects on the victims. The cycle begins as the abuser becomes offended or upset by something we do or don't do. It can be anything that doesn't meet their standard or preference—for any reason at all. They attack, shame, blame, accuse, and put you on a guilt trip. We may set a boundary because we feel their actions are wrong, then they accelerate, becoming cruel. Eventually they soften and apologize with convincing pleas, a slew of apologies that are masked manipulation. We then open our hearts, believing they are sincere. And then the cycle repeats—endlessly.

Seeing this from my counselor's perspective was eye-opening. This was true. And it happened continuously. Especially since many of us struggle with a need for connection or have a fear of abandonment. Many times, we reinforce these behaviors unintentionally.

We reengage too soon after the cruel phase—well before their harmful behavior has genuinely changed. Sometimes compassionate people will take accountability for their partner's emotions. Then we change ourselves to please them or tiptoe around their emotions to not "cause" another outburst, and we take accountability for them.

What needs to happen instead is to learn to set proper boundaries. Boundaries aren't meant to control someone else; they are meant to establish what we will and won't tolerate. They are to protect us from harmful behavior. We must enact these clear, firm boundaries that cannot be manipulated. We may love the people who cross our boundaries, but love without boundaries is not safe. Boundaries are healthy for both individuals because it allows each person to decide for themself what kind of person they want to be. It is not about control; it's about protecting yourself from harm and letting others choose as they will.

There are many tools used by an abuser to gain control. Guilt-tripping is a very effective tool used to coerce one to change their mind and deny what they feel is healthy or right. It makes the victim feel like a bad person if they honor their "no." The victim feels they need to prove their love or loyalty by abandoning their own needs.

Passive aggressiveness and sarcasm are used to cut, hurt, or confuse. It stirs up confusion and guilt with the abuser not having to take personal accountability. Many times, it's manipulation disguised as victimhood.

Blame-shifting is used to make the victim sound like the aggressor; the tables are turned, the narrative is switched, and the abuser plays the victim. The biggest sign you are dealing with an abuser is they never take responsibility for their behavior. They will put the responsibility onto the victim. This is designed to keep the focus on the victim defending themself and off the abuser's unhealthy or destructive behavior.

Escalation is used when more subtle tactics don't work—yelling, name-calling, or swearing occurs, anything to raise the escalation until the victim is overwhelmed and exhausted. This goal is to intimidate so they can force what they want.

All-or-nothing thinking is used to be dramatic, to blow things out of proportion. This is used to make the victim think if they don't cave, you will lose them or something bad will happen—this is emotional blackmail.

Love-bombing after cruelty is used to break down defenses. Suddenly the abuser switches gears and it causes confusion. There will be a strong pull to believe them, because the victim desires to believe there is authentic change. It is important to hang on to your logical wisdom and not cave under pressure. This is not a real change. It is part of the abuse cycle.

Playing the victim is used to make the abuser sound like they are the victim. This is effective because it makes others feel the abuser needs to be rescued, and the victim is "mean" for having boundaries and not giving in to what is demanded–the victim is the difficult one. The clearer your boundaries, the more the abuser tries to paint themselves as the victim, to get others to join in defending them. From the outside, the victim may look like the mean one, when the victim is finished having boundaries crossed.

Endless-processing is used to push long, unending conversations until the victim is worn down and drained. This happens to coerce the abuser's own way, not to share honest perspective or find a compromise. Their purpose is to keep the victim engaged and exhausted until they give in.

The abuser knows the victim's deep desire is to be loved and to love, to be understood and to understand, and to maintain a mutual connection with those we love. These are good things, but when they are used to manipulate, that is wrong.

Understanding these forms of abuse was mind-blowing. I never had anyone explain this with such clarity. I struggled to process these truths. My mind had been re-trained to give in, to keep the peace. I believed that being a peacemaker meant doing whatever was necessary to bring peace, but I was realizing now, that isn't healthy. Abandoning my own respect and integrity to please someone else is not a healthy relationship. Mutual respect and reciprocity is.

It's hard to set boundaries and follow through. But it's key to maintaining respect for ourselves, establishing what we choose to be around, and what we will remove ourselves from to protect our mind, emotions, peace, sanity, and body. We've been programmed to believe enforcing healthy boundaries is selfish, when boundaries are healthy and necessary.

We need to stop sacrificing ourselves for a destructive and abusive relationship that is one-sided and instead, choose our dignity and peace—working to heal, to restore our mental and emotional health.

My therapist explained it's easy to choose a familiar path, even one that is unhealthy, and much harder to choose a new path, one we must carve out ourselves to create new healthy pathways toward healing, proper boundaries, and rebuilding identity.

I knew I had fallen into these pitfalls so many times, not seeing the cycle of abuse I was living in daily. My focus was on surviving day to day, trying to keep the peace, and trying to build a family—and I missed the bullseye and everything that was swirling all around me constantly.

Chapter Thirteen

The Silence That Screamed

Beautiful baby Mia was born. It was a quick birth this time, without complications. As I held tiny baby Mia, I reverently touched every finger and tiny toe. Exhausted but completely captivated by this tiny miracle, I tenderly kissed the top of her soft, downy head. I breathed in her fragrance, cradling her in my arms as she suckled, and I looked upon her with awe. Mia was perfect.

I spent a perfect hour admiring this tiny bundle. My heart was full, then my eyes closed in peaceful exhaustion. The nurse came and gently released Mia from my arms to bathe her. Reluctantly, I relinquished her. On the rare occasion of kindness, Lucas bent down to land a soft kiss on my forehead.

"Babe is there anything you need?" he asked.

"I am so tired," I admitted.

"Just sleep," Lucas offered. "I'll be here."

I dozed in a peaceful respite, my heart overflowing. I loved birthing my babies. They were the only loves in my life.

Morning had dawned very early with baby Mia mewing for my breast. As the nurses came and went, I cradled Mia close to my chest and nursed her contentedly. I had spent the night alone. Lucas couldn't stay by my side at the hospital but promised to come as soon as he finished his shift—he explained he couldn't miss work. I tried to hold onto that promise, yet the hours stretched long and heavy, and I longed to return home. As the sun began to rise, I rocked Mia, counting the minutes until he would arrive. Late morning Lucas finally showed, looking showered and refreshed.

"I've been waiting for you," I said yearningly.

"I am here now," Lucas assured. "How is Mia doing?"

"She's actually doing well; she slept for four hours last night, so I was able to get a little bit of sleep," I explained. "But it is hard with the nurses coming in and out all night long."

"I bet." Lucas gently stroked Mia's tiny foot. His eyes took in the bundle. "She is so tiny," he said, admiring. "I can't believe how little she is."

"I know, she *is* little, only five pounds, seven ounces! Our little Peanut!" I said smiling.

With the discharge papers in hand, we finally headed toward home. I missed my little Ivy terribly, and I'm sure she missed her mommy. Grammy and Grampy did their best to entertain her, play silly games, make yummy snacks for their little darling, and love her incredibly. I was grateful for having wonderful parents who were amazing grandparents. I didn't know what I would do without them.

As we pulled up the long driveway, the front door opened, and Ivy flew across the yard, running barefoot through the freshly cut grass. The second I opened the car door, she hurled herself into my arms. Her little chubby arms squeezed tightly around my neck, not letting go. Her love was wonderfully warm and comforting. Scooping her up in my arms, I cradled her lovingly. "I missed you, Angel girl!" And I rained kisses all over her sweet little face.

"Missed you too, Mommy! Bunches and bunches!" she replied, eyes wide open and a happy smile plastered across her little face. "Where's baby sissy? I see her?"

"Yes, baby! Let Mommy get her out of the car so you can see your baby sissy," I gently explained.

Mom swooped in to help with Ivy as we gathered the baby and newborn items.

Dad gave a warm hug, squeezing just a bit longer than usual as we all gathered into the cozy foyer with the happy chatter of Ivy swirling around us.

Seeing the pure adoration shimmering in Ivy's eyes—wide with wonder and overflowing with love—as she paused to reach out and tenderly trace baby Mia's tiny arm stirred a deep, aching tenderness in my heart. In that sacred breath-held moment, one angel recognized another, and a delicate thread of kinship seemed to weave itself between them as love passed from one child to another—fragile, instinctive, and already unbreakable. Their bond seemed to take root right before my eyes—a luminous beginning that would never be broken.

Learning to juggle a newborn and a lively toddler took quite a bit of adjusting—there was nothing easy about it, and hardly a quiet moment for myself. Either I was nursing the baby, changing her, or meeting the endless demands of a busy toddler. It felt as if my own needs had disappeared entirely. I couldn't even remember the last time I had taken a proper, relaxing shower or shaved. Each day was a relentless twenty-four-hour job of care, and yet amid the exhaustion, there were fleeting flashes of sweetness—a tiny hand grasping mine, a soft cooing from the baby, or a sleepy smile from my toddler. Still, these small treasures did little to erase the constant fatigue and the sense that I'd lost myself somewhere between feedings, tantrums, and diaper changes.

"Honey, can I get you a cup of tea or coffee?" Mom asked, placing a comforting hand on my shoulder. The gentle weight of her presence felt like a lifeline. Having her come over was a needed luxury—like a soft pause in the whirlwind of motherhood.

"Actually, some chai would sound amazing right now!" I answered, grateful whenever Mom was able to come over and lend a helping hand.

"I need something soothing, I just want to relax so badly."

"Okay, honey, coming up in just a couple minutes."

A few minutes later, Mom handed me a steaming cup of chai topped with whip cream and a dusting of cinnamon.

"Oh my gosh, Mom, that looks absolutely amazing!" I gushed. Taking the mug carefully, I sipped the creamy froth with enjoyment, treasuring this calm moment.

"This is just what I needed," I said as I sank into the sofa. I felt the tension in my shoulders ease ever so slightly. My body ached with exhaustion—the kind that seeps into your bones, leaving your muscles heavy.

I allowed myself this rare indulgence: a moment of pampering, of stillness, of being cared for. Mom carried in her own steaming mug of tea, settling herself comfortably on the sofa as we tucked ourselves beneath the warmth of the knit throw.

"So, how are you doing with two littles?" she asked, her brow crinkled in concern.

"I'm doing okay, you know that I love my babies," I explained, "but I feel like I am also . . . a little bit in over my head."

"How do you mean? "Mom asked, her eyes looking worried.

I hesitated before speaking. With Lucas away at work, I felt free to speak with openness. "I never know what mood Lucas will be in. He isn't really a hands-on dad." Saying it out loud felt difficult, as if I were betraying him—but it was the truth. And the only person I probably could admit this to was Mom or Charlotte.

Mom looked taken back, "Really? He really isn't involved, at all?" Her brows raised in surprise; she reached out to gently rest her hand on my arm.

Fidgeting with my coffee mug, I traced and retraced the patterns of leaves with my fingers. I went on to explain, "You know, childbirth does some things to you. It makes you reassess your reality. To be fully honest, no, he isn't. He isn't mean to them, but he's not attentive. He doesn't really *do* anything to help or care for the girls. He just exists and does whatever he wants. I feel the entire load of raising my children is on my shoulders. He is just there for the fun and easy parts. And I really don't think that's how it should be." Exhaustion had removed any filter that might have been in place.

"Well, no," Mom said, "he should be helping you, with feedings, diaper changes, running errands, and watching the little one so you can rest. That's normal parenting . . . he's not doing any of this?"

"No, he isn't, not really," I answered honestly. "He exists at home doing his own thing and expects me to have all the bases covered." I felt horrible for even saying this out loud, and it made me feel like a terrible person. But it was true. It was difficult for me to carry the weight of two little ones mostly by myself. And it was apparent that Mom was having a hard time with this truthful information.

"Honey, why haven't you told me all this?" Mom said, her eyed clouded with tears, as she reached over to enfold me in a comforting hug.

"Do you know how hard it is to admit that something is deeply wrong in your marriage?" I confessed softly, my fingers twisting nervously in my lap, sadness written across my face.

"I am so sorry, Joy," Mom said. "You need to be transparent with me, tell me what's going on. I'm here to help you. You know that Dad and I are always here for you." Tears clouded her sky-blue eyes. I brushed a trembling hand across my cheek, nervously pushing my hair behind my ear. "I just don't want to bug you and Dad about every little thing. I feel like I would be constantly complaining."

She reached out, tenderly stroking my arm, as if to deposit her compassionate energy into me.

"I really do appreciate you and Dad so much," I reaffirmed. "I feel so guilty that my marriage isn't working out the way it's supposed to. But I also feel it's wrong for me to quit." I was quiet for a long moment before I admitted, "I also don't know how much more I can handle."

"I understand," Mom said softly, holding me to her in a close embrace.

And I knew Mom really did understand. It was the unspoken communication that communicated the loudest. I knew Mom was there, no matter what. I leaned into her touch and cherished the closeness and comfort.

"You know, you can always come home. You and the girls always have a place with us. Please come home if it gets worse or even if it just doesn't get better. Okay?" Mom's eyes glistened, the sincerity in her voice wrapped around me like a comforting embrace. Her hands tremored as she held onto mine.

"I will," I promised as my eyes misted. I looked into her caring eyes and knew I didn't want to bring her more worry or pain.

I knew this was my journey to navigate, mine alone to decide when I had endured enough. A quiet premonition settled in my chest: it wasn't going to be smooth sailing, more like a tempest—unpredictable and relentless.

Four years later . . . I trembled violently, shaking, hidden in my closet.

I needed to breathe . . . In . . . out . . . In . . . out . . .

The thunder of my heartbeat filled my ears, each beat crashed like a drum echoing through my skull. I could see nothing—suffocating darkness swallowed me. Thick. Heavy. Unyielding.

Breathe. I told myself. *Just breathe.*

I lay curled in a fetal position as time slipped away. One hour . . . two? A ragged cry tearing from my throat, hoarse and desperate. My ribs ached with every breath. I was spent–emptied, utterly exhausted. Slowly, I unwound my arm, stiff from holding myself in a small, protected ball and reached up to touch my neck. I traced the bruises that Lucas's fingers made on the tender skin.

My pulse pounded louder, and my heart slammed against my chest. It was the only noise my ears could hear. Boom. Boom. Boom. It was deafening, and the words rushed back.

They overlapped each other in an irregular sequence:

"I could squeeze your neck until you can't breathe . . . I wish I could just kill you."

"No one would ever find you . . . I have friends in low places who can get rid of you."

"I could bury you and no one would ever find you . . . No one will believe you."

"Useless. Worthless. Replaceable."

Breathe. Breathe. Breathe.

Heart pounding. *I can't do this.*

I was trying to survive. Every day, I had to act as if life was normal, but my body screamed the truth. My health was deteriorating. My emotions were shattered, a raw, jagged mess. I was the hamster on a wheel, a trained monkey . . . trapped in this repetition of insanity.

Day after day. Night after night. The same suffocating madness.

And two nights ago, it descended on me once more.

That evening, I was bone weary, every muscle heavy, my mind fogged with exhaustion, my spine aching from the weight of the day. After tucking the girls into bed with a silly puppet show, ending with a round of cozy kisses and a quiet song, I tiptoed silently out of their room. Downstairs, I moved through the monotony of chores, each motion heavy and methodical. I cleared the dinner dishes, washing an endless stack, and threw another load of towels into the washer. Two more piles of dirty clothes waited on the floor, demanding attention. My body begged for rest, every muscle trembling, yet I finished the tasks uncomplainingly. Dragging myself upstairs, I began washing my face, and paused, catching my reflection in the mirror. Looking deeply into my own eyes, I saw tiny wrinkles tracing the corners where laughter should have lived. The face staring back at me was taut and serious, instead of relaxed in ease.

I saw sadness. I saw loneliness. I blinked to change the view. Sorrow and worry lines etched, and hopelessness shadowed.

With a consigned sigh, I cleansed my face and applied moisturizer. Taking long, gentle strokes, I smoothed the skin and breathed in the fragrance of rose and jasmine, willing it to relax and refresh me. I glanced again at my sad, clean face, studying the misery for a long moment.

Then I tiptoed to bed, pulling back the covers and softly sliding into the cold bed sheets, barely making a dent on the firm mattress. Pulling up the extra blanket for warmth, I tried to cozy in, burrowing deeper into my half of the bed.

Lucas walked into the bedroom. Hastily, he pulled off his clothes, carelessly discarding them on the floor. I could hear the echo of his footsteps as he moved to turn off the lights. After a short moment, I felt the bed shift as he slid into bed and reached over to touch my hip. The only time he touched me was when he had a need.

"Please, no," I breathed. "I am so tired."

It was more than tiredness though. I could not say the truth . . . that he barely looked at me, he never hugged me anymore, never spoke gently to me, never preferred me or made me feel special, treasured, or loved.

He . . . didn't love me. That was the full, hurtful truth.

I longed to be desired, loved, and cherished. I longed to have a husband make love to me, passionately and tenderly. I longed for a partner, a lover, a best friend.

I wasn't even sure if Lucas had truly ever . . . made love to me. It just felt like sex.

Mating. Satisfying him. Mostly unsatisfying sex.

Non-consensual sex.

"I don't want to have sex," I stated very clearly.

"Really?" he said. "What am I supposed to do? We haven't had sex in over a week. If you aren't going to meet my needs, I'll have someone else do it."

"*What!*" I exploded, jerking to a seated position. "Why would you ever say that?"

"Well, if you are not going to do it, someone else will." He shrugged.

I feared he would cheat again.

Two years into our marriage, Lucas had an affair, and the fracture it created felt impossible to mend. Trying to rebuild after that betrayal was daunting. It awakened my greatest fear, the one place I was the most fragile. And Lucas knew how to weaponize that fear against me.

Lucas's hands began touching places I did not want him to touch. Revulsion surged through me as his grip tightened and his breath burned against my neck.

His whisper came hot and assaulting, "Learn to like it," he said as he pushed himself on top of me.

His hands yanked, pulling at my clothes, as I tried to tug them back into place. He shoved my top upward, squeezed my breast with an insistence meant only to prove his dominance. I stifled my cry as his body pressed against mine. Each sound he made was a reminder that this was about power, not love. He pushed himself into me, groaning and pleasuring himself. I turned my face away, shutting my eyes tight as a wave of disgust and shame rose within me, and my body betrayed me by being trapped.

This is not me. This is not love. He may command my body, but he will never claim my soul.

Inside I built walls—thick, cold, unbreakable. Each one rose higher with every demanded touch to protect my broken and vulnerable heart. So I endured, silent on the outside, but screaming within: *You will not win. Not all of me. I may be your wife, but you do not own me.*

I shifted my eyes to focus on anything else.

The chair. The dresser. Anything. The rhythmic pounding. The repeated motion kept pushing my head against the headboard. Thunk. Thunk. Thunk.

Squeezing my eyes shut, I willed myself to disappear. A solitary tear forced its way out, slipping free, despite my determination to stay strong. It traced a hot path down my cheek before it vanished and was lost. *Lost, like me.*

I did not feel like a wife.

I felt like a prostitute, forced to perform acts for survival.

Unwillingly.

My one consolation—my vow: I refused to kiss Lucas anymore.

I remembered once seeing in a movie that prostitutes never kissed the men they slept with, not intimately. It was their last defense, a way of protecting their heart. I wasn't sure if this was true, but at that moment, I decided, I would hold onto my last bit of self-preservation. He may force his way on me, claiming it is his right, but, I vowed, he cannot touch my heart. I will never kiss him again passionately. I didn't want his lips anywhere near mine.

I felt helpless, disgusted, angry, and violated as Lucas groaned with pleasure, his body shuddering as he collapsed his weight on me. He lay with dead weight, like a cow, pinning me in a silence I couldn't break.

His smell repulsed me; the touch from his body made me tremble. He shifted, rolling over on his side, and snugly pulled the covers over himself and began snoring almost immediately.

I remained frozen, my body stiff with shock. Only after long, trembling moments did I slowly ease myself out from the bed, careful not to let the mattress shift beneath my weight. Slipping into the bathroom, I closed the door, locking it with a swift turn of my wrist, and collapsed against the cold tile door.

My mind went numb. In a trance, there was nothing but the rhythm of breathing.

Inhale. Exhale. Breathe. Try again.

Tears slowly trailed down my cheeks in slow, trembling lines. I felt them slip from my jaw and fall—one after another—quiet, desperate drops falling soundlessly onto my night shirt, forming wet pools and turning the pale-pink fabric into dark, mauve blotches. I couldn't move. My body felt borrowed, numb, unrecognizable. Each tear carried the humiliation, the helplessness, the anger I couldn't voice. Lying there, I felt the reality of what had been taken settle over me, heavy and suffocating.

Furiously, I wiped at my nose. Not caring, I wiped the snot onto my shirt.

Who cares? I was a shell. I was not loved.

I cursed him. I hated him. I wished he would die.

I sat unmoving until my tears dried. Until I could breathe. Until the snot dried and crusted. Until the tear spots stained.

I pushed myself up from my immobilized position. I could not feel my legs.

Well, I couldn't feel my heart either, so . . .

I turned on the shower and waited with my back pressed against the cold wall until the room filled with steam. Stripping off my clothes, I let them fall carelessly to the floor and stepped into the pounding hot stream of water. As the water caressed my body, I hoped it would wash my sadness away.

Impossible.

The realization that my husband had forced himself on me, without my consent—that he had taken what I did not give—for his own selfish pleasure, made me angry and waves of nausea crashed on me. I was just an object to him, a body to conquer, *nothing*, but for him to abuse. I was not his partner, not his love, I was simply there to be taken, to be broken and controlled.

I turned the water temperature as hot as it would go. Almost scalding. And I scrubbed his touch off me. Water and tears streamed down my face, ran down my chest, over my breasts, down my stomach, to my feet, and was lost in the drain.

Wishing my sorrow to disappear down the drain, like the water, I begged—hopelessly.

The piercing-hot spray of water penetrating every part of my skin—until it ran cold. Resting my hand on the handle, I pushed to stop the flow. Leaning into the coolness of the wall, I looked up to the cream tiles above my head and rested my head against the wall, slowly sliding down to the floor. Wrapping my arms tightly around my naked body, I sat. Still. Unmoving. Until my body cooled and goosebumps appeared on my naked skin, spreading to my arms, my legs, my stomach and breasts.

Minutes ticked by.

This wasn't even close to the first time this had happened.

As my body trembled, I knew it wouldn't be the last. In broken resignation, I slowly unfolded and stood. Stepping out of the shower, I pulled a thick bath towel around me, letting its coziness warm my chilled body. Reaching for the clean nightgown hanging on the door hook, I slipped it over my head and smoothed it over my body, not caring about the towel or dirty, snot-crusted pajamas left discarded on the floor.

Soundlessly, I slid into bed, being careful to not shift the mattress. Although I closed my eyes, I knew sleep was far from coming. I tucked the covers tightly around my body, not wanting any part of my body to accidentally touch that animal.

Breathe. Breathe. Slowly, exhale . . . I hugged myself, trying to will myself to sleep.

Midnight. One o'clock. Two. Tick, tock, tick . . . Snoring . . . An endless night.

Finally, around four o'clock, I fell into an exhausted, desperate slumber. My reality was a prison of mind and body. How I wished for freedom from this living hell—from this monotony of an unchanging cycle.

It had a name I will never forget.

Fear.

Chapter Fourteen

Spring 2017, *Present Day*

Moisture streaked my cheeks, tears stirred by the memories that forced their way back.

The horrible act.

The one I dared not utter. The one that shattered me each time it happened.

I had spoken of this to no one. I didn't think I could ever share this ugly, painful, shame-filled part of my past. It belonged in my past and I wished it to remain there—buried. Stirring up even the memory of this trauma was more than I could bear, and I needed time to collect myself. The wash of memories opened Pandora's box.

Grateful the girls were playing at Mom and Dad's, I took the chance to slip away for a short walk. Feeling desperate to shake off the heaviness pressing against my chest, I meandered down the little dirt pathway leading to the river and tried to untangle the confusion of memories and pain. I followed the path to the water's edge and sat on the shaded, sloping bank. Dipping my toes in the cool, clear water, I relished the feeling of peace as it flowed over me like gentle waves of tranquility flowing over my soul. The grass, soft and mossy beneath my fingers, felt as though the earth itself was cradling me, its musky scent mingling with the delicate perfume of wildflowers.

Stirring the water gently with my feet. It was as if the Earth itself was speaking to me, urging me to pause, to center myself. I felt my muscles beginning to loosen, knot by knot, as if each breath untangled the hidden tension. I inhaled slowly and intentionally, letting the air fill me fully and I exhaled all the heaviness I'd been carrying.

Sometimes the memories that surfaced felt like they belonged to another person. Sometimes I could barely even believe the things I had experienced.

It was otherworldly, blurred at the edges, more like ghost stories than chapters in my life. Sometimes, I could hardly believe I survived them. It made my chest tighten to recognize I had outgrown the woman who once lived this daily suffering.

When the memories flooded, they came like broken, disjointed remnants of a bad movie, one you wanted to escape from badly. The pain struck sharp and deep. Leaving a bruise where an open wound once lived.

Why didn't I leave sooner? I asked myself. That was always the quandary. I always wondered about this. I truly felt fear had paralyzed me. The threats were so prominent in my mind, I believed he would act on everything he promised to enact upon me. I knew Mom and Dad urged me to come to them, and I had no doubt they would help me, but the fear of his threats kept me frozen. If he ever turned his rage on them, I could never forgive myself. I loved them too deeply to risk their safety, even if it meant sacrificing my own.

Maybe I wished, somehow, it would get better—if I could just be the perfect wife and mom, then he would finally be the man I knew he could be. I didn't want to do anything to make the situation worse, so I tried to be the peacemaker. I tried to smooth the edges of his harshness and not poke the bear.

"How wrong and unhealthy that was," I said aloud to nobody.

Looking at the chirping birds resting on the little branches, I listened to their symphony.

So safe were the little birds, trusting the branches to hold them, chirping happily, content in the rhythm of life and cradled by the tree's embrace. Cardinals, bluebirds, and sparrows flew about while merrily chirping, singing the song nature intended.

Lying back on the soft blanket of grass, I wished I had felt as peaceful as these little birds, feeling safe, without a worry or care. I propped my head up on my crossed arms and closed my eyes in relaxation, allowing sereneness to wash over me.

Now I was at peace. Now, I was safe. I no longer lived with constant, unrelenting fear.

I breathed in the intoxicating aroma of honeysuckle and wild wisteria growing freely around the riverbend. *So peaceful.* I felt myself drifting asleep and just let it happen as a gentle smile played across my face.

Exhale. . . Peace. Freedom.

Chapter Fifteen

The Monotonous Hamster Wheel of Abuse

I had spent the last couple years scrambling to shield the girls from any hint of contention. I became an expert at excuses—softening, minimizing, or completely inventing reasons for Lucas's aggression toward me. I didn't know what else to do except hide it and pretend it wasn't there.

Pregnant again, every errand felt like a small marathon with two littles in tow. If Lucas happened to be home, I'd take advantage of the moment—slipping out quickly while the girls played. Even then, a knot of anxiety always sat in my stomach; he was less than attentive to their needs, especially when they needed something.

That afternoon, in a rush to be home, I ran through the grocery store and a few short errands. When I walked back through the door, Ivy greeted me with a proud little smile. "Mommy, we were hungry, but we found chips in the cupboard for lunch. Daddy was too busy watching TV to make lunch. He told us to wait. We tried! I asked him again and he said go get a snack. So I found the chips!"

Her pride in solving the problem pierced me. Anger rose inside. *How dare he!* He left the kids to basically fend for themselves, eating crap for lunch.

After covering the girls with hugs and kisses, I nudged them toward their toys and waited until they disappeared down the hall. Then I walked into the living room and planted myself directly in front of Lucas, my anger barely contained.

"Why didn't you make them a proper lunch?"

He didn't even look away from the TV. "I asked them if they wanted lunch, they said no," Lucas replied, his tone flat, absent–like my question was so unimportant, it barely required acknowledgment.

"They are little kids!" I snapped, trying to steady my voice even as my pulse thundered in my ears. "That's your job to make them lunch; you don't wait until they *say* they are hungry. You make them something healthy. It doesn't have to be complicated, just not chips. You left them to fend for themselves. Do you not see how absurd that is?"

He shrugged without looking at me. "Then next time, you watch them. Take them with you. I don't care,"

"Lucas," I said with breath tight, "I need to be able to get things done without taking the girls every single time, that's impossible! You're their father. They're your responsibility too."

"Look," he said, turning his cold eyes toward me. "I do it my way. If you don't like it, figure it out yourself."

His dismissiveness and lack of responsibility hit me like a slap. I stared at him–at the man who couldn't be bothered to feed his own children properly–and felt a wave of disgust. Without another word, I turned away.

Being pregnant and trying to manage the girls almost entirely on my own-I felt in pieces, each demand pressing with a weight so impossible, I didn't know how I could hold everything together. Lucas's refusal to take even basic responsibility ignited a fury I could barely contain, but I knew pushing too hard would be like kicking a hornet's nest–I never knew what reaction I might unleash. So I swallowed it all: the anger, the frustration, the resentment, my need for partnership.

I forced myself to walk away before the pressure inside me erupted. The girls didn't need two parents simmering with rage. One of us had to remain steady, and that weight fell on me. As I stepped out of the room, I pressed everything down where it wouldn't spill over. I couldn't fix him. I couldn't make him a healthy parent or a good spouse. I could only manage the fallout.

I went upstairs and pushed open the girls' bedroom door. They were sprawled on the carpet, completely absorbed in their Barbies —tiny plastic shoes overturned, dresses scattered like confetti, little bits of furniture arranged in crooked lines. Their innocence hit me like a soft ache in my chest.

"What are we playing here? Can I play too?" I asked gently as I lowered myself onto the floor. I picked up a doll and began brushing her tangled hair. The simple repetitive motion grounded me. I tried to let the anger seep away, tried to breathe it down, and tried to be present with my daughters instead of drowning in anger and resentment.

Ivy brightened instantly. "Yay, Mommy, you can be the teacher!" she chirped, already directing the play. I followed her lead, letting their world pull me in, letting the laughter soften the hard edges.

And so, we played.

But underneath the play, the truth pressed heavy. Sometimes the weight of solitary parenting felt unbearable. I craved a break—not from the girls, but from the never-ending cycle of endless responsibility. I longed for a night out with friends, a peaceful moment of self-care. Anything where I could just be me. I wanted to walk into the house where the kids were fed properly, where their father had played with them, where memories were being made without chaos or tears.

I wanted to exhale—even once.

On the rare occasion I managed to slip out alone, I still had to meal prep every meal and return home to a mess waiting for me.

An unease stirred as I noticed Lucas's neglectful behavior and his sometimes overly harsh correction of the girls. It was becoming harder to ignore. Out of instinct, as much as fear, I started taking the girls with me almost everywhere. *This was my only option.* The only other alternative was relying on Mom and Dad, if they were available.

Waves of overwhelm and exhaustion crashed over me, leaving me struggling to catch my breath as my days blurred together: endless errands, doctor visits, dentist appointments, and grocery runs—all with the girls in tow.

There was no "tagging out," no partner to lean on. Every need, every demand, every cry fell squarely on my shoulders, from dawn until long past nightfall. Patience had to be stretched thin, pulled from reserves I didn't even have. By the time I finally sank into a chair, the clock would be nearing twelve. Life was an unrelenting rhythm of go, go, go—no pause in sight.

God, I thought, *how long do I have to parent with no one else to rely on?*

I needed to be at least three people–or at least have a few more pairs of arms. I was caretaker and cook, entertainment organizer, nurse, tutor, chauffeur, mediator, and referee. One moment I was wiping tears and tying shoes, the next I was chopping vegetables and answering a question about long division, breaking up a fight over a toy, and reading bedtime stories. Each task pulled me in a multitude of different directions, each demand carving away the small space I had to breathe. *This is crazy,* my brain told me. But my body obeyed what was expected, as if there was no other way.

Later that evening, I went upstairs to find a quiet place to hide—my bathroom.

Still and quiet, I sat for a few minutes, trying to breathe. Who would ever be there for *me*? Who do *I* have to run to and hide when *I* am overwhelmed and exhausted? Who is there to love *me*? Who would ever cherish *me*?

No one.

Panic gripped my throat, icy and tight. Unyielding. I gasped, trying to breathe past it. All I could see were the insurmountable tasks before me.

I was always . . . *alone.*

I had brought Lucas my concerns for the girls' growing needs, his ready answer was the same: "I don't have that kind of money," "I pay the bills," "Figure it out yourself, you have hands."

"Can we please make this work? It's not expensive. At the most, it's ninety dollars," I begged.

"Sorry, it's not going to happen. If you want it, figure it out yourself. Don't ask me again." He turned his attention back to the television.

"Don't you care? This is important!" I pleaded, feeling helpless.

"No, not really," he replied.

How was I supposed to feed the children and myself, buy personal necessities, school supplies, and still give the girls somewhat of a happy childhood? It felt like the walls were closing in. I couldn't leave the girls at home with him very often, nor would he allocate any money for childcare. The responsibility fell entirely on me. My mind spun in frantic circles. Every option collided with another impossibility. And there was the impasse—a mental and physical dilemma that had an impossible solution.

When summer faded into fall and the two older girls headed off to school, life shifted just enough to give me a sliver of breathing room. Three days a week, I could drop Rose off at Mom's before going to work. It wasn't much, but it was a lifeline.

I kissed Rose's forehead, wrapped her in a warm hug, and watched her toddle toward the playroom Mom had set up just for the girls. She had transformed the old sitting room into a colorful little haven—pink, lavender, and soft yellows scattered across the walls and rugs. Baskets brimmed with toys, and a small television hung on the wall for movie time, surrounded by cushy beanbag chairs. It was every little girl's dream.

Rose made a beeline for her favorite toy, giggling as the Elmo song started to play. She began to dance in that uninhibited toddler way, lost in her own joy. Seeing her content eased something tight in my chest.

I leaned down to give her a few more kisses, then hugged Mom—grateful in a way words never seemed to cover. Without her help, I had no idea how I would have kept everything afloat. After one last glance at Rose swaying to her song, I slipped quietly out the door, breathing a silent prayer of thanks.

Driving down their sloping driveway, I admired the vibrant colors of the maple trees lining the drive. Scarlet and fire-orange leaves graced the expansive lawn as nature showed off its outstanding elegance. I drank in its beauty and let it bring calmness to my soul.

On many autumn afternoons, the girls and I would wander down our winding, tree-lined road, picking wildflowers while chatting with friendly neighbors during bright afternoon strolls. We'd sift through the garden, collecting the last of the overlooked vegetables. Sunshine wrapped around like a gentle balm. With my hands in the soft earth, weeding among the vibrant mums, I felt a rare sense of calm. Nature was the one thing that let me breathe, bringing life and rejuvenation amid the everyday challenges.

Drawing on every creative instinct, I scavenged for fun, inexpensive ways to keep the girls entertained, racing against boredom. And to stay out of Lucas's way.

"Come, girls, let's make a water slide," "Let's run in the rain," "Let's take a walk," "Let's make muffins," "Who wants to go on a bike ride," "Who wants to go to Grammy and Grampy's house?" "Let's go to the snowball stand."

This was my every day. Evade. Hide. Distract. Be invisible. I had nearly perfected the art of slipping through Lucas's path unnoticed. And while it wasn't his hands that caused the hurt, the sting of his cruel indifference and unkindness still pierced deeply. *But was that any less of a hurt?*

As fall deepened into winter, and Christmas approached, there was no talk of presents. Once again, I was told we wouldn't have money for gifts until the week before Christmas. A familiar tight knot lodged in my chest, the panic sharp and tangible.

"How am I supposed to shop for the girls and our family only a couple days before Christmas? That is impossible. Either the shelves will be empty, or the sales will be gone, and that is hours standing in line!" I said, helplessness and frustration crashing over me, my chest tight and aching from the weight of anxiety.

"Sorry, I can't help you. That's all I can do," his voice flat, disinterested.

I felt the situation pressing down on me, impossible to solve.

The girls' little Christmas list, modest but still expectant, was an impossibility.

Why does every situation have to be so difficult?

Still, I was determined to try–for my babies. They mattered more than anything.

And so, my holidays would be as it was the year before, and probably years to follow: homemade Christmas cookies baked in the oven was one thing I could do, with borrowed eggs, sugar, and butter from Mom, a homemade gingerbread house created out of graham crackers, frosting, and dollar-store candy.

A Christmas tree would not be an option—yet Lucas seemed indifferent to the girls' feelings.

I have to do something! I won't disappoint my babies—not at Christmas! Determination fueled my creativity, I set to work, turning scraps and simple decorations into a winter wonderland from whatever I could find. I wound garland around the stairway railings, situating every branch to its evergreen perfection and weaving in twinkling Christmas lights and shiny ornaments that caught the glow. A few candy canes nestled among the branches for a festive treat.

"Look, girls . . . our Christmas wonderland!" I said softly, hoping they would remember *this*—the magic, not the struggle behind it.

Ivy's eyes widened, shimmering with wonder. "Ohhhh, it's so beautiful, Mommy!" she breathed almost reverently.

"Wow, I love it!" Mia squealed, racing forward to snatch the first candy cane she spotted. She tore off the wrapper with excited fingers, the sweet peppermint already melting on her tongue. Ivy joined her, both girls slurping happily, their faces lighting up with sticky, sugary joy.

"It's almost as pretty as a Christmas tree!" Mia declared, leaning her warm little body against mine in a soft hug.

They wrapped their arms around me—sweet, sticky, peppermint scented—perfect hugs. Happily, they cried, "Mommy, you make everything so pretty!"

A smile spread across my face as I bent to lay a gentle kiss on top of Rose's head. A wave of relief and warmth washed over me, sinking deep. For a moment, just one precious moment, the magic I had created was enough.

Bundled in my thick scarf, wrapped snugly around my neck, I braved the biting December wind. Hours stretched endlessly as I hunted for the least expensive–but still satisfactory–gifts, my feet sore and aching from standing in endless lines to secure a few simple treasures. The final week before Christmas arrived, and the world pulsed with a frantic energy. Parking lots swarmed with impatient shoppers and blaring horns as cars circled endlessly in search of even one open spot. The air felt tight, rushing, crowded, hurrying, leaving no time for a single pause.

Stumbling through the door—exhausted and hungry–I was barely able to stand, my legs trembled beneath me. I couldn't justify spending money on food when there were still presents to buy, so I pushed through the day on fumes. I collapsed onto the couch, my body sinking deep into the cushions as my feet throbbed in angry protest. For a few moments, I just lay there, listening to my own breath and trying to gather enough strength to move again. I finally pushed myself upright and hauled the shopping bags to the closet, tucking them away from curious little eyes and eager, searching hands. Only once everything was hidden did I allow myself to exhale.

Digging around in my purse, I pulled out the shopping list, each item carefully crossed off, noted substitutions scribbled in where I'd come up short. Somehow, I had found everyone a nice gift for Christmas. I was sure they would be happy. It was a Christmas miracle: the last-minute sales, clearance specials, buy one/get one and free samples and dollar-store specials. I'd take every miracle to make this work.

As I tucked the last presents away, cheery voices called from upstairs, "Mommy, come tuck us in!"

"Okay, girls, give me a few minutes," I answered, my voice lifting with a grateful sense of relief. "I'll be right there!"

Stuffing the list back in my purse, I hung it in the closet and sprinted up to the girls' bedrooms. Snuggling in between them, I showered them with sweet butterfly kisses amid their giggles and bursts of carefree laughter.

"I love you one, I love you two, I love you three, I love you four, I love you more and more and more and moooore!" I belted out a happy, silly lilting melody.

Their giggles and belly laughter worked magic on my heart, and their radiant smiles brought a soothing joy. *So worth it. I'd do anything for my girls!*

"Good night, my little angel," I softly whispered to each one and tiptoed out of their rooms. Leaning against the narrow hallway wall, I let myself rest for a moment– tired, but happy that I had found small treasures for my little angels.

I knew then that birthdays and holidays would likely always look like this, and I didn't know how to change it. So I poured myself–heart and soul–into everything for my girls, trying to make up for what we lacked. Even if I couldn't give them all I desired, I could surround them with tenderness, joy, love, and care. Every day, I tried to be the best version of myself, hoping, it might somehow be enough.

December flowed into January. The days dragged under a crushing weight. Lucas's moods shifted without warning, doors slammed harder, his voice sharpened, each word was edged with criticism, and the air turned as cold and brittle as the January wind. My body stayed on alert, panic lodged in my throat, and I braced for any unexpected reaction. By nightfall, my nerves were scraped raw, my chest tight with unshed tears, as my strength was nearly gone

Every night I lie on edge—listening to his breathing, his snoring, and the constant shifting beside me. I'd watch the clock tick past two a.m., then three a.m., trapped in utter frustration. By nearly five a.m., my mind would finally slip into a restless, shallow sleep, while the rest of me fought to stay wired and alert.

Evenings became a time I dreaded. As night drew near, the tension settled into my shoulders and knotted in my stomach.

Will I fall asleep tonight or not? The question looped endlessly in my mind, even when I tried to not think about it. Sleep felt like a mocking stranger, and relaxation felt impossibly distant.

I felt constantly unwell, my body rebelling in ways I couldn't understand–aches that wouldn't fade, restless nights, tension coiling in my stomach. Every day was a tightrope: navigating Lucas's sudden explosions and selfishness, tending to the girls' endless needs, and my own unresolved health issues. I was stretched thin in every direction. There was no respite, no quiet moment to just–*be.*

I was trapped, sinking in a storm I couldn't escape. Exposed. Helpless.

And the months slowly crawled by . . .

One early summer evening, I sank to the kitchen floor, the cool tile pressing against my bare feet, grounding me for a brief moment. My head rested against the cabinet as I let out a long, silent breath. Utterly spent. Every ounce of my energy had drained out of me, leaving only the thick, suffocating weight of stress layered thick on my skin.

How did other mothers do it? How did they look carefree—grabbing coffee with friends, laughing easily, unbothered by the chaos of life. . . Why can't I have at least a little of this?

I couldn't remember the last time I had felt light or free.

Was there something wrong with me?

The timer blared, yanking me back to reality—dinner was ready. My small moment of stillness vanished.

With a heavy sigh, I pushed myself up from the floor, forcing my emotions back into place, as I adding the finishing touches to dinner–fresh basil scattered over the pasta, a squeeze of lemon, and thyme tucked around the chicken.

Once everything looked perfect, I called everyone to the table. We gathered, and I made sure to keep the mood light, even if it meant hiding the exhaustion clawing at me.

"Guess what, girls," I announced. "Outdoor concerts start now that summer's here. We should go—slushies and cotton candy! What do you think?"

Their faces lit up. "Yay!" they squealed. "Can we go?"

"Yes! Let's do it! It starts tomorrow night!" I added, following their excitement.

"Oh, Daddy, that will be so fun!" The girls clapped their hands, bouncing in their seats.

"I'm not doing that. I have plans," Lucas kept his eyes on his phone, replying flatly.

"Daddy, please, we want you to come!" Ivy begged, reaching out to grasp his arm.

Lucas ignored the gentle tug and continued eating.

"Lucas . . . please, it would mean a lot to the girls. They miss doing fun things with you . . . can you try?" I offered.

"But why, Daddy?" Mia implored, her luminous eyes bright with unshed tears.

"No," he said firmly. "I work all day, that's not how I want to spend my evening."

"But Daddy, tomorrow's Friday! It's family night," Mia pleaded, her eyes sorrowful.

"Lucas, it's your girls," I begged. "Spending time with them is important. They just want to have fun with you."

"Someone has to have a real job to support this family. You don't. Stop trying to force your way. I'm not going," he said with cold finality.

I let the cruel jab pass without a word, but it pierced deeper than I wanted to admit. I forced myself to focus on the girls—their tender hearts, their innocent joy—and tried to shield them from the sting I felt.

The girls' faces crumbled as sniffles filled the air, and dinner ended in a somber silence. When the meal was over, I pushed back my chair and forced a small smile, swallowing the ache that pressed in my chest.

"Come, girls, let's go upstairs—I have an idea!" I said, my voice brighter than I felt.

As I led them upstairs, I plastered on a mask of excitement. *They deserve joy,* I told myself, even though my heart ached. *They deserve to laugh, to feel loved.*

"I've got a fun idea!" I said, once we reached their rooms.

"What do you think about dressing up like princesses? Let's make tomorrow an adventure! How about we make it a girls day?"

After a few moments, their sadness melted to wobbly smiles. Their eyes lit up with contagious joy, and I clung to that spark—determined to give them magic, even while my own heart was bruised. And soon, happy chatting and echoes of laughter filled the room.

"Let's bring a big blanket and art supplies! And who wants slushies and cotton candy?" I asked.

"Me! Oh, me!" Mia squealed, bouncing on her toes in eager happiness as her little feet drummed against the floor in a rhythm of pure excitement.

"Okay! Can we pick out outfits for tomorrow?" Ivy asked, anticipation bubbling over as she dove headfirst into the trunk of princess dresses, pulling out sparkling gowns and scattering them left and right.

"Absolutely!" I replied, adjusting the pair of Cinderella shoes Rose was struggling to wiggle onto her tiny feet. She had squatted on the floor, trying to shove her toes into the glittery shoes backward. I couldn't help but laugh at her quiet determination to succeed.

We rummaged through the trunk and closet together, hunting for the perfect outfit for each girl. Beaded necklaces, sparkling bracelets, hair bows, tiaras, and tiny sandals completed their looks, transforming them into radiant princesses. The girls became a happy, chattering whirlwind of excitement. I felt a comforting warmth in my chest, knowing I could bring joy to their hearts–but a pang of sorrow lingered too, a reminder that Lucas wanted little interaction in our lives.

After tucking the girls in and planting playful kisses on their cheeks, I slipped quietly from their rooms. That evening, I moved through the house on autopilot, keeping my hands busy with routine tasks–scrubbing counters, folding laundry, rearranging things I didn't need to–doing anything to avoid Lucas at all cost. His presence pressed down on me, and I felt every action scrutinized, measured under his calculated gaze. A hollow weight pressed against my chest, a sharp ache growing where joy should have lived.

I'd always imagined happy family outings–children laughing, family picnics in the park, a loving husband whose smile blossomed just for me–but in my life, it never unfolded that way. Most days, I felt like a single mother, carrying a weight that should have been shared. My heart ached for companionship and fullness, for the warmth of someone who truly saw me. Even still, I poured every ounce of myself into the girls–puppet shows with silly voices, forts made out of bedsheets, elaborate and fun hairstyles, movie nights with homemade popcorn–orchestrating little adventures and memories–even if that meant doing it alone.

The last thing I wanted was for them to feel the harsh rejection I carried daily.

So I lived in a careful balance, burying my own emptiness behind routines, masking the truth, doing whatever it took to make up for what he lacked. The girls were my whole world, and I hoped with all my heart that all they ever felt was love.

The girls burst out with the morning sun, their laugher spilling into the quiet house. Happy feet padded across the floor and voices tumbled over each other as they chattered about the treats, the music, and the new friends they would meet.

After a full day, we headed toward town, the girls bouncing curls, glittery necklaces that captured the light, and layered lace dresses swishing with every step. Side by side, they skipped down the cobbled street, their pigtails bounced in rhythm to their canter. The town center glowed in colorful lights and golden lanterns, while soft music drifted from nearby restaurants, wrapping the evening in a gentle, festive warmth.

Laughter mingled in the air—families gathered, children darting around lounging adults, and couples strolled slowly with their little dogs in tow. The soft summer evening wrapped everything in a gentle warmth. We spread our quilt on the grass, choosing a spot near the center—close enough to hear the music, yet near enough to the playing children.

"Mommy, can we go play?" Mia asked, tugging on my shirt.

"Yes, honey! Just stay nearby where you can see me. We'll get slushies in twenty minutes," I reminded her.

Mia and Ivy racing across the grass while I settled Rose on the blanket, surrounding her with colorful toys to keep the busy toddler engaged. The girls' smiles stretching from ear to ear as they darted in and out of a fast game of tag. A sense of peace settled over me, warmed by their blissful happiness. Music drifted through the evening air, and I let it carry me, tapping my toes to the rhythm as a glimmer of joy and calm seeped in.

The night ended in sticky fingers, bright laughter, beaming smiles, and pink-dyed lips, all set to the melody of music and playful chatter. That night, I kissed the girls a happy goodnight, and I tucked these memories into my heart as cherished treasures.

It was worth it, for them.

Water spilled from the edges of the washcloth into the sink as I held it loosely, pausing the familiar motion of cleansing my face, letting the droplets trail down unnoticed. My gaze locked on my own hazel eyes, and I found myself drifting in quiet contemplation.

So, this is how life is going to be—just me and the girls. I'll always have an absent husband—a missing father for them. No connection. No partnership. Few shared moments. A widening emptiness stretched where love and support should have been.

I let the water run over my hands, each movement slow and deliberate, a fragile attempt to anchor myself as sadness crept into the few corners of my heart that had once known happiness. Beneath it all, a heavy longing pressed against my chest, an aching, a yearning for more than this, for a life that seemed just out of reach.

Slipping out of the bathroom, I cast one last glance at the girls, their chests rose and fell in steady rhythm, and their faces softened in peaceful slumber. Muffled echoes of the TV drifted up the stairs, nudging me toward the sanctuary of my bedroom. I grabbed my newest novel and a small snack, and buried myself deep into a story, the one place I could escape, forget, and taste a little romance.

One late-summer evening, Rose's cheeks burned with fever, her small body restless and unsettled. Her cries pierced the still house long past midnight. After a sleepless night of whispered lullabies and rocking the crying toddler, my eyes blurred with exhaustion. When morning dawned, I walked robotically into the sunlit kitchen and began brewing a cup of coffee–necessary, desperate for anything to awaken me. My gaze fell on the large pile of dirty dishes left from last night. I stacked them into the dishwasher with brisk, mechanical motions–efficient, too drained to linger over the task. Exhaustion pressed heavy and tears threatened to spill, but I knew Lucas wouldn't lift a finger to help.

The kettle began to sing, and a speck of relief flickered through me as I poured the boiling water over the waiting grounds. The rich, decadent aroma curled around me, and I inhaled deeply, savoring the peace in this stolen moment. I closed my eyes, drawing in a slow breath, and lived in the small space of this fragile sanctuary.

But far too quickly, a sharp cry from upstairs shattered the moment. Clutching my strong coffee, I climbed the stairs to Rose's room, bracing myself for another long, relentless day.

"Mommy is here," I said softly, bringing comfort to Rose. "How are you feeling, baby girl?"

"Yucky, Mommy. Hold me!" Rose pleaded.

I scooped up her hot, sticky little body, and swayed with a peaceful rhythm, singing softly in her ear. Her fever raged, and her skin burned under my touch. I had used the last of the baby medicine, we needed more. It was the weekend at least, and Lucas was home–hopefully, I wouldn't have to manage it all myself.

"Lucas!" Rose is burning up! We need more baby Tylenol. Please watch the girls and get them breakfast." I pressed Rose into his arm, her body burning against my skin. "Keep a close eye on Rose. She's really hot."

I snatched my purse, yanking on the closest pair of shoes, and flew out the door with only one quick backward glance.

Returning home, the door swung open and I was hit with loud, heart-wrenching cries. My heart surged into my throat as my gaze found Mia, standing in the center of the living room clutching her shoulder, her small frame shaking with uncontrollable sobs. The grocery bag hit the foyer floor as I rushed to her side.

"What happened?" I cried, folding her tightly into my arms. My eyes darted to Lucas, sharp with accusation as I held Mia close. My own chest pounded as if it might burst.

My words stumbled out again, insistent and jagged, "What happened?"

After his silence stretched too long, I demanded answers. He looked at me indifferently–detached, as if he were not a part of the situation.

"She wasn't listening. I just tried to guide her to the couch and she tripped. It's not my fault she's clumsy. She should be more careful."

His words hit the room with a cold, callous finality. He moved into the kitchen and began rummaging in the pantry, as if the situation was of no consequence.

"That's not what happened!" Mia's sobs of unbelief tore loudly. "You pushed me!" She buried her face in my shirt, shaking.

"She's lying," he scoffed. "She lies all the time, you know that. She wasn't listening. She tripped and hurt herself." His words hardened, deliberate.

He stepped closer, shoulders squared, chest lifted, occupying every inch of space as his presence filled the room. His gaze was sharp and unwavering, piercing, and each movement measured, controlled, as if the room itself bent to his will. Sheer, determined insistence radiated from him, trying to make his version of events true. His power wasn't just physical, it was a force that overtook–demanded, pressing me into silence–daring me to contradict him.

I knew nothing could not be solved in that second. Every instinct screamed–to protect, to deflect, to hide. Anger coiled in my stomach, but beneath it, a focus stirred.

I needed creativity.

Kneeling in front of Mia, I cupped the sides of her face in my hands, "Honey, it's okay, let's go upstairs." Every tremble in her body anchored me to protect her.

Gently holding her hand, I guided her upstairs, as I forced myself to stay calm. Nestling Mia on my lap, I held her until her cries slowed to soft interrupted breaths. "What happened, honey? Tell me what happened."

"What Daddy said isn't true. He did push me. He pushed me hard, and it hurt!" she pleaded. Her big eyes continued to fill with tears, looking deeply into mine. She rested her head gently on my chest and breathed a sad sigh.

"It's okay, baby, I believe you. Would you like me to get you a popsicle, would that help you feel better?" I asked, trying to distract her.

"Yes, Mommy," she replied, between crying hiccups.

"How about you go hang with your sissy and read a book with her, and I will be right back with your yummy popsicle?" I suggested, stroking her back gently.

"Okay, Mommy," she said quietly as she slid off the chair and walked across the hall to Ivy's bedroom. She scooted in to sit close to Ivy, who was sitting quietly on her bed reading her book.

I looked at Ivy, searching her face. "Honey, did you see what happened?"

Ivy looked up at me, shaking her head. "No, I didn't see anything, I just heard Daddy yelling at her and then Mia crying." She paused for a long moment, then continued, "I didn't think I should go downstairs. It scared me, and I didn't know what to do. I wanted you to come home." Ivy's eyes filled with tears, and she quickly brushed them away.

I enfolded both girls in my arms, kissing them on their little cheeks. "I'm going to get you both a popsicle, okay, girls? I love you. I'm going to check on Rose, and I'll be right back," I said, trying fill my voice with comfort and artificial cheer.

After checking in on Rose, I found her asleep in the bed, cheeks flushed and still warm. I rushed downstairs and was back moments later with their favorite flavors. Gently,

I checked Mia's shoulder, being careful of the tender area. After landing a soft kiss on each of their foreheads, I slipped the fruity popsicles into their waiting hands and gently pulled the bedroom door closed. With Rose sleeping soundly, I went downstairs, resolve settling in my chest, to confront Lucas.

With barely restrained anger, I walked into the living room and saw Lucas deeply engrossed in his show, not even sparing a glance for me. I planted myself deliberately in front of the television, hands on my hips, letting my presence fill the space. "Tell me exactly what happened," I firmly insisted. "I don't believe she just tripped in thin air and hurt her shoulder."

"I don't have to answer to you," he said, coldness dripping from his words. "If I said she tripped, then that's what happened! She's the one who tells lies. Who are you going to believe, a child or your husband?" he demanded, his steely eyes glaring into mine, daring me to contradict him.

Uncomfortable silence surrounded us. My body was trembling as my brain furtively tried to make sense of what was fact and what was a lie. *How was I supposed to choose between my child and my husband?* Mia appeared honest and sincere, while Lucas appeared uncaring, arrogant, and insistent. I should be able to believe my husband; I shouldn't have doubts constantly overriding my thoughts. I didn't know what I should do or how to prove what happened.

If I accused him of lying, I knew he would erupt into dangerous behavior, accusing me of misconstruing facts or making it seem that I was on a wild witch hunt.

When needed, he could appear calm and competent on demand, with the intention of having me seem irrational or crazy.

I was furious if he *had* shoved Mia! That is not tolerable behavior. Children should be treated with kindness and respect, not with anger. I looked at him with cold, seething scorn, then turned and walked away. It was a battle I knew I could not win.

Hearing Rose beginning to stir, I gathered the forgotten grocery bag and headed upstairs to give her the much-needed medicine. Her skin was still flushed beneath my touch, damp with fevered sweat. I carefully measured the prescribed amount in the medicine syringe and coaxed her to swallow all of it.

After cooling her body in a lukewarm bath, I gently picked her up into my arms, wrapped her in a thick, fluffy towel, and then carried her in to see the girls.

"Girls, do you want to hear a story?" I suggested.

"Yes!" they replied, as a small smile began to appear on Mia's face.

"Okay, let's pick a fun one. Bring me a story," I suggested. After rechecking Mia's shoulder, I felt relieved it no longer caused her pain. We spent the next hour together, and I wrapped them in magical stories of princesses and far away lands. Rose curled warm and heavy in my arms, the other girls pressed close on each side, as I carried them through worlds filled with flying unicorns, pots of gold at the end of rainbows, beasts becoming princes, and good conquering evil.

When the night was quiet and still, my thoughts came rushing in, like a wave I could no longer hold back. *How am I supposed to handle these situations? How can I prove what is in my gut?* I would look like a horrible accuser if I'm wrong. *Who should I talk to? If I say something to anyone, he's going to be furious with me . . . What if he didn't do it? What if, unlikely as it is, Mia's did just trip and land on her shoulder?*

I know it sounded improbable, but how could I bring up an accusation that I feel in my gut may be right, but might not? And, *why would a father lie about this?*

Heavy dread settled in my stomach. Little things had been happening, alerting my concern. But I had no proof. I didn't know what to do.

It's not like they accused him of something horrendous. They seemed like weird accidents. *But then, were they?* I needed to talk to someone. I wanted to confide in Charlotte. Yet I thought, *was it wrong to say what I suspected of Lucas?* It wasn't all the time. It was random. But still, these situations kept happening.

Also, his behavior toward me was what made me suspect what the girls were saying may be true. If he was a kind and thoughtful husband, then maybe it could be an exaggeration. But I knew better. He was rough with me, not just in words but in the way he handled me—demanding, unkind, sometimes physically hurtful. Aggressive. Angry. Mean. *Was it such a leap to think that he wouldn't be that way with the girls when they were misbehaving or challenging?*

I felt if I uttered these honest thoughts, it would open Pandora's box. I wouldn't be able to shove everything back into the box and let it remain in the dark because, what if it exploded out in all directions? I feared it would completely change my life, in a terrifying way.

Accusations I had heard for years flooded my mind. I'm a bad wife. I exaggerate. I'm overly sensitive. I imagine things. I don't believe my husband. I don't have the right to question my husband.

It had been drilled into me that he was always right, he was the head of the house. He made the final decision; I only get to make suggestions. I am supposed to submit to his final word.

No questions.

I heard this hundreds of times. And these struggles assaulted me.

What was truth? What was manipulation? What was a lie? Did I have the right to challenge him? Could I confidently say he was wrong? Was that okay?

The following week, Charlotte texted, "Coffee, girl?"

Instant relief filled me. I needed my friend. "Yes!" I immediately responded.

I called Mom and asked if she could babysit—I desperately needed this break. Rushing to get ready, I showered but skipped the hair wash. I slipped into a cream linen dress, letting the fabric fall effortless over my shoulders. Pulling my hair into a neat bun, I secured it with a few pins, smoothing the sides into a slick finish. Simple. Quick.

I slid my feet into straw sandals, grabbed my big, straw tote from the side table, and hurried to gather the girls to drop them off at Mom's.

After quick kisses, I was back on the road heading toward our favorite coffee shop.

Seeing Charlotte sitting across the coffee shop, relaxed and happy with a serene smile on her face, brought a rush of mixed emotions to me. Feelings of joy, wistfulness of missing my friend, relief at finally getting together, and a jumble of things I needed to share with her all pressed on me as if they would all explode out.

We embraced for a long, tight hug. "Oh god, I missed you!" I said.

"Me too!" Charlotte replied. "Let's order and catch up, we have so much to talk about."

Getting cozy on the brown chic leather sofa, I cupped the steaming mug of a frothy caramel latte as Charlotte blew gently on her steaming spiced chai.

"It feels so nice to escape away from the kids!" I gushed, relief evident upon my face.

"I know!" she agreed. "It's been so crazy busy. How has everything been going? It's been a few months!"

"It's okay . . . It's hard to juggle everything, but I'm trying my best. The girls are so precious to me, they deserve it," I answered.

"They are the cutest, but you are only one person. I hope you aren't wearing yourself ragged. I hope you take some self-care time; it's very important," Charlotte said.

"I try, but you know how it is. It's just me. I'm thankful Mom and Dad are close by. They help a ton. It sort of makes things . . . bearable," I admitted.

"Are you going to stay with him forever if this is how it's going to be?" Charlotte pointedly asked, leaning toward me in concern. "I honestly wish you wouldn't."

"I don't know," I admitted, looking down. I picked at my fingernail, pushing a flecking piece off the edge. "I really need to talk to you. I don't know what to do."

I paused, summoning up the courage to get the truth out.

Charlotte waited patiently. Her calming presence propelled me to continue.

"I . . . I hate to say this out loud, but it's gotten worse. I think he is being rough with the girls." After a long pause, I continued, "When I am in the room, things seem to be fine, but when I leave or am in another part of the house, sometimes I hear a ruckus or a lot of crying. Yet whenever I walk in the room, he always has a reason for what happened. But it seems insincere to me, too happenstance or fabricated. Last week, something happened with Lucas and Mia. I had just gotten home, and I saw Mia holding her shoulder sobbing. Lucas said he was 'guiding' her to the couch, and she tripped and landed on her shoulder. That sounded too happenstance, like, that never happens. Mia immediately said he was lying. He became very defensive. He put me in the position of having to choose who I should believe, my daughter or my husband. Do you know how hard that is? How do you even do that?"

I looked deeply into Charlotte's eyes, trying to express my inner conflict. "I feel disloyal either way. Yes, I know sometimes kids do lie, but that also doesn't mean he never lies or that he is blameless. I don't know who to believe because I wasn't there. And Mia seemed very authentic. Lucas, as usual, seemed to brush it under the rug like it wasn't that big of an issue. Except, in my gut, I think Mia was being honest and Lucas was lying and trying to manipulate me. But I can't prove it. He tried to make me feel terrible for not believing him and instead choosing to believe Mia. Like, why should I have to think that my husband is lying to me about hurting my child!?" I blurted out in utter frustration.

"That sounds crazy," Charlotte responded, taking in all in. She paused to think, then continued, "That is odd, and he wasn't super comforting to her?"

I shook my head.

"I do think his behavior is concerning. That's a big red flag. Have more things like this happened?"

"Yes, there've been a few things, but I'm now trying to be more aware. I think some of the things might be hidden, or maybe the girls are afraid to say anything. It's difficult because

I should be able to trust my husband. He and I should be a team, we should work together at parenting. Also, when we do make mistakes, we should own up to it and fix it. But in my gut, I don't feel like I can believe a word that comes out of his mouth. Yet in front of me, he acts fake and inauthentic, and it makes me feel like a bad wife for not believing or trusting my husband. He can be very convincing when he wants people to believe him. Or he gets loud and puts pressure on me, acting intense if I don't automatically believe him or do what he says."

"I do know what you mean, he can be very persuasive and convincing." Charlotte paused to sip her chai. "But honestly, I think you should, in a sense . . . investigate. If the girls say something that concerns you, I think that should raise a level of caution to you. Maybe privately talk to them and tell them it's okay for them to talk to you about things they may be afraid to share. Assure them that they're not going to get in trouble. Maybe he's said something threatening. See what kind of information you can get from them. I think you should do this, and I think it's very important. Now that you're noticing really concerning behavior, I bet some things have been going on." She paused. "I am so sorry." Charlotte wrapped me in a warm hug.

"The fact that you and the girls are going through this, it's not fair and it's not right! A father should be loving and kind, imperfect, but still, obviously doing his very best. A father and husband should be the protector of his family, leading and guiding with gentle strength, love, and sacrifice. A man who is a good leader leads to serve. He is purposeful in giving of his time, his resources, and everything—for his family. And Lucas is not. Is there anything about him that you admire or respect? If not . . . that's something to think about. Why stay with a man who is unkind to you, dismisses your needs, belittles you, is hurtful and mean with his words over and over again? How is that good or right? And then he threatens you? How is that even healthy for your girls? I know it's difficult and makes you scared to even think about possibilities, but *you* have to choose. You can't let fear dictate to you. Because it may and probably will get worse. Jake and I are here for you. You can come to us, and your parents. We love you all a lot. And I don't want to see you or the girls hurt. You need to be careful, be smart and keep your eyes open. And think about what I said. You're going to have to make a choice."

I knew in my gut she was right. I knew what I'd been sensing was spot on. I had been controlled for so long, it made me question my intuition. I couldn't trust what I believed to be true. Somehow, I had to push past this for my daughters and myself and get to the bottom of this. I needed to uncover the truth.

Inhaling a huge breath, I sighed, expelling all my air.

I looked at Charlotte with a knowing look. "So it begins," I stated. "I'm scared out of my mind. But at least I'm not crazy for how I've been feeling. And I'm not a bad wife." I hugged her again tightly. "Thank you for being here for me. If I didn't have someone to talk to openly, I honestly think I would go crazy!" I admitted. "And I will really think about what you shared."

Charlotte held me tightly, communicating the depth of her understanding.

"Hey, come over tonight," she suggested. We're going to have a little cookout. See if your parents can watch the girls longer. You deserve a night off. And you already got all dressed up!"

"You know what? You're right. I never get out to have fun. Let's do it!" I agreed.

"Perfect!" Charlotte exclaimed, "We're having a couple friends over, and I'd love for you to be there. I've really missed you."

Pulling up to Charlotte and Jake's charming, mid-century townhome, I felt excited to be out with friends, and happy that Mom and Dad were more than thrilled to have pizza and movie night with the girls. Knocking on the door, I was immediately pulled inside by Charlotte and wrapped into a tight hug amid the laughter filling the room.

"I'm so glad you are here!" she exclaimed, still engulfing me in a warm hug. "I was hoping nothing would change your mind."

"Nope. I'm here. Ready to get out and have fun!" A smile spread across my face. I was looking forward to a stress-free night, a night to relax and talk with adults and not worry about anything. Moving into the living room, Charlotte introduced me to the few people I didn't know. Then she turned to catch the attention of a handsome, broad-shouldered guy standing with his back to us.

He turned and Charlotte said, "Joy, it's Sebastian, he just finished his second tour in the Marines."

Sebastian smiled as his blue eyes lit with warm recognition.

"Oh wow, it's been forever! How are you?" I asked, realizing how many years it had been since I'd seen our old friend.

"Really well." A smile spread broadly on his face. "How are you, Joy?"

"I'm doing pretty good. Life is crazy busy, but good," I replied, deciding to keep my answer to a minimum.

Sebastian had really grown into himself. He stood at least six-two, broad shouldered, his muscles well-defined. He was handsome, yet he carried himself with an understated confidence. I remembered how kind he had been when we were in college, how he was always thoughtful. I found myself wondering if he had ever found someone. He would have made a wonderful husband–funny how that thought drifted so casually through my mind. We chatted for a few minutes more before moving on to mingle with others.

After catching up with a few friends and meeting new faces, I finally turned my attention to the spread of delicious food, my stomach growling in response to the tempting aromas. Moving to the table piled with hamburgers, brisket, and marinated chicken, I piled my plate full and found an empty seat on the couch.

"Mind if I sit?" Sebastian's voice broke through my thoughts.

I looked up, startled. "No, of course—please." The words came out a bit rushed, my surprise evident.

Of all the people around us, he chose to sit next to me—though surely there were others far more interesting than me. As he started talking, I remembered how easy he was to be around, and within minutes, we were chatting as if no time had passed at all. He told me about his adventures in the Marines, the places he traveled, and the experiences that had shaped him into someone seasoned and mature. I didn't have much to add that was interesting, but he seemed to enjoy the conversation anyway. His kindness was disarming, and it felt good to simply be spoken to with interest and thoughtfulness. His eyes sparkled as he talked, and I couldn't help but notice: he didn't seem to talk to anyone else.

Before I realized it, the night had slipped away. Mom and Dad were happy to have the girls, so I wasn't worried, but still, I shouldn't have stayed out so late. A flicker of guilt tugged at me for enjoying myself. Nearly ten o'clock now, and Sebastian and I were among the last to linger. Jake, Charlotte, Sebastian, and I had talked far longer than planned, laughing as we caught up and rekindled old college memories.

"I really should go. I know the girls are fine with Mom and Dad, but I need to get back to them. It's been such a wonderful night—thank you for inviting me," I said, smiling warmly at each of them.

"It's late—let me walk you to your car," Jake offered.

"I've got to head out anyway. I have an early morning tomorrow," Sebastian added with a kind smile. "I'd be happy to walk you out."

"You sure? You don't have to," I replied quickly.

"I'd like to," he said softly, his eyes meeting mine for a fleeting moment.

Charlotte shot Jake a knowing look. "Well, we won't keep you."

Jake kept his expression neutral while heat crept up my cheeks.

Flustered, I gave Charlotte a quick hug as Sebastian held the door open.

"I'm parked just down here a bit," I murmured nervously, fidgeting with my hands.

"Lead the way," he said lightly, falling into step beside me. His hand brushed against mine as we walked the narrow sidewalk, a casual touch that made my pulse quicken.

At my car, I glanced at him, uncertain. "Thank you for walking me out. I appreciate it. It's been so nice catching up . . . It's been a long time."

"I was happy to," Sebastian said, his voice sincere. "I wanted a chance to talk to you. I just moved back . . . and I hoped I might see you again."

Blushing furiously, I stumbled over my words. "It's been really nice talking with you, Sebastian, but . . . I'm married," I blurted, unprepared to handle the weight of this situation.

His eyes softened, shadowed with sadness. "I know," he said quietly. "Jake told me."

His pause said more than words could. "Joy, if you ever find yourself in a situation—if you need anything—please don't hesitate to reach out. Jake has my number." His gaze held mine, kind and steady. "I always thought you were an amazing woman. Whoever won your heart had to be one hell of a guy. Can't say I'm not a little jealous. But remember what I said, if you need anything . . ." His voice trailed off as he leaned in, pulling me into a gentle, friendly embrace.

His broad figure retreated into the night. I stood there for a moment, stunned, unsure of what had just transpired. Then he glanced back with a small wave before fading into the darkness.

Driving home, my emotions were a tangled mess. No man had treated me with such kindness—or tenderness—in years. I knew the kind of person Sebastian was; he was a good man, a loyal man, steady, one whose actions reflected his character. He was steadfast, reliable, and full of integrity. The kind of man I had wished for in a husband. But I could not change what was.

Sadness welled up, and a longing filled my heart. *If only.* It would take a miracle to change my life. I could never betray my vows, but that didn't stop my heart from aching for the goodness I saw in him. I wondered what might have happened if life had unfolded differently—if I had noticed the quiet strength in Sebastian before Lucas swept in with his grand gestures and fast-moving charm. Sebastian left to follow his dream in the Marines eight years ago, and I was caught up in Lucas's spell. I sensed Sebastian was the kind of man I should have chosen, respectable and good, the kind who saw people clearly and treated them with dignity. But the timing was never in our favor. We were like two steady stars in the same sky—close enough to notice, but never to align. Whatever connection we shared was real yet restrained by circumstances, by life, and by choices I wasn't ready to question.

I drove on in silence with a solemn acceptance. Fate has chosen a different road for me. At least destiny had been gracious to give me my daughters—my greatest gift, my whole world. For them, I would endure anything.

Spending the night at Mom and Dad's gave me a much-needed respite. I knew I needed to look at my situation differently and approach the road ahead with clarity. It wouldn't be easy. I had to think objectively, stay in control, and not let Lucas continue to undermine my confidence or spin my emotions on a hamster wheel.

Talking with Charlotte had given me courage—the courage to try and do what was right for my girls and me. They deserved it, and so did I.

The next evening, after tucking them in bed, I sat with the girls for a little chat. Lucas rarely bothered to tuck them in, so I knew this would give us a moment uninterrupted. Nestled between Mia and Ivy, we chatted about the girls' fun adventures at Grammy and Grampy's. Ivy described, with sparkling excitement, wandering along the little stream with Grampy searching for frogs hidden among the stones. And Mia described in vivid detail how she and Grammy made waffles from scratch, even creating extravagant waffle sundaes, topped with "bunches and bunches" of sprinkles. Her enthusiasm was contagious—her big eyes wide, her cherub face animated with exaggerated expressions that could only make me smile.

"Girls, I want to chat with you about something important," I explained as I snuggled them closer. "I've noticed some things that I am not okay with, and I want to ask you a few questions. First, I want you to know, you don't need to worry, you won't get in trouble, but I want you to be super honest with me. I want you to tell me your real feelings. I want to know how you truly feel. And second, it's very important that kids know they can always go to an adult they trust and tell them anything that's bothering them. You always have a safe space to talk with me. I love you both with all my heart." I squeezed their little bodies in a warm hug. "You both are so precious."

"What are you talking about Mommy?" Ivy inquired; her little forehead scrunched with worry lines.

"Have you noticed that Daddy sometimes gets upset and angry? And sometimes he says or does things that seem mean or not very nice? I'm not trying to say bad things about him, but you live here too, and you girls see and hear a lot. Just because someone is an adult doesn't mean they are always acting in a way that is good, respectful, or healthy. Some mommies and daddies do wrong things. Not every mommy and daddy chooses to be kind," I gently explained. "So, please tell me, has anything happened when I am at the store or not in the room that upsets you or worries you, or makes you confused?

I waited quietly with a calm, understanding look upon my face, giving them space to think and share.

The girls were silent. Ivy fidgeted with her fingers, looking nervous. And Mia scrunched up her brow, visibly upset.

"What's wrong, honey? You can tell me." I gently squeezed Mia's hand.

"I don't want to get in trouble!" Ivy stressed. "I'm not supposed to tell!"

Dread formed in the pit of my stomach. "Oh my gosh, baby, you can tell me!" *What in the world had Lucas done?* I thought as I cradled her in my arms.

"I try to be good, but sometimes it's hard. Daddy gets really mad if we don't do what he wants right away. Or he gets mad if Mia or Rose are taking up his time. I try to help them a lot," Ivy admitted, her voice quivering.

"Well, what happens?" I said, asking for more specific details.

"He said . . . he will lock me in a closet if I am naughty!" Mia blurted out.

"What?" I asked, my voice raised in alarm.

Ivy explained, "If we are not listening, he gets mad and tells us he'll lock us in the closet if we are bad. He said we are not allowed to tell you, or we will get in more trouble. We're supposed to obey and not be naughty." Ivy eyes went wide, unblinking.

Her chin trembled as tears began to fill her eyes. Large tears escaped and dripped down her flushed cheeks onto her pink nightgown, turning it blotchy with dark-pink wet spots.

Mia tugged on my arm, begging, "Mommy, please don't tell on us! We don't want to get in trouble."

"Baby, I won't. I am so sorry!" I cried as I smothered them with hugs, kissing their cheeks and drying their tears. "It is *not* okay to say that. It is never okay to threaten a child. Even if a child is naughty, good parents don't hurt or threaten to hurt their children. That's very wrong!" I explained, then I paused and gently cradled their faces in my hands.

"Okay, here's what we are going to do. I want you to tell me any time something happens that seems not okay. Promise? And I want to tell you how very proud I am of you girls. You are very brave to be truthful."

"Yes, Mommy," they answered, nodding their heads in understanding.

"I am proud of you girls for being open with me. I love you very much."

In that moment, the decision became settled—I would always take the girls with me or drop them off at Mom and Dad's every time I had to run out. No longer was it a chance I was willing to take.

"Is there anything else you should tell me?" I asked.

"Well, he said if we are bad, he will make us sleep in the attic with the spiders. I'm scared of spiders!" Ivy whispered in terror.

"Oh, babies! That is terrible. Horrible! That will *never* happen! I can't believe it, I'm so sorry!" I held them tightly to my chest, as the weight of disbelief, anger, and heartbreak crashed over me like a rising tide.

Singing a soft lullaby, I brushed their hair back from their round, sleepy faces and stayed nestled close till both girls were fast asleep. Gently, I slipped out from between them, adjusting their blankets for warmth and tucked them in with gentle kisses before turning on the night light and soft music to fill the silence.

My mind raced with many thoughts . . . anger, rage, and injustice at the magnitude of wrongness.

Tossing and turning all night, I was unable to fall asleep, wondering how this should be handled. I was furious, but I didn't want it to seem like the girls tattled. I didn't want them to get threatened again, I decided to say I had overheard him talking to the girls and address it from that angle. It was important that I communicate and make clear this behavior would not be tolerated. I would not sit by and let my daughters be treated badly.

After countless restless hours, my eyes finally grew heavy, my breathing slowed, and I fell into an unsettled sleep. Morning sunlight eventually found me, its warm rays pressing against my eyelids. I stretched, wincing as I worked out the kinks in my back, then tiptoed to check on Rose. She lay peacefully, her cheeks flushed with a healthy, rosy glow. Relief washed through me—her fever still hadn't returned. Downstairs, I brewed myself a strong, inviting cup of coffee. Still drained from the night before, I paused, listening for Lucas, careful to gauge his mood before approaching.

I needed to have this important conversation with him, but timing was everything with Lucas. He didn't seem to be in a bad mood—not yet. I settled myself on the cozy chair, sitting between the throw pillows and slowly sipping my frothy brew. Lucas was sitting across from me, drinking his coffee, his attention focused on his phone.

"I've been thinking . . .," I began, "the girls are getting older, and I know it's important we are wise with how we handle the girls, especially when it's a frustrating situation. I know, it can be frustrating for me, I get it. I did overhear you . . . say something to them. I heard you say that you would lock them in the attic or a closet if they were bad. I'm sure you didn't mean it, but those things can't be said. It isn't healthy to threaten our children, whether joking or not."

"Where did you hear those things?" he challenged.

"I overheard you the other day," I responded.

He paused, looking at me with cold eyes that bore through me. Several seconds passed while he just stared.

I felt a chill pass through me, as if he could read my mind. I needed to act convincingly, or he would know.

"Look, I get it, kids can be challenging, but can we agree to be careful with what we say?"

"Oh, I am careful," he said slowly and purposefully, his gaze hostile.

"Okay," I responded. "I just want to make sure nothing is said to threaten the girls. That's not okay." I spoke with a catch in my throat, closely watching his response, but knowing the words I spoke were very important and the message had to be clear.

"I'm their father. I know what to do. I don't need you interfering."

With a quivering breath, I said, "They are my daughters too, and I won't have anyone hurting them, do you understand?" My legs began to tremble, shaking uncontrollably as I sat frozen to my chair. I felt as if the floor would swallow me up.

Lucas pushed himself up off his chair and was in front of me before I could take my next breath. "Do you understand, no one threatens me." He leaned down, his face a mere inch from mine. Hot breath fell upon my face as he squeezed my forearm. His fingers dug cruelly into my tender skin.

"No one!" he emphasized with steel in his voice. He shoved my arm and the coffee cup lurched, splashing scalding liquid across my chest. The hot brew seared through my sweater, burning the skin beneath in sharp, stinging pulses.

I lurched back, gasping, a jolt of shock rippling through my arms and torso, my throat tight as if it were closing. Steam curled upward, mingling with the acrid smell of spilled coffee as it soaked into the chair cushions and pooled at my trembling feet.

Lucas walked away, his face twisted in disgust. "You should be more careful," he said, eyes cold and scathing.

I stood, trembling. The empty cup dangled from my fingers as the heat continued to sting and the dark liquid crept across the fabric and floor, marking the chaos in his wake.

I stumbled toward the kitchen, legs quivering beneath me, chest tight, jaw clenched. I couldn't stop the shaking. I clutched my sweater to my chest and pressed against the hot coffee burn, trying in vain to rub away the piercing sting. A frozen bag of vegetables against the scorched skin brought a fleeting relief; my hands trembled violently as I struggled to stay upright. In a desperate attempt to reclaim control, I wiped down the clean counters and rinsed out the spotless sink, the motions mechanical, forcing myself to feel "normal" for a moment as I held the frozen bag tight to my chest.

I collapsed against the counter. *Focus on breathing* . . . one breath, two, slow exhale, again. I glanced at the key rack, noticing Lucas's keys were gone. He had left—probably out for the rest of the day. Relief mingled uneasily with lingering fear.

At least I can breathe.

Upstairs, I gingerly peeled off my sweater. Red, angry blotches stared back at me, marring my pale chest. The raw, stinging skin burned with every touch. I soaked a washcloth in cold water, pressing in gently against the burn, letting the icy weight soothe some of the ache. After several long moments, I set the cloth aside and stared at my reflection in the mirror. Jagged, crimson inflammation stared back. Helpless. Exposed. Unable to protect myself, no matter how much I wanted to. The pain in my heart hurt as deeply as the burn.

I pushed my vulnerable, raw emotions to the back corner of my mind. I could not let his anger and rage win over me. Desperate to forget the chaos swirling inside me, I carefully pulled a shirt over my head and headed into the girls' rooms, grasping for a way to make the day feel normal—at least for them.

"Girls," I called gently, peeking inside with a smile I had to force. "How about a trip to the park today? And maybe a movie afternoon? Doesn't that sound fun?"

I tried to insert cheerfulness into my voice as squeals of excitement filled the room. Ivy's bright, carefree face gave me a flicker of peace—fragile but so needed in the middle of my storm.

"Okay! Let's get up, brush your teeth, and I'll call you down for breakfast in twenty minutes, okay?" I directed.

"Okay, Mommy!" Mia enthusiastically agreed.

Softly, I closed the door to their happy chatter and gathered my attention to making a special breakfast. Waffles . . . they love that, sliced strawberries with whipped cream, topped with a generous amount of rainbow sprinkles. *I can do that.*

Forcing my attention ahead, I hurried to begin the day. The girls' silly laughter and smiles filled the atmosphere. As the day progressed, a bit of lightness began to fill my heart, and by the evening, I joined the girls in genuine laughter at the *Ice Age* movie, their favorite and mine. Cuddling with my girls brought true joy. I savored every moment; their warm, tiny palms caressed my cheeks, and their constant wiggles and giggles filled the room. Their love and happiness helped ease the sorrow that was growing invasively in my heart.

As the evening drew to a close, I stood and stretched. "Okay, ladies, time for bed. Brush your teeth and put on your pajamas. I'll be up in ten minutes to tuck you in."

Sleepy yawns answered. Tiredly, they climbed the stairs for bedtime while I cleaned our messy celebration.

I called up, "The tooth police is coming up to see who has the cleanest teeth and is ready for bed! The winner gets to pick the story!"

Hearing the scampering of feet run back to the bathroom brought a small smile to my face. As usual, they had forgotten . . . or skipped that detail.

I called, "You're lucky I need to fill the dishwasher. You have two extra minutes!" Climbing the stairs with Rose, I heard their scampering settle. I peeked into their room. "Who's ready?"

"Me!" they both echoed.

"Okey dokie, let's check!" I replied. After a thorough teeth and bedroom check, I awarded a first and second place. I deposited Rose on the bed, and she crawled over their legs with loud giggles.

"Let's read! What book are we reading tonight?"

"*Stephanie's Ponytail!*" they echoed.

Apparently, they were in cahoots for choosing the book. "Good choice. Love that one!" I answered.

Settled between the two munchkins with Rose crawling between, we enjoyed the hilariously surprising story for the one-hundredth time. With bedtime kisses given and lullaby music in the background, I settled Rose into her cozy bed and blew soft raspberries on her little round belly, bringing squeals of joy.

The door shut firmly downstairs. Lucas had arrived home. My stomach immediately clenched, and tension crept into my whole being. I finished tucking little Rose in, but mentally my brain was trying to figure out how I should act and what I should say or do.

Turning the light down, I quietly slipped out, leaving only the soft lavender glow of the princess nightlight. I closed the door and paused mid-step, subconsciously rubbing my chest and arm–still raw and tender from the coffee burn. I held my breath, releasing an anxious rush of air.

I walked into the kitchen, reaching for the box of chamomile tea, hoping maybe it would settle my nerves. My nervous hands stayed busy, tidying the pantry cabinet into a more orderly appearance. The kettle's sharp whistle cut through my thoughts. Steam curled as I poured the water over the tea bag and set the mug aside to steep. Lucas entered the kitchen without a glance in my direction, as though I were invisible. Turning my back to him, I braced myself, the only comfort being that—for now—he wasn't acting aggressive. My stomach clenched hard—I hated unkindness and disharmony. I wished he could be kind, without the shadow of his short fuse. It was hard being the only parent constantly monitoring the atmosphere in the home.

I settled onto the living room couch, a small sense of relief washing over me knowing I had the downstairs to myself. Lucas ignored me, as he had all evening. I adjusted the pillow until they rested comfortably and let out a slow breath. The glow of Netflix filled the room as I picked up where I'd left off, telling myself it was a solo night and I might as well try to enjoy it. But even as I tried to lose myself in the show, my mind drifted, and worries pressed in on every side. All I wanted was to feel safe– unguarded, relaxed, and at ease.

That was impossible.

I almost never felt peaceful. There was always tension. Stupid reactions, excessive anger, and constant huge emotions surrounded our home. I was beginning to seriously wonder if it was even worth it.

Being a single parent might be easier.

I realized I needed to talk to someone, a person who wasn't involved—a clear voice. But did I dare? If Lucas discovered I confided in another, he would be livid. And how much should I say? I felt nervous about revealing anything. Would I sound like I was complaining? An ungrateful wife? Or would my concerns be valid?

I began to consider reaching out, researching who I could confide in. The emotions had been building for too long; I needed to hear a voice outside my own thoughts, an objective voice.

I needed help.

Chapter Sixteen

Summer 2017, *Present Day*

Running my fingers through the sand, I let the coarse granules slip by carelessly. I sat on the beach, my beach, the one that held a host of treasured memories and remembered the summer days with Charlotte spent in careless joy throughout our teenage and young adult years. I remembered the hot sun shining down upon us, the fat, fluffy clouds in the blue sky, and the endless crashing of the waves . . . this was my happy place. It was where I loved to go when I needed to think, and the ocean drew me with its alluring pull.

I had been reflecting on many weighty things. The last decade of my life, in so many ways, shattered me. Yet amid the loss and pain, I had been given three beautiful gifts—my daughters. I couldn't fully grasp the depths of my trauma, nor could I untangle all I had endured, not just for myself but for countless women who had also walked a similar path. Still, I had begun my healing journey. There was so much more I needed to learn and understand. But each step forward was still a step toward freedom. It was a journey. And one I needed to go through to heal.

As the ocean waves curled up on the sandy shore and lapped around my toes, their cool touch felt like a gentle reminder: healing was possible, even if it came slowly, one wave at a time.

I sat in reflection. Why is it that women who live in an aggressive, harsh, and volatile environment almost always turn the harshness inward? We judge ourselves so severely, more than anyone else could. We hold ourselves to impossible standards, as if perfection might keep the peace, instead of seeing abuse for what it is. We truly believe that if we could just be better, calmer, more patient, the storm might pass. Yet it never does. It returns with greater fury. It is as relentless as the ocean waves upon the shore. You may think there is a break or respite. But there never is. It continues into infinity. And yet we still think there will be a pause or change.

This belief traps, binding us inside a prison. Any minor flaw or unaccomplished expectation invites an onslaught of anger and criticism. This intense pressure keeps us on a hamster wheel of performance. It is a learned survival strategy and is ingrained in us to survive.

So often I heard comments like, "I wouldn't have done that if you just didn't make me so angry" or "It's your fault." Words that shifted the blame and convinced me that I was responsible for his outbursts. And somehow, I came to believe it must be my fault.

Many times, the abuser will choose to intentionally shame, undermining confidence and self-worth. That constant undermining leaves you carrying the heavy burden of internalizing shame and the haunting belief of being deeply, irreparably flawed.

Living in abuse means carrying an unshakable weight of shame. It was as if my very existence was the reason for the cruelty I endured. It's as if we aren't good enough, or somehow our very existence promotes negative treatment, or we aren't worthy of being treasured or loved. Deep down, I wondered if I had somehow fallen out of grace, if I had unknowingly caused this shameless treatment. Maybe I asked too much. Maybe I wanted more than I was owed. Somehow, I must deserve it.

Therefore, we fall into the flow of less-than-human treatment, and we work harder, try harder, love more, forgive more, and require less. We push the plow until our shoulders ache. We grind the grain until our hands bleed. We churn the butter long after our strength has left us. We wear ourselves to the bone, believing if we could just give enough, then finally, they would meet us with love, with kindness, and with tenderness. But how much more can we give? What else is left, except the very lifeblood draining from our veins?

And deep inside a voice still whispers softly: You were made for more.

Chapter Seventeen

A Mirror Without Judgment

After sifting through what felt like endless counseling options, I finally discovered a program that offered scholarships. I had no way to afford therapy on my own, and I couldn't risk Lucas finding out. As I submitted the online form, I hoped it would reach a compassionate person who could read between the lines and see the desperation woven into every word. Breathing a huge sigh, I said a prayer upward: *Bring me help, please.*

I erased my search history then shut down the computer and headed upstairs to bed. Entering our room, I saw the rigid silhouette of Lucas sleeping. I didn't want drama, so I undressed and tugged on my cozy sweats as quietly as possible. Slipping between the sheets, I barely made a dent in the bed. I lay silent. Alone. Just hearing my breathing. Inhale. Exhale.

At last, after a long battle, sleep won, and I drifted away. Morning dawned bright as I dragged myself out of bed, groggy and half-asleep, craving the sharp kick of strong coffee. As the girls' happy chatter drifted downstairs, I knew my moment of peaceful solitude was over.

Time to begin the day, I told myself as I headed upstairs to greet the chaos of bouncing, happy girls and the rhythm of another day already pulling me along. The day rushed on and each one following blurred into the busy monotony of parenting.

After several busy days had come and gone, constantly rushing from one task to the next, one late afternoon the laughter and noise had faded and was replaced by the quiet hum of a therapist's office. For a long while, I had sat frozen in the seat of my car, contemplating if I should even walk inside. Anxiety, nervousness, fear, and a hint of the possibility of release all flooded through me. *Would I be disloyal for disclosing what was happening? How transparent can I be? Will I get in trouble?*

Pushing out of the car, I shoved my fear back inside, closed the door with a slow click, and moved tentatively toward the therapist office. From the moment I stepped inside, I was wrapped in a quiet comfort. A faint glow flickered from well-placed candles, their gentle scents of neroli, vanilla, and floral blending in the air, soothing my nerves before a word was spoken. Knitted throws were draped on plush chairs, inviting one to rest. The space felt safe. I let out a breath I didn't realize I had been holding. Soft light spilled across the room, casting golden warmth on the walls, making it feel like a sanctuary carved out of the life's debris, chaos, and quandaries.

I slipped into a solitary chair, tucked between cushions of soft cream and muted sage, but the solitude only made the pounding in my chest louder. My hands betrayed me, twisting anxiously in my lap, unable to be still. I tried to steady them, but the peace in the room only made my internal storm more intense. I had never been to therapy before. Never had a truly unfiltered, safe place to vent my doubts, fears, or concerns. Now, in this quiet space that seemed almost too calm for the chaos inside me, my doubts churned, my thoughts collided, and questions pressed in.

A sick churn rose in my stomach, and my bowels clenched. I thought I might have to run to the bathroom. *How much should I say? How transparent can I be?* I didn't want social services involved. I'd rather die than let them take my girls away. I decided to focus on myself. I would share what was happening with me, my confusion, my questions, and seek objective insight. I didn't even remember what my rights were as a wife or woman. *Was I supposed to obey him? Was I a bad wife to challenge him? Should I keep the peace at all costs?* I lived in this swinging pendulum of a contradictory reality because no matter how hard I tried, nothing made him happy, peaceful, helpful, or kind.

He always found a way to convincingly shift the blame: I was too sensitive. I didn't do enough. I put the girls before him. I was lazy. Incompetent. My opinion didn't matter. I didn't honor him. I had to ask his permission to do anything. I couldn't work outside the home, or he would sabotage it, yet I wasn't doing enough to contribute.

I might go crazy with this reality.

Startled when I heard my name called, I looked over to see a kind, open face. Her demeaner lent me a feeling of hope. *Maybe I can do this.*

For the first time, I wasn't running. I needed to be here—I *had* to be here. Following her into the small room, I let myself seek, ask, pour out.

I needed to find myself again, needed to know how to think, needed to swim out of the grey fog into something solid, concrete, something black and white. Something true. I needed clarity. And so, I let it spill out, every question that could form on my lips, tumbling over each other during those sixty minutes, and by the end, a half a box of tissues lay discarded and crumpled beside me.

I pleaded for help and direction—but I couldn't bring myself to say everything. Not the worst of it. I skirted around the truth of Lucas's rough hands, the moments that left me breathless with fear for myself and the girls. I didn't dare cross that invisible line. Lucas made sure I knew the risk—he would say they'd take the girls from me, and he'd make sure they believed it was *my* fault if I ever opened my mouth. So, I spoke with careful fragments, desperate for direction and truth, paralyzed by the fear of losing everything I was trying to protect.

"What decisions am I even allowed to make? How do I even know my own thoughts when I've been told how to think for so long? How do I know what is right or best, when all I have believed to be right, has been minimized, dismissed as stupid or unimportant, or told is untrue?" I begged the therapist.

Her council brought a flicker of hope: "What you are living through is not love—it is control. You're not imagining these things. You are being conditioned to doubt reality. You're being conditioned to question yourself, your thoughts, your worth, your sanity, and your very purpose. You are not weak, or useless, or stupid . . . the very fact that you are here shows your courage and your strength. You deserve safety, freedom, and joy. Even if you can't see the way out yet, there is a path forward, and you don't have to walk it alone. Hold onto the truth. You are worthy of more than survival. You are worthy—of dignity, of peace, and a life that brings you fulfillment and love."

And in her words, I found a strand of serenity. A very small glimmer of peace. I felt more like a human who had found a life-saving connection.

Please, God, let this help me. I threw a desperate prayer upward as I walked out, leaving the safety of the peace-filled room back to the chaos of my life.

Several months into therapy, I was beginning to discover my voice. I was realizing I had rights—rights I'd long forgotten I had possessed. The right to insist on certain preferences. The right to disagree. The right to challenge wrong behavior. The right to make decisions for myself, to reclaim the authority over my own life that had been stripped away for so long. Only Charlotte knew of my journey. Her support meant everything—her gentle encouragement gave me the courage to keep showing up. When she offered to watch the girls for a playdate, it was more than a kind gesture, it was the lifeline I needed to slip away to my session without fear of interruption.

Even in the midst of my growth, Lucas's rages grew more frequent. I could feel the storm approaching before it began. I flinched at the sharp edge of his voice and the sudden flare of his temper. The unpredictability made my chest tighten and stomach twist. Even small confrontations left me jumping at shadows. Every raised tone or harsh look was a reminder of how fragile my peace was, and I found myself wondering with bated breath, *Will he hurt me again?*

My mind raced through every scenario: What if he threw something? What if he shoved me or screamed at me until my spirit broke? Questions circled endlessly, gnawing at my calm, suffocating me with fear I could neither quiet nor still. I was trying to step forward and claim my own life, yet every step felt like walking on a tight rope over a deep pit.

"What is this?" Lucas demanded, waving a letter in my face with seething anger.

His rage was palpable, filling the room like a suffocating fog.

He threw the letter at me, and I flinched as it hit my face. I bent to retrieve the crumpled paper off the floor as my heart pounded in my chest. His volatile anger radiated from him, a barely contained storm coiling through his body. My eyes widened as I recognized it—details from my therapy sessions, the number of appointments, the donations I had made in place of regular payments. *Oh my God.*

I was frozen in fear.

How stupid could I be to not change my contact address!

"What the hell is this?" he demanded, eyes glaring.

My body shook. Trying to control my voice and not reveal my fear, I opened my mouth to speak, but nothing came out. I tried again.

"It's about the therapy I've been attending," I answered, speaking slowly with effort, concentrating to keep my voice level.

"Why are *you* in therapy?" he demanded, his chest rising and falling with barely contained fury.

"I needed an objective voice, someone I could talk things through with, someone who might help me with some issues," I answered. My legs trembled uncontrollably, leaving me on the edge of collapse.

"Did you ask my permission to talk about us, to air out our dirty laundry?" His eyes, dark and intense, pierced through me as he took a step toward me.

"No." I paused for a long moment, trying to hold my ground. "I don't need to ask your permission to talk to another woman about things I need guidance and direction on," I said.

"Excuse me! You don't *think*? . . . How dare you talk about our family to someone else. That is betraying. You don't reveal our private details to a stranger. You're going behind my back and sneaking this . . . this is the same as having an affair! You sneak, you hide, and you lie. You have no integrity. You spend all your time spewing lies. *You* . . . will pay for this."

He drew menacingly closer until he was a mere breath from my face. I could feel his foul exhale. "I have no respect for you. You are a betrayer. You have never respected your husband," he spat.

I felt the spittle spray hot across my cheek as I held my feet to the ground. I wiped the spray off my cheek and looked Lucas straight in his eyes. Although I trembled, I did not waver. "I do not have to ask permission from you. I am an adult, and I can seek help whenever I feel it is necessary. This is not a betrayal, that's ridiculous. Maybe if you chose to be a kind husband and father, I wouldn't have to seek help."

I paused to breathe, trying to work around the lump swelling in my throat. "You want respect, but you do not live respectfully," I uttered as I fisted my hands.

He erupted like an exploding volcano. "How dare you speak back to me!" His pulse pounded in his neck, veins throbbed, and eyes bulged as he inched his face a mere centimeter from mine.

Angry red veins streaked through his eyes, and his breath spat sour on my face.

I shook. I had awakened a monster.

Lucas narrowed his eyes, and before I could react, he lunged and gripped both sides of my head. His fingers dug in with a crushing force. I flailed, my arms useless against his strength.

"Stop! You're hurting me," I screamed, but he only tightened his hold, compressing my skull between his huge hands.

White-hot panic surged through me. My head felt like it would cave under the vice-like pressure. Every nerve screamed; every heartbeat pounded in my ears. All I was aware of was the pressure—the gripping pain and the throbbing. The world shrunk to a single piercing point of pain, and my mind clawed desperately for release. I realized with terror that I was on the verge of losing control of my bladder. My body trembled helplessly against the suffocating force and terror that had taken over.

"I could just kill you. I could crush your skull. I could squeeze your neck. I could bury you, and no one would ever find you."

I was dizzy. Reality seemed far away. His eyes locked onto mine like steel. "Remember what I said. Nobody can stop me. I have friends in low places, and no one will ever find you."

Then, with a violent shove, he sent me sprawling to the floor. My body pitched off balance, legs tangled beneath me, arms flailing uselessly as I tried to steady myself—but the force was too sudden, too powerful. He turned and walked away as if I were nothing more than a shadow, a speck beneath his boot.

Everything blurred with the force. I was stunned, reeling and disoriented. After a moment, I cradled my head in my arms. My head ached and throbbed where he squeezed. I could feel the tender, inflamed skin on the sides of my face where his fingers left angry bruises. Pushing up off the floor, I ran into the bathroom, bolted the door, and collapsed on the floor. A crumpled, helpless mess. My shoulders heaved with wracking sobs until my eyes were mere swollen slits. My face burned, blotchy and tender, a mess of raw and puffy skin. My eyes—wild and desperate—stared back at me.

A tiny knock sounded on the door.

"Who is it?" I answered, forcing my voice to sound normal, but failing as it came out more like a whimper.

"It's me, Mommy," a timid voice answered. "Are you okay? We were watching our movie, but I could hear you . . . crying."

"Oh, baby. I'm okay. Just give me a minute, and I'll be right out. I'll meet you in your bedroom, okay?" I answered, forcing my voice to sound as normal as possible.

With great effort, I forced myself off the floor, every movement heavy and uncooperative. I stumbled to the sink, splashing my face, even though lifting my arms felt like dragging weights through water. The first rush of cool liquid was a shock on my flushed skin, cooling the fire that raged beneath the surface. I pressed my face deeper into the cold, clinging to the numbness it offered. Patting my face dry, I hastily dabbed on a layer of foundation to conceal the reddened blotchiness of my skin and puffiness of my tender, swollen eyes.

Looking myself deeply in the eyes, I stopped and stared. I did not deserve this. A flashing remembrance of Sebastian popped into my mind. Would he ever do this? He wouldn't. He would be a good and kind husband. He wouldn't threaten and hurt his wife. I knew Jake would never do this to Charlotte. So why did this happen to me?

I needed to be strong. *You can do this. You are strong.* Exhaling slowly, I counted out five slow, relaxing breaths, opened the bathroom door, and walked down the hall.

Pushing open Ivy's door, I peeked my head in. "Hi, baby . . ."

"Mommy, you were crying," she said, her eyes huge with worry. "I heard you."

"I'm sorry," I answered. "Sometimes mommies have a hard time. But I'm okay. Want to cuddle? I need cuddles right now."

"Yes, Mommy," she said, her big, luminous eyes filled with concern.

Crawling next to her on her bed, I wrapped my arms around her, cradling her close to my chest, and breathed in her little-girl scent of sunshine and innocence.

"I love you, baby," I whispered again and again into her ear as I softly kissed the top of her head and breathed a prayer into her hair. She burrowed into my arms and nestled herself next to me. Her arms clung to me.

Softly, I sang a lullaby, and after several minutes, I felt her body relax and arms slacken. Her breathing slowed, and I knew she had fallen asleep. I continued to hold her, cherishing her love and closeness. My eyes grew heavy as I drifted to sleep. When I woke an hour later, I found Ivy still curled in my arms, her small, warm body safe against me. I tucked the blanket snugly around her sleeping form and pressed a soft kiss to her hair before slipping away. My own body ached, and I stumbled to my room, pulling back my covers and collapsing into the bed, surrendering instantly to sleep.

I awoke with a pounding headache. My stomach tightened, and the question rose unbidden: *What will Lucas be like this morning?*

My gaze landing on the unmoving lump on the far side of the bed, his body stretched in stillness—yet the sight did little to ease the tension coiled in my chest.

Remove yourself. Talk to someone. These thoughts arose in my mind. I decided to obey my thoughts and planned to drop the girls at my parents' and go talk to Charlotte. I knew I could confide most things to Charlotte, but I was too afraid of what Lucas might do to my parents, after his threats, if I told them the full truth. Yet, I needed to confide in someone. Nervously, I packed one large bag with hastily gathered changes of clothes for all three girls, pajamas, a few toys and art supplies. I stocked the diaper bag and secured both bags behind the girls' bedroom door where they would not be noticed by Lucas.

Stealing a few more minutes, I crept quietly into my closet, hastily packed for myself, not thinking of what matched but grabbing random snatches of jeans, shirts, undergarments, and toiletries. Once my bag was filled, I slipped on my shoes, not even bothering to tie them and hoisted the girls' bags and mine into my arms, not caring as the weight of the straps dug into the skin on my shoulders. Lugging them out to my car, I walked ever so carefully down each step, desperate to avoid the old, creaky spots.

Collecting the mail on my way in, I wanted to avoid drawing suspicion. I set the few envelopes on the kitchen counter. I could hear my pulse pounding like a loud drum in my ears. I tried to exhale, but my heart continued to pound loudly in protest, and I realized I had been holding my breath almost the entire time.

Taking a few moments to collect my thoughts, I formed a plan. I was afraid of confrontation and preferred avoiding it at all costs. After a pause, I headed upstairs to collect the girls.

Kissing their little angelic faces, I whispered, "Time to rise and shine, girlies. I have a surprise for you. We're going to go to Grammy and Grampy's to surprise them for breakfast! Let's get ready quickly, okay?"

I helped three barely-awake girls into comfy outfits, easily grabbed from the closet.

"We can brush our teeth there this time, okay? Let's go!"

As I walked down the stairs, I spotted Lucas sitting in the kitchen chair. Our eyes met, and dread filled my stomach.

"Where are you going? Where are you taking them?" he demanded in a cool, even tone.

"We are going for breakfast," I answered quickly, averting my eyes and prodding the girls gently toward the door with Rose balanced on my hip.

"With what money?" Lucas moved to stand.

"I got it," I answered, not wanting this to end in an interrogation.

He looked at me with a raised eyebrow and sat back with a look of disgust on his unpleasant face.

I can't believe I ever found him handsome. His cruelty made him ugly to me. Breathing a sigh of relief as he looked away, I ushered the girls outside and closed the door quietly behind me. I buckled the girls in the car, jumped in the front seat, slammed the door, and raced out of the driveway.

It took several minutes for my heart to stop pounding louder than the roar of the engine. It pounded in my head, louder than the girls' voices, like a relentless drum.

Just breathe, I told myself. Rolling the windows down, I focused on inhaling fresh, clean air to clear my mind. As the cool air hit my face, tears began to roll down my cheeks.

I can't have that right now, I told myself, forcing the anguish back down. I had to be strong. My features trembled as I struggled to compose them. The remnants of cool tears clung to the ends of my lashes. I pushed my emotions deep inside—it was like trying to cram a storm into a small box, expecting it to not explode.

Focusing on the girls, I searched my mind for a distraction. "Let's sing a song!" I suggested. Choosing their favorite pop song, I started belting it out loudly while the girls joined in a few lines later and sang at the top of their little lungs.

Fake it till you make it, I told myself with steely determination.

Looking in the rearview mirror, I saw the blissful joy and unencumbered lightness on Mia's face, her innocence and trust fully displayed. She closed her eyes and sang with all her heart, swaying to the beat, feeling the music in her soul.

Ivy sang with exuberance and passion in her eyes. Deep understanding written on her face as the words rang out and meaning clear with the message in *Brave* by Sara Bareilles.

Oh, to feel such freedom! I let the music wrap its warm, comforting arms around me.

I let courage build within my soul.

I breathed.

"I just want to see you be brave."

I let the message permeate as it resonated deep within.

I texted Charlotte, "I'm coming over."

She immediately responded, "Is everything okay?"

"No," I responded.

After taking the girls to Mom and Dad's for a yummy breakfast of homemade waffles and fresh fruit, I left shortly after with a quick hug and thank-you, and drove directly to Charlotte's house. The drive felt endless, every mile heavy with weight bearing down on my chest. My hands gripped the wheel, slick with sweat, as doubts and fear assaulted me. Yet beneath the fear, a fragile thread pulled me. Maybe, just maybe, I would not have to carry this alone.

Pouring everything out to my best friend was a lifeline. My fears, my hurt, my anguish, the unexpressed terror.

"You cannot stay with him!" she pleaded, her face a picture of pained worry and distress. "You have to leave." She gripped my arms tightly as if to push the message deeper.

"He is hurting you! And the girls. What if he does something worse? How will you live with yourself if you stay?"

"I know! I just . . . have to figure out how to do this. I can't just leave! I have no money, no credit cards, and no real job." I paused, trying to form the words that expressed my anguish. "But I can't . . . live like this either." I stared and uttered unthinkable words, "I keep dreaming how life would be if he . . . died—I would be free."

Feeling guilty for saying such horrific words, tears poured from my eyes, forming trails down my cheeks. I scrubbed them away vigorously, but more just replaced them. My tears became a faucet I could not shut off. Like a dam that broke, my tears fell, exploding in a violent rush. Like a flood, they came. Pouring. Erupting. The ache inside me burst into hoarse, wracking sobs. Charlotte wrapped her arms around me, and we rocked and rocked until all my anguish and tears were spent. Until all that was left were shuddering, exhausted sighs.

I breathed. We sat. And an hour or two passed in comfort and support.

"We need a plan," Charlotte decided. "Here is what we are going to do." And she fleshed out a probable scenario. "Plan ahead. Save every penny you can. Pack an emergency bag for you and the girls. Set aside important documents for each of you. And stay out of his way. Be busy with the girls and don't say anything to spark his rage. Be invisible. And leave the second you think he might hurt you or any of the girls. Do not wait until he does."

With the plan in place, I left shaky, afraid, hopeful, petrified, and yearning for a chance at freedom and peace, hoping I would have the courage. Sometimes, I reasoned, it's better to hide in plain sight. Other times it's best to disappear altogether to save yourself and your kids.

Lose yourself to save your life.

I felt like a raw gem, cracked and marred before it could shine, or a priceless vase shattered and broken.

This was my life. This was me.

I was like a bird who had just learned to fly, eager for adventure. But instead of soaring, I was captured, my wings cruelly clipped.

Freedom was something I felt I had never tasted. I never learned to dance with the wind, to dream boldly, or embrace my strengths or understand weaknesses. My mind spun with the realization. Everything sharpened into focus—intense, blinding.

Every part of me yearned for deliverance. I could taste the promise of escape. And I desired it with every fiber in my being. I had to do whatever I could to attain this freedom for me and my precious daughters.

Driving to my parents, I decided, firm and resolute, nothing was going to alter my path. No fake apology, no threat, and no misguided advice. I must stand for what is right and not be manipulated, deceived, or controlled by evil.

It had been a long few months.

The seasons had changed and so had my life. Every step I took toward help made Lucas tighten his grip. The more I reached for therapy, the more Lucas's need for control swelled. Trying to get my sessions became a guilty weight upon me. I would apologize to myself for taking time to breathe and seek help—like it was a selfish crime. This guilt settled in my bones, a shame for wanting help, revealing secret things, and keeping it from Lucas. His suspicion shadowed me everywhere, twisting even the simplest outing into proof against me. "*Where are you going? Who are you spending time with? Why did your 'errands' take you so long? What are you doing while you're out?*" It became an interrogation each time I left the house, insinuating wrongness. I couldn't bear the weight of his endless provoking interrogations the moments I stepped inside the door, so after canceling one appointment after another—I stopped going.

He won.

I told myself it was easier this way; keeping calm is better than drowning in the storm. Yet day by day, I began to fade. Again. I sank under the control of his fist while my heart ached for the comfort I had found in that little room. I felt myself caving and folding into the shadows, quieter, more apprehensive, more tentative, more unsure—until practically I had once again vanished. Only occasionally would my true self lift her head and dare to peek out.

I did whatever I could to keep busy—just to let my heart survive, to forget the freedom I longed for. I rewrote my life one careful step at a time, surrounding myself with those who truly loved me, trying to stitch together a fragile version of happiness. Every move was calculated, every day a silent dance around Lucas's shadow—pretending in my mind that he didn't exist.

We chose to spend crisp fall evenings with my parents around the cozy fire pit. While Dad oversaw roasting marshmallows to perfection, I sat and observed the happy commotion. Ivy and Mia ran and played, happy and carefree, while Rose toddled about with Mom shortly behind her busy, racing steps. The girls flew about, capturing flitting fireflies and echoing silly camp songs.

Endless days were spent with Charlotte while the kids filled the afternoons with childish games and imaginations. Often those days would turn into a girls night, a much-needed escape from my reality. Netflix, a bottle of wine, and laughter shared between us while the kids slept, was the usual. Jake would graciously "escape" to his office or make late runs for ice cream and treats for the kids—anything other than sitting through girl talk or yet another replay of *The Proposal* or *Runaway Bride*.

Sometimes Sebastian and Jake would hang out for the evening, giving us girls a chance to visit without interruption. On rare occasions when Sebastian and I exchanged a few words, he was always kind—courteous without prying, gentle without pity. He would ask how I was doing, but it was his eyes that lingered, carrying questions and understanding his words never voiced. Our conversations never strayed from the casual, but his presence carried a quiet steadiness I had long forgotten men could hold. He was every bit the gentleman, thoughtful and restrained, yet now and then I'd catch the curve of his smile or a fleeting look in his eyes that stirred something deep inside me. It was in those moments, against my will, I found myself imagining—dreaming of another kind of life, one where kindness and tenderness weren't fantasies but everyday truths. But I knew what I dreamed wasn't meant to be, so I buried it deep inside and tried to forget.

In the beginning, the girls would beg Lucas to join for family fun, but after repeated refusals, they asked less often and instead looked forward to their playdates with their friends. And after some time, they stopped asking altogether. I felt relieved.

I noticed the shift in my feelings for him. No longer did I desire any closeness.

I did not miss his affection or attention. That part had died. It died with his cruelty and unchanging behavior. I existed near him, two strangers in a home, giving him a wide berth and choosing to be away when I knew he would be home. I stopped cooking meals for him or doing his laundry, and I no longer tried to please him. It didn't help anyway.

No matter how much I used to accomplish, he would still find something to complain about or insult. When I pushed myself to clean the entire house, cook a huge meal, and take care of the girls with great attentive care, there would still be something I "forgot". "Useless" had been the slur thrown too many times. So I stopped trying.

As fall settled in, our visits with Mom and Dad became a steady rhythm; we shared dinners together several times a week. It fit easier with the girls' school schedule and gave us the gift of a peaceful, happy atmosphere—an escape where we could simply relax. We would chat, play board games, or watch a movie until bedtime drew near, then I'd pack three sleepy girls into the car, and carry them through quick baths and bed routines, and finally sink into my own moment of peace. Nestled in my cozy chair with a steaming cup of fragrant tea—sweetened with a spoonful of honey—I would get lost in my latest novel, savoring the stillness.

Most nights Lucas was out doing whatever he desired, and by then, I had stopped caring. It gave me some peaceful nights. And time to dream.

Red and green Christmas holly draped across the mantle, white twinkle lights casting a soft glow, and the mingling scents of fragrant cinnamon and cedar drifted through the house. These were some of my favorite things about Christmas. But it was the girls' radiant smiles, their eyes alight with wonder, that made the season feel warmer, deeper, more profound. I wanted every moment to carry its own kind of magic, to wrap them in joy that would outshine any shadow. So, I poured myself into the season—caroling through frosty evenings, rolling out dough for Christmas cookies, baking a gingerbread house with sticky fingers and laughter echoing. It was my promise to my daughters, a way of weaving beauty into their memories and sharing these moments with my parents. With each glittering light and frosted cookie, I strove to make Christmas shimmer with as much magic as humanly possible.

Lucas never really engaged; he lingered on the edges of our lives. Even as my heart longed for a husband who desired to share in our joys, in the end, I had to relinquish that longing and hold tight to the happiness still before me. The girls sparkled with excitement, thrilled at the promise of staying to open presents with Grammy and Grampy this year.

Christmas dawned bright and beautiful with newly fallen snow. Delicate flakes covered the ground and adorned the trees, draping them in a soft, frosty veil. The sun shone brightly as it radiated its luminance on the glittery powder, and the branches took on an angelic glow.

"Girls! It's Christmas!" Excitement filled my voice.

The thunder of feet hitting the floor and happy scampers echoed through the house as they scurried down the old, beloved stairs. Amid the joy and laughter, the presents and happy hugs, the decadent homemade cinnamon buns and necessary coffee topped with mounds of whipped cream, our hearts felt light and refreshed, peaceful yet joyful.

I was thankful for a safe place. The girls were cherished, loved, and a bit lovingly spoiled, and the day was spent in blessed happiness.

Winter slowly released its icy grip, and the first hints of spring unfurled like shy blossoms. Ivy and Mia were buzzing with excitement, eager for the outdoors, the fresh air and the soft grass beneath their feet. Even Rose was itching to play beneath the gentle sunshine. Crisp spring air felt mild after the chill of winter. Crocuses peaked their gentle heads up toward the warm sun, and daffodils bravely made their early appearance. Afternoon walks became an everyday occurrence, and picnics became planned. Life had settled into normalcy with me and the girls.

One sunny afternoon we took a long stroll to our favorite mulberry tree where we picked handfuls of the rich purplish blackberries, standing on tiptoe to capture every last one. We stripped the limbs bare and gorged ourselves on the succulent dark berries, while lips became stained purple and smiles spread resplendent. Happy laughter and skipping followed us as we made our way home and tumbled into the house, a joyful mess.

I barely noticed Lucas until I abruptly encountered him in the kitchen; he looked bothered and irritated, his presence sharp against our energy. I quickly tempered our excitement, ushering the girls upstairs to wash.

"Ivy, take Rose with you and help her wash her face and hands, please. Hold her hand while you walk upstairs," I directed with caution.

I watched until they safely climbed the stairs and entered the bathroom, then turned and calmly began unpacking our tote bag.

"What the hell were you doing?" Lucas demanded, as he strode over to stand in the middle of the kitchen.

I looked up, confusion evident upon my face. "We went for a walk," I said simply, and continued arranging the items on the shelf.

"All you do is live in a dream land. You know nothing of responsibility," he accused. "You're out gallivanting around.

You have no idea what it means to have a job. Stop sponging off me and get out there and get a real job. I am not giving you any more money until you start contributing. You are a lazy excuse for a wife." He was yelling by now, and his arm swung wide to display the less-than-perfect area. "*Look* at this mess!"

Remnants of finger-painting were on the table. The brushes soaked nearby in a cup of water, and the colorful creations were laid out to dry.

Having no idea why he was flipping out, I responded, "I let the girls paint this morning and left the pictures to dry while we went for a walk. It's not messy. When the pictures are dry, I'm hanging them up."

Lucas ripped the pictures off the counter and hurled them at my face. I stumbled back as they scattered across the kitchen floor.

"Stop!" I cried, my voice cracking, the plea lodged in my throat. "Stop being so cruel! The girls are just trying to make pretty spring paintings!" I dropped to my knees, gathering the pictures into my arms as gently as if they were the girls themselves, desperate to protect each one. A familiar anger rose in me—the realization that he couldn't bear even a moment of our happiness without trying to destroy it.

Above me, Lucas loomed—arms crossed, shoulders squared, his stance radiating cold determination, intent on crushing what little peace I had left. His boot firmly planted on one of Mia's little creations. The sunny-yellow flower was mostly hidden by his dirty brown boot.

"Move . . . your foot," I demanded, my voice trembling as I knelt on the floor, staring up at him. Fury rose inside me, hot and unyielding at his unjust rage. He looked down on me with a curl of disgust, refusing to budge.

"Move," I insisted, my anger surging. I tried to push his shoe off the picture so I could rescue it.

"Don't touch me," he spat, his voice sharp and venomous. Lucas's eyes burned into mine, narrowed to slits, filled with nothing but contempt. He lunged, his hand clamping onto my ponytail and yanking my head back so hard my face was forced upward.

A stifled scream clawed at my throat as pain seared across my scalp—his grip burning, merciless. Tears blurred my vision.

"Don't you ever push me. You piece of shit. You're worthless. Useless," he snarled, each word dripping with venom as his fingers twisted tighter in my hair.

My scalp throbbed as hot tears streaked my cheeks.

"Stop! You're hurting me!" I sobbed. My fingers dug helplessly into the hard cords of muscle in his forearms. He refused to budge. His grip only tightened until my vision blurred.

With a violent thrust, he shoved my head downward, and my head struck the corner of the table leg. Exploding pain shot through my head as lights danced in the peripheral.

Cradling my head in my hands, I rocked back and forth, sobs tearing through me as pain and terror blurred the edges of everything.

I could hardly piece together what happened next—the rage had been too sharp, the fear too consuming. Fragments came back in flashes:

Mia's tiny body hurling itself against Lucas's leg.

Her desperate strength throwing him off balance.

The fragile weight of her small frame draping protectively over mine.

"Stop hurting my mommy!" Mia's voice cracked through the chaos, small yet fierce, shaking with sobs.

Silence followed—a long, suffocating silence that stretched like an eternity.

I strained my eyes to open, to see her—to see him. I needed to know he wouldn't turn his rage on her. But my vision stayed blurred, trapped behind pain and fear.

Finally, his footsteps moved—slow, measured. Leaving the kitchen, treading over the girls' painting. Each step up the stairs thudded through me like thunder.

The bedroom door slammed.

Only then did the world come back into focus.

Mia stood frozen—tear-streaked, her little face contorted in terror.

I lay curled on the cold floor, rocking with suppressed sobs, my body trembling beyond control. Pain throbbed through my skull, each pulse a cruel reminder of his grip. I was broken, stunned, and hollow, shock sealing me in silence.

Mia threw her arms around me, her tiny body trembling as she whispered through her tears, "It's okay, Mommy, I love you. It's okay." Her sobs shook against my chest, her hot tears spilling onto my face, mingling with my own.

Moments later, Ivy came stumbling down the stairs, clutching the stair railing with one hand while struggling to steady Rose in the other.

"Oh, Mommy . . . oh, Mommy," Ivy cried, her voice breaking.

The sight of their terrified faces shattered me further. My sobs deepened, raw and broken, as I realized all my girls had seen and heard. I wanted to shield them, to spare them the cruelty I endured, but I had failed.

"I'm so sorry!" I wept. "I didn't want you to see this!"

"Mommy, it's not your fault. Daddy was being mean, so mean!" Ivy sobbed, her voice breaking with far too much heartbreak for her tender years. She and Mia collapsed into my lap, clinging to me with desperate little arms. Rose whimpered softly between us, as if she too felt the weight of it all. We clung to each other, a trembling knot of sorrow—a huddled mess. Our limbs were all entangled, and our tears mixed as we rocked together on the floor, bound tightly by the only refuge we had—each other.

For a long while, we sat huddled, rocking and holding each other as the last waves of sobs began to subside and the final hiccupping cry finally passed. A sense of calm began to settle, and I whispered, "Come on, let's go upstairs. You girls can take a bubble bath and get cleaned up, and I'll make mac and cheese for dinner. Then we can snuggle in bed and read some stories together, okay?"

"Okay, Mommy," they responded softly, their voices tentative but trusting. Slowly they disentangled themselves from my arms, and together we began picking up the scattered papers and tidying the mess. As the familiar rhythm of cleaning took over, their shoulders relaxed, and their breathing evened out. The tension that gripped us began to lessen.

The throbbing in my head was relentless, each pulse sending a blinding, shooting pain deep in my skull. It hammered sharply, and the feelings of nausea became overwhelming. I swallowed two ibuprofens with a small sip of water and hoped it would ease the pain.

"Come, let's go." I gently led them upstairs, slowly and carefully to not exacerbate my blinding headache.

After dinner, the sharp pain dulled to a low ache. Choosing to try and ignore it, I crawled in bed with the girls, and we clustered around their favorite stories. Ivy, Mia, and I took turns reading until their eyelids became heavy with sleep. After they drifted off, I carefully tucked the soft comforter around their sleeping forms and gently pressed goodnight kisses to their flushed cheeks, softly tiptoeing out the bedroom door.

All night my mind twisted itself in knots, cycling through the relentless threats and controlling words. I worried over the safety of my family and friends, haunted by the bitter memory of all the times I tried to find space—retreating to my parents' house, sneaking refuge with friends, grasping for peace in therapy sessions. But every escape was temporary. Fear held me captive—every threat, words spoken to control, interrogations to intimidate, decisions to tether me—was another link in a chain that wrapped itself tighter around my will. *"I know where you'll go . . . Do you think you can escape me?"*

"I'll tell the police you kidnapped the girls . . . I have friends in low places . . . Do you think you can ever get away from me? . . . You belong to me. . . You are nothing without me . . . No one else would ever want you . . . I will take everything from you."

Every threat pressed deeper into my chest, heavy and relentless, leaving me immoveable, a prisoner, unable to truly seek help and flee.

Morning dawned with a heavy atmosphere, the clouds grey and low, mirroring my mood. By the time the girls returned from school, their small footsteps were hushed, their movements cautious with uncertainty. They kept their distance from Lucas, moving past him without a word, retreating to their rooms as though it were a refuge. I watched as they played half-heartedly, and their eyes flicked to mine for silent reassurance throughout the evening.

When Lucas walked past, my body tensed instinctively, I gripped the edge of the counter as every nerve was on high alert. My stomach churned with anxiety, and nausea was a constant, unwelcome companion.

He ignored me completely, brushing past without a word, as if he was punishing me . . . for *his* behavior.

Lucas stormed into the kitchen, irritated and upset. He slammed the cupboard doors, then stood staring into the refrigerator for a long, tense minute before slamming that door as well.

"What the hell did you do all day?" he demanded, turning his eyes toward me in a cold accusation.

Taken aback at his accusation, I had no answer.

Lucas continued, "You have no job, your only responsibility is the kids and the house. Is it too difficult for you to make dinner, clean the house, and watch the kids?

Do I have to do everything for you? How about you get off your ass and take care of your responsibilities!"

"I . . . I have been busy all day with Rose," I answered, as I took several steps back to create more distance between us. "But honestly, I didn't want to make you dinner. You have been horrible to me. You can figure it out yourself. You can't treat me like crap and hurt me, then expect maid service. I'm done with your disgusting behavior."

I knew I needed to stay under the radar, but it was impossible to not let myself rise and defend. Sometimes my true self would break through and not allow myself to be forced into silent submission.

Rage built on his face as I spoke, turning from red to flaming dark crimson.

He squeezed his fists, clenching and unclenching as his nostrils flared. Eyes black as night glared at me with hatred.

He stormed back to the refrigerator and threw open the door, rummaging through the items on the shelf. I could hear containers being moved; he was probably pushing the leftovers to the side because, of course, he would never want that. He yanked out the hydrator drawer then shoved it closed. Staring into the chasm of the refrigerator, he slammed it shut again. He walked over to the cupboard, apparently frustrated with his findings, and went back to the refrigerator. He grabbed a loaf of uncut French bread and tossed it on the counter with the pack of deli meat and the block of cheddar cheese.

Sifting through the filled laundry basket to the couch, I kept a wary eye on the kitchen from the corner of my eye and saw him grab a knife to cut the bread.

Things weren't going well with the non-serrated knife. His actions had taken on a distinctly aggressive edge as he struggled to cut the bread. I was nervous, unsure of what he would do.

"Damnit!" he yelled. "You can't even make a simple dinner, and I've got . . . what . . . a lousy sandwich for dinner! I work hard, and all I get is a lazy wife!" His voice cracked with fury as he slammed the knife into the wooden counter, driving it in at least a full inch. Startled by his explosive rage, I froze, eyes fixed on his fist gripping the knife, knuckles white, and veins bulging blue and ugly. My heart beat wildly, feeling it might burst, and my mind struggled to process his fury.

Lucas hurled the half-cut loaf of bread against the wall, crumbs scattered on the floor. He snatched his keys from the counter and stormed out. The front door slammed with such force, the walls shuddered in response. The thick silence that followed felt heavier, sharper, more suffocating than his rage.

The accusations spiraled through my mind, each one sharper than the last. No matter how I tried, it was never enough. *I wasn't good enough.*

I poured everything into being a good mother, but he reminded me daily that I was a failure as a wife. To him, his needs came first—I was meant to attend, to please, and to serve. Yet he was a terrible husband. *So where is the line?*

Every attempt to stand up for myself backfired. Hindsight mocked me, whispering its cruel question: *Do I keep the peace at any cost?*

I couldn't move. Couldn't think. I was frozen—trapped inside the moment replaying in my mind. The knife, buried in the wood. His face—twisted with rage. His eyes—deadly, cold, menacing.

Nothing about him felt safe. He was always this way—a volcano on the brink of eruption, the slightest spark could trigger a storm.

My body understood before my mind caught up. This wasn't just another outburst. Something big just happened. *Oh god, had he just stabbed a knife into the counter to intimidate me? To show me how easy he could control me with fear? Or was it something darker—was he so angry he could drive the knife into anything . . . or anyone?*

I couldn't do this again.

I couldn't keep babysitting his emotions or monitoring his needs. *I'm okay,* I whispered to myself, barely believing the words. *Just breathe, you're okay.*

Only a minute had passed. It felt like an eternity. My mind raced as I climbed the stairs. I needed to check on the girls. I paused outside their door, praying they didn't hear anything. Praying somehow, this nightmare was mine alone to carry.

Pushing open the closed door, relief washed over me. Inside, the girls were immersed in their own world. A princess movie blasted its songs, and Ivy and Mia sang along—voices bright and innocent. They sat cross-legged on the floor, dressing their Barbies in glittery dresses and tiny, sparkly plastic shoes. They had no idea what just occurred.

Thank God.

I'd do anything to keep it that way. Ignoring my frayed emotions, I smoothed my expression into something gentle, something safe, and stepped fully into the room, slipping back into the role of sole caretaker.

"How's the movie, girls?" I asked, forcing false cheer into my voice.

"Good, Mommy!" Ivy answered, glancing up briefly as she tugged a dress onto her Barbie.

Mia grinned, eyes bright. "We love princesses."

I sank down between them, wrapping my arms around their small bodies. I pulled them close, feeling their warmth, steady and real, receiving comfort from their genuine love.

Rose played in front of the girls with a Barbie she borrowed, struggling to fit its legs into the dress. Then she ran over and plopped into my lap, exclaiming, "Mommy, help me!"

"I'll help you, honey. Mommy loves Rose!" I answered as I nuzzled her neck and blew raspberry kisses, then continued to help her dress the doll.

Her squeals emanated with bubbling laughter and the girls' joy slowly seeped into my heart. Their love was a catharsis for the soul. I lived for my girls, and I would do anything for them.

Jagged flashes of emotions and scenes abruptly appeared in my mind—this is how life was going to play out. And it wasn't changing . . . for the better at least.

I had been so willing to love, yet I only reaped buckets of trauma, indifference, and cruelty. No matter how much I pleaded for Lucas to understand or change . . . he never did. The physical bruises he left on me were less visible than the bruises on my soul.

Tomorrow, I would begin my plan to leave.

After tucking the girls in bed with extra kisses and love, I slid into the cool cotton sheets and cuddled into my downy comforter.

I was startled awake by the bumping of drawers and a door shutting noisily. Lucas returned home and inconsiderately went about preparing for bed, dropping the toilet seat with a loud bang, completely indifferent to the sleeping household. Firmly plopping on the bed, he pulled the comforter toward himself, not caring the little he left for me.

I could smell a drifting sweet perfume emanating off his body.

It wasn't mine.

My heart turned cold. I knew the signs. Again. Another betrayal without remorse. He created more ways to break me. Glaring into the darkness, silent tears escaped my lids. They slid sideways across my face and down into the pillow, forming a wet puddle beneath my head. I didn't love him anymore—not the man he had become. Yet somehow the betrayal still found a way to burrow in, to wound.

You are not good enough. You are undesirable. No one wants you. You are replaceable. It reinforced my rejection. Tonight, he added another layer of betrayal and hurt. While I was trying to hold the last pieces of myself together, he kept tearing them apart. While I clung to my remaining dignity and honor, he indulged his darkness.

I felt my heart splinter—not into a million pieces, but into something quieter. Numb. A breaking that barely made a sound.

A silent crushing.

The next morning, lilacs were in full bloom and their fragrance floated up, greeting me, but even their sweet fragrance couldn't touch the depth of anguish in my soul. I felt like another piece of me had died. I didn't feel like myself and couldn't throw off the pangs of sadness. I was left vulnerable—desperate for peace.

After some time, I heard Lucas moving about upstairs. Heavy footsteps, drawers slamming. I stayed rooted in my chair, letting the warmth of the sun soak into my skin. I didn't want to see him. I pretended not to hear the clatter. He came downstairs and began rummaging in the cupboard. I said nothing. *Calm. Be invisible.*

"Where's breakfast?" Lucas demanded as he strode into the living room, his voice slicing through the quiet moment.

I didn't look at him, but a long breath escaped—thick with disgust. After a long pause, I finally answered, each word measured to keep from shaking.

"I'm sure you can manage that."

The words tasted bitter in my mouth. The anger and betrayal of the affair cut, but in some twisted corner of my heart, I was also relieved it wasn't me he was forcing. The hatred for the man he was—charming to the world but cruel and entitled behind closed doors—rose in me like bile. He saw me as nothing. Less than nothing. A placeholder for his rage. The fact that he could sleep with other women without a thought . . . that I wasn't even worth being faithful to . . . it hit me harder than the infidelity itself.

He didn't care. *I didn't matter.*

Such an ass, I thought.

"Excuse me?" he snapped, eyes bulging with offense. He jabbed a finger toward my chair, voice dripping with contempt. "You do nothing but sit on your butt, and you want *me* to make my own breakfast?"

Anger surged through me like static. Each word struck a match. Deep inside I felt a shift—something coming awake. Something like—*No more.*

And the words broke free. "You expect me to serve you after you were with another woman? Are you insane?"

"What the hell are you talking about?" Lucas demanded, voice rising like a warning. "Stop making up shit. You're always lying about me, trying to make me look bad." He shook his head, playing the victim, his face a mask of false innocence.

Then his tone shifted, slicing like venom. "And even if I did, you are a terrible wife," he sneered. "You don't even know what it means to be a good wife. Go ask your friends—they know. They've talked about it. Everyone knows what kind of person you really are. You try to act so perfect, but everyone sees right through your act. You don't even have any real friends."

He leaned in, his eyes glittering with cruelty. "Honestly, you get what you deserve. If I end up with someone else, it's because of *you*. You are a cold, selfish woman. No man would want to sleep with you anyways." A vicious smile curled at the corner of his mouth. "Just watch, you'll get exactly what you deserve."

His words struck like arrows.

"What are you even talking about?" I cried, genuinely stunned. "That not true! Why do you talk like this? Why not talk about your lack of character?" My voice broke despite the fire rising in my chest. "You don't even know what honor means!"

His expression hardened into something sinister. "When Rose turns five, I'm replacing you. I am done. You better start prepare yourself."

Silence fell. I stood frozen. *How dare he!* Hatred burned behind my eyes. My thoughts raged. The audacity—the sheer delusion. He could cast me aside like I was disposable . . . and then blame me for it?

Fury burned within me—a sense of injustice surged within me. I had persevered to always do right, to never misstep, to be the best wife and mother I could be. No matter how deeply I longed for love, I never betrayed my integrity. Meanwhile, he cast loyalty aside as easily as shedding a coat.

God, I hated him. I *despised* him.

His very presence made my skin crawl—yet the betrayal still hurt like a fresh wound every time. I couldn't understand how a person could live a double life.

I glared at him, my mind flooded with a million angry thoughts—venomous, sharp, justified.

I told myself I didn't care—but I did care. *I cared too much.* I wanted a husband who loved and desired me, who found fulfillment in our marriage. Instead, I was bound to Lucas—a man who, through his actions, showed he cared nothing for fidelity, nothing for me.

I was disposable.

It tore at me—being married to someone who sought the image of family but none of the sacrifice. No honor. No kindness. No love.

He wanted the *title* of husband and father—without the weight of commitment. And I was left raw and aching under the truth—rejected, deeply wounded, yet still longing for the warmth and tenderness I deserved.

Chapter Eighteen

Fall 2017, *Present Day*

A part of the healing journey is enduring the onslaught of a million thoughts—doubts, regrets, questions, and longings—that plague that floods the mind without mercy. They come like waves, relentless and unbidden, demanding to be faced. Memories resurface, fears whisper, old wounds ache to be understood. It feels endless, as though the mind is caught in a storm of what-ifs and what-nots. Yet healing means sitting with each one, answering them patiently, one by one. Every struggle, every fear, each fragment of the past that the brain insists on untangling becomes part of the process. It is exhausting but necessary. This is the slow work of forgiving myself, of loosening the grip of shame, and of learning to gently gather the broken pieces so the soul can begin to mend.

I had begun journaling to work through my pain. I found it giving shape to the swirling emotions, giving voice to the unspoken. It helped bring clarity to the overwhelming thoughts in my mind. Sometimes my brain would get stuck in survival mode, cycling through memories, fears, and emotions too impossible to organize. Putting words to my feelings helped me feel safe to process without just reliving it, bringing me a much-needed sense of calm. My counselor shared how important this was in my healing journey. Yet it was not easy. Sometimes the journaling stirred up pain before it soothed the ache. But over time, the act of writing became a safety to emotions that were too heavy to carry alone.

With my pen paused midair, I came back to myself tucked in the corner of my favorite coffee shop. Beside me sat my half-drunk latte. I'd gotten lost in a swirl of memories.

It was my first quiet hour all week, and I had nowhere I needed to go. I was practicing just simply being—letting myself contemplate and heal. And I promised myself I would start listening to my body. This was an experience I now relished, having time to be alone and journal.

It couldn't erase the trauma or sadness, but somehow, putting pen to paper was a catharsis, a healing journey. It somehow gave me control over my own story, something that trauma often takes away. It was helping me reclaim my voice and listen to my story with compassion. It was like gently peeling back layers of a wound, not to re-open it but to let it breathe and clean out the infection. It was my safe space. The pages were a place where my voice was no longer lost. With every word I penned, it was me choosing to face the past without letting it define my future.

As I enjoyed my peaceful afternoon, the hum of conversations swirled softly around me. At a table beside me sat a young man and woman, unremarkable in appearance, but for some reason, my gaze kept drifting toward them. Something kept drawing me to observe them. I noticed the man's voice rose, not in anger but in something worse: control. Sugar-coated control. He continued to redirect the conversation, correct and interrupt. He treated her like her thoughts were irrelevant. His behavior was demeaning, yet he made it sound like he was just caring, like he knew better.

The woman across from him was a younger version of me. She continued to smile through it, ignoring his overbearing behavior and agreeing with whatever he suggested. She smiled, too much and too often. She looked unsure, pensive and pleasing . . . like she would say or do whatever to please him.

My pen hovered in the air; the sentence in my journal remained incomplete. I had seen this before—lived this before. I saw myself in this woman. And just like that, the coffee shop became a mirror to the past.

How naive I had been, I realized as a sickening feeling gripped my stomach. Why do we think if a guy is romantic, handsome, and charming, he is a true gentleman?

What makes a guy a “good guy”?

Just because he smiles a certain way . . . flirts adorably . . . captures our attention . . . acts like he can’t spend a day without us . . . showers compliments or makes you feel like the sun rises and sets on you . . . How is this anything but puppy love, infatuation, or just a new conquest?

Just because a guy seems like Prince Charming doesn’t mean he truly is genuine, deep-down, through-and-through good. Too many times guys come on strong and heavy, sweeping a girl off her feet, yet he is nothing like the image he presents.

I began putting my pen to paper and furiously writing—this was my message-in-the-bottle moment.

And I began to write everything I wish I had understood ten years ago.

If I had read a clear warning, I hope I would have listened. I’m going to take that chance and write this letter to a stranger, hoping she will see the truth, or at least have her eyes opened.

I know we are strangers, but I had to write you this letter. I was you—some years ago, and I wish someone had told me what I’m going to tell you. I can tell that you are a kind person, and it moved me when I saw how your smile faded and how your words died on your lips. I saw how your partner talked over you and corrected you like what you had to say wasn’t valued. I can tell that was hurtful. I can imagine you are a very caring person, possibly someone who would do whatever it takes to save a relationship—even sacrificing yourself. I was too. I used to sit exactly where you are, thinking, this must be love.

I wish someone had handed me a warning back then—I wish I had known that respect isn’t just compliments and grand gestures. Respect is listening, honoring, and sacrificing. So here

I am, writing you this spontaneous letter, hoping you'll see what I wish I had seen so many years ago . . .

I continued to write as thoughts flooded my mind. The past whirled back like a tsunami, crashing over me with mind-blowing truths I had now learned. Even though I had gone through therapy, I still struggled with the aftermath of abuse. I understood much, but I still had a very long way to go.

I wrote about authenticity and the importance of boundaries. And how you should watch someone's life to see if they are genuine in how they present themself. I continued to explain that your partner should respect your boundaries—emotional and physical. His actions should match his words. He should be able to handle disagreements without blowing up or withdrawing. The relationship should be reciprocal. He should also want to know about your life—your values, your interests, and your life goals. It shouldn't just be all about how you make *him* feel. You should never feel that you are walking on eggshells. You should be yourself without needing to perform or be "perfect." You should feel at peace with him—at home. I wrote about the importance of feeling free to express yourself without censure or judgment.

I continued to ask her some important questions . . .

Is he the kind of guy who is flexible or controlling? Does he respect your requests and boundaries, or does he blow past them? Does he respect and enjoy your friends and family, or does he act jealous? Does he respect your opinions and feelings, or does he make you question reality or tell you that you're too sensitive or you're overreacting? Is he possessive of your time and who you're with, or is he respectful? Does he let you be yourself or does he try to change you? Does he take accountability for his actions and change when he messes up? Does he practice patience, or does he have issues with anger? Does he think more of himself than others, or is he truly present in moments and not emotionally absent? Are you both working on improving yourselves?

These are things I never thought about. When I was younger, I never realized how important emotional accountability was—that each should apologize—and change actions when hurtful. I didn't realize that both of us should be working on our own issues, not blaming the other for moods or problems. It's important that you feel you both are building in the same direction with similar goals. It's most important that the relationship is not one-sided. Both should invest, value, and work toward building your relationship.

I know this is heavy, but it's important to think about. You need to be aware of red flags. The person you choose as your partner will indelibly make their mark on your life, and you want it to add to who you are, complement you, build you, not tear you down or destroy you piece by piece. Your relationship should be a safe place. Please be vigilant. Assess character. Don't look through rose-colored glasses. Look at the life, not just the words, and promises . . .

I paused writing. I realized how little I had understood as a young adult. How was this young woman supposed to fathom all this? It's mind-blowing all that should be understood to find a healthy, lifelong partner. Now I realized that a healthy man and woman choose to lovingly respect their partner—no exceptions. Even in arguments, a healthy couple fights fair—they choose to civilly disagree, without explosive or rejecting behavior, no manipulation or unsafe behavior. I hadn't realized that many unhealthy partners' behaviors may appear flattering at first but often signal control or emotional insecurity.

I had known so little of boundaries. But a good partner respects your no the first time without trying to manipulate you or getting angry.

Love-bombing is also huge in a toxic relationship. When a guy says things like "You are my soulmate" or "I've never felt this way before" so quickly after beginning dating, it's a sign.

When you barely know the guy, but you feel emotionally overwhelmed, swept off your feet, or pressured to reciprocate deep feelings, that's also a sign.

When he showers you with compliments and words of love that soon turn to criticism or passive-aggressive comments, that's also a red flag.

All these thoughts swirled, there was so much I hadn't known or had unintentionally overlooked. My head hurt thinking of how foolish I had been, so naive and too trusting.

And why is it that controlling men target empaths—sweet, kind women who love to serve and give? It seemed the more gracious and loving one is, the more she is targeted.

I continued to write, closing my letter . . .

You deserve a relationship where you feel safe, are respected and valued. Please trust your gut when something feels off and never apologize for protecting your well-being. Don't be afraid to stand up for what you know is right. And in the end, you will be thankful. You are much stronger than you even know. I know my letter is most unusual, and I have never done this before, but I could not walk away saying nothing.

I wish you a happy, loving, and peaceful life with a partner who cherishes and loves you more than anything in the world.

From,

A Caring Stranger

It felt surreal penning this letter to a stranger. But I knew it was the right thing to do. Discreetly, I ripped the pages from my journal, folding them in half, and half again. Observing cautiously, I waited until the man stood and headed toward the restroom. And I knew this might be my only moment to interact with the young woman.

Gathering my journal and now-cold latte, I clutched the letter nervously in my hand, fingers tightening around the edges as if it were both a lifeline and a weight. My eyes fluttered shut, a heartbeat of hesitation, the world narrowing to the rhythm of my pulse. Then, drawing in a deep, steadying breath, I released it, and with renewed determination, I opened my eyes, squared my shoulders, turned, and spoke.

"Excuse me . . ." I softly said as I walked the few feet to the young woman's table.

"I am so sorry to interrupt, but . . . here, this is for you." I handed her the letter, slipping it into her fingers.

Her hands froze around the pages, delicate fingers trembling slightly as she turned it over. Her eyes, wide and bright, flicked up to mine, a mix of curiosity and caution shining in their warmth. "For me?" she whispered, her voice soft, hesitant.

"I know this seems most unusual, but please read this later, when you are alone. It's very important. It's what I wished someone had told me. I wish you the best," I continued, smiling softly, then turned and walked toward the front door.

Casting a glance behind me, I saw her bewildered expression as she met my eyes. Then she lowered her gaze to the letter, interest flooding her eyes. Relief softened her features, like she couldn't believe someone was thinking of her in that way. She folded her fingers over the letter protectively and slipped it into her pocket.

Good, I thought. *She'll read it.* And I hoped she'd reflect deeply upon what I shared, letting it impact her life.

Heading home, I found myself mentally tracing the path of the last decade. My life had been a slow breaking—beginning with confusion and self-doubt, followed by isolation and disconnect, loss of identity, emotional collapse, and finally, I became a shell of who I was authentically.

I realized that women like me—who lived through this kind of life—may survive but don't truly live. We become invisible. Our worth diminishes. We may carry shame or believe the lies that we are to blame. Physically we are present, but emotionally we are faded. This woman who once was—her laughter, her light, her fire—is buried.

This progression doesn't happen all at once. It is a slow unraveling, yet even in the deepest collapse, there is a flicker of her somewhere—waiting for rescue or the courage to escape. This was me for too long.

What a battle it was to be free, to find the courage to stand up against tyranny, to fight for freedom and pick up the pieces of my life amid the wreckage and begin again—building one piece at a time. This rebuilding takes years, and the results may look much different than the original—but maybe, it could be better.

Later that night, I crept quietly into Rose's bedroom, each step muffled against the carpet. I saw my youngest curled asleep under the covers, her golden curls spilled across the pillow, cheeks flushed with dreaming, lashes resting like dark whispers against her skin. I lowered myself onto the edge of the bed, letting my hand hover for a moment before gently brushing a stray curl from her forehead. Carefully, I nestled beside her, making sure not to disturb her slumber. The night light bathed the room in a soft, warm glow, casting a halo over Rose's peaceful face.

Pressing a soft kiss against her hair, I whispered a silent prayer—thankful for the peace that now filled our lives. The healing, the growth, the blossoming each girl had done in the last couple years was nothing short of a miracle. Their resilience—remarkable. Gratitude swelled in my heart knowing my daughters now knew the safety and peace they deserved. I pressed one more gentle kiss on her soft hair before rising quietly.

I drifted to Mia and Ivy's rooms, pausing at each bed. Leaning close, I brushed their foreheads with a soft kiss and whispered prayers of gratitude. Their youthful faces were relaxed in sleep, hair fanned out across the pillows, chests rising and falling in a steady, peaceful rhythm. The fierce love and protection I felt for each of my daughters swelled in my heart, imprinting a memory of love that filled my heart.

Chapter Nineteen

The Beast Uncaged

In so many ways, I wanted to make Lucas suffer for his mistreatment—for the lies, the hurt and the betrayals. He continued to revel in his power to catch the eye of any woman, and I couldn't deny the sharp sting of brazen betrayal. I tried to shut off my heart, knowing that if I didn't, I would be swept away in the tsunami of mounting waves of rage.

I tried not to care and went about my days on autopilot.

His moods would fluctuate with terrifying speed, like I was living under a storm cloud ready to crack open at any moment. I jumped at every sharp noise: keys dropped on the counter, a dish clunking loudly in the sink, a sudden slam of a door, a cupboard firmly shut, a voice rising. My muscles stayed braced. Ready. My nerves tightened, prepared for the threat of the impending eruption. And it wasn't just the loud noises—it was the unpredictability, the constant sense of threat. He didn't even need to raise his voice; the probability of it was enough to keep me frozen, on edge, under my own skin. Instinct screamed at me to fix his mood, jump to serve him.

But I refused.

I focused on survival and finding a way to leave, a way for us to escape.

I was done being his maid. If he wanted to act like a child, he could do it alone.

I had forgotten what peace felt like. One moment I could be sitting quietly and the next he would tower over me, his voice erupting like a storm, his face inches from mine, the air thick with anger. Or cruel jabs and insults would be flung at me, said to wound. He didn't even have to touch me to break me. His rage hit harder than any blow. No hands. No bruises. Just a sudden crushing force, like standing in the path of a violent storm, knocking me to my knees. It shattered something inside me every time. Even without a hand raised against me, his words were weapons, fired relentlessly. His anger was a wrecking ball, swinging without warning, as my soul absorbed the blows. His fury was a violent riptide, dragging me under.

As my self eroded and my confidence melted away, somehow, I kept surviving in a space between his explosions. But then, a fragile, unsteady moment opened—a small crack of light appeared, as his footsteps retreated down the driveway. An engine roared to life, then faded. The house went still. Silence . . . real silence. Not the tight, waiting silence that held its breath for anger. But stillness. A gap. A window. That's when instinct snapped into movement.

Go. Now. Run.

Before I could refuse, I was already moving to grab this opportunity. Fighting back nausea, I bolted up the stairs two at a time, my heart hammering against my ribs. I checked the girls—still asleep, peaceful, unaware. *Keep them safe, keep them sleeping.*

My hands shook violently as I grabbed bags, flung open drawers, clothes, underwear, random toys, their favorite teddy bear, mismatched socks, a pair of shoes —nothing made sense, I couldn't think—I packed whatever I touched. I packed like I was drowning and every bag was a lifeline. I didn't have time to think.

All I could pray was that for just one moment, we would be invisible. And gone before the next storm hit. The girls were deep in slumber, their peaceful sleep a stark contrast to the chaos churning inside me.

The plan replayed in my head: *Get the bags in the car. Come back. Gather the girls. Ten minutes. Ten minutes and we'll be free.* I could taste the freedom.

Heaving the bags into my arms, I struggled under the weight as I dragged them out to the car. I couldn't live like this anymore. I needed to breathe. I knew if I stayed, my spirit would wither and die. As I shoved the bags into the trunk, desperation fueled me.

The sharp crunch of tires on the gravel.

My stomach dropped like a stone.

The slam of his door. Footsteps—rapid, deliberate—pounded from behind. I didn't even need to hear his voice; my body already knew before he spoke: There is no escape.

A wave of panic hit like icy water. I felt on the verge of vomiting, helpless and small, wishing I had been just five minutes faster. My pulse pounded in time to his footsteps, closing in, relentless.

"What the hell do you think you're doing?" His words pierced my soul, cutting through me like a blade.

There was no denying what I was trying to do. I thought he would be gone longer. My jaw trembled. I didn't know what to do or say.

I could see the bloodshot veins in his eyes and the pulse hammering in his throat. "If you think you can take my kids, you are dead wrong. You can leave, but my kids will never leave with you. I will strip you of everything, until you have no one and nothing. I will make sure no one believes you. I will see you homeless and on the street. You want to test me? Go ahead. Try me. Try me!" Hot spittle struck my face. He looked like a man possessed, his eyes wild in unhinged rage, and I knew it would take almost nothing for him to cross the line into something unspeakable.

Terror rooted me in place.

"You will never take my kids, do you understand?" His voice rose, harsh yet controlled as he shoved me hard against the car, the handle cutting into my back. He leaned in close, his voice dripping with menace. "I will destroy you."

He held me there for what felt like an eternity, his grip unyielding, like iron. His steely gaze bored into mine, cold and merciless, locking me in place. With one final shove for emphasis, he released me and turned away, certain of his power, certain he had the upper hand.

Broken, I crumbled to the ground as the gravel dug into my bare skin.

There was no way out.

A sharp, desperate cry tore from me, primal, steeped in agony. It carried the weight of my helplessness, the depth of pain. My nails dug painfully into my tender palms, sharp enough to draw blood. Dread hollowed my chest as my only option loomed before me—walking back into that house. Back in his grip. Back in my prison.

With each step, I felt my dignity slip away, leaving me worthless, stripped bare. Every piece of me splintered. In one silent motion, I turned the knob. The door creaked open, and I stepped across the threshold, each movement slow, deliberate, as though my body itself resisted, into what would be my prison with no way of escape.

Inside, the air hung heavy, thick with his shadow. I pressed my back against the rough wood, my breath ragged, summoning whatever courage I could muster—for the girls. For their safety. For the fragile net I alone could hold beneath them. Their last and only protection.

Walking into the kitchen, I dropped onto a stool, collapsing my head deep into my arms. My heart hammered wildly, refusing to steady, and hot tears slipped down my cheeks, falling onto the cool countertop and pooling in the small space between my folded arms.

"Make yourself useful and make breakfast," Lucas barked behind me.

I jumped at the sound.

"Move." His demand cut through the air like steel. His power and cruel intimidation evident.

I tried to avoid looking at him as tears blurred my vision. Slowly, I stood, determination igniting every fiber of my being. *I will do whatever it takes to keep my girls safe. The very second we can, we will escape.*

Turning away, I blinked hard, willing my eyes stop the rising tears and moved to the cupboard, scanning for something easy to make.

Pancakes. *I can do that.* I clung to that thought like a lifeline.

My hand reached out, trembling, closing around the box mix as the colors on the box swam through my tear-blurred vision. I didn't dare wipe them away. I couldn't let him see me cry. Tears were proof that he could break me at will.

Keeping my back to him, I set a pan on the flame, trying to steady my breath as panic clawed up my throat. My hands shook violently as I began collecting the ingredients.

I grabbed a large bowl. Flour mixture. Eggs. Water. One by one, I dumped them into the bowl, each movement robotic. My hands shook, my resolve was unwavering.

Tears spilled unbidden, hot and relentless, dripping onto my lips, down my chin, and into the batter. I couldn't stop them. I wasn't sure I could stop anything anymore. After what felt like forever, I turned to the stove. Fighting to swallow my silent sobs, I dragged a towel across my face—hiding the evidence, trying desperately to erase every trace of the truth he must never see.

I finished stacking the pancakes onto a platter just as the creak of the stairs announced the girls were coming down. "Good morning, ladies!" The smile I plastered onto my blotchy, red face felt fragile, like it might crack apart. "Who's hungry for some yummy chocolate chip pancakes?" I asked, my voice bright and sugary—so far from the heaviness crushing my chest it felt like a lie spoken by someone else.

"Me, I am!" Mia answered quickly.

"Me too!" Ivy chimed in. "Rose is up. I could hear her. I bet she wants some too."

"Thank you, honey. You two come sit and eat. It's all ready, and I'll go get Rose and bring her down," I said.

They hopped onto their stools, eager for their towering stack of mini pancakes topped with syrup and chocolate chips.

I kissed both girls on their cheeks and headed upstairs to tend to Rose. Pausing at the bathroom first, I soaked a washcloth with cold water and pressed the cool fabric to my inflamed skin, wishing it could erase not just the redness on my face but the anger and ache etched into my broken soul. Hastily, I applied lotion, then went to care for Rose.

I could hear her happy chatter and childish play as I entered her room.

"Good morning, my sunshine!" I greeted, leaning over the bed to see her smiling face. Holding Rose, I breathed in the scent of lotion mixed with lavender. Soothing. Calming. So desperately needed.

After a quick change, we headed down to the sunlit kitchen filled with the girls' chatter. In no time, Rose had more syrup on her face than on her pink plastic plate, and I managed a small smile as her cuteness. I wanted to feel light, to share in the girls' joy, but it felt almost impossible. Lucas's overwhelming presence dimmed whatever happiness tried to grow.

I noticed he had helped himself to the pancakes, taking all but one as he ate alone at the dining room table. My eyes fell on the last lonely pancake left on the platter, and I didn't care—I had no appetite anyway. Turning away, I began cleaning up the breakfast mess as the girls' voices swirled around me, and a hollow ache settled deeper inside my chest.

Throughout the day, I made it my purpose to avoid Lucas, doing everything I could to keep my distance. The very sight of him made my stomach churn. I detested him, feared him, and loathed him. Each time I caught sight of him, my chest tightened. I moved carefully around the house, quiet, measured, doing my best to stay occupied with the girls, trying to preserve whatever peace I could. More than anything, I longed to be free—completely, utterly free from him, and that thought of freedom became the only thing that kept me moving.

As much as he lived with a mask of pretending that he was a good and decent person before others, I lived behind a mask of pretending to my girls that I was okay. I didn't want them to see my brokenness, my fear, or my anguish. I hid it, burying it deep within me. I lived on high alert, constantly scanning for potential explosions, smoothing over every sharp edge he created to protect the girls. I protected the environment in the home with every breath, shielding the girls from his moods, masking the chaos behind forced calm. Everything revolved around him—while my needs and the girls' well-being disappeared in the shadows of survival.

I was desperate for a breath of fresh air in the form of friendship; it had been a few months since I'd had time to connect with Charlotte. She called, trying to plan a play date, and I was in desperate need.

"Yes!" I said without hesitation. "Let's meet this afternoon."

"Perfect! See you soon," she responded happily.

The girls were excited to help, eager to play with their friends. I felt a rush of determination toward our small escape. Together, we packed the stroller with toys, lunches, and toddler supplies, tucking Rose in, and set off toward our favorite spot.

Happy smiles and energetic boys greeted us. After a quick hello, the kids ran off to play, leaving me, Charlotte, and Rose, who was as happy as a clam to run about while we chatted.

"I've missed you so much!" I burst out to Charlotte.

"Oh my gosh, me too! It's been a whirlwind with these boys. If it's not one sport, it's another. I swear they never stop running. I can barely come up to catch a breath of air! I wish just one would be happy to sit and do a craft or project long enough for me to enjoy one cup of coffee!" she laughed.

"Oh, I get it." I laughed along.

"So, how has . . . *everything* been going? I've been worried about you," Charlotte asked, concern filling her voice.

"Well." I paused as the heavy weight settled over me. "Not good. At all."

"Really? What's happening?" she asked.

"It was really bad. It's not like I don't know I need to leave," I whispered, my voice trembling. "I know. Deep down, I know it's bad—worse than I ever say out loud. It's terrifying. But when I've tried to go, he stops me and threatens me. Or he says I can go, but the girls will never leave. I *cannot* leave the girls! I have to be there to protect them and take care of them. I would be the cruelest mother if I left them to stay with a father who manipulates them, intimidates them, ignores their needs, scares them, or threatens them . . . I would rather die. I just don't know how to make it happen. I tried to pack a bag for the girls for an emergency exit, and he caught me loading them in the car and exploded. He was aggressive and said I can leave, but I'll never be able to take the girls. I was scared out of my mind. His threats terrify me," I explained in desperation. "I'm afraid of what he will do if I try to leave. He doesn't bluff. He will do something crazy; I know it, I sense it. And I don't think I should ignore this warning."

"No, you are right," Charlotte affirmed, "Oh my god, this is crazy. This is unsafe. I am so sorry." Charlotte wrapped me in a huge sympathetic hug, her arms tightening around me. It felt comforting and safe. "All right, we need to make this happen." She bit her lip. "He has been aggressive with you? What about the girls?"

"I don't know. I mean . . . sometimes he shoves and pushes me, but he hasn't punched me in the face or broken one of our bones. Mostly he is intimidating, reactionary, mean, and demanding toward me. And sometimes he is rough with the girls," I explained, my mind a blur as I tried to remember specific instances, yet they seemed to get lost in a blur.

"Ya, that's not okay. You need to get a protective order. It's important," Charlotte insisted, her face lined with worry. "If he touches you aggressively—or the girls—or threatens to hurt you, go get a protective order!"

"I'm honestly afraid of what he will do *if* I go and get a protective order. I think he will explode even more," I admitted.

"You can't think that way. The protective order is to protect you *from* his rages so he doesn't flip out. And if he does, then he goes to jail. Period. You must do what you can to protect yourself and the girls. You can't be afraid to get a protective order because of how he *might* react. You must protect yourself and pursue all the legal avenues that hold him in check—before he goes too far. And you cannot allow him to act like a king; he doesn't have power over you. If that means seeking the legal system, then you need to do it!" Charlotte pressed, as she held tight to my arms. "I'm really concerned about you and the girls. There's been a lot of things that have happened that are seriously dangerous and disturbing. I know you are scared and worried, but you must step outside the box and think about what is best for you and the girls long-term. You need a safe environment. You need to be able to live authentically, not constantly in fear!"

"I know," I agreed, I wrapped arms around myself, holding tight. "This is the hardest thing I've ever done in my life. I'm constantly having to walk on eggshells to protect the girls and avoid confrontation. But holding him legally accountable scares me out of my freaking mind." I pressed my palms to my cheeks, trying to hold myself together. "I'm so afraid that he's gonna go batshit crazy. And he might, to be honest! And what am I supposed to do if he does? What *if* he retaliates and does something horrific? What am I supposed to do then?"

"I would be scared out of my mind too. You have reason to be very concerned," Charlotte affirmed. "I think it is very important to be wise. You can't brush things under the rug and ignore dangerous behavior. If you and the girls feel in danger, you must leave immediately or call the police. You can't stay when he is explosive. Come to us, you know that! You are not alone. Honestly, you should just stay with us now. Don't go back. You don't have to wait until another explosive incident happens. We can go get your belongings. Your and the girls' safety and sanity is most important. It's your choice. You are going to have to make this decision sooner or later. Things are not important; you and the girls are! We'll figure it out. You can't be manipulated and live under control and fear." Charlotte stressed, her eyes wide in worry.

I felt the warmth and sincerity emanating from Charlotte. She was a safe friend for me, and her presence made me feel at peace. I needed to be around people who helped me feel safe, where I could be myself. I truly needed to emotionally reset, to figure out who I was. I needed to stop being afraid of people's reactions or them being displeased with me and relearn how to be true to myself. To just be me.

Every time Charlotte and I hung out, I went away feeling like I could breathe more easily. Her presence helped me feel that things would be okay and I wasn't a complete mess. Somehow, being around her righted my world.

Watching as the kids played together, their laughing, joyful squeals, and exuberant behavior made my heart smile, and I soaked it all in. I could do this every day. I yearned to be in an environment that was safe. Free. I longed for peace, for myself and my girls.

I glanced at Charlotte, letting her feel the seriousness in my gaze. "I know what I have to do—but the thought of leaving, of what most likely will happen, terrifies me. I can't risk him hurting the people I love." I played with a blade of grass, twisting it nervously around my finger.

Charlotte rubbed my arm. "I understand. That's why we are here for you, any time. We can come over and help you too. You are not alone."

I almost told her, *let's do it now*. But a part of me froze and held the words hostage in my throat. I knew I may have to take her up on her offer. I wasn't sure I could do any of this on my own. I wanted to stay—right here, in this small pocket of comfort—forever. And never go home. But the sun was already sinking; shadows stretched long as they chased away the last of the warmth. The evening chill had settled in by the time we packed up and hugged tightly, holding each other extra-long—an unspoken promise, a quiet ache, and a reminder that sometimes strength comes from the arms willing to hold you up. Then, with her warmth still lingering in my chest, I gathered three tired girls and herded them home along the short walk home.

Entering the house, the heaviness hit me immediately—the atmosphere thick with Lucas's spirit pressing down on everything. It made me second-guess every move, every breath. I braced for a reaction to any perceived misstep. My stomach twisted into knots as I ushered the girls inside as casually as I could manage, pretending everything was normal while my nerves screamed otherwise.

"Where were you?" Lucas asked, shooting his eyes toward me.

"We had a playdate," I answered passively as I guided the girls upstairs for an early bath.

Avoidance was my answer. I forced a cheerful mood, bathed the girls, and sent them to play while I busied myself with dinner. All the while, Charlotte's words pressed heavily on my mind, replaying again and again. I resolved to live by avoidance, staying out of Lucas's way. Charlotte called it the Grey Rock Method. She explained it as a way to protect yourself when you are forced to interact with an abusive person. The purpose is to make yourself as emotionally unresponsive and boring as possible—as boring as a simple grey rock. Only respond with short factual answers, keeping calm, neutral expressions, purposing not to justify yourself or correct them. Stay emotionally detached. She explained it's not about fixing the other person—it's about protecting yourself.

Heeding her advice, I poured all my energy and love into the girls and tiptoed through each day with quiet caution. The house hung heavy with unspoken tension, yet I clung to small pockets of peace I could find with the girls. And then, almost without notice, the season shifted—summer's heat gave way to crisp mornings and the gentle, quiet joy of fall.

Fall was once again settling with chilly mornings and golden, warm afternoons.

I loved being outdoors with the girls. It was my escape. Hearing their innocent laughter and youthful exuberance brought a sense of peace amid the chaos. Afternoon walks brought us armfuls of riotous colorful leaves, each one brighter than the last. We chatted about new project ideas, sang silly songs, and smelled a nearby bonfire drifting over us in the wind. The fragrance of burning wood, drying leaves, and crisp autumn air seemed to awaken my inner self, even in my weariness.

Back home, we carried our treasures into the sundrenched backyard, settling in for one more hour of golden play. Brilliant red leaves, a stack of construction paper, and a jumble of crayons soon covered the table. I loved these moments: art projects with the girls, laughter spilling over as we made memories I prayed would last forever.

"Let's make leaf trees and turkeys!" Ivy chimed in, as she began selecting her favorite leaves.

"I want to trace my hands!" Mia replied, eyes lit with excitement.

"Okay, girls, we can do this together, I'll help you," I replied patiently. "Let's show Rose how we can make fun pictures with the leaves, crayons, and our fingers!"

Together we drew, laughed, and created a slew of silly, crazy fall pictures. Some of the turkeys resembled chubby elephants and scrawny dogs, yet I loved seeing their lively expressions and carefully concentrated faces as they worked to create their masterpieces.

After a happy afternoon, we settled into our evening routine. As evening wore on, I noticed Mia began to cough, her runny nose now constant. I rested my hand against her flushed forehead, the heat seeping through my palm.

"Baby, you are so hot!" I asked, concerned. "How do you feel?"

"Not good, Mommy." She looked at me with sad eyes. "My throat hurts a lot."

Her little face looked mournful.

"Baby, I'm so sorry, let me get you medicine," I responded, kissing her hot forehead.

Searching through the medicine box, I found a bottle half full of liquid Tylenol.

"That will do for now," I reasoned and measured the amount into the measuring cup. "Take this, honey, I'll make you some tea," I instructed, as I settled her on the couch.

"Okay, Mommy." She rested her head against the fluffy cream pillows. Her flushed-red cheeks contrasted sharply against the pale pillows, the burning flush evident on her pale skin as beads of sweat began to glisten on her brow. Rinsing a cloth in cold water, I pressed it against her forehead, hoping it would help bring down her fever. It always worried me when the girls became sick. Mia's eyes fluttered closed in exhaustion, her eyelids heavy with fever. Draping the thin beige throw across her little body, I tucked her in as comfortably as possible, knowing this was going to be a long night.

Days slipped into a week, and I was still nursing a sick Mia. Her fever lingered, her little body heavy with congestion, her face pale, and her energy nearly gone. She picked at her food, appetite fading with each passing day, and my worry grew heavier with every hour she remained the same. A week of missed school only deepened my anxiety. Finally, I called the pediatrician. She needed more than rest and fever medicine.

Bronchitis was the diagnosis—antibiotics and strong congestion medicine were what was needed. Sickening dread filled my stomach as I thought of the cost of it all. With three girls in tow, I headed straight for the Target pharmacy, determined to make this trip as short as possible. I knew Mia's capacity was limited; even walking a short distance would be taxing for her. After barely ten minutes, Mia's little legs were already dragging. She tugged at me, arms lifted in a plea, and I scooped her up, balancing her weight against my hip while trying to steer the cart. As we turned into the cold and allergy aisle, the cart jolted as it bumped into a man standing there, scanning the shelves.

"Oh my gosh, I'm so sorry!" The words tumbled out of my mouth, a rush of apology laced with embarrassment.

"It's okay, no problem . . .," he said, just as my apology spilled out. He startled as recognition hit. "Joy!"

"Sebastian! Oh my gosh, hi!" I exclaimed, recognizing him as he turned around.

"How are you?" he asked, taking in my disheveled appearance, frazzled demeanor, and panicked expression.

Setting Mia down for a moment, I replied honestly. "Mia is sick with bronchitis. We just came from the doctor—it's been a week, for sure." I ran my free hand through my hair, pushing it out of my face as I spoke.

He paused to take it all in. "Here, let me help you," he said as he offered to carry Mia in his arms.

"Oh, you don't have to . . .," I instinctively said.

"I don't mind. Would it help?" he earnestly asked, his eyes communicated compassion.

"If you are sure . . ."

"Please, I would be happy to," Sebastian said with a smile.

"Girls, this is my old friend from college, Sebastian, Mr. Jake's best friend," I said, turning to face them as they stood on either side of the grocery cart.

"Hi, girls," he greeted kindly, a broad smile on his face. "So, are you the little princess who isn't feeling so good?" he asked, crouching down to meet Mia's eyes.

"Yes," she replied.

"Can I give you a piggyback ride? Would you mind? Would that be fun? We can walk with your mom and maybe get some treats . . . you know, I've heard that ice cream is the magic medicine for bronchitis, did you know that?" he asked as a sparkle of fun lit his eyes.

"Ok . . .," she said tentatively, a small smile playing upon her lips.

"Here, let's help your momma! She looks like she could use some ice cream too, what do you think?"

The girls laughed.

"Yes, she does!" Ivy chimed in, her face lit in a smile.

"What kind should we get her—olive ice cream, ketchup ice cream, pickle ice cream . . . what kind would she like?" Sebastian asked, his voice rising with each sillier flavor.

"Pickle ice cream!" the girls chimed in together, laughing hysterically.

"Heeey! I don't want pickle ice cream! I want coffee ice cream," I argued playfully, and my heart began to lighten.

"Nope, it's pickle for you. The girls decided," Sebastian exclaimed, laughing alongside the girls as I pushed the cart next to the silly bunch. And Mia rested her tired head against Sebastian's broad back.

"Let's get this little missy her ice cream so she can rest," Sebastian offered.

After the ice creams were selected, Sebastian added a few extra treats for the girls and snuck a large tub of coffee ice cream into our cart as well, with a quick smile at me.

"You really don't have to," I countered.

"I don't even know what you are talking about," Sebastian said with a goofy grin.

I looked at Ivy as we rolled our eyes and smiled. With a cart full of snacks, ice cream, and medicines, we joined the checkout line.

"Oh my gosh, Sebastian, you didn't even get your items," I blurted aloud.

"It's fine, really. I came for pickle ice cream, but apparently, they were out," he said with a straight face. "I'll have to try another Target."

The girls broke out in giggles. "Pickle ice cream! That's so gross!"

"Heeey, it's one of my favs! Don't knock it until you try it," Sebastian insisted with a serious expression pasted on his face.

"Are you sure you don't need to get your items?" I questioned.

"Absolutely! You girls made my afternoon!" he said with genuine happiness.

"Let me get this," he offered.

"Oh, no, I can't let you." A bit of embarrassment creeped in. "I'll get the medicine at least."

"Okay," he said softly. "I'll get the treats. That's more fun anyway."

I rolled my eyes in mock annoyance as the girls stood by grinning in anticipation of their much-awaited treats.

"Ladies, say thank you to Mr. Sebastian for the treats, please," I instructed.

"Thank you, Mr. Sebastian, for the yummy treats," Ivy and Mia said in unison, then broke out into silly giggles.

"You are very welcome," Sebastian answered with a little bow. "Princesses should always have ice cream to make them smile!" And he drew a louder giggle from the girls.

"Well, we don't want to take up all your time, but thank you, so much," I earnestly replied to Sebastian. "Let's go, missy," I said, hoisting Mia into the back of the cart among the shopping bags. Rose sat happily in the front, chatting away while Ivy helped me steer from the front.

Sebastian continued to walk me to my car, kindly helping load the bags in the trunk as I buckled Rose into her car seat and the girls climbed into theirs. After Sebastian closed the trunk, he walked next to me, looking seriously into my eyes.

"Are you doing okay?" he honestly asked.

I paused, then honestly admitted, "I'm doing the best I can. That's all I can do." Tears began to fill my eyes. I tried to stop them by widening my eyes, but I didn't want to be embarrassed by the show of emotion.

"I don't want to be nosy or rude—please forgive me if it comes across that way—but why do you stay if he isn't good to you?" he asked with genuine concern. "Jake said Charlotte is really concerned. You are a good woman, Joy, and you deserve to be treated with kindness." His eyes held such sorrow as he expressed his care.

Sebastian's words cut through the chaos in my chest. For the first time in a long while, someone wasn't judging me, lecturing me, or dismissing my struggle. His honesty and concern stirred something fragile inside me—a mix of relief, sadness, a sharing of the burden and a spark of hope I hadn't felt in a while.

"I honestly don't know if I can do this anymore," I blurted out, my voice barely above a whisper. "I've tried to hold everything together for the girls, hoping he'd change, hoping it could be different—but it's exhausting. I want the girls to have their father, I'm just scared, scared of what might happen if I leave, scared of failing the girls, and scared of making the wrong choice. Yet a part of me continues to hope. And I know it's probably stupid."

I wanted to believe that love could fix the cracks, that the family we built could survive. I told myself it was wrong to divide a family and that leaving would hurt the girls more than staying. That fear constantly plagued me, the instability of not knowing what would happen hovered, and the fear of failing my children was constantly on my mind. And yet, somewhere deep down, a small voice whispered that I deserved better—I didn't have to sacrifice being loved to be a good mom. I deserved to be loved, and the girls deserved a mother who was whole and free.

"Joy, it's not wrong to leave. You aren't dividing your family; if he is treating you wrongly, then he already is doing that. It's never too late to start over, to find a life where you and the girls are safe and treated with the respect you deserve.

That must be the most important thing—your safety, your well-being. Please, really think about that. You don't have to stay where you are being hurt." Sebastian reached out and gave my hand a gentle squeeze, then let go.

As Sebastian left, I sat in my car and thought about the words he shared, and my thoughts lingering on them as I drove home.

Was I staying too long? Or was I doing what was right to save my family?

I didn't know the answer. I guess I had begun to believe much of what Lucas had said to me over the years.

Maybe I didn't deserve to be loved.

What about not quitting when it's hard? My head hurt thinking about this.

Setting the girls up with their favorite princess movie, I let Rose play under Ivy's watchful gaze as I went to put together a quick dinner. Kissing Mia gently on her forehead, I crooned, "It's gonna be okay, babes, you'll be better soon." Her tired eyes, ever so trusting, closed in exhaustion.

By the time the girls' bedtime came, I was completely exhausted. And it was barely eight p.m., and I had noticed my own throat was beginning to feel scratchy and hoarse.

Seriously, just what I need right now.

Wishing I could fall into bed, I still had the dishes to wash by hand—the dishwasher was broken . . . again.

The front door opened with a gust of wind as Lucas entered the kitchen, shutting it loudly behind him, his face set in a scowl. I didn't have the energy to comment; I just continued washing the dishes.

"What the hell did you think you were doing?" he erupted, standing intimidatingly close to me. "What gave you the right to charge thirty-five dollars without asking me? You do not touch the bank account without my permission." He pointed his finger in my face, nostrils flaring.

Taken back with the sudden onslaught, shock stole the words away from me.

I heard the loud raging voice, but his words dimmed to the background. All I was aware of was his beady eyes glaring hatred into mine, his finger jabbing at me, his nostrils flaring in rage, and the intense volume of his voice that brought me to tears.

His words came back into focus. ". . . You have no right to touch my money. I will remove you from my bank account if you spend even one dollar without my permission. If you want to spend money, get a real job!"

I forced myself to breathe. "Mia is really sick," I said slowly, my voice unsteady. "I had to take her to the doctor. She has bronchitis and isn't getting better. They prescribed antibiotics, and we needed to get congestion medicine too." I hoped the explanation would register as common sense, that maybe he would feel the paternal concern for our child.

Instead, his eyes burned into me with a chilling intensity as he stepped closer, his nose almost touching mine, and he spoke in a guttural, steel-edged voice, "Did you ask me?"

"No, I am buying medicine—something Mia needed." I said, feeling like a child having to defend their actions.

"Did. You. Ask. Me," he repeated with low intensity. "You will respect what is mine. Do not touch my money. You ask permission, do you understand?" His voice rising in intensity, he drew his fist back, and I cowered as he slammed it onto the counter next to me.

As I fell back into the edge of the counter, Ivy wrapped her arms tightly around me.

"Don't hurt my mommy!" she wailed as she buried her face into my stomach, tears streamed down her face. A look of terror plastered on her delicate features.

I held her tightly in my arms as Ivy turned and faced Lucas, now between us. The back of her body pressed into mine, hands gripping the sides of my shirt tightly. Lifting her face, she boldly stared her father in the eye. "Leave my mommy alone. You are mean. I don't like you." She spoke with quavering authority.

Lucas looked down at Mia with a cold stare, then looked back to my eyes. Ignoring Mia's presence, he demanded with a cold finality, "Tell her to go upstairs, handle it now."

I didn't tell her to leave, and my feet stayed frozen to the floor.

Narrowing his eyes in an icy glare, he demanded, "Go to your room."

"No," she answered with a challenge, and I felt her body tremble as she pressed harder into me.

"Go to your room right now!" his voice boomed louder. "You are being disrespectful, and you will be punished." The force of his words made us both shake.

"I don't care! Don't hurt my mommy!" Ivy shouted back. "You're being bad. I don't have to listen to you if you are being a bad daddy." Her small fists clenched tighter in my shirt.

Lucas's face darkened with rage. He hated nothing more than when he was defied.

"Get upstairs right now or I will take every one of your toys and throw them in the trash! Do you hear me?" His words came like a growl, sharp and threatening, eyes piercing and wild.

I could see the explosion building. A rush of emotion tore through me, pride at the courage of my little girl, heartbreak that my precious child would try to protect me even against her raging father, and terror at what his fury could do.

How I wished I could make all this go away. But no matter how hard I tried, I could never change him.

But there was one thing I knew for certain: I would not let him turn his anger on my precious girl.

I quickly shifted, kneeling in front of Ivy so we were eye to eye. "Sweetheart, I love you so much. I'm okay. Please go upstairs with your sisters. Watch them for me. That would help me more than anything. I'll be okay."

Uncertainty flooded her eyes as they shifted back toward her angry father. "Are you sure, Mommy?"

"Yes, baby, go," I gently insisted, staying between them and prodding her toward the stairs.

Lucas clenched and unclenched his fists, his knuckles tightening as if ready to strike. His eyes darted wildly around the room, fury radiating from him—palpable, suffocating. Once Ivy was gone, his face twisted into a snarl of pure revulsion. "This . . . is your problem. You spoil them, and now they don't know how to show respect. I am their father, and they will obey me immediately." He turned, stalking toward the stairs. "I am going to teach her a lesson she won't forget."

Terror gripped me, and in a rush of panic and instinct, I sprinted to the staircase and threw myself in front of him, arms braced wide across the railings.

"You will leave her alone!" I demanded, my voice shaking but firm. A fierce protectiveness for my daughter surged through me, a fire I had never felt for myself. For my girls, I would stand unmovable. "If you so much as touch her, I swear to God, I will call the police and send your ass to jail."

He stared at me for what felt like endless minutes, his fists clenching and unclenching in a rhythm of barely contained violence. Then he exploded.

A torrent of venom poured from his mouth, each word meant to break me apart. "Fine—*you* raise them, I don't want any part of it. Don't come crying to me when they don't respect you. You made this mess. You will pay for this. You will get what you deserve!"

His shove came so sudden, so brutal, I flew backward onto the staircase. My spine slammed against the wooden riser with a sickening crack. White-hot pain tore through me, stealing my breath, stunning me where I fell. Tears streamed down my face as my mouth twisted in silent agony. I couldn't cry out; the girls would hear and come running. I swallowed my sobs as my shoulders convulsed and I fought to keep the sound locked inside, even as the blazing pain consumed me.

Looking down in disgust, he said, "Look what you make me do. You always bring out the worst in me." And with barely a backward glance, he turned and left, the door slamming shut behind him.

I collapsed as stifled sobs wracked my body, and I lay heaving over the steps. Silently and agonizingly, I cried until no more tears would come.

Pulling myself up, I went into my bedroom and lay carefully across the bed, wrapping my arms around my pillow and burying my face into its comfort, almost disbelieving what I had just endured. I felt an out-of-body experience.

Did this really just happen? My brain screamed no, it couldn't have– but my body demanded the truth.

I can't believe it. My brain kept replaying the moments in jagged, terrifying fragments, over and over, searching for another path, reexperiencing the trauma over and over. *Was there something else I could have done? Could I have stopped it? Defused it better?*

The answer came back hollow and final: nothing. Absolutely nothing. Nothing can force someone to be a good person. Nothing can make him change. Unless he desires it.

And he did not.

And still he lived—like a tyrant on his throne, king of the hill, dictator of his family. Judge, jury, ruler of every decision, untouchable and void of all consequences.

Nothing could fix this.

I carried the heaviness in my spirit, like a shadow that clung. I yearned to escape, yet every time I left the house, Lucas would give a thinly veiled threat, strong enough for me to fear extreme retribution.

Lucas's behavior over the following weeks showed no remorse or simple silence; it was abandonment. He fully pulled away from the girls, withholding attention out of spite, a punishment for defending wrongness.

As his neglect grew, so did our needs. The cupboards emptied faster than I could fill them, and pride was a luxury I could not afford to cling to.

Through eyes blurred with tears, I dialed Mom.

"Can you help us with grocery money again?" I begged, "I have no idea when I can pay you back."

"Of course, honey," she instantly replied. "Come by tomorrow."

Feeling the wave of panic lessening, a thin flow of oxygen began to make its way into my lungs. I responded, "Thank you, I really appreciate your help. It's so hard when I'm not sure if I can pack them lunch or give them breakfast," I admitted. The pit in my stomach lessened.

"Of course. We are here for you," Mom reassured me. "Please let us know any time you need something."

Walking up Mom and Dad's long driveway, I rehearsed again and again the excuses I could give to ask for help. *We are a little short this week . . . we had extra bills to pay . . . I miscalculated the budget . . .* I felt embarrassed to have to ask. But what other option did I have? I couldn't let my girls go hungry. At least their basic needs needed to be met.

I was thankful for my parents' love and support; even still, I didn't want to ask for help unless I was in a desperate situation. And I couldn't fully share the reason why. I couldn't say, "Lucas cut us off, he controls all the money and won't allow me to buy sufficient groceries." If I said that plainly, it would make him look like a completely terrible person. *But he was.*

After purchasing two full bags of groceries, I felt more at peace knowing the girls would have the food they needed. That evening as my head was deep inside the refrigerator, deep-cleaning the inside and organizing the slim contents, Lucas arrived home.

"What's for dinner?" he asked, his tone flat, as if the only thing I should be occupied with all day was what would be on his plate. I had already decided: I wasn't cooking for him. *If he feels entitled to withhold financial support for our food and needs, then why should I bend over backward to cater to him?*

I would not.

When I walked down the aisles of the grocery store, every choice was deliberate. I filled the cart with what the girls needed—cereal for breakfast, bread, deli meat and fruit for school lunches, easy snacks and simple dinners, with a few small treats to make them smile. I didn't buy big cuts of meat or heavy proteins. I couldn't afford it, and more than that, I wouldn't sacrifice our needs to make sure his every preference was met. I was done checking boxes just to keep him comfortable.

After pausing for a moment, I replied, "I am making the girls chicken nuggets and veggies." Not bothering to look in his direction, I stayed focused on my task.

"What about my dinner?" he insisted, irritation edging into his voice.

"I'm sure you can figure that out," I said lightly, trying to sound casual. "You told me this week we didn't have grocery money, so I couldn't exactly focus on that."

"Really?" He swept his arm toward the grocery bags. "And somehow you managed . . . *this*." He arched an eyebrow in mock interest. "How'd you manage *that*?"

"I had to ask my parents." I admitted, steadying my voice, "You left me no choice, you wouldn't allow me to buy what we needed, so I had to do what was necessary."

"Oh, of course," he sneered, leaning in with mock sympathy, "When times get hard, you run back to Mommy and Daddy? Don't you think it's time to cut the apron strings? Or are you so dependent on them that you can't even stand on your own as a family? Tell me—how do you expect us to function if you are running to your parents every time things get difficult for you? Act like an adult and stop letting them interfere, or I will have a conversation with them!"

I was livid—done with his rudeness, twisted logic, never taking responsibility, and his refusal to see our needs. His words made no sense, and for a moment I just stared at him, stumped by how far from reality he had drifted. Then, steadying my voice and holding back the heat boiling in my chest, I answered with controlled anger.

"If you would be serious about providing, not withholding our necessities, I wouldn't have to ask them to do *your* job."

The words landed hard. His eyes bulged.

I didn't flinch. I was finished coddling his pride.

"What did you just say to me?" he demanded. "What do *you* do to contribute to this family? Nothing! You are useless. You just sponge off me. I do everything for you. I take care of you. I shouldn't give you a cent. Well, I'm cutting you off from my bank account, let's see how you manage then!"

Panic flared inside me. How could I watch the girls and still find a way to provide for their needs if he cut me off completely? I forced myself to keep my expression still, refusing to let him see the storm inside me. I would not apologize. With trembling hands, I turned back to the refrigerator, focusing on the ordinary task of organizing the items. I shifted condiments to wipe underneath, sliding them back in neat rows as if the order in the fridge might create some small sense of order in my life.

He grew angrier the more I refused to take his bait. His words turned sharp, crueler.

"I could kick you out of my house—*my house*—and you'd be homeless. Let's see how you like that—you'd have no one, nothing. No one would ever want you." His voice dripped with venom, a twisted kind of satisfaction as he savored the threat given.

My mind spiraled. *What if he meant it? What if he forced me out? How would I care for the girls?* The utter humiliation, the helplessness—it pressed on me like a weight I couldn't shake. I was exhausted and tired of the fighting, tired of walking on eggshells, and tiptoeing around his moods. I had enough to carry.

My thoughts hardened with resolve; it was time to let him man up and take the consequences of his own decisions.

If he wanted to rage, let him.

If he wanted to threaten, let him.

I wasn't backing down. Let him try to kick me out—I was still a human being, and I had the right to be treated as an equal.

I kept ignoring him, my silence louder than anything I could have said.

I jumped at a sudden, violent slam, spinning around to see what had caused the loud crash. Lucas had grabbed my Italian decorative bowl from the center of the counter and hurled it on the floor.

Dozens of jagged pieces spun across the floor, some slamming into the baseboards, others flying under the refrigerator. His booming voice followed, filling the space, and I realized I was frozen in place—the ketchup bottle held up in the air.

"Did you hear what I said?" he screamed, eyes wild with madness. "I will take everything from you. You will have nothing—*nothing*!"

Swallowing the panic, I steadied my breath and answered as evenly as I could.

"I heard every bit of your madness, and I'm done cleaning up your messes. I am done with your crap. Grow up and act like an adult."

I held his gaze—unflinching, for a long moment before walking past him.

I didn't bend down to clean up his mess.

I didn't pick up a single shard.

Instead, I stepped over the wreckage, over the jagged pieces of pottery scattered across the floor and walked up the stairs, leaving the mess exactly where it belonged—at his feet.

My legs threatened to give out beneath me, but I forced them to move anyway, even while I trembled with the weight of terror. At any moment I half-expected him to storm after me, to lash out, or unleash whatever rage he'd been sharpening for years. But I had reached the end of what I could endure. Being accommodating hadn't worked. Nothing had worked.

They say insanity is doing the same thing over and over and expecting different results—

and I was done living in insanity.

For once, I didn't care what he called me—bitch, idiot, or crazy—all the words he used like weapons to break me down. The fear was still there, humming against my ribs, but beneath it burned something fiercer. A spark. A hardened resolve. A quiet, rising roar that said *no more*.

I was ready to push back.

I pushed into the girls' room, my hands shaking as I threw together overnight bags, randomly grabbing outfits, shirts, pants, socks, diapers, whatever my mind could grab amid my frantic rush. I wasn't packing. I was escaping. Within ten minutes, the girls were dressed and ready to go.

Calmly, I said, "Let's go, girls, we are going to spend the night at Grammy and Grampy's."

"Okay, Mommy, why?" Mia asked.

"We will talk in the car. Let's go. Now," I said, firmly. "Get your bag and follow me now." Their small eyes searched my face as if they could feel the ground shifting beneath us.

And still, I kept moving.

Lifting Rose onto my hip, I grasped Mia's hand and motioned Ivy to follow close to me. Terror crawled up my spine of what awaited me downstairs. Every nerve braced. Each step felt like dragging lead beneath my feet as my heartbeat flooding in a relentless rhythm. I moved quickly—silently—holding the girls tight, praying my own fear wouldn't spill over them.

When I reached the bottom of the stairs, there he was—rooted in place, his posture rigid, radiating threat.

"Where do you think you are going?" he demanded, his voice slicing through the air like a deadly warning, the kind of tone that made my stomach drop.

"Out," was all I could manage, the words barely more than a breath as I locked my gaze on the door, refusing to even look at him.

"I'll ask you one more time," he said, each syllable radiating an impending terror. "Where are you going with my kids?" He took another threatening step closer, slow and deliberate, the kind of step meant to intimidate—meant to remind me who he believed held all the power.

I tightened my grip on Mia's hand, pulling her closer until her shoulder pressed against my side. Ivy stepped behind me, clutching the back of my sweater with trembling fingers.

"I am going out," I repeated, my voice steadier than I felt. "And if you want to discuss it further, clean up *your* mess and think about *why* I am leaving," I said firmly.

"Come on, girls," I said, firm and low. "Let's go." I marched them straight toward the door, every step powered by something deeper than fear—something that refused to back down this time. Something that refused to bow to him anymore. Something that refused to disappear. Something that whispered, *I am done being small.*

I don't know if it was courage or simply the exhaustion of having to survive enough terror to fill a lifetime of brokenness. Maybe it was both.

"You'll be sorry," he threatened, with a voice that cut like steel.

Ignoring his threat, I walked forward—straight through the shadow of his fury, straight through the weight of every threat he ever used to keep me quiet. For once, fear wasn't steering me—resolve was.

And I didn't look back.

I yanked the door wide and hustled the girls through, shutting it behind us with a sharp, final click that felt like a line drawn in stone. Only then, with the barrier between us, did I drag in a deep breath and realize how long I'd been holding my breath—bracing for the worst—and how tight fear had coiled inside me. I rushed them to the car, buckling Rose with shaking hands as the girls climbed into the backseat. Sliding into the driver's seat, I firmly locked the doors, and the echo of that click carried the first hint of relief through my chest.

The engine roared to life, and I backed out of the driveway without a single glance behind me—because looking back meant feeling everything all at once. I was trying so hard to outrun it, to outrun the terror, the control, the hurt and pain—all that had marked every step of our lives.

Silence filled the car like a fragile canopy. The girls' eyes were wide, brimming with concern. I could almost see the many thoughts flooding their minds—confusion, fear, questions they didn't know how to voice.

I turned the radio to soft music, letting the gentle notes fill the space between us, a fragile attempt to soothe the coil of anxiety winding through the car. We rode like that, in quiet solidarity—each one alone with their swirl of thoughts and fears until we pulled onto Mom and Dad's road.

"Girls, do you know why we left?" I managed to say, my voice trembling despite my best effort to stay steady. I glanced in the rearview mirror, meeting their eyes—Mia's uncertainty and nervous fidgeting, Ivy's wide, searching gaze, and Rose's small, unsure expression. My chest felt tight, my words catching in my throat, but I continued. I had to be their anchor even when I felt like I was barely holding myself together.

"Because Daddy was being mean," Ivy answered somberly, eyes filled with unshed tears. I swallowed hard. She was the oldest, and the weight she carried was heavier than any child should bear. She had learned the unspoken responsibility to protect her sisters and keep them safe—as safe as a child can.

I wanted to wrap her in my arms, to shield her and the other two from the unnecessary pain and burden that abuse thrusts upon children. I kept my hands steady on the wheel and told myself to be strong. My chest ached with a mix of sorrow and resolve—to show them safety, even as fragile as it was.

"Yes," I said softly, my voice trembling. "It wasn't safe. It's not okay to throw things, break things, or be angry like that," I explained as simply as I could, my words steadying the girls even as my own heart raced. "We're going to stay at Grammy and Grampy's tonight. It's going to be okay."

I said the words, hoping—praying—if I said them aloud, it would be true.

As we stepped into Mom and Dad's house, it was like we were racing toward our safety, tumbling through the door in one frantic, desperate motion. It was our refuge, the place that had always held the promise of calm and protection. The girls piled around me, pressing close. The familiar warmth wrapped around us, the scent of home, freshly baked cookies, the steady ticking of the wall clock, the sharp, comforting fragrance of cinnamon and clove. Their tense bodies slowly began to loosen, shoulders unclenching, breaths easing. And in those moments, the sharp edge of fear began to fade, replaced with the quiet comfort of a space where we could finally breathe.

It felt safe—truly safe—in what felt like forever.

"Hey!" Mom said as she appeared around the corner. "What are you all doing? I'm glad you popped in!" she said as she enfolded us in a warm, lingering hug.

"Where's Dad?" I asked, as I scanned the room.

"He ran out to the store for a minute. Should we ask him to bring home some ice cream?" she asked the girls, eliciting smiles and yeses all around.

She locked eyes with me for a heartbeat, then turning to the girls said, "How about we get your bags upstairs and set up the living room for a movie . . . and ice cream sundaes?" Her knowing gaze met mine again, silently taking in everything that couldn't be spoken aloud—the fear, the exhaustion, the relief, the escape, the fragile thread we were clinging to, a sense of normalcy. And a quiet reassurance passed between us: here we could finally begin to heal.

"Yes!" the girls responded, their voices bright with relief. They followed Mom upstairs like little ducklings, their smaller feet padding softly on the stairs, their earlier tension slowly melting away. I watched them go. A small smile played on my lips as I saw their tentativeness give way, replaced by a sense of safety and love. Relaxation and the first shy peeks of joy began to surface, fragile but real.

Mom turned her head, looking down the stairs at me. "Want to make a pot of tea and we can chat?"

"Sounds good," I replied, exhaustion closed in as my emotions pressed heavily.

"Take a few minutes and try to relax. I'll get the girls settled," she offered, her eyes taking in my overwhelm.

I paused just long enough to steady myself, then headed to the kitchen to fill the water kettle. Slumping into the kitchen chair facing the open window, I looked out over the fields of green, taking in the peaceful view. I tried to exhale and not let my mind go in a million directions.

I craved peace, desperately.

Lost in my thoughts, I didn't notice Mom's returning footsteps until her warm hand settled on my shoulder. I startled at her touch, snapping back to the present.

"What's going on, honey?" she asked, her eyes soft with concern as she pulled out the chair beside me and turned to face me fully.

"Oh god, Mom, it's just so much. I can't do this anymore," I burst out. "Mom, it's like an explosion all the time now. It used to be occasionally, but now, it seems like it's almost every day. There is nothing I can do to stop his aggression or avoid his explosions. I hate to admit it, but I can't keep doing this!" Tears began to escape, and I couldn't stop the flow. "He threatened to take everything from me! And I know he will do it. He is so vengeful. So cruel." I wiped the flowing tears with handfuls of tissues.

"I can't let the girls live in the middle of all this anger and rage. I see the fear in their eyes, and I know they are terrified, no matter how hard I try to shield them. I've hidden what I could, but it's impossible to hide it anymore."

Just as Dad set the groceries bags on the kitchen counter, he turned and caught sight of me—tears streaming uncontrollably down my face, shoulders shaking with the force of it. In an instant, he crossed the room and wrapped me in his arms. The moment he pulled me close, the dam inside me shattered. Sobs tore out of me unrestrained, my chest heaving as though I could not draw in enough air. My legs gave way, too weak to hold the weight any longer. Still holding me tight, Dad lowered us both to the floor, his strength anchoring me.

Mom's arms came around us, encircling us both. I clung to Dad's shirt, my fists gripping the fabric, all the while soaking it with every inch of my sorrow I had carried inside. The waves of suppressed pain hit me relentlessly, leaving me gasping, unable to stop, unable to breathe, yet somehow, finally, able to let it out.

When the torrent finally began to fade, all that remained were trembling shudders, leaving me hollow. Dad's gentle hand kept moving in soothing motions across my back—steady, patient, radiating a father's love that seeped into the broken places inside me. Mom's comfort and understanding lent the strength I needed to breathe as she tenderly brushed tear-soaked strands of hair from my face, tucking them softly behind my ear with the tenderness only a mother could give. And Dad was the rock we desperately needed and had come to rely on. And it sorrowed me that the girls would never know a tender father's love.

"Honey, please come home. We love you, you don't have to carry this alone." Mom's voice trembled with both urgency and tenderness. "Let us be your safe place. I know it feels embarrassing, even humiliating, when a marriage doesn't turn out the way you desire, but it's not your fault. None of this makes you less worthy of love or respect. You don't have to stay trapped in a place of unkindness or the pain. It's not weakness to walk away—it's strength. Please, honey, it's okay to come home. We are here, waiting, so ready to help you and the girls," she shared, looking deeply into my eyes.

I knew I needed to let them help me, but it was humiliating to admit that my marriage was a failure. I alone felt like a failure. After several long, trembling moments, we slowly stood. I grabbed a handful of paper towels, dabbing at the clear trails of tears on my face, trying to regain a fragment of composure. After a few steadying breaths, the three of us walked into the living room. There, the girls were nestled together on the couch, fast asleep after watching *101 Dalmatians*, their arms intertwined in a protective little circle. My chest ached with both relief and gratitude. They were still little, young enough to heal quickly, small enough for love and safety to begin knitting the pieces back together.

"Well," Dad began, his voice carrying relief and determination, "Your mom and I are here to help you with everything." He leaned forward, his fix-it-all tone softened by worry. "We've been so concerned. You need to move in with us. We'll help you pack, whatever it takes."

My throat tightened as his words sank in. "I appreciate it, Dad. Very much. I don't see another way. I can't do this without you both. Thank you." I squeezed his plaid-covered shoulder in gratitude.

"That's good. Let's get these sleeping girls to bed. I'll help you carry them," Dad kindly offered.

After settling the girls in bed, tucking extra blankets snugly around them, I slipped away for a much-needed shower—desperate to wash away my stress. As the hot water cascaded over my cool skin, a long sigh escaped my lips, and my tense muscles slowly began to release. For once, I willed my mind to stop spinning through the endless what-ifs and looming possibilities. I chose to allow myself this moment of peace and to enjoy the luxury of a calm atmosphere.

The days at my parents' house unfolded in a rhythm both soothing and strange. For the first time in so long, I allowed myself to exhale. The girls adjusted quickly, their laughter filling the rooms as they trailed after Grammy and Grampy, planting flowers after school, baking cookies on the weekend, and playing card games each evening—soaking in the joy of being doted on without tension or raised voices. Each evening, I felt some of the heaviness ease from my chest, the sharp edges of panic dulling a bit as I settled into the steady love and support.

Still in the quiet moments, my thoughts wandered to Lucas—his face, his voice, the gnawing ache of what could have been. But no matter how deep the pull of memory, I reminded myself again and again: I was done. I would not go back.

By a few weeks' end, relief had begun to mingle with resolve. I was breathing without fear, not bracing for the next blow. Charlotte had been a pillar of strength, lending her ear for hours while I worked through my feelings, struggles and fears.

I felt lighter, more myself, and I caught myself laughing—at the girls' silly antics, at a funny movie—without inner angst. Yet I still couldn't remember what *I* felt like—*who I was*.

Now a new weight settled in—what came next. The following week loomed before me with the daunting task of going back to my house and gathering every piece of my life from the house I had called home. It felt like an ending and a beginning—painful and liberating, all at once. But I knew I did not have to face this alone.

And so, the plan was set. Mom would stay with the girls while I returned to the house, boxes in hand, to begin the painful process of packing our lives away. I knew I could accomplish much while Lucas was at work, and part of me needed to do this first day alone—the part that required quiet strength, the part that had to face goodbye.

I knew every drawer I planned to open and every picture I took down from the wall would be like peeling away pieces of a life I had once believed in.

It would be gut-wrenching, packing away one's entire life. These weren't just things; they were fragments of a dream—moments etched in time—being carefully folded and sealed into cardboard. These square containers with no memory, no heartbeat, and no feeling—would be holding our entire world.

My books, the girls' toys, photographs of memories, pieces of a home that once carried dreams—all would be inaccessible—packed away, out of sight. It felt cruel, insulting, to reduce our world into cardboard boxes, to be stacked in a garage and left to sit in the shadows for God knows how long.

I gripped the steering wheel tighter as I drove toward my street and thought of the momentous and heartbreaking task ahead of me. *When I remove each item, will the walls mock me, or whisper echoes of what will never be?*

Chapter Twenty

Winter 2017,
Present Day

Many wonder why women wait so long to leave. Why do we return time after time to the grip of death? Why do we not see what is clearly in front of us? Are our minds so programmed that we cannot think for ourselves? Must we run every thought through the gamut of what he will think, say, or do? Why do we think we must obey? Conform? Or change to appease a monster?

As I sat in a circle of broken women, women trying to heal, trying to find themselves again, others like me—precious, sweet, wonderful humans who lived through trauma and found the courage to leave—these were the questions circulating.

In this therapy group we listened to each other and agreed that reality is not so simple, it is much more complicated; our minds do become programmed, rewired, reshaped by constant control until we no longer hear our own voice. Conformity becomes our second nature, like breathing, until we forget what freedom feels like.

Fear becomes our leash.

Shame our chain.

And obedience the cage we live in.

Each tear shed, every story that was spoken aloud was a mirror reflecting my own. We all carried the same ache—the fear of leaving, the guilt to return, the hope that one day he might change and the quiet, crushing truth that he never would.

It is not weakness that keeps us in an abusive relationship—though the world might think so—it is survival. It's a distorted kind of strength we're conditioned to believe we need—so we adapt, we shrink ourselves, we endure, and we mold into shapes we hope might stop the rage—yet monsters are never satisfied.

And when we finally leave, when the fog begins to lift, questions flood in, sharp enough to wound but also necessary enough to heal.

As each woman shared their journey and struggles, one heartbreaking truth that echoed from many was a hurt that paralleled the abuse, it cut almost as deep as the abuse itself. It was the wounds left by others, the doubts and judgments, the careless questions, the cool glances and thoughtless comments. It was the cold shoulders and silent rejections and friendships lost. It was those who believed the hurtful words that there are "always two sides to every story," which twists the truth to force the victim to accept blame for causing a portion of the abuse. Many say how wrong it is to break a family apart, yet the truth is, better a broken family (broken by the abuser's actions) than being broken in a family.

People have no idea. Many have never lived within walls where every action is monitored, where you have no choices, where every spoken thought must be measured against the threat of what he might say, or do, or take away. Many cannot fathom the devastation of abuse. What does it cost to silence your own voice just to keep the peace–to bend, shrink and twist yourself into something unrecognizable simply to survive?

It is a slow kind of heartbreak, the kind that hollows you out from the inside.

That is not marriage.

That is not reciprocity.

That is not two individuals free to live and move within the fullness of themselves.

It is the quiet destruction of a soul forced to live small—silent—numb.

One woman shared through her tears, "You can't reach out to your friends because they don't believe *you* could be living in abuse. "Where are the bruises? He would never do that. He's a nice guy, that's too hard to believe," they say.

But the bruises aren't always visible. Sometimes you carry them on your heart.

Living under abuse—oppression—is living as a prisoner.

It is stripping—of dignity, of safety, and of hope. Of you.

It is a shaming, until you begin to believe you deserve the cruelty. It is the slow breaking of individuality, until you no longer know where *he* ends and *you* begin.

Your autonomy is shattered.

When people ask why did we stay or why did we go back, I want to scream, "Because escaping takes a miracle. A miracle for each one of us, every single one of us sitting on these unpadded chairs, every single woman who dared to step outside those chains and say, *No more*."

Here we sit, in this circle of chairs, each of us cradling a cup of lukewarm coffee, lending an ear to each other's grief and struggle. We speak the questions that haunt us and fears that hold us prisoner. Then slowly, over time–in this shared space, something remarkable began to happen.

We gave each other hope.

We reminded each other that we are allowed to dream, allowed to pursue our lives free from fear. We encouraged strength where doubt had lived for too long. We whispered truths that our hearts had been silenced to hear: *Your future can be better. You are worth it. You are allowed to leave the pain behind. You can heal.*

We were asked to go around the room and share, if you could give advice to your younger self, what would you tell her? What would you say to spare her the pain of this journey? And what are some of the greatest struggles, so others can understand?

One woman shared, in a small, timid voice, "I would tell my younger self, Believe in yourself, know how worthy you are of being loved and respected. Know your worth."

Another courageously spoke up, "It's not just important to know that you need to leave a harmful situation, we need to learn—every young person needs to learn—that we all have incredible value, we have purposeful lives, and we should never be okay with someone treating us in less than a respectful way. And if you're in a relationship where your partner starts diminishing your value or treating you disrespectfully, you need to have the courage to step out of that relationship. Don't stay in a relationship that doesn't have mutual honor, respect, and love. Love that controls-isn't love, that's coercion. Forced submission isn't submission—it's subjugation."

There were many "yeses" and nods to that statement.

Hearing these truths made me realize so much. It's so important to not allow someone to force you to change. Choose someone who wants you to shine. Choose someone who encourages you to be your best and believes in you. Choose someone who sees your value. Because love should never take away your freedom—it should protect it.

Another brave woman added, "The most important thing I wish I knew when I was young is that your boundaries matter. Love isn't controlling, and respect isn't optional. If someone doesn't honor you and pushes past your no, that is them showing you who they really are. Believe it. They are not demonstrating good character.

If someone tries to dictate your choices, makes you feel guilty for being yourself, or tries to dim your voice, that's not love. That's control. If someone mocks you, belittles you, or dismisses your feelings, that's not love-that's a lack of respect, and it will get worse. If you feel you must walk on eggshells just so they don't react, that's not love. That is control, fear, and manipulation. Love makes you feel safe and supported. Love lets you be free to express your authentic self. Love encourages you to blossom and grow. Love is your safe haven."

The last woman who spoke shared hard truths: "What many don't understand about living through years of abuse is that it's not just the abuse itself that the victim must come to understand, grieve, and heal from. It's also coming to terms with all that surrounds the abuse. We must deal with real feelings toward people who looked the other way, refusing to believe it was 'that bad'. It's also having to work through the abuser dismissing what they did to us, as if it never happened. It's working through the hurts from people who made excuses for the abuser's behavior, yet there is no excuse. It's working past the unthoughtful comments people make who believe we should easily let it go and stop dwelling on the past.

It's having to work past the crimes committed against us that will never see justice, and those who assume the victim must have done *something* to cause it to happen. It's painful, the betrayal from people who remained friends with the abuser, while the abuser has smeared our character with lies–yet no one cares to hear our story or seek out the facts. Then having to deal with isolation after escaping abuse because of the abuser's alienating lies. On top of that, we must deal with financial ruin. We have to work through the trauma and try to regulate a destroyed nervous system while also grieving the person we used to be—who is no longer.

And how do we function in a world where we don't feel safe, or we struggle to trust anyone? And what of the shame we feel for not having the courage to leave sooner or not understanding we were being abused until it progressed so terribly? And then, there are our precious children who need to heal from so much damage done to them by manipulation, lies, and abuse. Victims not only have to heal from the 'actual' abuse—we must learn how to survive after surviving. And few talk about that."

It was a long, somber silence after she finished. We sat with the truths that had been spoken—truths we wished our younger selves had understood, instead of ignoring them out of naivety from young love or believing it couldn't be true. It would have spared much heartache, if only we had known—or listened. The effects surrounding abuse ripple through everything it touches. Abuse is like a spider's web: it entangles, you can't unravel it without it touching something else. It affects all it touches, and there is never a clear, easy path out.

As the weeks turned into months, sharing in the camaraderie and therapy slowly softened the doubts and shrank the shadows as we leaned on each other. I felt hope as we lifted each other's arms when we wavered, spoke courage into trembling voices, and celebrated each small step forward. I found in the reflection of others' eyes the glimmers of freedom, fragile yet unmistakable. And with every story we shared, every hand we held, every box of tissues soaked with tears, every quiet word of encouragement given and received, I began to understand truth. Even in the aftermath of trauma, even after enduring what no one should, we could take baby steps—and one by one, they would lead us back to rediscovering ourselves.

Women gathered around us—women who had gone before, women who had summoned their courage and strength to show us the way—and in them I saw mountains of magnitude in this room, despite the simple grey walls and unpadded chairs. Here were mighty women, brave women, women willing to reach out to us, to lift each other up, to help another find their identity again. These women shared their courage for us to choose freedom and healing.

As they shared their stories, as they laid bare their journeys, their bravery became a map for us. Their voices echoed in the quiet corners of our hearts, helping us to discover our own paths, our own strength, and our own hope. And in this place, I learned healing.

After several months, I took the courage to speak my story–my journey, why I struggled and went back again and again to the very source of my suffering . . .

Chapter Twenty-One

When the Monster Says Sorry

Pushing open the front door, I was met with silence. The only sound was the furious pounding in my head, each pulse reverberating like a drumbeat echoing in the stillness.

I glanced around—the floor was shiny and clean, everything was tidy and put away, no dishes were visible in the sink. I felt I had walked into someone else's house. Lucas never cleaned up after himself, at least not well. *What's going on?* I asked myself.

I shut the front door with a soft click and moved tentatively, further into the house while boxes and tape filled my arms. I could barely peer past the mountain in my arms. As I turned the corner into the living room to unload my arms, there sat Lucas.

There he sat, slumped on the couch, as though the weight of the world had finally crushed him. His head was buried in his hands. The sight of him shook me—I hadn't expected him to be home. He was supposed to be at work; his car wasn't even in the driveway. Fear instantly gripped me, yet what I saw wasn't intimidating, it was . . . sad. He hadn't shaved, and the sharp smell of stale sweat hit me. His shirt was wrinkled and stained, as if he'd slept in it for days. He looked broken.

When he lifted his head, I caught the rawness in his eyes. Bloodshot eyes stared back at me, ringed with exhaustion, but something behind that misery flickered. Hope? Relief? For a fleeting second, it almost looked real.

"You're here!" he breathed, as if he didn't believe what he was seeing.

Seeing his vulnerability cautioned me to my core. My empathy began to stir. He looked broken—human.

"Yes," I responded suspiciously, feeling alert. This wasn't the normal Lucas.

"I didn't think you were going to come back." His voice breaking. He looked at me for a long moment, then dropped his head into his hands, shoulders shaking. In a whisper, he added, "I'm so sorry. I've been terrible to you, and you don't deserve the way I've treated you." His body trembled with the confession, the weight of his remorse almost palpable in the air between us.

I froze. I felt like I'd been dropped on another planet—gravity gone. Everything tilted sideways.

I had never seen Lucas broken. Never seen him remorseful. It was surreal.

Not believable.

The room seemed to warp around us, the edges blurring, as if my mind refused to believe what my eyes were seeing. I was silent while my brain scrambled to figure out what to say.

After several long moments, I finally spoke—my voice flat, void of emotion.

"Yes, you have been horrible to me—to us. And I am not living like that anymore. I deserve better and so do the girls. I'm going upstairs to pack, then I'm leaving. Give me space to get our things."

I turned and began walking up the stairs. My brain was jumbled with thoughts, a chaotic scramble. Everything collided at once—shock, anger, confusion, disbelief—knotting together so tightly I couldn't pull a single emotion free.

I hadn't expected *any* of this. Not from him.

I'd only taken two steps up the staircase when I felt a soft touch on my hand. Lucas had shot to his feet and followed me, closing the distance in a short stride. His fingers clamped around my hand as if he could anchor me in place.

"Please," he begged, voice cracking. "Please don't leave. I was wrong. I'll change—just don't go." He then dropped on his knees. Right on the stair steps.

I had never seen Lucas collapse on the ground before-begging. I didn't even know how to respond.

My brain said nothing. My gut offered nothing.

Just a single, sharp thought cut through the haze.

More than anything I wanted him to change, for good. I desired him to be a loving husband and father. I would do anything for that. Confusion swirled at the drastic shift in his behavior. I couldn't find a single word to say.

"Please," he continued to beg. Tears left angry streaks down his unshaven face.

"I will do anything. I don't deserve you. Please let me try one more time."

His hands fell to my ankles, clinging to them in desperation. I stood on the stairs, gripping the banister with one hand to steady myself. Three steps up, an arm full of deconstructed boxes pressed against my chest, I looked down at my husband sprawled across the lower steps—his body stretched along the staircase as he clung to my ankles, as though I were the last lifeline left for him.

A storm churned inside me. Fear prickled up my spine. Confusion swirled in my brain, pity tugging at my chest, and anger simmering just beneath the surface.

Was this real remorse—or just another act?

Part of me wanted to pull free, to break away from him. Another part ached at the desperation in his grip, at the raw sorrow in his eyes. I didn't know whether to scream, cry, or collapse beside him.

I didn't know how to handle any of this.

"Please . . . just give me one more chance," he cried, his voice breaking into messy sobs. His fingers clutched at me with frantic need. "Do you love me?"

Frozen.

My mouth went dry, my chest constricted.

What am I supposed to say?

The truth was unbearable: I didn't feel love for him anymore. His anger, his cruelty, and his endless unkindness had ground it out of me until there was nothing left but ugly dust.

And yet, he was my husband—the father of my children. Of course, I wanted our family to be whole, to be healthy and loving and flourishing.

Maybe . . . maybe if I said yes, it would ignite something in him. Maybe it would be the spark that would finally prompt him to change. But even as those thoughts flickered, guilt twisted in me.

If I said no, I was cruel. If I said yes, I was a liar.

His eyes—wet, wide, pleading—*What an odd time to want to change—when it's already too late*–begged me for an answer, searching my face like they were a lifeline. The weight of his desperation pressed down on me, heavy and unrelenting, a boulder pinned to my chest. His fingers trembled against my skin, his breath hitching, his whole body shaking with a grief so intense it felt almost violent.

The guilt hit me hard. A sharp nauseating twist in my stomach. I felt like a monster for even thinking it—for letting the thought form at all.

But the truth ached through me, clear and cold, cutting through the chaos swirling inside my head.

No, I do not love him.

And yet, before I could stop myself, I heard my own voice betray me.

"Yes."

"Okay," he wept in a mix of relief and unbelief, tears streaming down his face. "Just—just let me try, one more time. Let me make it up to you," he begged, the words shaking loose between ragged breaths and choking sobs. "I swear it'll be different, I promise."

I couldn't help but hope. More than anything, I longed for a loving, healthy family. Maybe—just maybe—this was Lucas's breakthrough.

I had wished for this miracle for so long that the hope made my chest ache, a bittersweet weight pressing down on me.

I slumped onto the steps beside him. The weight of all the years—pain, anger, and fear—crushed down at once, making it impossible to separate longing from doubt, love from exhaustion.

Were his actions genuine or just an attempt to erase his guilt and keep me from leaving? My mind raced—searching, scrambling for signs of honesty, for some truth I could hold onto.

Each thought tugged me in a different direction, leaving me raw and unsteady, like a shipwreck adrift in a storm, wreaking havoc on my heart. I didn't know if I could trust my own judgment.

I collapsed on the steps. The boxes I'd been gripping lay discarded across the floor, scattered in the chaos—I didn't even remember when they slipped from my arms. Tears dripped down my face, a silent witness to the storm inside me as Lucas begged and wept below.

I was burdened by the inhuman weight of deciding whether to keep our family together or let it shatter as Lucas's arms engulfed me.

My body instinctively stiffened, unsure of his touch. Wary. I didn't know what to do. There had been too much pain, too much history of anger and betrayal—I couldn't see a way back.

He held me anyway. His hand moved slowly across my back in a comforting rhythm, the kind of touch I'd always longed for.

My mind screamed, *Is this even sincere? Can I trust him?*

Every fiber of me wanted to recoil, to run, to protect myself from the possibility of being hurt again. Despite the fear and suspicion, I felt my body starting to loosen—not completely, but enough to notice a subtle shift. My shoulders softened. I exhaled a long sigh, releasing some of the crushing anguish I'd carried inside of me for years.

And in this fragile moment, a small flicker of something I hadn't felt for far too long—*hope*—stirred within me. But it was cautious. Unsure. Shadowed by the memory of every time I'd trusted him before . . . and been burned.

Yet I couldn't help but lean into his arms as they surrounded me. He kissed my face, my cheeks, and my hands, over and over, tears falling on my skin.

I felt my body responding to the tenderness I had craved– for so very long. Tangible love.

Love that was real—something I could give back fully, with my whole heart. The warmth I had yearned to feel again wrapped around me, and I drank in his kindness, his acceptance, the gentle tenderness that made me feel seen and safe.

I knew that if a man loved me wholly—unreservedly—I would give everything I had, every fragment of my heart without hesitation.

And amid all this inner turmoil—swirling fears and doubts —I still longed to be loved. My heart ached for it, even as caution whispered warnings. And inch by inch, I felt myself giving in to a dream I had carried for years.

Lucas leaned toward me, his movements careful and tender, as if he knew just how fragile my heart was. Softly he pressed his lips to mine. For a long moment, the years of pain seemed to fade, replaced by a delicate, fragile sense of belonging.

My body responded before my mind could question it, leaning into the warmth and reassurance of his touch. And yet fear hovered like a shadow, a quiet reminder of the heartbreak that had come before.

Lucas stood, his eyes gentle and pleading as he pulled me to my feet and led me slowly into our bedroom. His gaze never left mine, the tears he had shed still lay wet upon his cheeks.

Silently, he closed the door behind us.

Lying with our limbs intertwined, a rare sense of peace and love washed over me.

His arms wrapped tightly around me, holding me close to his chest. I could feel the steady rise and fall of his breath against my neck and the coarse bristles of his unshaved cheeks. Every fiber in me longed to believe this was his changing moment.

A small part of me trembled, remembering too vividly the years of pain and broken promises. And the fear lingered.

Could I trust this tenderness? Could I let myself fully hope? Could this heal what had been broken for so long?

I prayed he would finally see what he'd been missing and choose to become a better man—kind and caring.

"Baby, let me try again," Lucas said softly. "I have been horrible to you. You deserve so much better. You deserve to be loved. I don't deserve a wife as wonderful as you."

Tears began to spill—first a tremble, then breaking like a dam I could no longer hold together. The flood came fast, raw, unstoppable. Heartache, hopes, dreams, every shattered piece of me surged to the surface at once, spilling into the space between us. Lucas pulled me into him, his arms tightening as if he could somehow keep me from falling apart. I sank into his chest, sobs tearing through me like waves. Time blurred.

It seemed hours had passed. The storm eased, my tremors stilled, leaving behind a quiet shaking, the aftershock of a body that had held this crushing weight for far too long. I drew in a breath, thin and trembling, my chest rising and falling in slow breaths, each exhale carrying away a fraction of the anguish I had been holding inside.

For a moment, the air around me felt lighter, the world quieter, as if it paused to let me simply breathe. I clung to that fragile sense of calm, savoring it, letting it seep into my bones.

Untangling our limbs, I pushed myself upright and turned toward the window. The tall tree outside swayed, its branches softly tapping the pane in the gentle breeze.

What should I do? I whispered to myself.

More than anything, I wanted our family—one stitched together with love and tenderness, a place where we could finally be happy and safe, the kind of safety I'd been aching for my whole life.

Should I trust him? Should I take this risk?

Lucas reached over, grasping my hand with a gentleness that surprised me. He lifted it slowly, bringing each finger to his lips, kissing them one by one as though they were sacred.

"I love you," he whispered between kisses. "I'm sorry. Come home . . . please bring the girls home. Let's be a family. Let me start again."

His eyes locked onto mine—desperate, pleading, full of longing.

He tugged me back against him, his arms tightening as if trying to anchor me to the moment, to him. His touch awakened something deep inside me—a hunger I had buried for far too long. A longing to be loved by his heart, his soul, and body.

Against all the doubts—and what-ifs screaming in my mind—I let him draw me closer, wondering if surrendering to him could be the first step toward healing. I let him love me as the birds chirped outside, their delicate melody threading through the quiet room like a melody.

Dusk had settled as I pulled into my parents' driveway; the soft glow of the approaching evening washed over the flower-lined walk. I hurried up the path, heart racing, and pushed open the door, calling out, "I'm here!"

Little voices answered, bright and urgent, and small feet scampered toward me.

"Mama!" Rose exclaimed, as she threw herself into my arms, holding tight to my neck. Ivy and Mia's arms surrounded me. I pressed kisses to their soft faces again and again, treasuring their happily given hugs.

"How is everything?" Mom asked, her eyes wide with concern. "Were you able to pack a lot?"

I could only smile through the fluttering ache in my chest, as the weight of years of pain and fear continued to lift. The love of family surrounding me, the memory of Lucas's promise to love me fully, filled me with a fragile, radiant hope—hope that finally the future would be different, safe, and full of love.

"Can we talk in the other room?" I suggested, a small smile played on my lips despite myself.

Popping on a short video for the girls, Mom and I stepped out to the back patio. I sank into the wicker chair, hugging the cozy sage throw pillow to my chest, and turned to face her, my eyes bright with a shimmering hope that felt almost new.

"Mom, Lucas is . . . different. He happened to be home when I was there, and I barely recognized him. He was so broken—sobbing on the floor. I doubt he'd even taken a single shower since we left. And yet . . . he had completely cleaned the house. When has he ever done that? It was like walking into my home and seeing a stranger.

"I have never seen him like this. I think . . . maybe us leaving really impacted him—or finally broke him. Whatever it is, something was drastically different. He wasn't angry or rude. He wasn't loud or insulting. He was just . . . a pile of regret and brokenness. I have to believe . . . something has changed."

"You actually believe him?" Mom asked slowly, eyes filled with caution.

"I do," I answered, my voice steady despite the flutter in my chest. "I think he's different. I *know* he's different. I think he's finally realized that he could lose us . . . and that broke him. Otherwise, why would he be like this?"

"Joy, I beg you—please be careful," Mom warned, her hands gripping the sides of my arms, as if holding on could keep me safe. "I'm glad he wasn't rude or mean to you, but just because someone apologizes and seems contrite doesn't mean they've truly or fully changed. You must be very wise, Joy. A heartfelt apology isn't proof of a complete life change. It must be shown in the way he lives, over time—not just for a week or two."

"I think he really wants to be different." I said softly, "He's never been this sincere . . . or this broken. Mom, I understand what you're saying, I do—but you didn't see him. He was sobbing, lying on the floor, holding onto my ankles like I was his lifeline. Who does that? I can't ignore it." I reached for her hand. "I'll be careful though, I promise. And I really appreciate you and Dad so very much. You've always been there for us, and I don't know what I'd do without you."

"Of course, honey, we're always here for you," Mom said, her voice gentle but firm. "But please, I beg you, I know how desperately you want this to be true, and you *deserve* it to be—but do you understand how rare a complete life change is? If he's truly changed, it will show consistently over time. This isn't a quick fix, not the way he's been treating you and the girls. This isn't a small 'bad habit' we're talking about."

She gripped my arms tightly, eyes searching mine. "He hasn't had time to prove his change. You need to give him a few months—at least a few—to show whether his change is real. I'm glad he's shown remorse, that's good. But you need time to see if the change is genuine and not a temporary display meant to keep you. No one changes instantaneously. Please . . . wait, be cautious, and stay with us for a few months. Test it out. See if his actions are consistent with his words. You'll know—if you wait."

Dad stepped outside with us, his expression lined with worry. He had overheard our conversation, and it was clear he wasn't pleased.

"Joy, honey," he began, his voice firm but full of love, "I know you feel this is a huge step for him. And I know how badly you want your family whole again. But I have to be honest with you—he has *not* changed. No one changes their entire life instantly. Going back now . . . isn't wise."

He paused, letting the words settle. "We love you. We'll always support you and the girls, but we've seen you broken and hurting. We've been scared for you and the girls. And we don't want to see this happen again." He took both my arms in his hands, holding me steady, his eyes locking onto mine. "I'm asking you to wait. Let him prove his change over time. Give him six months. Watch how he lives his life. Don't rush back. And yes, of course, we hope he's had a change of heart. But thinking this happens instantly? You must be very careful.

"I'm not saying this to be unkind, or harsh," he continued, his voice softening, "but we love you more than anything. We know the size of your heart, how deeply loving and trusting you are. You always see the best in people, and that is one of the things we love most about you. It's what makes you so beautiful." He squeezed my hands gently.

"But it's also important to temper that with wisdom and caution. You owe it to yourself—and the girls—to protect your heart. To make sure the hope you feel right now, is matched by truth and action—that Lucas is willing to do the hard work to prove he doesn't just *want* you but loves you and the girls enough to live every day with selfless love and sacrificial kindness. That is the test." Dad held onto both of my arms as if to let the full measure of his words sink into me.

"I will be careful, I promise. I'll really think about what you said. And I appreciate your words. You didn't see him though—he was a mess, broken, sobbing . . . he has never been like this. I can't ignore it. I have hoped and prayed for so long that he would change. And I can't throw this away, after all I've gone through and waited for—it would have been for nothing. I know you are worried and concerned, and I'm thankful for that. I just have to give him one more chance," I explained. "I really believe this is the right thing to do."

"Joy . . ." Dad's voice trailed off, caught somewhere between pleading and heartbreak. I saw the struggle written across his face—the tremor in his jaw, the tension in his shoulders. Tears welled in his eyes, unspoken fear shimmered in their depth.

He didn't believe it was true.

Beside him, I could see Mom's own heartbreak, the tight set of her shoulders and the gentle catch in her voice. Her eyes, so full of love and compassion that mirrored my own. She also believed the best in people, saw the goodness where others might not, and wanted to see hope flourish. But beneath the hope was a fierce protection, a mother's fear of seeing her daughter hurt again, her longing to shield me from pain she knew could happen. "We love you tremendously," she whispered, voice trembling with love and warning. "We just . . . caution you. We don't think you should go back."

I sank into their arms, holding them tightly, feeling the full weight of their love, their worry, and their hope pressing against me. A slow tear slipped down Dad's cheek as he closed his eyes in the embrace.

It felt like a premonition, a warning etched into the very air around us.

And yet . . . I wanted this so badly. I wanted them to be wrong. I *knew* Lucas had changed, and I couldn't wait for them to see it.

Three months had passed since I had returned, and I felt our marriage was finally finding its rhythm again. Happiness settled over me like sunlight shimmering through the open windows, light and warm, carrying me back to the carefree days of our blissful youth. Lucas was thoughtful, kind, gentle with the girls, attentive to me in ways that made my heart ache with gratitude and relief. I watched the girls begin to trust him again, their laugher blooming in response to his tenderness, and it made my heart overflow. I didn't want to hinder any of that growth, so I poured myself into the family—planning meals with little touches that made ordinary moments feel magical, organizing game nights, and having weekend special outings. I didn't mind the work I took on. In my mind, Lucas didn't have to do anything except be present, be kind, and live in the moment with the girls. I was happy to carry the weight of planning, entertaining, creating, parenting, cleaning, and errands . . . all of it—as long as there weren't explosions.

I saw it as a way to prove—to show, that he had changed. I was just happy there wasn't cruelty, explosions, or obvious unkindness. I clung to every small moment of gentleness, blind to how little it really was. I didn't see them as crumbs of kindness; I only knew they were better than the storms I'd lived through. And yet . . . the truth lingered in small, quiet ways. He didn't have to shout to be unkind, he didn't have to be loud to be rude, he didn't have to be forceful to still get his own way, yet he wasn't really proving he has transformed. He left tasks undone, didn't lend a helping hand, dismissed concerns I had, and slipped in jokes at my expense. He couldn't make time to help with the girls' homework or projects, and offered to help with tasks but didn't follow through. He would often sitting back while I handled everything, letting his inaction slide beneath the surface. It twisted something small inside of me, a whisper–a warning at the edge of my mind. *What if something big happens? What if his kindness doesn't last?*

Still, each day flowed by, mostly peaceful, convincing me that perhaps he had truly changed. My spirit felt hopeful. Family evenings became celebrations of small joys—sharing meals, laughing at the girls' silliness, and building new memories.

I cherished the cuddles on the couch, the laughter spilling from the room, and the way Lucas laughed with the girls, easing into their world.

I wanted so desperately for the girls to have their father. Every smile, every laugh, every moment of connection made me believe change was possible. I knew it wouldn't be perfect, but it could be good. I knew cracks and old habits would remain. But I truly believed Lucas's heart has shifted and that he was a changed man. I was willing to overlook little things that concerned me—the subtle sarcasm, the unhelpfulness, the tiny selfish habits, still steering things according to his liking—because the big explosions still hadn't come. I was willing to look past these small signs of unhealthiness to focus on the hope of what we could become. And I wanted it so badly that my hope stretched wide, carrying all the dreams of our family being whole, full, happy, and safe with a love that could last.

My day had been slammed with appointments. I was just starting a quick dinner as Lucas came home from work and tossed his keys casually on the counter.

"Hi, honey," I greeted with a smile on my lips.

"Hey, how was your day?" Lucas leaned in, giving me a short peck on the lips.

"Good, just busy with the girls. I'm almost done with dinner, then I thought after we get the girls in bed, how about we watch the movie we were talking about? The new one I've been dying to see is finally out." I was eager to have the evening to relax, cuddle on the couch, and watch a movie together. I couldn't think of a better ending to a busy day.

"Oh, sorry, babe. I'm going out with the guys. We're going to grab dinner." He scrolled on his phone.

"Oh, I didn't know," I responded, confused. "I thought we were going to hang out." The feeling of being left out crept in. "We talked about doing something fun tonight . . ."

"Sorry, can't this time. Do something fun with the girls," he instructed.

Feeling disappointed, I just muttered, "Kay."

"Don't wait up," he threw over his shoulder after he quickly changed, then grabbed his keys and walked out the door as the scent of strong cologne lingered after him.

My jaw hung slack.

Oh, please don't let him be doing something stupid. Not again.

A pit of dread settled in my stomach. Robotically, I went through the evening with the girls, forcing a smile on my face when all I felt was impending doom.

After getting them settled in bed, I grabbed my book and snack and settled into bed, trying to relax. As the evening wore on, I checked the clock and saw it was almost 11:30, and still, Lucas was not home.

He slipped through the front door a little after one in the morning. By the time he crawled into bed I was still wide awake, waiting, staring at the ceiling, anger burning in my chest at the fact that he chose to stay out late when we had planned to spend the night together.

He pulled the covers over himself and within ten minutes was snoring as if the night had been perfectly ordinary.

What am I—invisible?

My chest tightened. A foreboding settled as I willed my body to relax enough to sleep. Morning brought no relief—only a fresh wave of frustration. I shoved back the covers and padded downstairs, purposeful—needing a cup of coffee in me to help me think. As I was pouring the steaming coffee into a mug, Lucas walked down the stairs and ran his fingers through his freshly showered hair. "Where's the coffee?"

"I only made one cup," I answered, focusing on adding sugar and cream to my brew.

"Really? You didn't think to make coffee for your husband?" he asked.

Not liking the intent of his comment, I decided to speak honestly, "Do you think I appreciate you disappearing all night even though we have three kids? And we had plans?"

He shrugged like it was obvious. "Well, you're the mom. It's not that big of a deal. It was just one night."

His casual dismissal cut through me. "Why are you being this way?" I asked, confused at the shift in his behavior. "Why aren't you being kind?"

"I am kind, I just wanted a night with the guys," he snapped back. "And it's your job anyway. I work hard all day, you're home with the girls, I deserve to go out and relax. Look, I make it pretty easy for you; you don't even have to work. I don't think going out one night is a big deal. And I don't appreciate being questioned."

My stomach dropped.

Again, he was being rude. Why couldn't he stay kind? Why did he feel he had the right to berate me? I looked at him with sadness in my heart, realizing he hadn't really changed.

"I don't know why you are being rude, but the way you are talking to me is not okay. You promised you would change, that you would be kind, loving, and respectful. *This* . . . is not that." I walked out of the kitchen, leaving Lucas alone.

Lucas trailed me into the living room. "You have the responsibility of our children. You don't have a real job. This is your job. Stop complaining—be an adult, and don't be so sensitive."

Tears filled my eyes. I felt all my hopes were crushed. My mind turned numb, trying to drown out his voice as the words came like arrows, piercing my heart. One after another they flew until my heart was once again riddled and raw.

Nothing with him was sincere. The realization came with a familiar dread of what was about to unfold.

"You need to change," Lucas lectured. "All you do is point fingers at me. You don't even look at your own flaws. I'm telling you now, if you don't work on yourself, it's going to hit you like a rude awakening. You act like you're perfect, but you're controlling, self-centered, and you always want your own way. When is the last time you haven't complained or found fault in me? Fix yourself before you start poking fingers at me. I work hard. I have a job. I carry this whole family. What do you do? Not much."

Unwanted tears streaked down my stricken face.

My heart splintered into pieces as his words struck my heart; the truth was finally sinking in.

His change was not real.

Maybe he longed for his family—but not enough to do the hard work on himself. Maybe he wanted me—but he did not love me. Maybe he craved the illusion of a happy home—but he was never willing to do what it truly took to build one.

My brain fought back, refusing to accept this defeat. It denied the unraveling before me, denied that my dream would never materialize.

This can't be, I whispered to myself. *I refuse to accept it.*

I drifted through several weeks in denial, clinging to the illusion I knew deep down was never true. But denial had an expiration date. It was a matter of time before the next explosion came.

It only took three months to prove he had not really changed. With each passing day, I was forced closer to a goodbye I never wanted to say. Goodbye to the hope of happy family holidays—laughter around the table with a mom and a dad. Goodbye to family fun, to special evenings shared, to the happy memories I wanted my girls to have with their father. Goodbye to everything I once believed and hoped our family could be.

My heart ached as it answered with truth.

I pushed through the weeks on auto pilot, carrying the grief of an ideal I had been willing to sacrifice almost everything for.

One evening, Ivy and Mia sat in the living room playing Candy Land. Ivy had been quiet all day, more than her usual contemplative self. And Mia had been irritable and easily frustrated, dissolving into tears every time something went wrong. Their opposite moods had collided all day, and I spent the whole day caught in the middle, trying to find balance.

Ivy instructed Mia, "No you can't do that. That's not how you play the game."

"Yes, I can," Mia insisted, determination written plainly on her face.

"No, that's cheating," Ivy explained, crossing her arms in a firm, deliberate stance.

"Well, I want to do it my way!" Mia's voice rose in pitch and volume as her anger swelled. With a sharp cry, she hurled the cards across the room.

"You're being a baby," Ivy snapped. "Stop throwing fits."

Mia's cries only rose, breaking into desperate wails, her voice louder and louder as it filled the room with her frustration.

I sighed and gathered myself to intervene between the girls. Before I could move, Lucas flew out of the kitchen chair and stormed into the living room. He grabbed Mia by the shirt, hauling her up off the rug as her feet dangled helplessly in the air.

Her eyes bulged, and terror filled her eyes as her cries became wails of panic.

"What are you doing?" I yelled, lunging for her. "Stop—this instant!"

I yanked at his arm, pulling hard, desperate to free Mia, but he shoved me back—hard—sending me stumbling away from him. I fell backward, my foot catching on the game box, and I hit the floor with a cry of pain that went unnoticed.

Lucas's hand only clamped tighter, his fingers twisting the fabric of Mia's shirt into a fist. "I've had enough of this crap. Stop being a brat!" he thundered. "When I come home from work, I don't want to hear fighting. Do you understand me?"

Mia eyes were wide in terror as tears streamed down her cheeks. A strangled sob broke loose.

"Do you understand?" he bellowed again, shaking her little frame so hard her head snapped back like a ragdoll.

My body surged with terror and protectiveness. Launching myself from the floor, I threw all my weight against him, desperate to free her.

Out of the corner of my eye, I saw Ivy curled on the carpet. Her arms trembled, her small body shaking, eyes wide—drinking in the horror she could not unsee.

Don't interfere when I am dealing with my kid. Stay out of it. It's none of your business," he bellowed.

"It is my business; they are my daughters! Let her go!" I yelled, as I pushed between them.

"Worthless, lousy job as a mom you're doing. You can't even handle the kids. Do I have to do your job for you? Stupid," he spewed, dropping Mia to the floor.

He turned in disgust, kicking the game across the rug as the pieces scattered.

He stomped into the kitchen, grabbed his keys, and stalked out the front door, slamming it with a resounding thud.

The girls and I trembled—stunned, suspended in a silence so sharp it felt unreal.

Did this just happen?

It all had erupted and collapsed in under a minute—forty-five seconds, maybe sixty—yet the shock rippled through us as if time had fractured itself.

Can we rewind and erase?

Still unbelieving, I sat frozen with Mia clutched against me, her small body shaking. Ivy inched closer, eyes wide and glassy and then folded into me, burying her face into my chest until her tears soaked through my t-shirt. I wrapped my arms around both girls, holding on as if anchoring us to something solid. And there, I rocked them back and forth, back and forth, for what felt like forever until our sobs softened and all that was left was raspy, uneven breaths.

Stroking their little faces with trembling fingers, I whispered words of comfort. My hip throbbed where it had slammed against the floor when Lucas shoved me, but the pain barely registered. All I could think of were my precious babies—my girls—and the unshakeable truth that I could not, would not, let Lucas hurt them.

I wanted this all to disappear.

I cupped their cheeks gently, guiding their frightened eyes to mine. I steadied my voice, reaching for the strength we all needed.

"Girls . . . I am so, so sorry." My voice cracked in a broken sob. "This is not your fault. Your father is not being kind. He is being very hurtful and very angry, and that is wrong. It is *never* okay for a parent to hurt their child or be cruel."

A tear slipped down Mia's jaw. I wiped it with my thumb, wishing I could erase everything. "I'm sorry," I whispered again. There was nothing else I could say, no magic phrase, nothing to erase what transpired—just the desperate hope that my love would shield them from the damage his anger had already done.

After some time, I led the girls upstairs and tucked them gently into bed. I eased myself between them, being their comfort, their little arms clinging desperately around my neck. I began to hum a lullaby—soft and low, the kind meant to soothe nightmares—and slowly their bodies loosened. Their arms grew limp as they slipped toward the edge of the mattress. Finally, they drifted to sleep.

Careful to not awaken them, I slid off the bed and crept out, pulling the door closed behind me. Still in shock, my mind replayed the terrible moment over and over, bending and twisting it, desperate to imagine a version where it had ended differently. My heart ached with the impossible weight of what had happened.

My thoughts spun out of control, refusing to quiet—as if my own mind had turned against me, hurling unrelenting questions faster than I could breathe. They crashed over me in violent waves, each one sharper and more blunt than the last, demanding an answer I didn't have.

How can a man be so cruel and horrible?

How can someone claim to love his family yet treat them like they're worthless? How can he spew hatred almost daily?

What makes him explode with a fury far beyond anything normal?

If he loves us, why won't he change?

Why is it so easy for him to hurt the ones who love him the most?

Does he enjoy seeing us afraid?

How can he act like his rage isn't that big of a deal—like the chaos he leaves behind is insignificant, like we should swallow our fear, pretend it never happened, and move on, as if it was our fault?

I crept into Rose's bedroom, relieved she had slept through the chaos. I'd left her nighttime music on, and it drowned out the noise. Leaning close, I pressed a gentle, almost featherlight kiss to her little pink cheeks and watched her breathe in peace.

Inhale, exhale . . . that's what I needed for my girls—peace.

As the truth settled over me, I knew I *had* to leave.

And as truth always does, it roared. It shone a merciless light, exposing the darkness, and revealed the undeniable, brutal truth that could not be ignored. I could not run from it, and the memories surged back, each one steeped in its own raw anguish.

The rage.

The violence.

The insults.

The control.

The manipulations.

The servitude.

The unfaithfulness.

The accusations.

The intimidation.

The neglect.

The threats.

The rejections.

The lies.

The subjugation.

The fear.

The isolation.

The cruelty.

The helplessness.

They crashed on me like an unrelenting tide, pounding again and again until I could barely breathe. How could I possibly erase what had happened to them—what had happened to us?

This was the final straw.

I had to leave.

Chapter Twenty-Two

Day One

This would be our last day ever with Lucas. The decision was final, carved into me like stone from the moment I woke. I told the girls to pick their favorite toys, and while their small hands clutched dolls, stuffed animals, and trinkets, I packed their clothes and books with trembling fingers. Suitcases lined the wall in each bedroom, taped shut with the weight of finality. With every latch closed, a strange clarity surged through me—determination tempered by grief, sorrow for what we were leaving behind but relief for what lay before.

I packed quickly, nerves stretched taut, every sound in the house making me flinch. I forced small smiles for the girls, but inside I was a whirlwind of fear, anxiety, and anticipation. My stomach twisted with sickening dread. Any second now, I thought, I might have to grab their hands, snatch the suitcases, and dash—before the door opened, before his voice filled the house again, before our chance at freedom slipped away.

I had chosen this path deliberately. We would go to my parents, at least for now—a sanctuary, a place where protection and support would surround us. And if he came after us, I would report him. No longer would I allow fear to control us.

I moved fast once the girls had their small treasures in hand. Slipping them out the door, I buckled them into their seats with quaking fingers, smoothing their hair back, telling them everything would be okay. I shut the car door gently and hurried inside to collect the last two suitcases.

I was halfway down the stairs when the front door opened.

Lucas walked in.

I froze mid-step, breath trapped in my lungs. The girls were outside. Alone. Buckled in. Waiting for me.

I stopped on the stairs with the last two suitcases, caught between escape and danger, my heart hammering so hard I could barely think.

His eyes swept over the bags, the empty rooms. "What's going on here?" he demanded.

My voice rose before my courage could falter. "You've crossed major lines, Lucas. I'm done sitting back while you treat me and the girls terribly. I've given you so many chances. You haven't changed." I delivered the words steadily, but my legs trembled beneath me, my body shaking with cold sweat.

His jaw tightened. "You do not want to do this," he growled, taking a slow predatory step toward me. "You're making a huge mistake."

"Oh, I do want to do this," I answered, surprising myself with the steel in my voice. "And you will be held accountable for the horrific way you've treated us."

For a moment, I thought I saw something flicker in his expression. Disbelief . . . surprise, maybe. Then it hardened. "If you do this," he hissed, "there is no going back."

He leaned closer, eyes dead and glinting. "I will destroy you. There will be consequences for going against me. You have no idea what I am capable of."

My mind raced through a dozen possible outcomes—none of them good. But something pieced through the fear, clean and sharp: truth. The same thing that had roared at me this morning.

"We're leaving," I said, my voice calm, cold, resolute. "And if you do anything—anything—I will call the police. I will tell them *everything*."

He smirked, lifting one eyebrow. "You can't prove anything. It's your word against mine. Go ahead and call the police—they won't believe you. Everyone knows you're crazy. I'll take the kids from you. You won't get away with this. I have friends everywhere. Everywhere!" He spat the words with a sneer, as if disgusted by the air I breathed. "I will destroy you."

I met his stare head-on. I [illegible]ooked into his soulless, heartless [illegible]ack orbs for a full minut[illegible]—long enough to see there was [illegible]ing in them left to save.

[illegible]rned, clutching tightly the last two suitcases and [illegible]ast him.

[illegible]d out the door, closing it behind me, and with [illegible] single, steady motion, I closed the part of my life that belonged to him.

The girls were buckled in, wide-eyed and silent. Relief struck me like a wave when I realized Lucas hadn't seen them. Thank God for the dark tinting on the windows. Such a small detail but so important. They were invisible to him, shielded, protected for one precious moment.

Nervous energy surged through me, propelling my body into motion before my mind could catch up. I scrambled into the driver's seat, tossing the suitcases into the passenger seat—not caring where they landed. My hands shook so violently I nearly missed the door handle. I yanked it shut and slammed the locks down, the click echoing like salvation.

I couldn't breathe.

I didn't dare.

I threw the car in reverse, my foot trembling on the pedal. The tires skidded, spitting loose gravel as I backed out onto the road. For a heartbeat, the wheels spun, fighting for a grip—and then we shot forward. My pulse thundered in my ears as the house shrank in the rearview mirror. Every cell in my body screamed, *Go.*

We sped away, leaving the shattered pieces of our life behind us, heading straight for my parents' house—the place of safety, of refuge, of something that felt like hope, where we mattered.

"Mommy . . . what's happening?" Ivy's small voice broke through the roar in my head, thick with concern. She could see it—the terror etched on my face.

I glanced in the rearview mirror. Her hazel eyes were wide, unfiltered, shimmering with fear far too big for her little body.

"We are leaving," I said softly. "Daddy has been very dangerous. It's not safe to stay any longer. We're going to stay at Grammy and Grampy's."

She nodded as though she understood, though confusion still lingered in her eyes—a child trying to make sense of a world already too damaging.

As we left the neighborhood, my body rebelled. I jerked the car to the curb just in time. I barely pulled the door open before vomit hit the gravel and the side of the car in a shameful spray. A vise clamped around my throat, squeezing until I could barely breathe.

He will chase me down.

He will make me pay.

He could kill me in a blind rage.

The assaulting thoughts crashed over me as more waves of sickness wracked my body. Nothing was left but burning bile and humiliation. When the heaving finally eased, I wiped my mouth with the back of my hand, trembling.

For a moment, it felt like I floated above the scene, seeing myself crouching on the roadside, vomit streaking my shirt, splattered across the car and ground.

The girls watched from the back seat, their scared little faces watching the scene unfold before them, unsure, scared, confused, absorbing the trauma they could not name. Maybe even believing this kind of chaos was normal.

And something in me froze.

And then it hardened.

A resoluteness formed in my chest, sharp and unbreakable, like steel forged in fire.

I will not be controlled by fear.

I am doing what is right.

I am protecting us.

No longer will we be treated like useless possessions. No longer will we be raged at and threatened, broken down. My daughters are everything—and they deserve peace. They deserve safety—emotionally and physically.

They deserve a life where love doesn't hurt.

This was not running away.

This was saving our lives—each one of us.

The steel in my chest held firm as I pulled the door shut, resolve no longer wavering. I wiped my eyes, swallowed the last of the stinging bile, and eased the car back onto the road—not a woman running, but as a woman reclaiming her life.

He never believed I would seek freedom on my own.

He never believed I would *fight*.

He was wrong.

My jaw was tightened, set like stone. My eyes narrowed on the road ahead as determination surged through me, hot and unyielding. Try to cross me now, I thought, gripping the wheel. You have no idea what I am capable of.

Truth crystalized in that moment.

I have survived his narcissistic cruelty. I have already endured years of his rage, manipulations, and cold indifference.

If I could survive *that,* I can survive anything.

I wasn't weak.

I wasn't broken.

This woman—trembling, breathless, covered in sweat and vomit—is a survivor.

I will survive. And flourish.

My soul is stronger than his cruelty, stronger than every attempt to silence me.

I gripped the wheel until my knuckles blanched white.

Just watch me—despite all you have done.

Nothing will stop my quest for freedom.

I will survive. My daughters and I will be free.

We tumbled into Mom and Dad's house like desperate runaways—shaken, crying, undone. A broken, sobbing mess. And instantly we were caught. Held. Wrapped in the kind of love that steadies trembling hearts. This was our refuge, our shelter from the storm.

All four of us curled together on the guest bed, a small island of safety.

Thank God for my precious girls. They are my life, my breath, my everything.

I would go through hell and back for them—*And I have.* I will do anything to shield them from unnecessary pain.

When the pain exceeds the joy, something has to change.

When my girls are grown, I want them to know—truly know—that no matter what their father claims about me, their mother was brave. Strong. Their mother stood up to a giant with nothing but her bare hands and her sheer will and a fight for justice, love, and truth.

And if it had cost me my life, so be it.

But it wouldn't. I had the determination and courage of Joan of Arc—I would not give up.

I had the unrelenting endurance of Harriet Tubman—I would overcome.

I would survive.

Chapter Twenty-Three

Day Two

Sirens wailed. Cold brick walls pressed in on me. People crowded into hard, metal chairs, shoulders touching, each of us waiting for our number to be called—waiting to be seen, to be believed. This was the next day, and fears still clung to me like a second skin. I had come for one reason—a chance to petition for a protective order. My mind raced with thoughts . . . *What if this doesn't work? Maybe there isn't enough proof. What if I can't remember all I need to say?*

I reached for the blank white paper taunting, provoking me. There it lay, its empty lines daring me to write the words I couldn't even speak aloud, waiting for me to write all the details I buried just to survive—the proof I needed a protective order.

My thoughts split into a thousand directions, frantic and clouded, racing with plausible reasons it would not work . . . Would my evidence hold up in court? Were my reasons enough proof that we lived with a truly dangerous man—a man whose charm hid something monstrous, a man fed on fear, one who thrived off our pain? Would I be able to prove he loved to rule over and destroy the ones he should have guarded?

A tyrant? A narcissist? A destroyer of the very hearts he was meant to protect.

A blue pen trembled between my fingers. I hovered above the page, but my mind went utterly blank—emptiness swallowing every word.

Not a single thought came individually; instead, they all crashed into me at once. A thousand jagged, painful memories jumbled together, poured into my brain like a bursting dam.

Where in the world was I supposed to begin?

I closed my eyes, reached into the darkness of my past, and forced myself back—back through the moments I had tried so hard to forget. And then, with one breath that shook down to my bones, I pressed the pen to the page and began to write . . .

> *I was forced into a closet. He squeezed my head with his hands. He threatened to kill me. He forced me to have sex. He attacked me, leaving red, gouging claw marks from his fingernails across my chest. He shoved me into the wall. He threw dishes across the room in violence. He stabbed a knife into the countertop. He threatened to bury me. He choked me. He threatened that he has friends in low places to get rid of me—promising I would never be found. He shoved my daughter. He threatened to lock my daughters in a closet if they were naughty. He shook my daughter violently. He screamed threats in our faces. He shoved me into the stairs in rage. He refused to allow us to buy food, refusing money for essentials.*

I continued to write—all the verbal abuse, emotional abuse, mental abuse, financial abuse, sexual abuse, and physical abuse.

I filled the front and back of the paper, my brain hurt from all the remembering.

I walked to the counter, lost in a daze. I felt I was in someone else's nightmare.

I handed over the simple piece of paper that contained much of my trauma written only with ink, while the trauma had been indelibly written on my soul with pain and blood. My hands shook violently as the woman behind the counter reached to receive the piece of paper. She waited for me to release it.

Ten seconds, two minutes . . . time dissolved.

I had no idea how long it took for me to let go—for me to surrender the page that contained the whole of my sorrows, fears, rejection, terror, and pain . . . all of it compressed into too few lines written on parchment. Something so fragile, so insignificant, yet somehow burdened with the weight of my entire world.

It's crazy—the irony that a nearly worthless piece of paper could hold the words and proof that might grant me the most valuable thing I ever fought for: *freedom*.

Slowly—so slowly—my fingers uncurled, releasing it. And as the paper left my hands, I prayed with everything in me I would be believed. Nausea surged up my throat, an overwhelming rush of fear and trepidation flooding my body. My mouth filled with saliva while my throat remained impossibly dry. I stood there trembling, suspended between terror and hope.

As I walked back to my chair, the room sharpened with clarity. I became aware of every noise—the loud, uneven breathing of those around me, muffled crying, soft pleadings, hushed assurances shared to strangers who both shared the same silent terror.

Tick.

Tock.

The clock on the far wall marched on, indifferent to the lives unraveling beneath it. More women walked in—seeking refuge, scanning for available chairs, clutching forms, searching for available pens—pens used to write down their trauma. Some looked hollowed out, worn, broken. Some, I knew, had suffered far worse than me. And still, I waited. Two hours crawled by.

Finally, my name was called.

My destiny hung on the weight of one word.

Would I be granted freedom? Or remain bound to a man who had broken me piece by piece.

I stood on trembling legs and walked the twenty feet toward the official who held my future in my hands. My throat tightened until I could barely breathe. A wave of fear crashed so hard I thought my knees would buckle.

I forced my voice past the thick lump wedged in my throat. "Y-yes . . . I'm here. Do I . . . do I have the protective order?"

The unknowing was unbearable.

Tears gathered at the corners of my eyes and spilled over, tracing hot, helpless lines down my cheeks. Dread lodged in my chest, gripping me with a suffocating force.

I closed my eyes.

The air around me felt thick, cold, tangible. My body braced for the worst.

When my eyes lifted, I looked pleadingly into theirs.

Compassionate eyes met mine. "Yes . . . you've been granted a temporary protective order. The judge will hear your case tomorrow," the official answered gently.

Granted. Freedom.

I sank into the weight of it.

My eyes closed, only reopening when my heartbeat finally slowed.

I can do this.

I can take the long walk.

To freedom.

Chapter Twenty-Four

Day Three

Above me glowed the ancient architecture. Surrounding me was the rich smell of old wood, stale paper, strong lacquer, and leather as it permeated the courtroom. The chair creaking in protest to movement, the quiet rustle of papers, the muted outdoor noise of the traffic and emergency sirens all dimmed when the judge entered the courtroom.

"All rise. The Honorable judge presiding," the bailiff announced.

I stood, every muscle trembling. The judge's eyes settled on me—measured, expectant—before I sank into the chair, my hands clutching the hard wooden arms of the chair as though they were the only things keeping me upright.

Across the room, Lucas sat at the defense table. Just seeing him stole the air from my lungs. *How was I supposed to open my mouth and speak?*

And there I felt her—Charlotte, sitting right behind me. Solid. Steady. Unwavering. Her presence grounded me, a lifeline in the storm of my fear. Feeling her strength seep into me, I straightened my spine and gathered my voice. Even when my mind screamed at me to be silent, to shut up, to swallow the truth as I had done for so long, I refused.

Faint, trembling, but mine. I had to find it. Years of intimidation had buried my voice, telling me it was safer to stay quiet. But silence had already cost too much. I swallowed hard, feeling the weight of everything I'd endured press against my throat. And yet, there it was—my voice.

A soft touch grazed my back, a simple touch that lent me courage. A steadying reminder that I wasn't alone, enough to remind me to speak. Enough to remind me that I deserved to be heard.

"We have a protective order request today," the judge declared. "Please present the court with reasons and proof for your imminent need for a protective order."

I opened my mouth. Closed it. Opened it again.

Nothing came out. Every thought scattered, dissolving before I could grasp it. The air felt heavy, almost suffocating. *What repercussions would I get for speaking up to protect myself and the girls? Something bad . . . I knew something bad would happen.*

I tried to speak again. Failed.

Maybe my experiences weren't "bad enough" for the court to give us protection . . . *This is stupid. Why am I doing this?*

No. I have the right to be safe. To not be traumatized. To be treated with dignity. For my daughters to be treated with kindness, not with rages of anger.

I can do this.

The judge waited. The truth waited.

My hands shook as I tried to focus on the trembling paper I had written this morning.

"It's okay, take a moment to breathe. We will hear you when you are ready," the judge graciously spoke as his kind eyes looked down upon me.

And then I understood. If I didn't name what he had done, his power would follow me out of the courtroom and into every last inch of my life.

And I spoke.

"Thank you, your Honor," I began, my voice small, fragile. "This isn't easy for me. I'm scared."

I focused on the paper in my hands, the one that held every piece of my pain, every memory I had survived. I gripped it tighter, and the words began to flow. Slowly at first, then with more confidence. Each sentence, each truth pulled me onward. Each word of truth stripped a little more of his power away.

I was speaking, I was naming the truth. I was shining a light on the darkness.

And for the first time in years, it mattered.

" . . . squeezed my head in his hands, threatening he wants to kill me, threatened to have me buried, slammed me against a wall, hurt me when I was pregnant, threatened and shoved my daughters, terrorized them, slammed the knife into the counter, squeezed my throat, leaving marks all over my neck and chest . . ." I paused.

Panic surged, and I squeezed my eyes shut, forcing my breath to slow, to find the center in the storm raging.

"It's all right, take your time," the judge said kindly.

Grateful for patience in those words, I glanced up, then dropped my eyes back to the paper trembling in my hands.

Summoning every ounce of courage, I began again. "Lucas would neglect the girls' care . . ."

I continued on as my voice quivered. Every act of cruelty, every violation of trust, every moment of fear we endured all poured out. The paper in my hands felt weighty, yet also, with every word spoken, somehow lighter, as if the truth spoken lifted the weight of the secrets I'd been forced to endure alone.

The judge's face remained serious, carefully controlled. But I could sense the quiet anger simmering beneath the calm exterior—the depth of our suffering understood.

Finally, I sank into the chair, utterly exhausted. Every ounce of strength had been spent unearthing the trauma that had been submerged deep in my soul.

And now . . . the waiting.

What would the verdict be?

"Please, please let it be enough," I whispered under my breath. "Give us peace. Take this out of our lives. We can't live like this anymore. My children can't . . ."

Then the words came, steady, final:

"In light of all I have heard, I find the petitioner's request justified. A permanent protective order will be issued immediately for all that has been requested. This has been extremely disturbing information for the court to hear. The responder must cease all abuse, threats, and harassment toward the petitioner. The responder must stay away from the petitioner and the children—including the home, school, and homes of family members. The responder must have no contact with the petitioner directly or through a third party. Finally, the petitioner is granted full custody of all three children."

As the judge's words sank in, a tidal wave of gratitude and release washed through me. I collapsed into the chair. Every wound, every scar came rushing back. Flashes of all I had endured—the fear, the dread, the pain, the endless nights of tears, the helplessness, the suffocating weight of anger and hurt, the heartbreaking betrayals, and the broken memories—spilled into my chest all at once.

My chest rose and fell in racking breaths. And then, through the trembling, through the tears, one word echoed, steady and unshakable.

Free.

It is finally *over*. It is *finally* over.

I pushed myself up from the scarred, wooden chair and rose taller than I had in years. My eyes locked straight ahead—past Lucas, past the shadows of everything he had stolen from me. I walked out, not just from the courtroom but from the grip of the man who had stolen my youth, crushed my joy, broken my heart, beaten down my individuality, defiled our marriage, lived hypocritically, enslaved my choices, terrorized my daughters, treated us ruthlessly, and tried to shatter my spirit with cruelty and lies.

I left behind his narcissism, his rage, and his endless belittling. I stepped through the courthouse doors into the blaze of sunlight, feeling the warmth touch my skin without fear clinging.

I was free.

I walked into the sunshine. Into the light.

Truth. Accountability.

I had let the truth burn away the lies. I let the light reveal what the darkness tries to hide.

I was exposed by the sun, where the truth doesn't whisper.

It roars.

What a difference three days can make.

Grab that rope, hold on for your life. And climb. Don't let go, not when the rope burns your hands with coarse texture, cutting your skin. Not when your muscles scream in protest. Not when the skin peels raw. Not when your arms quiver with fatigue and every ounce of strength is gone.

Grit your teeth and climb.

Climb out of hell.

You will make it.

You will find joy.

"I have learned that courage was not the absence of fear, but the triumph over it."
Nelson Mandela

Chapter Twenty-Five

Summer 2023, *Eight Years in Freedom*

The front door swung open and in came my husband, nudging it wider with his foot as he lugged an overflowing bag of groceries and a vibrant bouquet of blossoms tucked under his arm.

"Here, babe, these are for you," Sebastian announced as he carefully set the bouquet in my arms, leaning in to brush my lips with a sweet kiss. "Love you, babe. I even grabbed your favorite coffee!"

"Thanks, honey," I replied, as I buried my nose in the delicate blossoms, inhaling the rich perfume of hyacinths, lilacs, and tulips. He always remembers.

Strong arms wrapped around me from behind, enveloping my smaller frame. I had found my home, my peaceful place, the space that allows me space to grow, to breathe, and to heal.

As he nuzzled my neck with a trail of soft kisses, goose-bumps rose along my arms.

"Ewww . . . get a room. Gross, PDA!" the girls called out, bursting into the kitchen just as we were wrapped in embrace. Years later, they had grown into their own, beautiful, unique selves. Ivy, blossoming at seventeen, radiant, strong, and resilient; Mia, fifteen, spunky, smart, and beautiful; and Rose, my baby at thirteen, still sweet, cuddly, and full of innocent curiosity. Together, they joined in teasing us about our "overly affectionate" marriage.

The trio of girls left the kitchen in peals of laughter, their voices echoing down the hallway, joking about how we still acted like teenagers even after a few years of marriage—even though, in their eyes, we were "old."

Seeing my daughters flourishing, vibrant, and free makes every second of my courage worth the battle. I am thankful, for their worth is far beyond measure. I fought to be free, so they can live free—free from fear, free from trauma, and free to grow to be the women they were meant to be. Their future is priceless and protecting it has been the greatest victory of my life.

As I leaned into Sebastian's embrace, we exchanged a quiet, knowing glance, our smile saying everything words could not. For a moment, we just simply breathed it in—the laughter, the joy, the happy chaos, the life we had built together—and I felt profoundly grateful.

"You just wait until you find someone who loves you so wonderfully, then you'll understand," I laughed, calling out to the girls.

"Well, they just left the room . . . so how about we dig into that caramel ice cream I just bought?" Sebastian suggested with a sly grin, pulling out the girls' favorite ice cream. He fished out two spoons and pressed one into my hand, his triumphant smile contagious. "Let's dig in!"

"Why not?" I replied, a conspiratorial smile spreading across my face.

After barely one bite, the girls came rushing into the kitchen, socks slipping on the shiny wood floor as they skidded to a stop.

"No way!" Mia laughed, pointing at the ice cream.

"That's for us," Ivy declared, grabbing her own spoon.

"I got bowls!" Rose announced with a smile, holding them up for all to see.

And just like that, after planting quick, affectionate kisses on Sebastian's cheek, and shooting us a playful smile, they scooped up their spoils and disappeared, their delightful, joy-filled laughter echoing down the hallway.

"Well, we tried," I said, looking up into his smiling blue eyes. He wrapped his arms around my waist, pulling me close and kissing a bit of caramel off the side of my lip. Behind him, I caught sight of the *other* tub of ice cream peeking from the grocery bag—coffee ice cream, my favorite. The sight made my heart lift.

Glancing up into his eyes, I leaned into him just as he whispered softly against my ear, "My Joy . . . you are my greatest blessing. Loving you is the best part of my life."

Responding to his love was effortless. My heart, once fractured, felt full again.

My journey has been hard—almost impossible. At times I did not want to go on, when survival was my only goal. Never did I imagine I would find love like this. When it came, it caught me by surprise.

The depth of a good man's love is deep, rich, powerful—sacrificial and kind.

I am thankful for our family. A family not born only from DNA but born of the heart.

A love chosen.

A love fought for.

A love sacrificed for.

A love protected.

My children treasured, safe, loved, and wrapped in gentleness.

That was more than I wished.

I am Joy.

No longer a shadow, I have been reborn.

I am kintsugi, broken pottery that was mended with gold.

Healing gold is now painted on every crack and broken piece fusing together my spirit, my heart, and my life, making it more beautiful than it was before.

My husband had been a part of my healing gold. To me, he is rare, invaluable, and precious.

Together we are imperfectly perfect.

And when light strikes all the broken pieces of my life,
all you see is the glow . . . of Joy.

The end.

Isaiah 60:15

"Whereas you have been forsaken and hated,
with no one passing through,
I will make you majestic forever,
a JOY from age to age."

Reflections from the Author

This book is more than words on a page for me. It is the outpouring of a journey I never thought I would escape or survive. There were years when my spirit felt shattered, when fear and doubt threatened to silence every bit of hope within me. Yet somehow, even in those fragile places, I found an anchor.

For me, that anchor was my faith. It steadied me when I felt I was falling apart and broken, reminding me that even in brokenness there is strength. It helped me believe even when I could not see a way forward. It helped me stand for truth, be courageous, and take steps of faith into the unknown, even when I was terrified. It gave me hope that joy could come again. I was able to see beyond my situation, to have faith and believe anything is possible. I can overcome. I clung to these promises as my lifeline—and it rang true for me. For that I am thankful, and I am a survivor.

I chose to name the character Joy because joy is one thing you lose when your very self is stripped away, when your voice is stolen, and you become a shadow of who you were. And joy is what returns in full measure when you find yourself again. It is what others see spilling out after you are free and begin to heal. It comes back a little at a time and continues to grow until you are a shining beacon of light to others.

The verses I share below became imprinted on my heart and were whispers of truth that held me together when everything else felt like it was falling apart. They called to the joy that had been stolen but now has been restored.

I want you to know this: no matter what your journey has looked like, no matter what you believe or where you stand, you deserve freedom. You deserve peace. You deserve to live a life where you are safe, seen, and cherished. You deserve joy. If the words that steadied me also speak to your heart, I hope they bring you courage and comfort.

My hope is still the same: that you will find your own anchor and well of hope that steadies you and helps you rise into the fullness of who you were meant to be—amazing, beautiful, joyful, *you*.

Instead of your former shame, you shall have recompense. Instead of dishonor you shall rejoice, and you shall possess double and everlasting joy. For I will faithfully give them their recompense in truth. I will make an everlasting promise to you. And your children shall have honor. All who see will know that these are a people whom the Lord has blessed. The Lord will cause righteousness and justice to spring up. And I will not rest until her vindication shines as brightly as the sun. Isaiah 61, 62 (paraphrased)

The Lord has redeemed them from the hand of him who was too strong for them. They shall sing and be radiant with joy. And their life shall become like a watered garden, and they will have no more sorrow for I will turn their mourning into joy! Refrain from weeping and see your restoration. There is hope for your future and an inheritance for your children. Jeremiah 31 (paraphrased)

I will gather them and I will make them dwell in safety. I will make an everlasting covenant. I will bring upon you all the good that I have promised. Call upon me, and I will answer you and show you great and mighty things, more than you even know. I will lay upon you health and healing. I will cure you and reveal an abundance of peace, prosperity, security, stability, and truth. And there shall be heard again the voice of joy and gladness. I will fulfill this promise I made to you. **Jeremiah 32, 33 (paraphrased)**

Final Caution on Moving Forward

Leaving a relationship marked by coercive control / domestic abuse is not the end of the journey–it is the beginning of recovery. Survivors are most often vulnerable **after** they leave, not because they are weak, but because control can distort boundaries, intuition, and self-trust.

Before entering another relationship, it is essential to allow time for healing. Regaining your voice, freedom, and independence is not something to rush. Safety is built slowly–through space, reflection, and rebuilding self-worth on your own terms.

Those who have experienced control may unconsciously be drawn to familiar dynamics. Control can disguise itself as charm, protection, intensity, or urgency.

Healthy relationships do not demand immediacy, compliance, or self-sacrifice.

Healthy relationships are marked by patience, mutual respect, emotional safety, honor, and freedom of choice.

As you move forward, pay close attention to **green flags:**

- Respect for boundaries without resistance or punishment.
- Consistent behavior over time, not accelerating or pushing intimacy.
- Encouragement of your independence, friendships, and personal goals.
- Accountability, empathy, and the ability to hear "no" without retaliation.

Trust is not proven through pressure or persistence. It is revealed through time.

Most importantly, give yourself permission to remain single if that's what healing requires.

You are not incomplete without a relationship. Your worth is not measured by companionship.

Choose yourself, again and again, until your voice is fully your own.

Finding your voice is the beginning of choosing freedom, and Shadow of Joy was written to walk beside you as you do. **You are worth it.**

Appendix 1:
Common Red Flags

Not every unhealthy relationship has all of these, **but any one of them in a repeating pattern is a red flag** worth paying attention to. Here are some examples of common red flags:

- When your no isn't respected, and you are pressured, manipulated, or made to feel guilty until you give in.
- When your past trauma is minimized, and are accused of being "too sensitive" or told "you should just get over it," – dismissing personal responsibility for their actions.
- They feel threatened by your achievements /special occurrences and aim to dismiss your successes or find ways to diminish your joy.
- When they behave with hurtful actions, then reverse the blame onto you–making excuses for their behavior or expect immediate forgiveness without changing. Zero accountability. Minimizing the abuse, denying it, shifting the responsibility.
- When you feel the constant need to filter your thoughts and feelings–you feel afraid of their reaction when you express your true self /thoughts / preferences/ desires.
- When your body signals distress around them: tension, stomachaches, nervousness, headaches, or constantly feeling on edge.
- When they deny actions or words, twisting facts, making you question your memory or sanity.
- When there is a double standard. They can do things that you aren't "allowed" to do (e.g., go out, spend money, talk to others).
- When they make all the rules.
- When there are serious mood swings–unpredictable, going from being cruel to kind without clear reason.
- When they use the silent treatment or withdrawal of love as punishment.

- When they belittle, mock, constantly criticize, or demean you—even labeling it as jokes–accuse you of being crazy, play mind games, humiliate you, and intend to make you feel guilty.
- When they threaten to do harmful or hurtful things to control your actions.
- When they behave with jealousy and possessiveness; needing to know where you are at all times, who you are with, or accuse you of cheating.
- When there is disrespectful communication–raising voice, name-calling, or swearing to gain control or intimidate.
- When they ignore your feelings or minimize your concerns.
- When they threaten to leave or harm themselves, you, or others if you don't comply.
- When they use isolation: he controls where you go, who you are with, what you do, who you talk to, what you read or eat, or uses jealousy to justify his actions.
- When there is physical intimidation: blocking doors, standing too close, entrapping you in spaces, throwing objects, and destroying property.
- Other intimidation–causes fear by using actions, words, and gestures, abuses or threatens to abuse pets, and displays weapons to intimidate.
- When they pressure you / threaten you into intimacy / ignore your no.
- Male privilege: when they treat you like a servant/ less valuable than him, ignores his own personal responsibility, or make all the decisions- he defines the roles.
- When they shove, grab, hit, restrain, even if they later call it "playful" or "not serious".

- Financial sabotage:
  - Limits your access to money, tracks every dollar, or makes you dependent financially.
  - Runs up debts in your name.
  - Prevents you from working.
  - Forces you to ask for money.
  - Doesn't allow access to money/bank account. Siphons mutual money into their private accounts.
  - Confiscates your money or earnings.

- Psychological Red Flags:
  - You feel anxious about their moods and avoid conflict at all costs.
  - You feel less confident, less "yourself," or that you are never good enough.
  - You feel afraid of their reaction more often than safe and comfortable.

If you see yourself in any of these situations of abuse or control, know this: You are not alone, and none of this is your fault. Please seek help. It is your first step toward safety, freedom, and reclaiming your power. **You are worth it.**

Appendix 2:
Definition of Coercive Control

Coercive Control is the invisible cage. It is a pattern of ongoing, intentional behaviors used by one person to dominate, manipulate, isolate, entrap, control and regulate another person's life. Rather than a single incident, it is the **cumulative, repetitive, and strategic nature** of these behaviors that creates *entrapment, dependency, fear, and loss of autonomy* for the victim. Coercive control may be harder for others to see, but it is indelibly harmful. It chips away at freedom without always leaving obvious external scars. It strips the other person of their independence, confidence, and sense of self.

It is entrapping and makes resistance feel impossible or dangerous, and can escalate *with or without physical violence.*

This pattern undermines free will.

It restricts basic freedoms and personal liberty.

It creates a pervasive climate of fear, confusion, and psychological harm.

It may include physical, sexual, phycological, emotional, financial, and technological tactics.

It often occurs in intimate or family relationships but can occur in other close relationships.

It is not defined by one action alone but by the pattern and impact over time–cumulative harm.

It can occur with or without physical violence.

It is often invisible to outsiders, but its effects–loss of freedom, isolation, fear, and self-doubt–are profound and long-lasting.

Recognizing and naming coercive control is critical to supporting survivors and holding abusers accountable.

Hallmark Characteristics of Coercive Control

Pattern over time:
Coercive control isn't a single incident; it is a course of conduct that repeats and intensifies, shaping the victim's entire life.

Psychological and emotional domination:
Abusers use tactics such as threats, intimidation, isolation, humiliation, gaslighting, and manipulation. They use unpredictable shifts between charm and rage to erode confidence and self-trust.

Isolation and social control:
The abusive person systematically cuts off support systems: restricting contact with friends and family, controls communications, creates jealousy, suspicion, or barriers to outside support. This deepens dependency and reduces options for escape.

Control of daily life:
The abuser regulates the victims: movements, and schedule, finances and economic resources, access to services, transportation, work, and housing. Such control deprives the victim of autonomy and opportunity.

Surveillance and monitoring:
Abusers often use technology or physical means to keep constant watch: tracking devices, spyware, or phone monitoring, checking accounts, messages, or browser history. This reinforces fear and restricts freedom.

Threats and intimidation:
Not all threats always include violence- they may include threats to harm the victim, their children, pets, or reputation; legal threats or threats to cut off resources. The abuser may also act on one or all of these threats–there is no guarantee it will stop at a threat. The abuser may use threats of suicide if the victim leaves or tries to get help. These tactics create a climate of fear and control.

Deprivation of resources:
Abusers may withhold money or control spending, steal the victim's money or resources, sabotage employment, deprive the victim of food, sleep, transportation, friends, family, or medical care. This deepens dependency and limits escape options.

Erosion of identity and dignity:
Over time, coercive control *dehumanizes* the victim with constant criticism and belittling, verbal and emotional abuse, controlling appearances, controlling behaviors, and controlling personal choices. This chips away at self-worth and agency.

Appendix 3:
Reader's Guide to Understanding Abuse and Control

This guide is here to help you put words to what may feel unexplainable. Abuse isn't always visible, and it doesn't always leave bruises. This gives language to the hidden patterns, allowing what's long been silenced to finally be seen and understood.

Abuse (Domestic Abuse)

It isn't just about anger—it's about power and control. It is a pattern of behavior used to gain and maintain power and control over another. Abuse can be physical, emotional, mental, sexual, financial, spiritual, or psychological. Its purpose is always the same: to make someone feel smaller, weaker, and dependent.

Brainwashing

Intense and continual coercive tactics to produce profound changes in the victim's beliefs, attitudes, and emotions.

Circular Conversations

Never resolving issues in a logical way, twisting arguments until you are confused and exhausted; overcomplicating or derailing conversations to make you feel lost.

Confusion Tactics

Changing stories, contradicting themselves, or shifting topics with the intent to destabilize your thinking.

Coercive Control

A pattern of ongoing, intentional behaviors used by one person to dominate, manipulate, isolate, entrap, control and regulate another person's life. Rather than a single incident, it is the cumulative, repetitive, and strategic nature of these behaviors that creates entrapment, dependency, fear, and loss of autonomy for the victim.

Cycle of Abuse

Abuse often moves in patterns: tension builds, incident happens, apology/honeymoon phase, then calm—makes it easy to hope things will change. This cycle keeps repeating and can trap victims in ongoing abuse.

DARVO

A common practice abusers use to manipulate: Deny, Attack, Reverse Victim, and Offender. They flip the story to make the real victim look like the abuser.

Emotional Abuse

This abuse targets the heart. It shows up in criticism, name-calling, silent treatment, threats of leaving, or withholding love and affection. Its purpose is to tear down someone's confidence, dignity, or self-worth.

Emotional Blackmail

A tactic used by abusers to control, manipulate and dominate their victims through fear, guilt, obligation, or shame. It is a core tool of coercive control. The victim feels pressure to comply with the abuser's demand by threatening emotional or relational consequences. This also effects children.

Financial Abuse

Money is used as a leash, controlling someone's access to money, employment, or resources to limit their independence. This may include stealing, restricting spending, sabotaging, or forbidding work. Without financial freedom, leaving can feel impossible.

Gaslighting

A tactic where the abuser twists reality to make the victim question their own mind. A form of psychological manipulation where the abuser causes the victim to doubt their own memory, perception, or reality. For example, "That never happened—you are imagining things."

Isolation

Cutting the victim off from family, friends, or support systems to increase dependence on the abuser. The smaller the circle, the stronger the control.

Love-Bombing

An early stage in abusive relationships where the abuser over-showers the victim with attention, gifts, and affection, making it harder to leave once the abuse begins.

Manipulative Kindness

When one uses acts of kindness, not out of genuine care, but with the intention to control, influence, or confuse the other person.

Minimization, Denial, and Blame

Abusers often downplay what just happened—using common tactics where the abuser downplays the abuse, denies it happened, or shifts responsibility onto the victim. ("It wasn't that bad, you are too sensitive") and making your feelings seem unimportant, silly, or overblown.

Physical Abuse

A form of intimate partner abuse in which one partner intentionally uses bodily force or a physical act to cause pain, injury, fear, or harm to the other partner. It can range from overt acts of violence to subtle forms of physical intimidation, and is used as a means to exert control, domination, or instill fear within the relationship.

Power and Control

The heart of every form of abuse is power and control. It is the central goal of abuse. The Power and Control Wheel is often used to illustrate the different tactics abusers use to dominate others.

Projection
Blaming you for the very thing they are doing (cheating, lying, lazy, being controlling).

Safety Planning
A practical, hopeful plan created to help someone in an abusive relationship to increase their safety. It may include ways to leave quickly, contact information for trusted contacts, or important documents.

Sexual Abuse
A form of intimate partner violence in which one partner coerces, manipulates, pressures, or forces the other partner into sexual activity without consent. This abuse violates the victim's autonomy, body integrity, and personal boundaries. It is often used as a means to assert power, control, and dominance.

Spiritual Abuse
Using religion or a belief system to control, intimidate, or harm.

Trauma Bonding
A strong emotional attachment between the victim and the abuser, created through cycles of abuse followed by reconciliation and affection. This bond makes leaving extremely difficult.

Triangulation
Abusers often pull in a third party to take side against the victim. This becomes a divide-and-conquer strategy to deliberately drive a wedge between the victim and others so that the abuser can stay in control.

Verbal Abuse
Attacking through words—yelling, insults, threats, humiliation—with the intent to harm emotionally.

Continue The Journey

This journey doesn't end on the last page. If something in this book resonated with you, know that you're not alone–and there are gentle ways to keep moving forward, at your own pace. The path forward is yours to explore and full of possibilities–trust yourself and enjoy what's to come.

Continue the journey in any way that feels right for you.

1. **Visit the website and access free resources**
   You've already said yes to yourself by reading this book. As a thank you, you're invited to access free bonus content, resources, and tools created to support healing, clarity, and reclaiming your voice. Go to **https://www.beyondtheshadow.me/book-resources** to access your resources.

2. **Invite me to speak**
   I speak from lived experience–surviving intimate partner abuse, navigating coercive control, and walking the long road back to self-trust, freedom and voice. My work blends compassion with education, offering hope, clarity, advocacy, and language to what so many feel but struggle to name.

   If you are looking for a speaker who leads with empathy and truth, I'd be honored to connect.
   Email me at **JenniferDean@BeyondtheShadow.me**

3. Connect on social media

Let's keep the conversation going! The journey doesn't end here. I share education, encouragement, and real talk about healing, boundaries, and reclaiming your life–one small step at a time.

You can find me on:

Instagram: JenniferDeanNovelist
Facebook: Jennifer Dean Novelist
YouTube: Beyond the Shadow (Jennifer Dean)
TikTok: @jennifer.dean.novelist
LinkedIn: Jennifer Dean
Threads: Jenniferadean6
Website: BeyondtheShadow.me
Blog: BeyondtheShadow.me/blog

Acknowledgments

This book did not come to life on its own. Shadow of Joy exists because of the people who believed, encouraged, challenged, and stood beside me throughout this journey.

These three years of bringing *Shadow of Joy* to life required patience–patience with late nights, inconvenient writing hours, sometimes stretching into early morning, and the thousands of hours it took to shape this story. I am deeply grateful for the space my family gave me to create.

First and foremost, my gratitude begins with my daughters, Alexandra, MacKenzie, Isabella, Lilly, and Scarlett, five remarkable young women, and the greatest gifts God has entrusted to me, I will forever cherish.

You have shown extraordinary courage, resilience, and grace—walking with bravery, choosing love amid struggle, allowing healing to take root. I am endlessly proud of you, and I hold you in the highest esteem. Every breath I take is marked with my love for you. You never quit. You keep pressing forward, setting your sights on the next goal, and accomplishing it with determination. You are women of incredible character, dignity, and courage—a living testament to what it means to rise above. This book is dedicated to you as a reminder that we can endure, overcome, and grow stronger. We are not bound by cycles of the past. We are free to create a future full of joy, purpose, and hope. Nothing can hold you down. I love you, my beautiful, strong, precious women!

Thank you for supporting me as I pursued something that required time, focus, and persistence. Thank you for your encouragement, prayers, and belief in my dream. And for listening to me go on and on about this story and why it's so important to me. And to Scarlett- my youngest angel, thank you for sharing me, even when it was inconvenient, and for your hilarious voice narrations of my book that always made me laugh. You make my heart smile. I promise to make it up to you with dozens of Dunkin runs!

To my husband, Christian Dean, thank you for your encouragement from the beginning, for having the vision to challenge me to write my story. Thank you for believing in me and for surprising me with the best Christmas gift – my first laptop, after seeing me handwrite my story for several weeks. You always see the need and strive to meet it. Thank you for supporting me –unquestioningly–through this journey. Thank you for letting me pick your brain, for reading hundreds of pages, helping me choose an interesting male character name, listening to ideas and countless research, interrupting your reading time to go off on tangents about what I've been learning, and helping me refine this novel into what it has become. Your support has been constant and unwavering. Thank you for granting me the space, time, and support to heal through my journey. I am forever thankful for you. You have been my Sebastian.

You are the love of my life, my best friend—and the man who convinced me that amazing men do exist. And as I relived many memories and felt the reoccurring wash of fear, you loved me. You pushed me to discover myself again, encouraged me to explore who I was meant to be, and gave me the best gift—the gift of letting me just be me. There is no greater gift, no greater love–than to love me fully as I am. And for your heroic, patient, and selfless love to me and our daughters, I am forever and eternally grateful. I love this man more than I thought humanly possible. And I dedicate this book to you, as it was you who encouraged me to write my story. And because you own my heart.

I am endlessly grateful for my loving parents, whose steadfast presence, patience, prayers, and support carried me and the girls through years of trials. Pop and Mom, thank you for all the ways you gave and sacrificed for us. Thank you for your unwavering support and encouragement. Thank you for every single act of love. You are the best parents, grandparents, and great-grandparents, and I am eternally grateful for you.

I dedicate this book to you, for your love, support, and endless prayers.

To my extended family, thank you for the openness, encouragement and support you offered as I spoke about this difficult yet important topic. Your support means more than you know.

In loving memory of my Grandmother Genevieve, who instilled within me a deep love and lifelong passion for reading. Her vast personal library, books embossed with her personal seal, and favorite reading snack of orange puffs and slices of white cheddar cheese, I will always remember. I hold dear the series of *Anne of Green Gables* you bought for me the winter I was twelve, sick with pneumonia and stuck in front of the fireplace. I inherited her uncanny ability to fly through books effortlessly and still remember every word and every scene . . . even decades later.

My sincere gratitude to Jake Kelfer and the entire team at Big Idea to Bestseller. Thank you for your guidance, insight, and steady support. I am deeply thankful and honored to publish this novel with a company that believes in both the story and its purpose.

To my friends, thank you for the many conversations, the timely encouragement, prayers, thoughtful advice, and the unwavering belief when I doubted myself. You helped breathe life into this vision. You saw possibility when it felt distant, and your faith in me carried me forward. And I am thankful for all the friends I made through this journey.

And to every woman who has lived, suffered, been broken, escaped, and survived intimate partner abuse -emotional, verbal, mental, financial, sexual abuse, and coercive control—and desires to be on the healing journey to wholeness, newness, and a discovery of themselves, I dedicate this book to you.

This book is written for every woman who knows what it's like to experience her voice being stripped away, her individuality stifled, and her hopes and dreams destroyed. This is for every woman who has had self-doubt—wondering what else she needs to do to make her relationship work. This is for every woman who has had to protect her children, despite her own safety. This is for every woman who has lived in fear—fear of eruption, fear of violence, fear of betrayal, fear of explosion, or fear of rejection. This is for every woman who didn't want to quit, who felt things might be okay if she could only give more. This is for every woman who has lost herself trying to save her relationship–who has lost the sparkle in her eyes, the joy in her life, and her vibrant, carefree spirit. Your freedom is a fight worth fighting for. It may seem impossible, but it is not. You are worth it. May you relearn who you are, who you were meant to be, the wonderful, beautiful gift that is . . . you.

Be free! Be alive to discover all that awaits you. Blessings will come.

A brand-new life awaits on the other side.

Although this story and characters are fictional, this is the life many are living, have escaped from, or have died trying to leave.

In some way, this is what we lived.

I cannot wait to see how far this story travels–and how this platform is used to change lives. It has changed mine.

And this is only the beginning.

#MyStory
#OurStory

About The Author

Jennifer Dean is an educator, storyteller, and lifelong lover of literature whose work is shaped by more than two decades of lived experience. She holds a Bachelor of Education and has spent several years working as a substitute teacher and volleyball coach—roles that deepened her commitment to resilience, growth, and meaningful learning.

A devoted mother of five daughters and grandmother to two, Jennifer's life is full and lively, shared with her husband, four cats, and one endlessly energetic dog. Her home is lined with hundreds of well-loved books, many of which she can recall in vivid detail, and she is often found reading late into the night with a cup of coffee close at hand.

Jennifer is a passionate advocate for women impacted by domestic abuse and coercive control, and she uses storytelling as a means to bring awareness to hidden forms of harm, amplify truth, and encou-rage healing.

Shadow of Joy is her debut novel, born from her deep belief in the power of story to illuminate difficult truths, foster restoration, and inspire meaningful change. Jennifer lives in Maryland with her family.

www.ingramcontent.com/pod-product-compliance
Lightning Source LLC
Chambersburg PA
CBHW031320230926
51848CB00001B/34
9781968164287